Desolation
Flats

Desolation Flats

Andrew Hunt

Minotaur Books
A Thomas Dunne Book
New York

This is a work of fiction. All of the characters, organizations, and events portrayed in this novel are either products of the author's imagination or are used fictitiously.

A THOMAS DUNNE BOOK FOR MINOTAUR BOOKS.
An imprint of St. Martin's Press.

www.thomasdunnebooks.com
www.minotaurbooks.com

The Library of Congress Cataloging-in-Publication Data is available upon request.

ISBN 978-1-250-06461-5 (hardcover)
ISBN 978-1-4668-7081-9 (e-book)

Our books may be purchased in bulk for promotional, educational, or business use. Please contact your local bookseller or the Macmillan Corporate and Premium Sales Department at 1-800-221-7945, extension 5442, or by e-mail at MacmillanSpecialMarkets@macmillan.com.

First Edition: November 2016

10 9 8 7 6 5 4 3 2 1

To Maddox and Aidan and Ruth and Tony

*The future belongs to those who believe in
the beauty of their dreams.*

—ELEANOR ROOSEVELT

Acknowledgments

Writing *Desolation Flats* was a fabulous experience. And, as was the case with the first two books in the series of Art Oveson mysteries, *City of Saints* and *A Killing in Zion,* I have a long list of thanks.

Thank you to Steve Ross, a wonderful, kind, encouraging, supportive agent—always an e-mail or phone call away, always responding with a positive, can-do attitude.

Thank you to the amazing folks at Minotaur/St. Martin's Press. The splendid copy editor, Edwin Chapman, handled the manuscript with great care. The helpful staff made the production of the book you're holding a pleasurable experience, from start to finish. Once more, in particular, I'd like to single out Peter Joseph, a fantastic editor with a meticulous eye for detail. Peter's levelheaded advice and deep belief in what I was doing brought tremendous satisfaction to this project.

Thank you to my colleagues in the history department at the University of Waterloo for being so supportive of me, and so patient with my endeavors in the field of mystery writing. I have the best job in the world and every day I feel deep gratitude.

To my kin back in Utah—my mother, Linda; my father, Kay; and stepmother, Jodie; my brother, Jeff; and my sister-in-law, Stephanie, and their wonderful family, and my amazing aunts and uncles and cousins (I love you all), and my other loved ones and friends in the Beehive State—a huge thank-you for all of your support and love from afar.

Thank you to friends closer to home—to John and Betty, Daniel and Laura, Charlie and Lori, Patrick, and to Gord and Linda.

Thank you to the love of my life, Luisa D'Amato, for everything—the long walks at Riverside Park and Mount Nemo, the amazing vegan cooking, the episodes of *Coast* and the latest election news on CNN, the read-a-thons, and for all of your patience and support and love. The next book, the one I spent all of those months reading out loud to you (you know the one I'm talking about), will have your name on the dedication.

Finally, I dedicate this book to my children, Maddox and Aidan, and Luisa's children, Ruth (Vienna) and Tony. The word "children" is actually no longer applicable in their case. What a profound experience it has been to watch all four of you evolve— in the most wondrous, awe-inspiring and moving ways—into four of the finest adults I've ever known. I get choked up thinking about it. You've all got amazing futures ahead of you.

And behind you, you've got my love.

The Mormon habitat has always been a vortex of legend and lie. Even today, as the state settles down to gray hairs, there lingers something wonderful and outrageous about Utah, a flavor of the mysterious and strange.

—*Utah: A Guide to the State,*
BY THE WORKS PROJECTS ADMINISTRATION, 1941

Desolation
Flats

One

The Silver Arrow, a speck on the crystal horizon, streaked across the desert under a cloudless sky. I braved the sparkling salt pan, walking on ground so hot it penetrated my shoe soles and cooked my feet. I approached one of the newly installed photoelectric devices, complete with a flip-clock timer, speed sensor, and a blinking red bulb to let you know the event was under way. In my left hand, I clutched a clipboard with a pink timing record form and a stubby No. 2 pencil. I halted at an orange cone that served as my marker and peered off into the distance. The shiny racer rose out of the shimmering earth like a phoenix bursting out of the desert floor. Moments later, a metallic streak thundered past me, its horsepower stabbing my eardrums, its wheels spreading a dust cloud that engulfed me. The flip numbers on the timing station began flapping away, until 238 MPH appeared, along with the timing. I tasted salt on my tongue as I jotted 1:12.5 at the appropriate place on the clipboard form.

Outside of the tent, a banner announced our new sponsor—
PERFECT CIRCLE PISTON RINGS, HAGERSTOWN, INDIANA—with
the company logo in front of a black-and-white checkered flag.
The banner ballooned outward like a sail in a gust of wind.
Murray Jensen bowed as he passed through the tent's open flap
door. He had a bottle of ice-cold soda pop with condensation
drops forming on the glass. Pudgy and short, with tinted sun-
glasses, a blue short-sleeved shirt, and khaki shorts that fell to his
knees, Murray was the younger brother of Hank Jensen, driver
of the Silver Arrow. The two men were my first cousins from my
mother's side, and their younger brothers, Gordon and Kenneth,
assisted as mechanics on our volunteer racing team out here in
the West Desert.

For years, all of the brothers had gravitated around Hank, a
brilliant inventor featured on the covers of *Life* and *Popular Mechanics*. He'd made a small fortune from his patents, nearly all of
which had to do with automobiles, including a revolutionary
anti-backfire device used by all of the big Detroit car companies.
Each time he cooked up an invention—from his Starterator
Coincidental Starter, which greatly enhanced engine-starting
performance, to his Universal Synchronizing Distributor, an item
that improved the flow of the current between the ignition and
the combustion chamber—he'd return from Detroit a million or
so dollars richer.

Hank kept busy throughout the summers, trying to break his
old distance and speed records. He had been coming out here to
the Salt Flats since 1912, when he first started racing cars while still
a teenager. Most observers agree that he was the man who made
this stretch of salty desert the world's preeminent destination for
land speed racing. And, being the ever-dutiful cousin, I volun-
teered, along with his brothers, to assist him in his endeavors.

As I stepped under the shade of the striped canvas awning, Murray polished off his Coca-Cola, placed the empty in a wooden bottle crate, and raised the binoculars draped around his neck to get a better look.

"How'd he do?"

"Two thirty-eight, at one twelve," I said. "And a half."

He lowered the binoculars, grimacing. "Any way we can erase that half?"

I leaned in the tent, tossed the clipboard on a folding card table, and popped back out, staying under the awning to avoid the sun. "He's got two more markers to pick up speed. Let's wait to hear back from Gordy and Ken."

"You know what your problem is, Art?"

"No, but I'm sure you're about to tell me, Murr."

"You're too honest," he said. He laughed and gave my shoulder a squeeze as he walked past. "Oh well. It's only the trials. He's just gotta get a faster start, that's all."

"It's six seconds better than he did in June," I said. "I'm sure he'll best his old record soon."

"It isn't *his* old record he has to beat," said Murray. "All these young Turks are leaving him in the dust, taking away sponsorships. We've even been dropped by Barr's Auto Supply, and they stopped paying us long ago."

"Well, he'll always be the first to race these flats," I said. "Nobody can take that away from him." I paused a second and looked around. "Where is everybody?"

"Ain'tcha heard?"

"No. What?"

He took a shot at his best British accent. "I say old bean, the good chap shall be here shortly, and after a spot of tea, I hear he'll go out motoring."

I glanced down at today's *Salt Lake Examiner,* held down on the table with a big, heavy rock to prevent the wind from blowing it away. A picture gracing A-1 showed a smartly dressed, aristocratic Englishman arriving at the Salt Lake municipal airport. He boasted a mop of curly hair, dark little round eyes, and an angular face. Perhaps the fact that he could rightly claim to be a distant relative of the royal family accounted for all the press fanfare. Or maybe it had something to do with his celebrity status in Great Britain as the nation's top racer.

Whatever the reason, the headline above his photo said it all:

BRIT SEEKING TO BREAK OLD RECORD
CAUSES STIR

"Don't look now," said Murray. "His majesty has arrived."

A convoy of vehicles swept across the flats, zooming past rows of tents and grease monkeys adjusting race cars. They slowed to a halt at a circus-type tent printed with a giant Union Jack. Murray watched through binoculars, chewing Black Jack gum and offering me a stick. I shook my head and told him I'd be back. I set off west, in the direction of the encampment, to get a better look at what appeared to be a bona fide brouhaha. Along the way, I passed colorful metal signs, thrown up in haste, wired to poles in the ground. CHAMPION SPARK PLUGS, SINCLAIR MOTOR OIL, GOODRICH SAFETY SILVERTOWN TIRES, 100% PENNSYVANIA VALVOLINE MOTOR OILS.

In the distance, a huge speaker perched atop a steel tower called out announcements that echoed for miles: *". . . timed trials . . . drivers Larrabee, Gomez, Napier, Mandell, and Lindquist . . . all assisting vehicles please report to the starting line . . . next qualifying runs begin in five minutes, five minutes. . . ."*

A hundred or so people gathered around the Union Jack tents as the motorist's entourage got out of their cars and trucks. Atop a long trailer pulled by a pickup, the speed demon's auto was kept a closely guarded secret by a tarp clamped down by metal fasteners. People clapped, and I worked my way to the front of the gathering to see if I could get a better view of what was happening. A British Pathé newsreel camera, emblazoned with a crowing rooster on the side, whirred away as a mustachioed British interviewer quizzed Clive Underhill, who looked every bit as debonair as he did in the papers and the Saturday afternoon news shorts.

"This is quite the welcome . . . Could you step closer to the microphone? Yes, thank you. As I was saying, this is quite the welcome, Mr. Underhill. Does this mark your debut at Bonneville?"

Mustache man tilted the microphone toward Underhill.

"No. I took part in my first run here in 1935, under the auspices of the Wembley Motor Club. Back then I came all the way out here to witness Sir Malcolm Campbell's land speed record in the Bluebird. Now, with three years behind me, I am ready to best Campbell's old record, and all subsequent ones."

The crowd laughed and light applause crackled, prompting a smile and nod from Underhill.

"Do you anticipate breaking any land speed records today, Mr. Underhill?"

"Not today. That will likely occur next week. Today is a test run using the Desert Lightning prototype, so that I can ascertain driving conditions. It's, uh, quite different here than it is at Daytona. Today's run will help me understand what modifications, if any, need to be made on the Spectre, which I'll unveil next week."

"Ah yes, splendid, Mr. Underhill," said the interviewer. "You are a long way from home. How do you find conditions here in the Utah desert?"

"Bloody hot. Dry as a bone. It's quite desolate. White crystals for as far as the eye can see, almost as blinding as snow. It always takes me a while to get used to the heat out here. The mercury never climbs this high back home. Right now, we're a hundred and twenty-five miles from Salt Lake City, so we're far from the amenities of civilization. We stand here on this rather stunning plateau, a hundred miles long, twenty miles wide, surrounded by distant mountains, to engage in friendly competition to see who can be the fastest man on earth. It is remarkable, this day and age we live in."

"Will you be kind enough to reveal any details about your racing machine to the ladies and gentlemen back home in England?"

"I've brought two versions of it with me to Utah," he said. "The prototype under the cover there is what I will be driving this afternoon. Next week, I will introduce Spectre, a bold new speeder that has been two years in the making."

"Will you be looking to break the last record set by Sir Malcolm Campbell?" asked the interviewer.

"No, as a matter of fact, Campbell's record of 301.129 miles per hour from the third of September, 1935, was beaten two months later, on the nineteenth of November, by British racer George Eyston, who reached a top speed of 311.42 miles per hour in his Thunderbolt. I understand Eyston has modified the car by narrowing the front-end intake and adding a new grille, and he'll make an attempt at the end of this month to break his record from last year. However, it is my goal to set a record next week that not even the talented Mr. Eyston can touch."

Underhill's remarks triggered light laughter and clapping, and he shaded his eyes with his hand to survey the scene. He noticed people growing restless in the terrible heat, and he faced the interviewer.

"Unfortunately, I must be saying farewell," he said. "My timed prototype trials are coming up shortly and I must confer with my crew."

"Thank you, Mr. Underhill, and I think I speak for all of England when I wish you the very best of luck."

The camera kept rolling as the audience swarmed Underhill while he was stepping down from the makeshift platform. I watched him shake hands with the adoring masses, pose for photographs, and laugh at jokes I am certain were stale. The man had charm to spare, no question about it. He struck me as the sort of fellow who, if he played his cards right, might very well wind up a movie star.

I set off back to base camp when I literally bumped into Roscoe Lund, the man who'd been my partner in the Salt Lake City Police Department for four years and, before that, in the Salt Lake County Sheriff's office. His eyes turned to saucers when he saw me, and his smile showed off the gap between his front teeth.

"Arthur Oveson, as I live and breathe! Get over here!"

He bypassed the handshake and went straight for the hug, squeezing tight, with plenty of backslapping. He smelled of Aqua Velva, but I also caught a faint whiff of his favorite chewing tobacco, Red Man. He backed away and gave me the eyes up-and-down treatment, with a nod of approval. Roscoe had put on a few pounds over the years, and while I definitely would not call him fat, I don't think beefy would be inaccurate. He still wore the same linty tweed sport coat and baggy green trousers that he wore back when he worked with me in the detective bureau.

"How the hell are you, Art?"

"I can't complain," I said. "And you?"

"Me? I'm on top of the world!"

"No kidding? Private investigating business treating you well?"

"Never better."

I smiled warmly at my old friend. "Good. I'm happy to hear. Hey, we need to catch up with each other. It's been, what, since Christmas when we last saw you? My kids keep asking, 'Where's Uncle Roscoe?' You've got to put in an appearance. The natives are getting restless."

"I'd like that, a whole hell of a lot," said Roscoe. "Hey, I wish I could stick around and talk for a while, but I'm on a choice detail."

"Oh yeah? Do tell."

"I'm working security for the Englishman," he said.

I'm sure my face went as long as the Salt Flats. "No kidding? You mean . . ."

"The top dog himself. Clive Underhill. He needs extra muscle, beyond what he's already got. Somebody who knows the lay of the land, I guess. If I had my druthers, I'd prefer to stand around and chew the cud with you, Art. But duty calls, I'm afraid. I don't want to lose this job the day after I landed it." His face lit up and that big smile came back. "Hey, come with me."

"What do you mean?"

"Underhill will be testing his prototype in a half hour," said Roscoe. "Keep me company. I got the best seat in the house."

"Sure," I said. "Let's see for ourselves what all the hubbub is about."

Two

I had never seen anything like it.

Clive Underhill's car—if one might call it that—appeared straight out of *Flash Gordon*: a twenty-eight-foot, eight-inch-long polished black teardrop of a machine, with a stabilizing tailfin and tires concealed under domes. The glass-like surface reflected clouds and mountains, mechanics and salt, and anything else that came close to it. Tiny uppercase letters spelled out DESERT LIGHTNING on the sides of the car, and on the front, a Union Jack flag and Old Glory crisscrossed each other. Unlike so many other vehicles here today, Desert Lightning let out a steady rumble when she idled rather than a loud chugging. A member of Underhill's crew crawled into the driving compartment and backed the car down a ramp attached to the trailer. Newsreel cameras perched on tripods filmed as his car was anchored to the support truck that would launch it.

Working for Underhill meant Roscoe had to remain near him at all times. I watched the Englishman charm admirers, mostly men but also a few adventurous women who came out all this way to gawk at the eligible bachelor. The shutterbugs got especially animated when world champion German motorist Gerhardt "Rudy" Heinrich shook hands with Underhill. We stood in the shade of the observation tent, and I bristled with excitement at the prospect of meeting the world-famous racer.

A man bearing a strong resemblance to Underhill, only shorter and younger, excused his way through the crowd and whispered something in Underhill's ear. Underhill opened his mouth and nodded, leaned toward the man, and whispered something back. Underhill handed a young boy an autograph book and pencil, then flashed his palms, as if to break up the gathering.

"Gentlemen, I am told I am due at Desert Lightning, so I'm afraid I'm going to have to cut this short," he said at the top of his lungs. That triggered disappointed "ahhs," and he grinned and tilted his head. "I am sure our paths will cross again soon. Good day!"

Underhill's younger doppelgänger came toward us, eyeing me suspiciously. "Who's he?" he asked Roscoe.

"This is my friend Art Oveson." Roscoe gestured to the man. "Art, this is Nigel Underhill."

"Good to know you, Mr. Underhill."

I held out my hand. He glared at it and refused to shake it. I pulled back, doing my best to muster a sheepish smile. He sneered at Roscoe. "What is he doing here?"

"I can vouch for him," said Roscoe. "He's a police detective."

"You know the rules," said Nigel. "This is a restricted area. Guests require advance clearance."

I said, "Look, I've got to go anyway. It was a pleasure meeting . . ."

"No, Art," said Roscoe, holding out his arm like a tollgate. "Stay. I don't work for this prick. I work for his brother."

Nigel moved in close to Roscoe. "You know, Lund, I don't care for your attitude. The only reason I'm letting you to stay is that my brother, for some inexplicable reason, seems to feel better when you're present. But I advise you to stay out of my way. Do I make myself clear?"

"Crystal," said Roscoe, in a sullen way, placing a fresh wooden matchstick between his teeth.

Before Nigel Underhill departed, he grimaced at me for good measure. He stormed off into the sun, in the direction of Desert Lightning, where his brother was putting on a helmet and goggles and consulting with his team.

"I'd better go," I said to Roscoe.

"Fuck him," said Roscoe. "Stay put. You're my guest."

"I don't feel too welcome here," I said. "Let's get together some other time, huh?"

"Don't let that little prick get to you, Art," said Roscoe. "He's a brittle sissy, that's all. Stick around. We've got the best seats in the house. Underhill's test run begins in five minutes."

I held out my hand. "Good seeing you again, Roscoe. Don't be such a stranger."

His expression turned forlorn as he gripped hands. "Aw hell, I was gonna introduce you to Underhill," he said. "He's a hell of a lot nicer than that bimbo brother of his."

"I appreciate it, but I don't want my cousins to think I've fallen off the face of the earth," I said. "See you soon, huh?"

"Take it easy, Art."

I started off in the direction of Cousin Hank's base along a route that took me past tents, blasting engines, crews in colored coveralls, refreshment stands, and the blaring loudspeaker. I took one backward glance at Clive Underhill's sprawling Union Jack encampment.

On my way back to base, I spotted a Utah Highway Patrol car parked alongside the long, wooden protective barrier near the main track. I knew the two patrolmen in uniform, Howie Bennion and Lowell Calder, from some past raids I'd conducted during my days with the Morals Squad. I wiped sweat off my palm and walked up to shake hands. "Hey fellas! You boys keeping things safe out here?" I asked with a chuckle.

"You know how it goes," said Howie. "Another day in paradise."

"We always get stuck on these lousy beats," said Lowell. "Got us workin' on a Saturday. Can you beat that? Saturday! So much for my fishin' plans."

"I hear the Englishman is gonna make history today," said Howie.

"It's a test run," I said. "He's saving the real show for next week."

Words echoed from the loudspeaker: *". . . Underhill is now at the starting line, waiting for the official flag to be raised, and he will commence in five . . . four . . . three . . . two . . . one . . . And he's off!"*

"Don't go anywhere, Art," said Howie. "You'll miss out."

"Yeah, there's a rumor that he's gonna top four hundred next week," said Lowell. "Ain't that something? Four hundred!"

I strolled up to the barrier near the black-and-white UHP sedan to watch Underhill speed across the massive salt track rimmed by stubby hills.

Cheers erupted in the distance as Underhill's car came rocketing out of the spot where the white crystal and azure sky touched. It shot past us, a giant bullet streaking from one end of the desert valley to the other. Nearing the finish mark a ways to the south, the vehicle left the earth for a few seconds, circled boomerang style, flipped upside down and skidded to gravelly halt. Light smoke turned black very quickly, and I spotted a flash of orange near the smashed tailfin.

"Good heavens," I whispered. Panicked cries came from distant bleachers as I turned to the two patrolmen. "Can you drive me over there, pronto?"

"Sure thing," said Lowell. "Let's go!"

I jumped the barrier, opened the back door, and my foot wasn't even entirely inside when the car took off in a mad rush across the flats. I pulled the door closed and leaned forward, resting my elbows on the seat top between the heads of the two patrolmen.

We arrived first at the accident scene, and by that time, the small flames had grown bigger and hotter. Because the car was upside down and full of fuel, I wondered how we were going to get Clive Underhill out before it exploded. I found an opening near the cockpit dome where Underhill's arm was waving around, desperately searching for help. The wail of sirens came closer, but I knew I could not wait for the emergency vehicles to arrive. I belly-flopped on salt and inch-wormed my way under the overturned car. I realized that the only hope Underhill had for getting out of the burning car was for someone to pull him out. My hand squeezed Underhill's hand, and that's when I smelled what I feared worst: gasoline fumes.

"Move away from it, Art!" shouted Howie.

Clive Underhill's upside-down face appeared between broken glass. "Don't let me go," he said, surprisingly calmly. "I don't want to die."

"Today's not your day," I said. "Are your restraining belts re-leased?"

"Yes!"

"OK," I said, taking a deep breath. "On the count of three. One, two, three. . . ."

One often hears that before you think you're about to die, you see your whole life flash before your eyes. It's not true. You only see a handful of snapshots—maybe half a dozen images total—because you simply don't have enough time to walk through your entire life again. With flames devouring car wreckage, gasoline fumes stabbing my nostrils, and a hand reaching out of twisted metal beckoning for help, I had no time for a stroll down memory lane. Still, scenes from my life—etched in the deepest recesses of my mind—took shape with crystal clarity: the morning when I was seven that my father took me fishing on the lake; the time I found out he'd been shot and killed; my first awkward dance with fifteen-year-old Clara Snow, whom I later married; the day I awoke from a coma-like state after battling the Spanish influenza of 1918; the births of my three children, Sarah Jane, Hyrum, and Emily. . . .

"Wait! I think my ankle's caught!"

"Your ankle? Well, can you get it . . . can you free it?"

"I'm trying, but it feels like there's something pinning . . ."

His words faded as he bent his upper torso to get a better look. I noticed an ominous puddle of gasoline expanding out-ward from the crunched tailfin, well on its way toward crackling orange flames. I never take the Lord's name in vain, but right then I couldn't stop myself from saying, "Oh god."

I jerked my head up. "Pull your ankle out!"

"I'm trying! The metal is digging in. . . ."

"Yank it as hard as you can! Do whatever you've got to do! We're both dead if we don't get out now!"

"Okay, okay. . . ."

A pained expression came over his face, his teeth clenched together, his skin color turned purple, and the veins on his neck bulged. His eyes opened wide and he let out a pained shout at the top of his lungs as his hand squeezed mine even tighter.

"It's free!"

I pulled with all of my might, groaning as I threw all of my strength into my right arm. To reinforce it, I instinctively lunged my left arm outward and grabbed his wrist. I redoubled my efforts and his body began to move toward me, like a tooth being extracted by a pair of pliers. We both yelled in a mix of agony and pumping adrenaline, and I tugged him out of that burning mash-up of steel and glass, rubber and gasoline and oil. The smoke had darkened, the flames crackled hotter, and that gas puddle at the rear of the car kept flowing outward. I placed Clive Underhill's arm around my neck and struggled to my feet, bringing him up with me. He wailed as he put his weight on his badly mangled ankle, but I managed to keep him upright by wrapping my arms around his chest and back. I charged forward as fast as I could, baking under a hot sun that seemed only fifty feet away, and Underhill limped and stumbled and jogged and generally fought to keep up with me. The force of the blast behind us struck our backs with a hot shock wave, swatting us to the ground. Slamming chest down into the solid salt surface, I felt the wind knocked out of me. That instant, with my nose pressed into the dry desert earth, I knew we'd narrowly survived a blast that would've incinerated both of us had we remained stuck back at the car.

A fleet of automobiles sped toward us from the south, accompanied by an ambulance and a big red hook-and-ladder with its bell clanging. (*What good is it going to do out here with no hydrants?* I wondered.) Brakes squealed, car doors flew open, and people swarmed around us, ungluing Underhill from me, leading him to the ambulance. A crowd enveloped Underhill, and I could no longer see him, which was fine by me. After my brush with death, I wanted nothing more than to get in my car, drive back to Salt Lake City, and spend the rest of the day with my family, where I belonged. I'd helped my cousin Hank, keeping a promise to him that I'd made some time back, and then I rescued a man from a flaming vehicle that seemed to be a cross between an automobile and a *Flash Gordon* spaceship. In short, I had done my good deed, and experienced more than my fair dose of the human race for one day.

I walked past tents, awnings, racing crews, cutting across a clearing to an area where rows of automobiles were parked, a sea of running boards, rear spare tires, shiny headlamps gleaming in the sun. I blew a sigh of relief as I neared my car, a blue '36 Dodge that I purchased brand-new a few years back. I reached for the handle to open the door when I heard a distant "Hello! Hello! You there!" I turned around, facing a plump man in a sweat-drenched yellow shirt with a striped tie, his trousers held up by suspenders, and a white Panama on his head.

"I say! You there! Hold up a moment, will you!"

When he reached me, he was panting, and his face was covered in a layer of perspiration. "So sorry, I'm not used to this bloody heat," he said, in a heavy British accent. He held out his hand and I shook it. "Hi there, I'm Albert Shaw, Mr. Underhill's manager."

"Good to know you, Shaw," I said. "My name is Art Oveson."

We released hands and Shaw jabbed a thumb over his shoulder. "Somebody back there said you're a constable."

"Constable?" I chuckled at the title. "Well, I am a police detective."

He smiled. "That was a brave thing you did back there, Mr. Oveson."

"Anybody would've done the same thing."

"That's where you're wrong," he said. "Only someone with tremendous fortitude would have done it."

"That's kind of you to say," I said, reaching out to open the car door.

"Mr. Underhill would very much like you to join him for dinner tonight at the Coconut Grove," said Shaw. "It's his way of thanking you for what you did out there."

"With all due respect," I said, looking Shaw up and down. "I don't think he's in any shape to paint the town red tonight."

"Oh, he'll be up to it," said Shaw. "Even if it takes crutches to pull it off."

"Really, there's no need for him to thank me. It's not a big deal, Mr. Shaw. . . ."

"Albert."

"Albert. Please tell him I said thanks, but he doesn't have to . . ."

"So he can expect you around half past six for cocktails, seven for dinner?"

"Well, if you must know . . ."

"Bring your wife, too! By all means, bring her!"

I shot him a quizzical glance. "How'd you know I'm married?"

"You're a policeman, and most American policemen are married," he said. "And I noticed the wedding ring on your finger, Mr. Oveson."

"Art."

"Art."

I thought it over. The Coconut Grove was a swanky down-town ballroom where big bands played. On certain nights, when some musical big shot was in town, radio station KDYL would broadcast live from there. I'd never set foot in the place. I was pretty sure Clara hadn't, either. For simple married Mormons like us, who dedicated our nights to parenting, the Coconut Grove seemed like a foreign country, an exotic place out of a Fred Astaire–Ginger Rogers picture.

There was something else—another matter I did not want to discuss with someone I didn't know. Ever since giving birth to our third daughter back in 1934, Clara had been suffering from what the psychiatrists called "mental disease." She'd been hit by a full-blown bout of post-natal melancholy. She experienced the same thing after she gave birth to Sarah Jane in 1923, and the doctors treated her with something called "hydrotherapy," which essentially consisted of lots of hot baths at the state mental hos-pital.

Unfortunately, after Emily's birth four years ago, her "blues" (as she called it) never subsided, and they could come on strong without any warning. Her condition, in fact, had actually resulted in a nervous breakdown two years ago, and she was forced to take time off teaching. Thus, I hated leaving her alone with the children at night, not because I doubted her abilities as a mother, but more out of my own personal concern for her well being. Her present condition made me reluctant to even leave the house today to come out to the Salt Flats to help my cousins. I did it anyway, out of a sense of loyalty. Now I was itching to get home, staring at a pudgy Englishman waiting for an answer and show-ing off his crooked bridgework in a hopeful smile.

"Seven, huh?"

He nodded. "If you don't wish to wet your whistle with a pre-dinner cocktail."

"I'm not much of a whistler wetter," I said. "A glass of lemonade is as wild as I get."

"So be it."

He held out his hand. I shook it. We went our separate ways.

Three

I swerved into the driveway of our bungalow on Sherman Avenue, a quiet residential street we'd relocated to last year. I parked next to our other car, an aging Oldsmobile. We treated it as Clara's car, and she used it to run errands, go to lunch with friends, and drive our kids places. She and I had three children: Sarah Jane, age 15; Hyrum, age nine; and Emily, now four. Clara and I were born the same year, 1901, and both turned 37 in 1938. The two of us made a conscious decision to stop at three kids. Three seemed a reasonable number. Not too many. Not too few. It allowed us to give each child plenty of individual attention.

I shut off the engine, pocketed keys, and walked up to my house, reaching in the mailbox and pulling out a few envelopes I somehow missed yesterday. *Bill, bill, bill, envelope containing brochure from the Ward Line ocean cruises that I'd requested a month ago. . . . Parcel pickup slip.* Looks like I'd have to run Sarah Jane over to the post office to pick up her latest record. She belonged to one of those clubs where you get half a dozen phonograph albums for a nickel and then you have to buy four more in the next two years. She loved classical music, and would save her allowances to buy the albums. The little pickup slip identified the newest arrival as BEETHOVEN: SYMPH #6 & BRAHMS: TRAGIC OVERTURE.

"Hmm, 'Tragic Overture,'" I said out loud. "Sounds peppy."

I entered the house and gave the front door a good, hard shove closed so everybody'd know I was home. I set the mail down on the little hallway table. A second later, my daughter Emily came bounding up and leapt into my arms, and I lifted her up and gave her a big hug.

"Daddy!"

"Eskimo," I said. We rubbed noses. "Butterfly." We rubbed eyelashes together. "And one old-fashioned . . ." I kissed her on the forehead.

"I miss you, Daddy!"

"Me too, sugar plum."

My son, Hi, peeked around the corner, cowboy hat planted firmly on his head, and fired one of his silvery cap guns. Two loud cracks sounded, and I lowered Emily to the floor and put my hand over my heart. Emily ran off to the living room, clearing out of the way for the frontier drama unfolding.

"You shot me, you dang varmint! Wait till I get my hands on you!"

"Meet me outside and I'll send you out in a blaze of glory, you desperado!"

"Not if I send you to Boot Hill first!" I looked around. "Where's Mom?"

"In the bedroom, resting," he said, lowering his gun. "Says she's not feeling good. Again."

"Why don't you go out in the backyard and I'll be along

soon," I said, giving the brim of his cowboy hat an affectionate downward tug.

"You'd better be there, or I'll hunt you down at the O.K. Corral," he said.

"Oh, I'll be there, all right," I said. "Now get a move on, pardner!"

"All right, Dad! See you soon, baboon!"

"Not if I see you first, hombre."

Hi took off running, cutting through the kitchen, and I could hear the back door slam. Emily was sitting in the living room, listening to an afternoon children's show on the radio. *"Send three box tops from any brand of Kellogg's cereal to me, Miss Jane, Box P, Chicago 77, Illinois. That's all. Send no money. We'll enclose your very own membership card, certificate, and magic ring. Miss Jane's Happy Saturday Kiddie Club is free to every boy and girl. . . ."*

I grinned wistfully as I started out down the hall. On my way, I stopped and picked up the envelope from The Ward Line, tore it open, and pulled out a glossy color brochure. It contained pictures of exotic shores, majestic cruise ships, and happy tourists. I took it with me, walking past the kitchen, the bathroom, the bedrooms, to a closed door at the end of the corridor. Sarah Jane's door was also shut. *Bad sign.*

For the past few years, a growing rift had developed between Clara and Sarah Jane. Personality conflicts and differences of opinion sparked repeated clashes. As the family diplomat—not a job I chose, by the way—I intervened repeatedly to try to neutralize the hostilities, but I usually ended up becoming the proverbial messenger repeatedly slain by the Oveson women.

At its most basic level, the tension reflected the divergent paths followed by mother and daughter. For her part, Clara's severe bouts of melancholy, brought on following the birth of our daughter Emily, were exacerbated by her decision to quit her job as an English teacher at East High School. Her resignation came only after years of intense pressure from members of her family, my family, and various folks in our ward ("ward" being a Mormon word for a congregation). Back when she was juggling the demands of teaching and motherhood, she faced a relentless barrage of disapproval for her attempt to do both.

Not everybody lobbied Clara to quit her job. I encouraged her to stick with it. So did a handful of others, especially her colleagues and the school principal. But when the bishop at our old ward weighed in and told Clara that he thought it was "unwise" for her keep teaching while she had three children to raise, she abruptly quit. She'd been an educator since her late teens. In her adult life, it was all she had ever known. She found it richly rewarding. Her students loved her, and every year she got emotional when it came time for her classroom to move on to the next grade. They held going-away parties with games and refreshments. Clara also organized fund-raisers to enable students to collect money for the less fortunate.

When she quit, she lost all of this, and it only worsened the depression she experienced after Emily's birth. At our doctor's recommendation, she saw a psychiatrist, who diagnosed her with "mental disease," saying that Clara suffered from an acute case of "melancholia." At his advice, I took time off of work during that period to look after Emily. Clara slowly recovered from her downward spiral, but her personality changed. She became more rigid and embittered. She began to place greater emphasis on order and decorum. She wanted the Oveson clan to be liked, and to that end she championed such things as fitting in, attending church regularly, avoiding political discussions, dressing nicely, and maintaining proper weight and a healthy diet. Some days, she'd "hit bottom," as she put it, falling into a deep state of depression that would leave her virtually immobilized.

Sarah Jane veered down a different path, embracing nonconformity. She began questioning lessons she was learning in the Mormon Church. She'd also developed her own politics over the past year. She kept a framed picture of Eleanor Roosevelt on her wall. Sarah Jane once shocked her mother by saying, "If Jesus were alive, he'd be a communist or a hobo riding the rails." Clara dismissed her from the dinner table and told her to go her room for that remark. Clara frequently insisted that I, as the family patriarch, needed to be harder on Sarah Jane than I was.

"She needs a firm hand guiding her," Clara told me. "I don't always want to be the witch, Art. You need to step up to the plate."

Now I faced our closed bedroom door, which usually meant that Clara had "hit bottom." A feeling of dread shot through me as I knocked lightly, turned the knob, and eased the door open a few inches.

"Come in," she said.

Lights off. Blinds closed. In the dimness, Clara was lying on the bed with her arm folded over her eyes. The bed was still made. She wore a dark skirt and a light-colored blouse, but in this darkness, I could not tell precisely what color they were. I crossed the room and sat down on the corner of the bed.

"Hi, honey," I said.

"What have you got in your hand?"

I looked down at a dimly lit picture of a cruise ship, wondering how she saw it in this darkness. "That Ward Line brochure I requested a while back."

"It's a pipe dream. We can never afford it."

"I know."

"Well?"

"Well what?"

She lifted her arm off her eyes and turned her head toward me. Even with the lack of light, I admired her pretty, shoulder-length hair, waved so nicely, like a motion picture actress. She rolled slightly in bed, propped herself up on her right elbow, and blinked at me.

"How did he do?"

"He didn't break any records," I said. "He's no competition for these new hot shots. Compared to some of these youngsters, Hank's a dinosaur, I'm afraid. Enough about him. How are you?"

"Not good. I had another episode. The stress from it gave me one of those awful headaches, and I've been throwing up all afternoon."

"Did anything bring it on?" I asked.

"I had an argument with our daughter," she said, plunging into the pillow. Her hair splashed outward. "She insists she's not going to church anymore."

"Did she give a reason?"

"She told me to my face that she doesn't believe in God anymore."

I needed a few seconds to take in that news.

"Well, I'll have a word with her," I said.

"Would you?" Clara asked, reaching over to squeeze my free hand in hers.

"Yeah."

We shared a silence.

"We'll never have the money for a Caribbean cruise," she said.

"All I ask is that you look at it. Just give it some thought."

I waited a beat, and then said: "I don't suppose you're feeling good enough to go out tonight?"

"I couldn't. I'm feeling too sick. It's this nausea and the vomiting. I'm not even sure I can sit up straight for more than a half hour. Why do you ask?"

"Well, when I was out at Bonneville today, I sort of—I, uh, saved a man's life, and he wanted to know if we wanted to . . ."

Her mouth dropped. "Wait! Back up."

"Yeah?"

"You saved a man's life? That's a big thing. When were you going to tell me?"

"I'm telling you now."

She sat upright in bed, propping herself up on her elbow. "Out with it! Who did you save?"

"He's an Englishman. His name is Clive Underhill."

Clara's eyes practically popped out of her head when she heard his name. "You're kidding me! *The* Clive Underhill? Tell me all about it!"

I recounted my experience of pulling Clive Underhill out of his burning car, and the encounter I'd had afterward with his manager, Mr. Shaw. The end result, I told her, was an invitation from Shaw for me—and my wife—to attend the Coconut Grove tonight, as Underhill's guests. Clara sat in rapt attention, hugging a pillow tightly against her bosoms, her pearly smile showing through crimson lips. When I reached the end of my tale, I waited for her to speak, but evidently I'd left her speechless. My tale seemed to exorcise her demons. She picked right up. She seemed almost dizzy with happiness.

"I don't think I'm going," I said. "Especially if you're not up to . . ."

"Pshaw! You're going to the Grove tonight!"

"What about you?"

"What about me?"

"You said you were sick."

"I'll stay here and recuperate," she said. "But don't let that stop you!"

I shrugged and shook my head. "I don't know . . ."

"Don't do this, Art."

"Don't do what?"

"The shrugging . . . The *oh, I don't know. Gee whiz.* That! Don't do it! You're going tonight, and that's the end of it."

"What am I going to wear?"

"Never mind that," she said. "But there is one thing . . ."

She hesitated.

I prodded. "What?"

"Sarah Jane . . ."

"I'll have a word with her," I said. "I can't promise anything."

"All I ask is that you try."

I nodded and rose to my feet with that sinking feeling of dread, though I hid it well with my "shucks" grin. My news had reanimated Clara, who now seemed full of purpose, despite her illness—getting out of bed and preparing me for my big night out. That left me with the task of confronting Sarah Jane about her waning spiritual commitment. On my way out, I set the Ward Line ocean cruise brochure on Clara's bureau drawer, and she gave it a glance.

"At least consider it," I said.

"You know we can't afford it."

"Please."

"OK. I'll look at it later. Right now, we've got bigger things to attend to."

I crossed the hallway and tapped on Sarah Jane's door with

my knuckles. Some sort of classical music played on the other side, and she responded with a muffled "come in." I opened the door.

From her desk by the window, Sarah Jane looked at me through wire-frame eyeglasses and smiled. She kept her honey-colored hair out of her eyes with the help of a thin black head-band. Her Admiral phonograph was spinning something melodic with a big string section and plenty of woodwinds.

I stepped inside. Her room contained a bed against the wall that she seldom made (to her mother's chagrin), a dresser, and a desk buried under orderly clutter: her typewriter, articles and pieces of paper, and stacks of books—some hers, some the library's. A wall once covered with paintings of ballerinas and framed engravings from children's books now played home to a cork bulletin board pinned over with layers of newspaper and magazine articles about striking workers and Nazis in Germany and lynch mobs in the South. To the right of the board was my daughter's beloved framed black-and-white Eleanor Roosevelt picture, signed by the first lady herself. Sarah Jane turned the volume down on her record player. Then she flipped her chair around.

"Have a seat," she said.

"Nice music," I said, walking to the chair and sitting down. "By the way, you got a pickup slip in the mail. Something about a Sad Symphony. . . ."

" 'Tragic Overture,' by Brahms," she said. "You're getting there."

She sat on the edge of her bed and rocked back and forth, flashing a quick smile that soon went back to a frown.

"Don't tell me, let me guess," she said. "It's about Mother."

"Well, it has to do with something she told me."

"Our argument?"

"She said you're having doubts," I said. "About your faith."

"Yes, that's true," she said.

"I was hoping we might discuss it." I gestured to the typewriter, which had a sheet of paper in the carriage. "Am I interrupting?"

"Oh that?" she asked. "It's a letter to Mrs. Roosevelt."

"Another one?"

"She replied to the last one," she said, beaming. "I'm going to get it framed, along with the picture she autographed for me. It pays to have an uncle high up in the FBI."

"Yes it does, doesn't it?" I chuckled. "So, what's this letter about?"

"I'm asking her to do what she can to help change the laws so the United States lets Jewish refugees into our country," she said. "Do you have any idea what the Nazis are doing to those poor people in Germany?"

"I have some inkling," I said. "I've seen the newsreels."

"Jews have been stripped of the right to vote," she said. "They can't own property. Their families are being forced into slums that are guarded by armed soldiers, like prisons. It's eating me up, I swear. I'm losing sleep over it, Dad. And all of these stupid leaders in our country are sitting around, twiddling their thumbs, doing nothing, hoping the problem just goes away."

"I agree it is awful," I said. "Maybe the first lady can do something to change things. But the real reason I came in here is to talk to you about this disagreement between you and your mother."

"Oh. That. Yeah. I'm not going to church anymore."

"So I've heard. That's a drastic change for you," I said. "Care to discuss it?"

"What's there to talk about?" she asked. "It's my decision. It's what I want."

"Of course, the choice is yours to make," I said. "You know by now that I'm not the type of father that's going to force you to do something you don't believe in. But I also want you to know that you should feel comfortable talking to me about this, or any other matters in your life, anytime you feel like it."

"Thanks, Dad."

I nodded. She nodded. I smiled. She smiled. We seemed to be at an impasse.

I drew a deep breath and said, "Mind if I ask you one thing?"

"Go ahead."

"Is it the Church specifically that you're having troubles with? Or is it a bigger philosophical issue with God?"

"Both."

She didn't elaborate. She was not making this easy.

"OK. That's a start. Let me ask you—"

"If it's all the same to you, I don't feel like talking about it right now," she said. "I want to finish writing my letter to Mrs. Roosevelt. Could we talk about it later?"

"OK," I said, nodding. "Just tell me this."

"Yes?"

"Did something happen recently that brought this on?"

"It was the school bus," she said, sure I'd know what she meant.

And I did. She was referring to a horrific accident on the first day of December in 1937. It happened in a hamlet called South Jordan, southwest of Salt Lake City. That morning, thick fog, combined with falling snow, caused whiteouts all over the valley. Around eight in the morning, a fast-moving train collided with a school bus at a railroad crossing. Thirty-nine students rode that bus to school. The Denver & Rio Grande Western locomotive hurtled through space at seventy miles per hour, slicing the bus in two, raining debris in all directions, and dragging the bus's front half more than two thousand feet before a brakeman could bring the train to a halt. Fourteen students survived, all seated in the rear of the bus. The driver, Gerald "Skinny" Wilson—who'd driven that same route for years— was mangled beyond recognition inside of wreckage that had to be separated from the locomotive by workers using acetylene torches.

The staff at Salt Lake General Hospital set up a makeshift morgue, and posted lists of the passengers killed. The youngest student, Victoria Morgan, was fourteen, and the oldest of the passengers, Tommy Larsen, was eighteen. On that bleak day, parents broke down and wailed when they read the names of their children on typewritten lists. Six of the teens killed lived within a few blocks of each other, in the small town of Bluffdale. Youths, children really, destroyed in the prime of life, their deaths random and senseless. In the weeks following the accident, people kept finding objects near the railroad tracks: ruined band instruments, textbooks with pages warped by snow, lunch boxes packed with uneaten food.

"Do you think it happened for a reason?"

Sarah Jane's question brought me back to the present. "What?"

"The bus accident," she said.

"Yes."

She winced. "What possible reason?"

"To test us."

"But it didn't test you. Your children weren't killed."

She was putting me through the wringer. She wanted an

answer I could not provide. I said, "Heavenly Father tested us as a people, as a community."

"Would you feel that way if one of your kids had been killed in the accident?"

"I don't know. I hope I never have to find out." I gestured to her typewriter. "I'll let you get back to your letter to Mrs. Roosevelt."

I got up from the chair and walked over to her bedroom door. Before opening it, I thought a change of topic might cheer her up: "Say, guess who I'm going out to dinner with tonight?"

"Who?"

"Clive Underhill."

Her face lit up brighter than a lighthouse lamp. "*The* Clive Underhill?"

"The very same."

She fell to the floor and pulled her revered box of movie magazines out from under the bed. At the top of the box was something called *Modern Screen* magazine with big-shot Hollywood actor Errol Flynn's picture on the cover. She held it in front of my face. "They're going to make a movie about Clive Underhill! Starring Errol Flynn! And my dad is going out to dinner with him! I can't believe it!"

I laughed. "It's true."

"Hey, can I go, too?"

"No. Sorry. It's at the Coconut Grove. They don't allow anyone under twenty-one," I said. I leaned forward and whispered, "They serve liquor."

Now giddy, she smiled and waved her magazine. "My dad's gonna tie one on with Clive Underhill!"

"Hey, who said anything about tying one on? I'm strictly a lemonade man."

We laughed, and I told her all about my ordeal out at the Salt Flats. Exiting her room, I encountered Clara, who was none too pleased that I'd failed to secure a commitment from Sarah Jane to attend church regularly. But the way I saw it, I made our troubled daughter happy, and that counted for something.

Four

One could not find a ritzier joint in town than the Coconut Grove on Main Street, between Fourth and Fifth South. An endless yellow building, with a row of palm trees lining the front, the Coconut Grove called itself "the largest ballroom in America" on its penny postcards, available for purchase at the cash register inside. I believed it. No other ballroom I knew of boasted a trio of interior waterfalls spraying mist on a garden of tropical plants, or a dance floor that would've taken a day to drive across. Maybe that last part is an exaggeration, but not by much. In front of the Grove, college-age boys in suits earned extra change as valets and manning spotlights, swinging beams across the night sky like dueling swords. I parked a couple of blocks away. Valet parking was a foreign concept to me. Discomfort overwhelmed me as I approached that colossus. Stopping in my tracks, I took a deep breath, checking my slicked-back hair in a shop window, and moved on. Why did I come? I didn't want to be here. Ascending those front steps of the Grove, I'd never seen so many tuxedos and ball gowns in my life. I was a plebe among the ruling class, one of the unwashed masses worming my way through a crack in the floor to rub elbows with the elite.

"May I help you?" asked a maître d' as I entered the front doors. He clearly adhered to a black-tie dress code that was far more upscale than anything I had hanging in my closet. I could only manage my Sunday best: a tweed jacket, frayed around the edges, a white shirt and bright red tie, a pair of dark trousers, and shiny brown patent leather shoes. I looked like a frumpy college professor.

High above, chandeliers blazed brightly from all parts of the ceiling. An orchestra played dance music that flooded every inch of the place.

"Sir, may I help you?"

"Huh? Oh yes. You may, as a matter of fact. Help me, I mean. I'm here at the request of, uh . . ." For a split second, I blanked out on his name. I licked my lips nervously as I searched for it in my faulty filing cabinet of memories. "Underhill! Yes. Mr. Underhill has requested—Clive Underhill has requested my presence here. So he is, uh, you know, expecting me, and whatnot."

"You are?"

I pressed my hand into my chest. "Me?"

He studied me through sleepy eyes. "Yes. You."

"I'm Art Oveson. *Arthur* Oveson. Like King Arthur."

"I beg your pardon?"

"I'm just telling you my front name."

"Art!"

I spun in the direction of Roscoe. I'd never seen him dressed in a tux before. With his shaven head and a face battered by one too many fistfights, he reminded me of a retired boxing champion, smiling his gap-toothed smile and moving across the lobby in giant steps. This time, instead of a skeleton-shattering bear hug, we exchanged warm handshakes.

"You know this fellow?" asked the maître d' in a tone of contempt.

"He's with me. He's my chum." Roscoe eyed me. "Right this way, Art."

I tailed him. We skirted the shiny dance floor. There must have been two hundred people out there tripping the light fantastic. Elegance sparkled in all corners of the place. Beelining through here, one would hardly guess that there was a Depression on outside. We passed a series of tables covered in green linen, many empty of diners yet covered with partially completed meals or appetizers and ice-filled wine buckets with bottle necks poking out the top.

We arrived at a long booth packed with men, and at the center of the action sat none other than Clive Underhill, debonair and smartly dressed as ever, with his brown hair deliberately tousled to give him the appearance of an Oxford lad. He looked none the worse for wear, as if the fiery crash I pulled him out of that morning had never happened. He smiled up at me with twinkling eyes, and when he spoke, he raised his voice high above the din.

"Art, my dear fellow! You've come to join us! Please, find a seat somewhere amongst these ne'er-do-wells!"

That remark triggered an outburst of laughter. The men inched together tighter in the crescent-shaped booth, freeing a spot on the end for me to sit. I took a seat beside Underhill's kid brother. Roscoe smiled down at me in an assuring way, as if to say, "You're on your own, pal," and then he walked away. I surveyed the scene around me. A table full of Englishmen huddled around plates of lobster and filet mignon and chicken cordon bleu, with buckets full of bubbly and half-full cocktail glasses galore. Underhill commenced with introductions.

"This is my brother, Nigel. I believe you two have met."

Nigel, the younger version of Clive, sneered at me without saying a word.

"Good to know you, Nigel."

"And I believe you know Albert Shaw, my manager. . . ."

Shaw smiled and dipped his head.

Underhill gestured to a square-jawed platinum-blond gent and introduced him as "my dear friend Peter Insley.

"He's recently returned from Spain," Underhill continued. "I'm sure he has some fascinating stories to tell about the gruesome bloodbath unfolding there."

Insley reached across the table and shook hands with me. "Mr. Oveson, it's a pleasure to meet you."

"Art," I said. "The pleasure is all mine."

Insley eased back into his seat, and my eyes moved to the next person, a lanky redhead with sleepy eyes and very little chin to speak of. Underhill nodded in his direction. "That is Julian Pangborn, my mechanic."

Pangborn pouted when I offered him my hand, as if leaning forward to shake it posed too much of a challenge. At last, he relented. I found his squeeze light and clammy.

I could only make out certain words as he mumbled, "Thor's lashins iv neet left, an' Ahm neet near mortal 'nough."

I smiled, not daring to ask him to repeat it.

"If it weren't for Arthur, I wouldn't be sitting here tonight," said Underhill.

"So we have him to blame," said Nigel. The men around the table laughed, but Nigel never graduated beyond an arrogant smirk. My eyes locked on his, and vice versa, and I knew then

I disliked him, despite my best efforts to embrace the "I never met a man I didn't like" philosophy of Will Rogers.

Underhill flagged the waiter, who zoomed over to our table. "Would you be kind enough to get Arthur a . . . How rude of me! What will you have, Arthur?"

"Got lemonade?" I asked.

The waiter replied with a soft yes.

"Surely you intend to sample something harder than that before the night is through," said Shaw. "Martini? Beer? Glass of wine?"

"Lemonade," I repeated. The waiter nodded and vanished as fast as appeared.

"You Mo'mon, Oveson?" asked Pangborn.

I nodded. "Lifelong."

He mumbled something again—at least I saw his lips moving and heard faint spoken words—but the music drowned him out.

"What?" I asked. "Can you speak up?"

"So whatsat mean?" he said louder. "No licka? No coffee? No fags?"

"I don't partake in any of those things," I said.

"Behold the live wire," said Nigel. "Quick, hide the cognac! Art is here!"

More laughter, but, once again, Nigel only smirked.

"And what of your ancestors, Arthur?" asked Shaw. "Were they among the pioneers that settled this area?"

"Yes sir," I said. "Some came here with the 1847 trek. First Mormons to set foot in this valley."

"How fascinating," said Peter. "You know, Nigel here is quite the family history buff. He's already visited the Genealogical Society here. Isn't that so, Nigel?"

"Oh?" I asked, twisting in the booth toward Nigel. "I'm impressed. You don't strike me as the genealogy type."

"Maybe I'm bored, killing time, trying to figure out why the devil anybody in his right mind would set up shop around here," said Nigel. "It's a God-forsaken wasteland, the most desolate place I've ever seen. But I'll give you this much: at least you screwy Mormons know how to run a world-class genealogical research facility."

"Nigel, please," said Shaw. "You're being improper."

"Am I?" asked Nigel, "I was only being honest. It's not as though any of you . . ."

"I love genealogy," I said. "I find it soothing to map out my family tree. The leaders of my Church encourage it. They think it brings us closer to our ancestors. That's why they opened the library, and why they send experts around the world to bring back research documents."

Nigel opened his mouth to speak, but Clive cut him off. "So, Art, I understand you're a police detective."

I replied with a nod and a soft "yes" as my lemonade arrived.

"No wonder you reacted so decisively today—and so heroically, I might add."

I sipped lemonade, ice clinked, and the tartness made me pucker and shudder slightly. "It truly was nothing, honest."

"You're modest—a rare quality in this day and age. Are you married?"

I peeked at my silver wedding band. "Yes."

"She couldn't make it tonight?" asked Shaw.

"She has a sour stomach, I'm afraid." I looked at Underhill. "I hope you're not injured too badly. From earlier today, I mean."

He tugged at his ear, to indicate that he could not hear me above the orchestra.

"I said I hope you weren't hurt too badly today!"

The song came to an end and applause crackled. The band-leader struck up something slow, an ethereal tune fronted by a smooth-voiced male singer. Underhill stopped clapping and turned his gaze on me. "My ankle is bandaged, thanks to a cut that required stitches. But I plan on returning to the flats next weekend to unveil my latest creation. It'll take a lot more than this to make me sit that one out."

"Come, come, you mustn't keep us on tenterhooks," said Insley, lowering an empty martini glass after polishing off its contents. "Tell him what it is that you'll be showing off to the world next Saturday!"

Underhill shook his head. "If I do, I'll be—what's the expression—*spilling the beans* too soon. Let me simply say that I've been working on a revolutionary new vehicle that will shatter all previous records. And we shall leave it at that. How are you doing over there with that lemonade?"

I held the half-full glass high so he could see it. "I'm quite all right, for now."

"Well, then, why not order dinner? Might I suggest the lamb chops and Saratoga chips? It comes with a side of fried green beans and cauliflower in cream sauce. It is divine, some of the finest cooking I've tasted on either side of the big pond, I must say."

"Sure," I said. "That sounds swell."

He caught the waiter's attention again and ordered for me. The waiter did not write it down. Instead, he darted off in the direction of enormous swinging doors to the kitchen. "What about you?" I asked Clive. "Are you married?"

An uneasy silence, accompanied by darting eyes, followed my question.

"Engaged," said Nigel. "To Dorothy Bliss, from Kensington."

"We're to be married next May," said Underhill.

Insley laughed as he filled his champagne glass, now that his martini was gone.

"Did I say something amusing, old boy?" asked Underhill, cracking a smile.

"No matter how hard I try, I can't see you walking down the aisle," said Insley. "It defies my imagination."

I looked at Insley and asked, "Why did you go to Spain? It's a dangerous place."

Insley raised his martini glass at the waiter, who nodded and hurried off to the bar.

"Why does anybody go to Spain these days?" Insley asked, lowering his glass. "I'm a writer."

"And a damn good one," said Clive. "Tell him about your novel."

"Novel?" I asked.

"Some other time," Insley said, fighting off a blush. "You were asking about Spain. I went there as a journalist, sent by a radical London newspaper. When the fighting intensified last summer, I took up arms on the side of the Loyalists resisting Franco. I must say I developed a whole new respect for the American volunteers in the Abraham Lincoln Brigade. Tough as nails, especially the fellows I met from Brooklyn. In fact, I rather quickly deduced that if you want to live to see the end of the war, the best place to stand is beside the man from Brooklyn."

"Once more, you chose the wrong side," said Nigel.

Insley smirked at Nigel, as if this were a routine between them. "Did I?"

Nigel nodded. "Why do you suppose fascists are winning everywhere? Hitler has given the German people hope and prosperity. That's something you and your band of armed, free-love bohemians can't fathom. Nobody wants your sickly sweet utopia. They want someone who's going to deliver in the here and now. They want a Hitler."

"Hitler won't last," said Insley. "Good men around the world will rise up and oust him."

"And what of you?" Nigel asked me. "What are your politics?"

"My politics?" I asked.

"How about it, Arthur?" asked Insley. "Are you a man of the left, like me, or the right, like Nigel?"

"I guess I'm in the middle," I said. "I try to keep my nose out of politics."

"Spoken like a true philistine," said Nigel.

"Sounds refreshing," chimed in Clive, his voice overlapping with Nigel's. "I suggest we take a page out of your book and steadfastly avoid the topic of current affairs for the remainder of our dinner."

"What an odd comment," said Nigel, "coming from a man who once supported Mosley's British Union."

I had no idea what any of this meant, but I felt a tension in the air.

Clive glowered at his brother. "I said no current affairs at the table. I meant it."

"I've had enough of this rot," said Nigel, picking his linen napkin out of his lap and throwing it on his plate. He looked at me. "You may be the only honest man at this table. Now, if you'll please excuse me . . ."

I squirmed into position to stand up, to give Nigel room to scoot out.

"Where are you going?" asked Underhill.

Roscoe came over to the table to check on things. Nigel rose out of the booth, clenched his fist, and leered at Roscoe, as if ready to start a fight with a man who was twice his size and could easily wallop him into the ground. He moved menacingly toward Nigel, but I inserted myself between them, to prevent an altercation that likely would've ended with Nigel's neck getting broken. The brief stalemate concluded with Nigel scowling at everybody at the table and then storming off. Roscoe and I exchanged glances, and I eased back into the booth, where the others resumed their conversations and drinking as though nothing unusual had happened.

My dinner arrived, and I listened to Underhill offer a long explanation about why the Bonneville Salt Flats were the best place on earth for setting land speed records. The man could talk, and he apparently surrounded himself with good listeners—men who laughed at his jokes and asked him questions that made him go on even longer. He explained high-powered engines, described what a "superlative" (his word, not mine) mechanic Pangborn was, and let me know exactly how the right set of tires could make all the difference in the world. An hour and a half passed of him talking and the rest of us men at the table sitting in silence, taking in everything he said. At one point, German motorist Rudy Heinrich—stately, angular, athletic, with a tan head shaved on the sides and back—stopped by our table. His swastika pin reminded me of a vicious little bug crawling up his lapel. He leaned over the table and shook hands with Underhill.

"Hello Clive."

"*Guten tag,* Herr Heinrich. Fancy seeing you here tonight."

Underhill launched into introductions, and when he reached

me (". . . and this is Art Oveson, Salt Lake City Police Department . . ."), Heinrich shook my hand.

"Kripo?" Heinrich asked, smiling and arching his eyebrows.

I released his hand and shot him a quizzical look. *"Kripo?"*

"Kriminalpolizei?" Heinrich asked.

"I'm a police detective," I said.

"I hope you do not give out speeding tickets," said Heinrich.

The comment provoked raucous laughter at the table.

"No, that would be the traffic bureau," I said, after the laughter died down.

Heinrich said, "What were you doing out at the flats today, *kripo?*"

"I was helping my cousin," I said. "He's a land speed driver."

"Oh? What's his name?" asked Underhill.

"Hank—er, uh, Henry—Jensen."

"Hold on," said Underhill, coming to life now. "You mean to say Hank Jensen is your cousin?"

"Yes."

"Bluh'ee legend," called out Pangborn.

"Thank you," I said.

"He started it all, you know," said Underhill. "If it weren't for Hank Jensen . . ."

"Bonneville would not be the world's chosen spot for land speed racing," said Heinrich, finishing Underhill's sentence. "Your cousin is a visionary and a pioneer, Herr Oveson. But I'm afraid his records cannot withstand the current crop of drivers. Before this summer is over, there will be a vehicle capable of reaching speeds in excess of four hundred miles per hour on the speedway. Next summer, that number will climb to five hundred, and by the next decade, the Führer will introduce an automobile capable of surpassing six hundred."

"Ah yes, we're all aware of your top-secret P9, Heinrich," said Underhill. "An impressive machine, no doubt. But it is, I'm afraid, no match for what I plan to reveal to the world next week."

"We'll see," said Heinrich, in a taunting way. He checked his wristwatch. "Well, I do not wish to overstay my welcome. Good evening, gentlemen."

Heinrich looked at me and bowed slightly. "Herr Oveson."

Underhill watched Heinrich leave, and then he turned his attention to me. I smiled as I puzzled over what must've been on that Englishman's brain of his. I found him a hard man to read. He clearly wished to be thought of as a man of wit, style, and intelligence. However, it occurred to me, as the night wore on, that what churned beneath the surface was complex. I sensed dark secrets lurking deeper down. I did not wish to be privy to those. I'd had enough of the Coconut Grove. This was not my world.

Five

"It's not enough!" he hollered at the top of his lungs. "You hear me!"

"Yeah, I hear you," I said. "There's no need to shout. We're inside a car."

A little past one in the morning found me driving north on Main Street, sharing the road with a handful of late-night jalopies. Clive Underhill eased his head inside the window and his upper body twirled slightly, as if he were about to fall forward into the dashboard. I extended my right arm and gave him a gentle shove back against the seat. My wife, Clara, always warned me that chivalry would be my downfall. She had a tendency to overstate her case, but chivalry has introduced much inconvenience into my life, such as tonight, for instance. Here I was, in the wee morning hours, on my way to drop off an inebriated Clive Underhill and his bodyguard-for-rent, Roscoe Lund, at the hotel where he was staying, when I really should have been home hours ago.

It'd been a strange evening, not at all what I expected. As the night wore on, the other men at our table, one by one, fell away. Shaw left around ten o'clock. Pangborn drank himself into a stupor and had to be taxied home at midnight. Insley wandered off with a blond lady in a green dress who I was pretty sure arrived with a different fella.

That left me alone with Underhill, while Roscoe loomed off to the side, keeping an eye on us. Underhill talked and talked— about his secret car that he was planning to reveal to the world next week, about his trip last year to Nazi Germany to inspect their race cars, about his favorite brand of cigars, about nearly everything under the sun—until all of the band members had finished packing their instruments. Why I stayed so long, I don't know. Eventually, I worked up the nerve to tell Underhill that I had to wake up early in the morning to go to church. On my way to the exit, weaving around tables of night owls, I spotted Heinrich and his table of raucous Germans laughing and toasting. He gave me a little wave as I went past him, and I mouthed the word "hello."

Exiting the building, I overheard the coat check girl calling the taxi company to request a cab for Underhill. I passed through the front doors, jingling my keys in my hand, watching a tipsy Underhill standing with the help of crutches next to Roscoe, waiting for a black-and-yellow sedan. I could not, in good conscience, let them ride in a taxi when I had a car of my own parked down the street. I asked them to stay put briefly until I could return and pick them up. I jogged into the night until I reached my car. As per my instructions, Roscoe and Underhill waited, and I soon pulled up at the curb across the street and gave a double honk.

En route to the Hotel Utah, Roscoe sat in the backseat while

Underhill resumed talking. He seemed to be a compulsive talker. He kept saying, "It's not enough!" I didn't know what he was talking about, and I quietly requested clarification. "It's not enough!" he repeated.

"Pipe down, Underhill," said Roscoe. "You'll get ticketed for violating the noise laws."

"Nonsense! They've no such things in America!"

"They sure as hell do," said Roscoe. "If you keep carrying on like that, they'll slap you with one to prove it. Three of them things and you'll end up in jail. I promise you the accommodations there aren't as regal as the Hotel Utah."

Right then, the Hotel Utah, a white, ten-story glazed terracotta tower on South Temple and Main, came into view. The building gave off an ethereal green glow, as if bathed in a mysterious light. I turned onto South Temple, steered into a U-turn, and braked in front of the entrance, where doormen in caps and long coats waited to assist.

"My home away from home," said Underhill. "Right here is fine."

I stopped, put the car in park and idled.

"It was good of you to give us a lift back, Art," said Underhill. "Come up for a drink, why don't you?"

Underhill was giddy. I couldn't take him seriously with his hair dangling in front of his eyes.

"I would, but I have to get up at the crack of dawn," I told him. "Thank you for dinner. The food was delicious and I enjoyed the company."

"What about tomorrow night?" asked Underhill. "We're planning on spending the evening down at the Old Mill for . . ."

"He's busy," said Roscoe. "Ain't that so, Art?"

"It's good of you to ask," I told Underhill. "Maybe some other time."

Underhill sighed. "You know what's wrong with this town? No nightlife! What if the desire to go out dancing should strike me at three A.M.? What am I to do?"

Roscoe's head popped between us, like a jack-in-the-box springing over the seat. "I'm under orders to get you back to your room by midnight, Cinderella. It's already past one. Let's shake a leg."

"She's up there," said Underhill.

"Who?" I asked.

"My fiancée. Her airplane came in earlier tonight."

"In that case, don't let me hold you up," I said. "You must be eager to see her."

Underhill blinked at me in the dim light. "Did you ever have the feeling that your life is a charade?"

"No. I can't say I have."

"You're fortunate." He bowed his head and whispered, "It's not enough."

"That's the fourth time you've said that tonight," I said. "What do you mean?"

"C'mon, Underhill, you've had too much to drink," said Roscoe, getting out the car. He slammed the rear door hard and opened the passenger-side front door. He leaned Underhill's crutches against the running board, then he seized him by the elbow, but Underhill jerked his arm free. Roscoe made an angry face. "Oh, it's gonna be that way, is it?"

"Give us a minute," said Underhill, looking up at him.

Roscoe eyed me. I gave him a single nod, to confirm it was OK.

Roscoe sighed and told Underhill, "Your crutches are here, when you're ready."

"Thank you, Mr. Lund."

Roscoe straightened and slammed the door. He strolled over to a maroon awning near the revolving door and lit a cigarette. After a long moment of silence, Underhill stared at me and his words came out slowly.

"I can't stand it anymore, Art," he said, almost in a whisper. "I'm beginning to despise it all. My greedy manager, my sniveling brother, my suffocating fiancée—I wish they'd leave me alone. I'm in love with somebody I can't have. I want to leave it all behind—the sycophants, the fast cars, the long nights of revelry. I want to go somewhere far away, where nobody can find me. Forget about the speed records and competitions, the money and the unattainable aspirations my parents have imposed on me. Far, far away from here." He reached out and pressed his fingertip against the dashboard clock. "I bet you think I'm mad."

"No, not at all. I'm sure a good night's sleep will help you see things differently in the morning."

He pulled his finger away from the clock, and he eyed me again. "Two years ago, when I first came here, I read about a young artist that went missing, a man named Everett something or other."

"Ruess," I said, pronouncing the name *Roo-iss*. "Everett Ruess."

"Ruess?"

"Yeah. He was from California. He disappeared in the fall of '34, down around the Canyons of the Escalante."

"Everett Ruess. I won't forget that name again. Sounds like you know his story. He wandered off into the desert and was never seen or heard from again. Search parties spent months looking for him, to no avail. It was as though he melted into the land, became one with the earth and sky. Four years ago . . ."

"Going on four, this fall," I said.

"No sign of him?"

"Not yet."

"What do you suppose happened to him?"

"There are theories floating around," I said. "Some say he drowned in a flash flood. Others think he might've fallen into a slot canyon. I remember the papers quoting one fellow who theorized that he took a squaw as his wife and went to live on the Navajo Reservation. Who knows where the truth lies? It's all mixed up in legend."

"I know I'm going to sound like a lunatic, but . . ."

He stopped in midsentence.

"But what?" I asked.

"Would you take me there?"

"Where?"

"To that place where he disappeared. Where did you say it was? Escalante?"

"Yes, that's what it's called. No, I can't take you there. It's late."

"I shall go on my own then."

"Do you mind if I pass along some advice?"

"By all means."

"If you really want to go down there and see it, hire a guide," I said. "I know a few I could recommend."

"What about *you*?"

"Me?"

"Have you been?"

"Yes."

"Would you guide me through there?"

I shook my head. "That country swallows people whole. It can erase a man as if he never existed. Half that area isn't even mapped out yet. I don't know the terrain well enough. We'd both get lost with me guiding us. Sorry. At least I know my limits."

"Suppose I were to pay you?"

"Pay me?"

"Yes, the sum of ten thousand dollars, to guide me through the Escalante and show me the place where Mr. Ruess walked off into the desert. Would you do it?"

"Like I said, I think you need a good night's sleep."

"Would you do it?" he repeated.

I looked at his earnest expression, turned blue by lights outside of the car. "No," I said. "If you're willing to fork over ten G's, you shouldn't have a problem hiring the best guide in the business."

"Nigel was right about one thing. You're honest, Oveson. I can't tell you how refreshing it is to encounter an honest man."

"It's late," I reminded him. "I have to go to church in the morning."

"Yes, of course!"

He opened his door, grabbed the crutches propped against the running board, and used them to maneuver to his feet. I stole a look at the bandages, wrapped thickly around his injured ankle, as he stepped onto the sidewalk with a crutch under each armpit. He closed the door, leaned into the open window and, for a few seconds, he seemed to want to say something meaningful.

"Thank you for saving my life," he said. "I'll never be able to repay you."

"You repaid me with that nice dinner," I said. "That's a whole lot more than I expected. Good night."

"Good night, Art."

He crutch-walked to the building and the doorman assisted Underhill in getting inside. That's when the tornado came spilling out of the lobby and onto the front sidewalk. By "tornado," I mean Roscoe locked in a ferocious argument with Nigel Underhill, voices shouting, arms flailing. I rushed out of the car to help the doorman break it up. Gripping Roscoe's stony bicep, I pulled him a few steps backward, and the doorman stepped in front of Nigel and eased him away.

"You're fired, Lund! You hear me? Fired! I've never known anybody so brazen and insolent! Don't bother coming back tomorrow!"

Roscoe broke past me and got in Nigel's face. "Fuck you! I oughta wring your puny neck right now!"

I pivoted in front of Roscoe and separated him from Nigel.

"Are you threatening me?" Nigel yelled.

"I quit this fuckin' detail!" shouted Roscoe. "As far as I'm concerned, you can go screw yourself, ya squirrely little tea-and-crumpets, Buckingham Palace prick."

"What a big man, spewing out such sophisticated insults!"

I continued to block Roscoe, but he nearly outflanked me.

"I want my money, you weasely little fuck!" Roscoe hollered.

"What money?"

"Don't gimme that! You owe me almost an entire week's pay! Cough it up, ya fuckin' chiseler."

"C'mon, Roscoe," I said. "You can pick it up later, after you've cooled down."

Clive Underhill now blocked his infuriated younger brother near the revolving door.

"What is this all about, Nigel?"

"That incompetent oaf was supposed to have you back here by midnight!"

Roscoe breathed hard between clenched teeth, ready for a fight.

"How 'bout I give you a ride home?" I suggested.

"Thanks," he said, his voice hoarse from shouting. "I'm gonna need one. My car is at home. These pricks sent a car to pick me up."

We climbed into my idling car, pulled doors closed, and I steered out into South Temple, heading in the direction of Roscoe's house in the Marmalade District, a quaint neighborhood to the west of Capitol Hill. Roscoe pulled off his bow tie, rolled down the window, and pitched it out onto the road. He cursed under his breath, and he took out a flask, unscrewed the top, and gulped down the remains. "Ah," he said, as he pulled it away from his lips and twisted the lid back on.

"What was that all about back there?" I asked.

"You saw what an arrogant prick he was at the Coconut Grove. Well, when we got back to the hotel just now, he ran up to me in the lobby and started shouting at me for not getting his brother back by midnight. Can you believe it? I've got a good mind to go back there and—"

"Leave it be," I said. "You're better off."

He nodded and let out a shaky exhale. "You're a true pal, in every sense of the word."

"You're welcome," I said. "How come they hired you in the first place?"

"Underhill was getting threats," said Roscoe. "Shaw didn't want to involve the police. He was afraid of unwanted publicity."

"What kind of threats?"

"Death threats," said Roscoe. "Shaw told me Clive was averaging three or four a day back in England, ever since he publicly quit some fascist group over there. Shaw was afraid for Clive's safety."

"Hmm."

"But I'm glad I'm no longer anchored down to that lousy detail," said Roscoe. "Let those high-and-mighty English ball-breakers hire someone else. I've had it with their snooty horseshit. The pay is decent, but it ain't worth the headaches."

I slowed to a halt in front of Roscoe's darkened bungalow at the end of an unlit cul-de-sac.

"Have you heard from Rose?" I asked.

"No. Still no word from her."

"Hey, why don't you come over for dinner tomorrow night?" I asked. "We'd love to have you. We miss you, Roscoe. Come on. Say yes."

"Can't," he said. "I'm busy. Some other time, though, huh?"

"Sure. Some other time."

He stared at me in the darkness. "Have you given any thought to my request?"

Last time I saw Roscoe, which was over lunch at the Chit-Chat Luncheonette downtown, he begged and pleaded with me to leave the Salt Lake City Police Department and go into business with him as his partner at Beehive Discreet Investigations. Tempted though I was to go the route of free agent, a steady paycheck was ultimately more appealing, and eventually won out.

"I have," I said. "I can't afford to leave the force now."

Roscoe grinned. "I thought you said you were fed up with the bureaucracy."

"I am," I said. "But I've got bills to pay."

"I understand. Say no more."

He got out of the car and closed the door, headed up the front walkway, and trotted up porch steps. I waited until lights went on inside. When they did, one after another, I felt a wave of pity for my friend.

Since going into business as a private detective four years ago, he'd been lobbying me to quit my job and join him. He knew I was tired of all the red tape at Public Safety—the forms that needed to be typed out in triplicate, having to account for every little detail of everything I did, witnessing the petty turf wars between squads. I'm pretty sure Roscoe thought I would turn things around by bringing more structure and efficiency to his agency. He probably also figured that having the names of two detectives on the frosted glass window of the office door— especially if one of them happened to be a devout Mormon— would instill greater confidence in potential clients. And knowing Roscoe the way I did, I'm sure he would've been all too happy to let me do the heavy lifting, thereby giving him a chance to relax a little more.

I worried about my friend. If it weren't for the meager pay that the Union Pacific and Denver and Rio Grande Western railroads threw his way, hiring him to police the rail yards and evict hoboes from trains that passed through here, I don't think he'd have any money at all. To add to his challenges, around the time he quit the police department four years ago, he traveled to Denver to meet a daughter he'd abandoned when she was an infant. Rose had been living with her grandparents for years, and when she hit her teens, Roscoe decided he wanted to make up for all those missing years by trying to be a good father to her.

She arrived in Utah in 1934, a brainy and reticent girl, not un- like my eldest daughter, Sarah Jane. Over the years, however, Rose developed into a rebel with a taste for hard liquor, aggressive boys, and fast cars. Her insolent streak was a mile wide, and she had little patience for her father's many short-term relationships. Women came and left Roscoe's life on a weekly basis, and such turbulence gained Rose's full disapproval, which she voiced often. She challenged her father by wearing provocative clothing and lots of makeup. She was always affectionate with me, calling me "Uncle Art" and hugging me whenever she greeted me. I never once saw her embrace her father.

Rose and Roscoe quarreled repeatedly. One night, in May of this year, following a particularly heated exchange, Rose lit out in the middle of the night to parts unknown. Her decision to run away left Roscoe a basket case. He paced the floors and took up smoking again. He worried something terrible was going to happen to his daughter and he'd never see her again.

I asked him what they had fought over. They'd had a bitter knock-down-drag-out about a lad that Rose was dating that Roscoe didn't approve of. The kid, a college dropout named Teddy Duncan, had been busted numerous times for shoplifting and thieving. Rose told Roscoe she was in love with Duncan. Roscoe called Duncan a "heel" and Rose a "fool," and he told her she didn't know what she was doing. Rose stormed into her bedroom and slammed the door behind her. At some point in the night, she climbed out her window and took off.

Two weeks later, a postcard arrived in Roscoe's mailbox showing a painting of the Chinese Theater on Hollywood Boulevard. Postmarked Los Angeles, May 16, 1938, with a return address on Franklin Avenue, it contained a short note from Rose:

> Hello Father: Writing to let you know I am okeh and staying with a new friend, Margaret, until I get my own

place. Newspaper is full of apartment ads. Will find one soon. Your loving daughter, Rose Sylvia Lund.

Roscoe gave me the postcard. Knowing I'd been transferred the previous year to the two-man Missing Persons Bureau in the Salt Lake City Police Department, he begged me to use my connections to locate her. I vowed I'd do my best, and assured him that the arrival of the postcard in the mail was an encouraging sign.

That was three months ago. Rose moved out of Margaret's apartment in June, but never sent Roscoe her new address. I contacted Captain Seton Walters of the Los Angeles Police Department's Lost Person Detail to ask for his help. Walters's specialty was finding missing would-be starlets who ran away from home searching for stardom in Hollywood. He was friendly enough and offered to "make inquiries," but warned me that his hands were full. He gave me the name of a private investigator with an agency dedicated to missing persons called Skip Tracers. I telephoned the detective, Arnold Cameron, and wired him fifty dollars out of my own bank account to secure his assistance. Until now, my investment had yielded no results.

And now, in the early morning hours, here was poor Roscoe, alone with his demons.

Six

Caroline Kimball, a nine-year-old pigtailed girl in a white dress with pink polka dots, interrupted me in the middle of my Sunday-school lesson. She told me a man was waiting for me out in the hall and wished to see me right away. I asked the children to excuse me, rose from my chair, and followed Caroline out of the room. In the dimly lit corridor, I came face-to-face with my partner, Detective Myron Adler. A diminutive, oval-faced fellow with a brown fedora and a subtle cleft in his chin, Myron gazed at me through thick spectacles that obscured beady eyes. A hint of gray was starting to appear in his inky black hair, and he kept his hands dug deep in his pockets, jingling change, a tic he often repeated when he wasn't entirely comfortable in his surroundings, which was nearly always.

"So this is what the inside of a Mormon church looks like," he said.

"Ward."

"Come again?"

"It's called a ward."

"Oh. Pardon me for using the wrong terminology."

"Don't give it a second thought," I said. I waited for him to say something. When he did not, I prodded. "I'm kind of busy at the moment."

"There's been a murder," said Myron. "Hawkins wants us at the crime scene."

I nodded. "Last I checked, we're not homicide dicks."

"He still wants us there."

"Did he say why?"

Myron frowned and shook his head.

"Where is it?"

"Hotel Utah. Seventh floor."

His words sucker-punched me. *Hotel Utah?* Clive Underhill came to mind. *Maybe it wasn't him,* I thought. *Maybe it was someone else.*

Myron drove to the Hotel Utah, ten minutes by car from my ward, which was located in the middle of a residential neighborhood. In the passenger seat, I silently speculated about why my old friend Buddy Hawkins—now assistant police chief of the Salt Lake City Police Department (which made him my boss)—would want us at the scene of a homicide. Myron and I specialized in missing persons cases, and in those unfortunate instances when they turned into homicide cases, we were under strict orders to turn them over to the Homicide Squad.

Myron suddenly broke the silence: "I thought you'd like to know that I've made some real headway in my genealogy research."

"Good. I'm pleased to hear."

There was genuine excitement in my voice. I'd shown Myron

how to do his family genealogy a few months earlier, because he was curious about his familial lineage.

"You were right about that Family History Library," said Myron, referring to a Mormon genealogy center downtown. "Even if you're not a Mormon, which I'm obviously not, there is lots of helpful information there."

"Well, genealogy is important to us," I said. "It's one way to connect with our ancestors. You needn't be a Mormon to appreciate something that meaningful."

"No, I guess not," he said. "I'm discovering a lot about my family tree. "

"Hey, I'd like to hear about your discoveries sometime. Maybe over lunch?"

"OK." Myron turned deadpan as he stared ahead. "Don't look now, but members of the Fourth Estate have come out to greet us."

Myron swerved to the curb on South Temple, near the building's entrance, and killed the engine. I got out and, briefly blinded by the sun, tugged my hat low to shade my eyes. Amelia Van Cott, a blond woman in a matching green hat and dress, stood by the revolving door, spiral notebook and pencil in hand, along with her gangly photographer sidekick, Ephraim Nielsen, a lad with a camera cradled in his arms. Van Cott worked as the crime beat reporter at the *Salt Lake Examiner.* I was certain she either owned a police radio or had a mole inside of the SLCPD, because she turned up at every single crime scene, long before we'd sent out word to the press. I found her to be aggressive, an asker of tough questions, and when she saw me coming, she rushed over to me, her high heels click-clacking on the sidewalk.

"Detective Oveson!"

"Hi Amelia."

I brushed past her, and she twirled and kept up with me as I headed to the hotel entrance. "That's a smart suit you have there, Detective Oveson."

"What brings you out here on this hot day?" I asked, ignoring her compliment.

"I heard you performed quite the heroic feat on Saturday," she said. "They say you saved Clive Underhill from a burning car. Now *that* is news!"

"There isn't a story," I said. "Anybody else would've done the same thing."

"Always so modest," she said. "Care to comment on Saturday's incident?"

"I just did."

"What brings you here?" she asked, with a flirty smile. "Rumors abound."

"What kind of rumors?"

"Something's the matter with Clive Underhill," she said. "Any truth to it?"

"Don't believe everything you read in the newspapers."

My hand pushed glass as I stepped into the lobby. A rush of chilly air greeted me, a relief on such a hot day. The clop-clop-clopping of high heels pursued me, and I glanced over my shoulder.

"Let me go with you, Detective Oveson," she panted.

"Nope."

"At least tell me why you're here today," she said. "Does it have anything to do with Saturday's crash?"

"It's police business," I said. "Now if you'll excuse me . . ."

"Aw, c'mon. I promise I'll stay out of the way."

"Sorry, Amelia," I said. "No can do."

An elevator operator in a maroon suit held the doors for me, and I stepped inside, followed by Myron Adler. The doors closed, we faced forward, and the operator threw some switches. We were quiet most of the way up, but as the little brass arrow above us neared the number 7, Myron gave me a sideways glance.

"Persistent, isn't she," said Myron.

"Very."

"Does she always do that?"

"Do what?"

"Switch on her ladylike charms to get what she wants?"

"Usually."

"Does it work?"

"Nope," I said. "I don't treat her any differently than the other reporters."

"Sure. Uh huh."

I glared at him. "I don't."

"That's what I said. *Sure* you don't."

A bell dinged. We stepped out of the elevator and crossed the hall to Room 703, where two officers, Elmer Dutton and J.T. Sanderson, stood on either side of the doorway in dark blue uniforms and peaked caps. Brass buttons reflected light from above, and they wore regulation jodhpurs with boots. Made me glad that I didn't have to dress so stiffly anymore. Being a detective came with benefits, chief among them the right to put on more comfortable clothes. The men stood at attention, treating me like a sergeant coming through to perform an inspection.

"Afternoon, sir."

"Hello, Lieutenant Oveson."

I nodded and tugged my hat brim. "At ease, fellas. Who's the poor soul?"

"Nigel Underhill," said Sanderson.

I tried to conceal my shock by keeping my expression changeless. I stole a peek at Myron, who side-glanced at me. I looked at the officers. "Who found him?"

"Hotel dick," said Dutton. "Dooley Metzger."

The name instantly rang a bell. Ex-cop. Used to be SLCPD, years ago.

"Step aside, gents," said Sanderson with a wave. "Coming through."

The uniformed men parted as white-clad morgue workers carried out a sheet-covered body on a stretcher. I raised my palm to stop them, and peeled back linen to see the victim. Hair still slicked back neatly, eyes closed, face colorless and waxy, Nigel Underhill appeared the spitting image of his live self last night, when he was animated and full of rancor. Myron peered over my shoulder. I stared at that lifeless face longer than I should have, and the morgue men eyed me expectantly, as if to prod me along. I could not tell for certain how he died. I guessed manual strangulation, because of the discoloration around his neck and jawline. But I reckoned I'd have to wait for a full autopsy to get my answer.

"Is Livsey in there?" I asked, pulling the sheet over Nigel's head. Tom Livsey, an old childhood chum, was now county coroner.

"He left," said one of the bearers. "He's expecting us."

"Take him out the back way," said Buddy Hawkins. "I don't want the press getting wind of this."

Deputy Police Chief Buddy Hawkins chose that moment to emerge from the room. An athletic, broad-shouldered bureaucrat with close-cropped hair that'd once been red before going blondish silver, he reminded me of Spencer Tracy in those lavish MGM pictures, with his penchant for fancy suits and freshly shined shoes. He always made me feel like a slumming pauper in my frayed church threads. I could tell he was in no mood for small talk, and after being summoned out of my Sunday-school lesson, frankly, neither was I.

"Buddy."

"Art."

"What gives?"

"Sorry to pull you out of church," said Buddy. "I need to have a word with you. In private."

"There somewhere we can talk?"

"We've set up shop a few doors down."

"OK."

Myron and I followed Buddy to 708. He double knocked, the door opened, and he led us into the room. Hatchet-faced Captain Wit Dunaway, whose scowl seemed to get worse the more his hairline receded, stood between two other homicide investigators: Detective Lieutenant Pace Newbold, nearly chinless and sporting an overbite, and his partner, Detective Reid Whitaker, a newcomer, clean-cut, freshly shaven, in a professorial tweed jacket. Both men wore hats, and Whitaker carried an open notebook and pen, as if ready to record someone's conversation.

We said our "excuse me's" as we squeezed past. In the spacious room, Buddy pulled up a pair of chairs, spun them toward the bed, and sat down on the bed's edge, motioning for us to join him. I took off my hat, Myron left his on, and we plunged into the chairs.

"Nigel Underhill is dead," said Buddy. "We've determined it's foul play. It appears he was strangled to death."

"Was a weapon used?" Myron asked.

"Hard to say at this point, but it appears manual," said Buddy. "Done by hand. Hell of a way to go."

"Are there any suspects?" I asked.

"We'll get to that soon enough," said Buddy. "First, I've got a few questions for you, Art. Hotel employees state you dropped off Nigel's older brother, Clive, at the hotel entrance around one o'clock in the morning. That so?"

"Yes."

"I also understand you were having dinner with the Underhill brothers at the Coconut Grove last night."

"Yes. Earlier in the day I—"

"You saved his life at the Bonneville Speedway," said Buddy. "Pulled him out of the wreckage of his burning car. I know."

"Go on," I said, uneasy with this line of questioning.

"I need to know what the two of you talked about at dinner," he said. "Start from the beginning, and give me as many details as possible—everything you can possibly remember."

"What's this all about? Am I a suspect?"

"I'll level with you, Art."

"I'd appreciate that."

"Nigel Underhill is dead, but then, you already know that," he said. "What you probably don't know is that Clive Underhill is missing. His manager, Albert Shaw, has no idea where he might be. You wanna know the real bomb?"

"I guess so."

"We've got three eyewitnesses who can place Roscoe Lund here, on this very floor, around three in the morning, stinking drunk, banging on doors, demanding payment for services rendered."

"Where is he now?" I asked.

"In jail, downtown, cooling his heels," said Buddy. "We'll wait for word back on the autopsy. I'm sure it's foul play, though. I'm hoping for a speedy arraignment, within the next two weeks, if possible."

I shook my head in stunned disbelief. "Surely you don't think . . ."

"We know for a fact that he got in a screaming match with Nigel Underhill last night, in plain view of the entire hotel staff. . . ."

"Nigel was being unbearable."

"So you can't blame Roscoe for strangling him?" asked Buddy in a wise-guy way. "Is that what you're saying?"

"Roscoe didn't murder anybody," I said.

"Did you drive him back here last night around three in the morning?"

"Of course not," I said. "I was at home, in bed."

"Then how do you know what Roscoe did when he came back here?"

"Who are these eyewitnesses?" I asked. "I'd like to talk to them."

"It's not yours. Don't even think about touching it."

"Why? Clive Underhill is missing. I'm the head of the Bureau of Missing Persons," I reminded him. "It makes sense that I would . . ."

"You're too close to Roscoe."

"I want to see the crime scene."

"Oh you do?"

"Yes."

"The answer is no."

"It involves a missing person," I said. "That means I've got a stake in it."

Pace Newbold picked that exact moment to barge into the room. He came over to where we were sitting and glared at me before stooping to whisper in Buddy's ear.

"Send him in," said Buddy.

"Yes, sir."

What came next was my second big jolt of the day.

Into the room walked my eldest brother, Frank, an imposing, 250-pound version of me, about a half a dozen years my senior, dressed in a three-piece suit with a fedora tipped at an angle. His cologne nearly overwhelmed my nostrils. The man must have dunked his head in a bucket full of it this morning.

"Frank," I said, rising to greet him.

He set his briefcase on the floor and threw his arms around me, giving me a vise-clamp hug, patting my back. Frank was head of the Salt Lake City office of the Federal Bureau of Investigation.

"How are you, kid?" Frank asked.

"I've been better," I said. "What brings you here?"

"May I?"

He gestured to the bed where Buddy was sitting.

"Sure."

Buddy stood up when he saw Frank coming. He walked over to the window and opened the drapes. Sunlight flooded the room, blinding me a second. I blinked the brightness out of my eyes and returned to my seat. Frank took a seat on the spot where Buddy was sitting a moment ago.

"Myron, this is my older brother, Frank," I said. "Frank, this is my partner, Detective Myron Adler."

They shook hands.

"Striking resemblance," said Myron, tilting his head at Frank. "Only you weigh more, have less hair, and look older."

Frank chortled. "Thanks a lot."

"Why are you here?" I repeated.

Frank studied me. "As Special Agent in Charge of the Salt

Lake City field office, I'll be working with the police on the Underhill case."

"Which one?" I asked.

"Both. If Clive Underhill fails to surface by midweek, two business days from now, the Bureau is going to regard this as a kidnapping and will formally take over and direct the investigation under the Federal Kidnapping Act of 1932."

"I thought kidnappers had to cross state lines before the feds stepped in," I said.

Frank shook his head. "The law stipulates that if a missing person is not found in twenty-four hours, federal agents may operate under the assumption that he or she has been taken across state lines. We're giving you extra time because we feel the police should exercise jurisdiction when it comes to matters of local law enforcement."

"What does that mean for us?" I asked.

"Your superiors will answer to me and coordinate their investigation with mine so we don't step on each other's toes," Frank said. "I'm in contact with a fella from British military intelligence who is here in town right now, and whose identity I am not at liberty to reveal. I'll be working closely with Deputy Chief Hawkins here, utilizing police manpower and sharing information. If I deem it necessary, I'm allowed to request additional federal agents to assist me in my investigation. But the presence of large numbers of G-men here in Salt Lake City will almost certainly draw attention to this case, and I would prefer to avoid that if possible. If the newspapers get wind of this, all hell is going to break loose, excuse the French."

"He's right," said Buddy. "We'll have reporters camped out here, hounding the living daylights out of us. As you well know, being under the microscope of the press dials up the pressure considerably."

"Is there any evidence of a kidnapping?" I asked. "Is there a ransom note?"

"Not yet," said Frank. "Tell me something, kid."

"Yeah?"

"You were with Clive the night he went missing."

"Yes."

"Did he say anything that might shed light on his where-abouts?"

I spent the next while describing what happened Saturday night at the Coconut Grove, and Clive Underhill telling me about his desire to leave town and go see the Canyons of the Escalante. Frank already knew about my rescue of Underhill out at the Salt Flats. Word travels fast in the Oveson clan. He listened intently, as did Buddy and Myron, and by the time I finished, Frank was nodding and gazing into space, as if carefully considering my words.

"I want you to stay away from this case," Frank finally said. "I'm aware of your friendship with the key suspect. You and Roscoe are close, aren't you?"

Myron and I exchanged glances.

"Not like we used to be," I said. "We don't stay in touch like the old days."

I was not entirely lying to my brother. I did not see or speak to Roscoe as much as I once did, back when we were partners on the force. But I opted to downplay our ongoing friendship, to avoid being taken off the investigation due to conflict of inter-est. Unfortunately for me, Frank responded with a skeptical raised eyebrow, and as soon as I stopped speaking, the silence became oppressive.

"I'll remind you that lying to a federal agent is a felony," said

Frank. "Even if you are my little brother, if you ascertain my meaning."

"Meaning ascertained," I said.

"Look, kid, this is a volatile situation we find ourselves in," said Frank. "In case you haven't noticed, Utah is playing host to two rival racing teams from countries that aren't exactly on the friendliest of terms with each other. Clive Underhill and Rudy Heinrich are celebrities back in their respective homelands, and the wrong incident at the wrong time . . . Well, let's just say we're sitting on a barrel full of gunpowder, and all it takes is one person with misplaced priorities to send it up in a gigantic fireball. Particularly if that one person happens to be an officer of the law who has a vested interest in clearing a key suspect."

"That's not the case with me," I said. "If Roscoe is guilty of committing a crime, no matter what it is, I'll personally bring him down. On that, you have my word."

Frank eyed Buddy, who was already looking at Frank. I noticed each man offer the other a subtle nod.

Buddy said to me, "You'll coordinate with Newbold. Exercise a subtle hand at all times. Refrain from putting your entire squad on it. Let Adler here and Beckstead work on other cases. Above all, keep it under wraps. You are to report directly to me, right down to the smallest of details. Is that clear?"

"Crystal."

"We're giving you a chance to prove yourself, kid," said Frank. "Don't blow it."

Myron and I stood to leave. When we were halfway to the door, Frank called out: "It's Sunday. You know what that means? I'll see you at dinner tonight. My place. The usual time."

Seven

The Salt Lake City jail is about as ugly as jails come. So ugly, in fact, the builders—in their infinite wisdom—chose to locate it away from the road. It opened its doors in 1903, constructed to the tune of a paltry $40,000, due to the excessive frugality of the mayor and city council. You don't get much for $40,000, not even in 1903. Where a sea of tall grass once undulated in the wind, a multistory brick eyesore went up, complete with bars over the windows and the kind of thick, arched wooden doors you'd find in medieval dungeons.

The inside wasn't any prettier. Poorly lit, kiln hot in the summers, icebox cold in the winters. Most occupants were either vagrants or suspects busted for public intoxication, so the place reeked of a vile mix of body odor and stale booze seeping out of men's pores. Cells on each floor specialized in different types of inmates: juveniles went in the basement, women on the main level, misdemeanors on the second floor, and on the third and top, felons who'd typically be transferred under heavy security to the Sugar House Prison down on 2100 South.

After passing through a big set of double doors, I walked up to the front desk and tugged my hat brim at a beefy guard in a peaked cap and police uniform. He lowered his copy of *Life* magazine and cracked a toothy grin. I instantly recognized him as Officer Leonard Stroud, a low man on the totem pole who got stuck with Sunday guard duty at the city jail. I sympathized because I'd had the duty before, too. It entailed hours of boredom, occasionally interrupted by some sort of fracas in the jail cells, depending on how crowded they happened to be. Fortunately for him, Stroud had a Bakelite radio playing the American League baseball game. He partially rose from his chair to shake my hand.

"Art Oveson, how the heck are ya?"

We clasped hands.

"Swell. How about you, Len? How's every little thing?"

"Aw, you know," he said, releasing his grip, slumping back into his chair. "Another day, another dollar, and all that jazz."

"Yep, yep, I hear you," I said. I gestured to the radio. "Who's playing?"

"Yankees and Indians," he said. "Three-game series, at Lakefront in Cleveland, and New York is winning yet again."

"Remind me where your allegiances lie."

He gave a slight shrug and resigned head tilt. "Injuns."

"So I thought," I said. "Sorry to hear."

"Ah, you know how it goes," he said. "I don't have a lot invested in it. I'd rather be hearing the Tigers/Red Sox game about now, but I'll take what I can get."

"I suppose it beats the other stuff on the dial," I said.

"That it does."

"Len, I've got a favor to ask. . . ."

"Shoot."

"You've got a prisoner here," I said. "Roscoe Lund."

"Yeah, I know him," said Stroud. "Ex-cop, in a felony cell. How the mighty fall."

"I'd like to have a word with him, if I might," I said.

"Sure, of course. I'm assuming you want an interrogation room?"

"Is one free?"

"It's Sunday," he said. "Take your pick."

"How about three-oh-four?" I asked.

"Three-oh-four it is," he said.

"That's dandy," I said. "Say, Len . . ."

"Yeah?"

"Do they still keep those big refrigerators in the chow hall kitchen stockpiled with soda?"

"Of course. What of it?"

I placed a trio of dimes on the counter. "Can you rustle us up a couple of bottles of cold pop? And one for yourself."

"I'd be delighted. Pick your poison."

"Nehi Grape for me, or Seven-Up if they don't have it," I said. "And a Dr Pepper for Roscoe."

"Coming right up. Keep your money."

"You sure?"

"It's no good here. You know your way up to the third floor, I presume?"

"I think I can remember," I said.

We shared a chuckle as I scooped up my dimes. He lifted the telephone to his ear and turned the rotary dial.

"Hey Dick, it's Len." Pause. "Yeah, Detective Art Oveson. Is three-oh-four free?" Pause. "Good. He wants to see Roscoe

Lund. Will you deliver the prisoner?" Pause and nod. "Much obliged." He hung up. He opened a cabinet behind his desk and pulled out an object. He handed me a rather large silver key on a ring attached to a chunk of wood with the number 8 etched into it. "You know the drill. Feel free to go up. Dick will bring Roscoe in shortly. I'll be along soon with those sodas."

"Thanks much, Len."

"See you around, Art."

I used the key Len gave me to get through several heavy steel doors, most of them painted dark gray. I could have used the elevator in the building, but it was ancient and slow, and I wanted to get up to the third floor while it was still 1938, so I went to the stairwell. Maybe that wasn't such a good idea. It was hot in that narrow, dark space as I trotted up steps. By the time I reached the third floor, I was breaking out all over in a sweat. I walked out into a corridor lined with interrogation rooms and a couple of administrative offices. If you kept going to the end of the hall and hung a left, you'd get to another enormous gray steel door that opened up to the felony cells.

I reached 304, let myself into the windowless room, and switched on the lights. Electricity buzzed in the globes above the rectangular table. I had my pick of chairs. I pulled one out, its legs groaning against linoleum, and I sat down facing the door. A minute later, the doorknob turned, and in walked Roscoe Lund, escorted by Officer Richard Chapman, who went by Dick. He and I exchanged quiet hellos as he pulled a chair out for Roscoe.

Roscoe grunted when he sat down. He rested his cuffed wrists on the ancient wooden table, marred from years of use. If I didn't know him better, I might believe he was a criminal, what with his five o'clock shadow, bags under his eyes, chapped lips, and some stains on his shirt. He glanced furtively over his shoulder as Chapman left the room and closed the door. He looked at me with those forlorn peepers of his, blinking slowly, breathing through his nostrils, waiting for me to say something.

"Tell me what happened last night," I said.

"I don't feel much like talking," he said. "I'm parched."

Three knocks.

"Come in."

Officer Stroud slipped inside with a bottle in each hand, and as soon as he put them on the table, he left without saying a word.

Roscoe picked up his Dr Pepper with his cuffed right hand and raised it to his lips. The soda churned and bubbled as the bottle tipped upward, gone in seconds, and he set the empty on the table and belched. I slid my Grape Nehi over to him, and he eyed it with confusion.

"Don'tcha want it?"

"Turns out I'm not thirsty," I said. "Go ahead."

He polished off the Nehi as fast as the Dr Pepper. He belched again, balled his right hand into a fist, and punched his chest. The handcuff chain rattled.

"Thanks," he said. "That's better."

"Good," I said. "Tell me everything—and I mean *everything*—you did last night. Take me every step of the way through it."

"Christ, Art, I'm not up for it."

"Listen, pal, I just finished talking to Tom Livsey before I came over here," I said.

"Ain't he a Mormon?" asked Roscoe. "What's he doing working on a Sunday?"

"This is a big one," I said. "Clear-cut case of foul play. Strangulation, if you want to get specific. So the way I look at it, you have two options. Talk to me and I'll do what I can to help. Or prepare yourself for a date with the firing squad. Your choice."

"I'll take the latter. They'll be doing me a favor."

"I don't think you really believe that."

"I'm sick to death of swimming against the current. Those pricks have it in for me. Buddy, Wit, Pace. They hated me when I was on the force. Now they're tripping over themselves to see me take the fall for this one."

"What about your daughter?"

"What about her?"

"How do you think she's going to feel when she learns that her father is a cold-blooded murderer? Whether it's true or not, that's what she's going to hear."

He leaned over the table and spoke low, yet intensely, for emphasis. "She's gone. Remember? I won't ever see her again. So who the fuck cares?"

"You can't give up," I said.

He stared at me, blinking in disbelief. "Doesn't it exhaust you?"

"What?"

"Being so goddamned optimistic all the time."

"You still haven't answered my question," I said.

"What was it?"

"What did you do last night after I dropped you off at your house?"

"It's all there in the transcripts," he said. "Newbold grilled me. Wit and Buddy were there. So was Reid Whitaker. There was a stenographer getting it all down."

"I'd prefer to hear it from you."

"All right. After you dropped me off, I got piss drunk. I started stewing over that money that Underhill's manager promised me. I was too blotto to drive, so I phoned for a yellow cab. I only vaguely remember making the call. The cab took me to the Hotel Utah and I went up to the seventh floor. I started banging like mad on his door. Probably woke up half the hotel."

He fell silent and I prodded: "What happened next?"

"He opened it. He was sore as hell at me for banging on it so late. I reminded him that I was promised two C-notes for two weeks of work, and I wanted a hundred for the week I'd put in. He told me to go to hell, but I grabbed him by the pajamas and threatened to stomp his scrawny ass to China if he didn't get me my money."

"I see. Can you grasp how something like that might not look good?"

"I only wanted what was owed to me, fair and square."

"Go on," I said. "Then what?"

"Nigel buckled. Scared shitless. Ran into his room. Came out with five twenties. Threw 'em at me. Yelled at me to leave, and slammed the door in my face."

"And then?"

"I left. The cab was waiting for me out front. And that was that."

"You didn't wring him by the neck?"

"No. If I were going to knock off the little prick, I'd put a bullet in his skull."

"Best to leave that last part out, Roscoe."

"If you insist."

"What taxi service did you use?"

"Green Cab," he said. "Their number is easy to remember."

"Oh yeah? What is it?"

"WAsatch seven-seven-seven-seven."

"Back to the confrontation," I said. "What time did it happen? *Roughly?*"

"Oh hell, I dunno."

"Take a guess."

"Three. Maybe a little before. Maybe a little after."

"Were there any eyewitnesses at the hotel?"

"I was too drunk to notice. Besides, I wasn't expecting the prick to go get himself knocked off."

"What else?" I asked.

"Next thing I knew, there was a knocking at my door this morning. Newbold was out on the porch with a couple of patrolmen. They cuffed me and brought me here. I spent two hours under the hot lamp answering questions. They told me I was being charged with the murder of Nigel Underhill, and I'd better confess if I knew what was good for me. At the time, I didn't even know how the murder was committed. You mentioned he was strangled."

"Yeah."

He grimaced. "Poor bastard. He didn't have that coming."

I nodded. "Did you know that Clive Underhill is missing?"

Roscoe appeared genuinely shocked. "He is?"

"He hasn't been seen since we dropped him off at the Hotel Utah."

"I didn't know that."

"I've got questions about this security detail you were working on with him."

"Ask away, Art."

"You were hired to guard him?"

"Yep."

"You said Albert Shaw told you that Underhill had been threatened."

"Yes."

"Did Shaw describe the nature of the threats?"

"No. All he said was Underhill had been getting threats. He

was short on specifics but long on dough. I was dodging evic-
tion notices and needed the work."

"Understandable. When did he hire you? What date?"

Roscoe raised an eyebrow. "Let's see, what's today . . . ?"

"Sunday the seventh."

"He dropped by my office in the Rio Grande at the end of
last month," said Roscoe. "It was on Tuesday, the twenty-sixth
of July, because everything was closed on that Monday, what
with it being Pioneer Day the day previous."

"And he hired you to do what exactly?"

"He wanted someone who could guard Underhill at events,
especially out at the Flats," Roscoe said. "He promised me it'd
be two weeks of steady work and I'd earn a hundred a week min-
imum. All under the table, of course."

"When did the actual job start?"

"When Clive Underhill got into town, on August the first.
Last Monday. A big crowd came out to greet him at the municipal airport. I was surprised to see all of those photographers
snapping pictures and the reporters filing stories about some English chump getting out of an airplane. I had no idea he was that
famous."

"When you were guarding him, did you talk to him at all?"

"Oh, you know, 'hello,' 'how are ya,' that kind of shit. He
wasn't the type to mingle with the help."

"What did a typical workday look like for you?"

"Get up at half past six, go to the hotel first thing, wait for
Clive to rise and shine, follow him out to lunch," said Roscoe.
"He tended to sleep late every day, till about ten or eleven. That
slimy Nigel would enter his room and wake him up each morning. Clive would get up and shower, shit, and shave, and put on
fancy duds."

"You'd go with him to lunch . . ."

"Yes. He went to Lamb's every day," said Roscoe. Lamb's Grill was a venerable old restaurant on Main Street, a favorite of the affluent. "He'd take long lunches. I'd sit near the cash register and wait. He always took his own sweet time. Afterward, he'd go exercise up at the university gymnasium for a few hours. They closed off an entire section of it just for him. Then he'd return to the hotel, get ready for dinner."

"What were his favorite places?" I asked.

"For dinner? He preferred clubs, where live orchestras played and booze flowed. You know, the Coconut Grove, the Old Mill, the Brass Rail, the Pinecrest. Crowds of autograph seekers would flock to him. He never once had a second of privacy. It didn't seem to bother him, though. He'd tell anyone that'd listen that one of the big studios is making a movie about him, starring Errol Flynn. Did you know about that?"

"So I've heard," I said. "Flynn looks nothing like him."

Roscoe shrugged. "He'll have to shave off his soup strainer."

I changed the subject: "Was there anywhere he went that struck you as out of the ordinary?"

Roscoe considered the question. "He met a man at the Old Mill. This was on, oh, Tuesday night. The music was too loud for me to hear what they were saying. They seemed like they knew each other, like a couple of old chums."

"Who was the man?"

"I don't know."

"Sounds like an exhausting detail," I said.

"Morning until night," he said.

"What time of night would your shift end?"

"It varied. Usually between midnight and one."

I said, "That night at the Grove . . ."

"Yeah."

"Did you happen to overhear Clive asking me to take him down to the Canyons of the Escalante?"

"No. That's a strange request."

"He'd read about Everett Ruess vanishing there," I said. "He offered to pay me ten grand to show him around the place. He wanted to go that night."

Roscoe whistled. "That's a hefty chunk of greenback. What did you say?"

"I told him to hire a guide," I said.

"For ten grand, I woulda given the prick the grand tour."

I smirked. "You don't know your way around there."

"How hard can it be to mosey up some goddamned canyons?"

Roscoe's comment made me laugh. Then it got me thinking.

"What?" he asked.

"I wonder if he went down there," I said. "By himself, without telling anyone."

"Try calling tour guides down there," said Roscoe. "Who knows? Maybe Underhill is down there right now taking in a little bird-watching or dipping his toes in some creek."

"That's a grand idea," I said.

I eased my chair backward and stood up.

"I need you to do me a favor," he said.

"Yeah?"

"My cats . . ."

"I'd be happy to take care of them," I said. "Barney and Millicent, right?"

"And Captain Jack," he said. "He's the one I got last month."

"I'll look in on them."

He held up his hand. I took it in mine and gripped it.

"I didn't do it," he said.

"I know," I said. "I'll see you soon."

I stood and circled the table, plucked up the empties, and patted Roscoe on the shoulder with my free hand before leaving. Out in the corridor, Officer Chapman stood against the wall, waiting. I thanked him, told him I was finished, and made my way to the stairwell. I thought of Roscoe all the way to the ground level, about how life had dealt him so many bad deals, and about the role he played—often a reckless one—in exacerbating his own troubles. Most of all, I pictured his sagging, defeated face.

On my way home, I stopped by Roscoe's residence. He shared it with three distinctive felines: the slow-moving orange tabby Barney, now getting along in years; the sprightly tortoiseshell Millicent, ready to duke it out with the toughest of alley cats; and paranoid newcomer Captain Jack, black as licorice, and constantly afraid of being followed. I gave the trio a mix of dry food and opened one of many cans of tuna Roscoe had stacked on the kitchen table especially for them. Once that was done, I filled a couple of bowls full of water and put out a saucer of milk for good measure. Barney and Millicent circled me, smacking into my legs like sharks thudding into the pillars of a fishing pier. Captain Jack put in a brief appearance, and I guess I spooked him when I called out "hello," because he took off in the direction of the staircase.

"Nice to see you, too," I said.

I went upstairs to look in on Roscoe's room. The door was ajar. I nudged it open. I found the bedclothes disheveled. Obviously, he didn't have a chance to make his bed before he was arrested. I don't know what came over me, but I began searching the bureau drawers. I rifled through socks, underwear, T-shirts. I opened a wooden box in the top drawer and found cuff links and jewelry. In the bottom drawer, beneath some undergarments, I found a stack of racy adult magazines with titles like *The Bachelor, Vim & Vigor, Silk Stockings Magazine, Spicy Tales Illustrated, Tijuana After Midnight,* and *Man about Town.* I put them back, tucking them under white cotton shirts, exactly where I'd found them. I closed the drawer and stood up.

I wandered around the house for another half hour, looking for something—anything—that might help me get a better grip on why Roscoe was in the situation he was in. I went through his daughter's room, too, and saw everything frozen the way she'd left it. A framed picture hanging on the wall of Fred Astaire and Ginger Rogers dancing. A bedside diary full of girlish handwriting. A neatly made bed with a pink bedspread and ruffled white skirt. A breeze blew in through the open window, ballooning the curtains. I came to a portrait of father and daughter from happier years. It made me sigh. I set the frame on the nightstand and left her room.

I probed rooms downstairs. I glanced at a picture of Roscoe and a trio of his comrades from his days as hired muscle with Donovan and Sons, a Denver-based company that hired out mercenaries to help companies crush strikes. He was great at his job, no doubt about it. In his youth, he was strong and handsome and had a head of unruly dark hair that spilled over shaved sides. I returned the photograph to the mantel and then left, locking the door to Roscoe's house behind me. Being in his house saddened me, but it also made me want to redouble my efforts to find who killed Nigel Underhill. I was sure it wasn't my best friend. Maybe I was blinded by my loyalty, but I was determined to find the killer and free Roscoe from jail.

Eight

A few years ago, after all of our families got to be too big and unwieldy, my brothers and I agreed that we would relocate our weekly family dinners to Frank's spacious farm in West Jordan. That way, we figured, we'd be taking some of the pressure off of our aging mother to hold these events every Sunday. Our mother still attended, although she seemed relieved not to have to plan such enormous undertakings so frequently. My older brother, Frank, always sat at the head of the table, beside his wife, the dour redhead, Margaret, who got to be more and more humorless with each passing year. My brother John, the gregarious sheriff of Carbon County down in the central part of the state, was seated near his wife, Eliza, a vocal woman who was essentially good-hearted, but didn't always filter her words before they came out of her mouth. And then there was Grant, the next-to-youngest Oveson brother, the police chief of Provo, Utah, athletic and angular-faced, with a portly, dark-haired wife named Bess, who could be a mix of charming and cold, sometimes all at once.

The huge, wood-paneled dining room in Frank's house, with its high rafters, was big enough to accommodate all of us—and all of our seventeen children. Frank accomplished this by placing two long tables together and draping linen tablecloths over them. In the corner of the room, near where the adults sat, was a short, round table for the youngest children, including our four-year-old daughter, Emily. Being closer to the adults, it made it easier to monitor the little ones.

Not surprisingly, I remained preoccupied throughout the evening. Clara kept eyeing me, likely frustrated by my aloofness. Truth is, I felt blue and bedeviled. The image of Roscoe languishing in a jail cell loomed large in my thoughts. In fact, nothing else mattered to me at that moment. All of the talk around the table about church activities, sporting news, the ongoing economic slump, or whether Clara would actually stick to her vow of having only three children and no more, all of those matters struck me as insignificant. As a result, I wasn't much of a dinner guest, and I knew it. Entire conversations happened without me hearing a single word spoken. Mouths moved, but my brain blocked out the sounds. I flashed back to Clive Underhill's car rocketing across the salt flats and flipping out of control and exploding into flames. I blinked the vision out of my mind, doing my best to chase away that grim memory.

"Well?"

John was eyeing me expectantly.

"Well what?" I asked.

"We're hoping you could help us settle this debate," said John. "I say President Roosevelt has saved our country from disaster."

"Cow dung," said Grant. "If you ask me . . ."

"Which I didn't," John mumbled.

". . . he's turning America socialist," said Grant. "Washington's taxing everybody to death, and spending it all on relief programs to help the indolent."

"Indolent, my foot!" snapped John. "These are decent, hard-working folk. Why, I'll have you know that at least half the people in my county keep framed pictures of Roosevelt in their curio cabinets."

"Oh, how do you know?" asked Grant, with a sneer. "Have you counted?"

"I just know it for a fact. Name me another president where people did that. And don't say Herbert Hoover or I'll laugh in your face."

"The only thing that proves," said Grant, "is that the lump-headed proletariat have been duped by the Washington Brain Trust."

"I wish you two wouldn't go on and on about politics over dinner," said Eliza. "There are more pleasant topics of conversation, you know."

"Like what?" asked Grant. "Which dish soap leaves your hands feeling smooth?"

John laughed and spoke with a full mouth: "Or where you get the best deal on hosiery?"

"Well, those are steps in the right direction," said Eliza.

"I have to agree with Liza on this one, dearest," said Bess. "It's not as though you're going to talk sense into John and turn him to a Republican."

"What do you mean 'talk sense into him'?" asked Eliza. She dropped her fork on her plate and it made a loud clank. "And what exactly have Republicans ever done to help ordinary Americans?"

"Now, now," said John. "Let's not start a catfight." John turned to me. "What's your take on Franklin D., kid?"

"I'd hate to be in his shoes," I said. "He's got a lot fuller plate than any of us."

"Well, isn't that a surprise," said Grant. "Old Mr. Neutrality gives an answer he thinks will make everybody happy. Remind me not to ask him to go door-to-door for me when I run for Congress."

Clara leaned toward me. "You OK?"

"Sure, I'm fine. I just don't care about politics, that's all," I said. "Never have, never will. I could use a little fresh air, I think."

"Go ahead," said my white-haired mother, staring at me over her bifocals. "We'll all be here when you come back."

"Yes, Mom."

As the conversation resumed around the table, I got up and headed out to the front porch. A cluster of wooden chairs formed a semicircle, and I pulled one aside and sat down. Inhaling warm air, I enjoyed the view of the Wasatch Mountains. The instant I got comfortable, the screen door clopped shut and heavy footsteps came my way. A shadow fell over me. I looked up. Frank stood there, hands in pockets, running his tongue along his molars.

"Mind if I join you?"

"It's a free country."

He pulled up a chair and sat down. He reached in his briefcase and fished out a thick file, creased in multiple spots, frayed around the edges. He passed it to me. The thing must've weighed a pound or more. I placed it on my lap, opened and thumbed through a thick mix of classified FBI reports on bond paper, newspaper articles, and case photographs. I noticed morgue photos. Dead men. Battered. Mangled. Most had open mouths and closed eyes. Flipping from front to back, I scanned headlines on yellowing newsprint.

LOCAL UNION LEADER DISAPPEARS

**STRIKE-BREAKERS BELIEVED TO BE
BEHIND KIDNAPPING**

THREE KILLED IN STEEL PLANT LABOR CLASH

I looked at Frank. "What is this?"

"It's a classified file from the bureau's investigation of Donovan and Sons, where Roscoe once worked. Look, kid, I don't like union agitators any more than Mr. Hoover. Most are either dirty reds or corrupt to the gills. But even the lousiest of 'em doesn't deserve to be on the receiving end of the kind of violence that your friend Lund and his associates dished out. Only the worst company bosses hired gun thugs from Donovan. Those men terrorized and intimidated strikers and their families in the worst ways imaginable. That file demonstrates conclusively that murder was standard operating procedure for Donovan's men. Roscoe Lund was no exception."

"What's your point?" I asked.

Frank held up three fingers. "Three eyewitnesses saw Lund return to the Hotel Utah in the middle of the night, demanding payment for services rendered."

"That doesn't prove anything," I said.

"Listen, kid, the eyes of the world will soon be upon us. The feds and the police will come under scrutiny. Catching the killer right away means we escape that. On the other hand, if we allow this case to drag on, it'll embarrass the bureau, the police, and the state. The outside world will see us as hapless bumpkins who can't tie our own shoelaces."

I turned through crime scene photos, newspaper clippings,

and investigation reports from the days when the FBI used to be called simply the "Bureau of Investigation." Frank waited in silence. Before long, I closed the file and gave it to him, and then he did something I was not expecting. He handed it back to me.

"Consider it a loan," he said. "I could get demoted for taking it out of the office. But it's worth the risk. I want you to see for yourself what Lund is capable of. You can drop it off by my office at the federal building when you're done."

"Thanks, Frank, but I don't need . . ."

"Uh-uh, I insist," he said, holding up a palm. "If you'll excuse me, I'd like to go finish my victuals. I think it'd be a swell idea if you were to join us."

On his way past me, Frank stopped to grip my shoulder. The bang from the screen door assured me I was alone again. The file weighed heavily on my knees. The last twenty-four hours had been a whirlwind. I needed to absorb it, make sense of it all, and figure out how I fit into the grand scheme of things.

"He doesn't want to see you crying. You've got to be strong."

"I'm trying."

"Try harder."

"I can't help it."

"You don't want your tears to be the last thing he sees, do you?"

"No."

"I didn't think so," Frank says. "Now, I ain't gonna let you near his bedside till you stop your blubbering."

It takes time for the tears to stop. Once they're out of my system, I return to the hospital room. My brothers stand against a whitewashed wall, waiting for word on our father's condition. Incandescent bulbs dangle by cords attached to the ceiling. The room is filled with dull yellow light.

Frank's arms are folded over his chest.

John keeps hands in pockets, staring blankly at the floor.

Grant bites his fingernails.

The room is cold and dim. Dad is gaunt, his eyes sunken, his thick mustache covering his upper lip.

My brothers have already paid their final respects. It is time for me to offer mine.

"You ain't crying anymore, are you?"

"No," I tell Frank.

"You're up, kid," says John. "Now is your chance to say good-bye."

I approach his bed in short, measured steps. The bed reminds me of a coffin, with its steel headboard, footboard, and rails on both sides. My glacial movements are due to my not knowing what to say. Should I thank him for taking me out on the lake early in the morning to fish for the first time on my eighth birthday? Or thank him for all of the special times he shared with me—the Christmases, the birthdays, the family outings? Maybe it is enough to say I love you. I'll miss you. Life won't be the same without you.

His breathing suddenly becomes labored. He gasps. He opens his eyes. His mouth falls open. Fear shines in his tiny pupils. His chest rises one last time. A final, crackly exhale is all that is left. He's gone.

The doctor comes in, checks Dad's pulse. Finding nothing, he takes off his stethoscope, closes Dad's eyes, and pulls the sheet over his head. The doctor leaves.

I am frozen in the spot where I stood when he died, taking in the outline of his body under the linen.

It is too late.

I awakened to darkness, pierced by moonbeams. Clara slept soundly. I checked my watch in the moonlight. 3:48 A.M. I kicked my feet over the bed's edge, stood, donned my robe, and left our bedroom, closing the door behind me.

In the kitchen, I switched on the light. I pulled a bottle of milk out of the icebox, and poured some in a saucepan. I set it on the stove's bluish-orange gas flame. Minutes later, I poured warm milk in a mug, went over to the kitchen table, and sat down. I never did look at the file. It was tempting. I stared at it long enough. Instead of going through it, I returned to bed. What little sleep I got was fitful. Next morning, I stopped off at my brother's office on my way to work to leave the dossier with the secretary at the front desk. She said Frank was in a meeting. I asked her to make sure he got the file. Scrap paper I clipped to the front said: *Thank You.* I left the federal building and headed to work.

En route, my thoughts swirled. I wanted Roscoe's past to stay irrelevant. I preferred to think of the man I knew now. Despite his flaws, he had a good heart beating in his chest. That's all I needed to know, I reasoned. Roscoe had been a loyal partner when we worked together on the Dawn Patrol—the midnight to eight A.M. shift—our first few years on the SLCPD, and before that, when we were deputies in the county sheriff's office. He'd always been there for me, saving my life twice. He was a regular visitor to my house on holidays and birthdays. My children knew him as Uncle Roscoe. I was closer to him than I was to any of my brothers. Even after he left the police force to start his own detective agency, I'd stayed in touch with him. I knew he had skeletons in his closet. It stands to reason that he would, given the nature of his prior employment. Roscoe had always been guarded about his past, but I'd discovered fragments of it, enough to know that he'd been present at some big labor battles. A man doesn't leave behind a profession like that without blood on his hands.

For the higher-ups in the police force, Roscoe made the ideal culprit, straight out of central casting. He'd been reprimanded countless times for insubordination. He cussed. He drank. He spat wisecracks like a Gatling gun, and nearly everybody got turned into grist for his mill at one point or another. Rumors circulated that he visited prostitutes. Pious Mormons—other than me—disliked him for obvious reasons. He wasn't one of them, and they thought he behaved reprehensibly. It did not help that he loved to turn their sacred cows into hamburgers, or that he showed up to work hungover on a number of occasions.

Non-Mormons didn't much care for Roscoe, either. He was a loner, forming few friendships on the force. His self-destructive streak led him to burn bridges. In the end, I was the only person on the police payroll that cared about him. To most of his superiors, including Buddy Hawkins and Wit Dunaway, Roscoe was expendable. They had no use for him. That he was an ex-cop would give them an opportunity to showcase their willingness to go after one of their own, if need be. The public likes it when the police punish bad apples, even if those apples had fallen out of the barrel, like Roscoe. It makes for good press.

I pondered such matters as I steered my car into the parking lot behind Public Safety, a marble and granite colossus with columned entrances and cathedral-high ceilings. Located on the southeast corner of First South and State, it used to house the local chapter of the YMCA when it first opened its doors in 1914. The Y relocated to more modest digs, and the police made themselves at home here. Back in those days, around the time of the Great War, the police chief opted to keep its weight room and swimming pool and indoor track open to encourage officers to maintain rigorous calisthenics routines. All of those rooms had been sealed shut by the time I got here, and newer generations of police chiefs encouraged the men under their command to exercise on their own time.

But that was all in the past, and I didn't have time to dwell on distant yesterdays. Monday morning beckoned me to start the week anew, and I faced far more pressing matters than the aging, labyrinthine building full of bricked-off rooms that I called work.

Nine

Back around, oh, 1934, maybe early '35, Chief Bill Cowley came up with the idea of creating a Missing Persons Bureau in the Salt Lake City Police Department. He envisioned it being a small squad, staffed by two detectives. He once confided in Buddy Hawkins that the inspiration behind the squad came from a Warner Bros. picture called *Bureau of Missing Persons,* starring Pat O'Brien and Bette Davis. I've never actually seen it, but I recall reading about it sometime back in *Photoplay* magazine. The film depicted a hard-as-nails cop with a heart of gold (what other kind is there in Hollywood?) played by O'Brien, who takes over the missing persons division of his police department, only to get mixed up with Davis, who is looking for her missing husband.

Even if a movie had served as its source of inspiration, starting the bureau was a good call on Cowley's part. It was long overdue. With economic hard times packing a particularly potent punch here in Utah, reports of missing persons were on the increase. So the bureau set up shop in a room only slightly larger than a broom closet, which had windows overlooking the dreary alley where cars entered and exited the parking lot. For the first few years of its existence, the bureau conducted its affairs under the able leadership of Detective Sergeant L.D. "Link" Andrews, an aging former Homicide dick who welcomed the change of scenery during the last few years of his career. Link retired in the spring of '37, and his partner at the time, Donald Smoot, pleaded with Wit Dunaway to be reassigned elsewhere. Smoot ended up in Homicide. And guess who took over Missing Persons?

Most detectives saw the bureau as a dead end, a place where the higher-ups put people like Link Andrews when they're approaching gold watch time. I guess I had a different attitude when Wit asked me if I'd consider taking it over and whipping it into shape. I said yes instantly. I'd grown tired of the dreary internal politics of the Morals Squad. My commander, Lieutenant Harman Grundvig, had the job for life if he wanted it, and he expected all of his subordinates to be slavish brownnosers, willing to drop everything to work overtime with no advance warning. Not only did he choose favorites, he also insisted on broadcasting his impressive Mormon credentials every chance he got, and he would often ask the men under his command about their church duties.

Now, you won't find a more dedicated member of the Church of Jesus Christ of Latter-day Saints than me. In all of my years as a worshiper, I can count on one hand the number of times I've missed church due to illness or some other unfortunate circumstance. But I've always been a firm believer that one keeps Church business out of police affairs. Grundvig's unfortunate behavior, I felt, only added fuel to the fire of the anti-Mormon faction in the force. That camp consisted of a tiny yet vocal coterie of men who insisted the Mormons were persecuting them at every turn and generally making their lives miserable. So when Wit Dunaway, a non-Mormon who got along well with Mormons on the force, asked me if I'd consider moving into the Missing Persons Bureau, I replied yes before he was even done posing the question. The next thing he asked is if I had someone in mind that I'd like to have as a partner. I also furnished a speedy response to that question. I told him Myron Adler.

Myron worked in the records division, located in the basement of Public Safety. He possessed an eidetic—or photographic—memory, which gave him an astonishing recall of the most minute details. Whenever someone paid a visit to records with a request for a box or file, Myron always knew precisely where to go inside of that labyrinthine storage area. He and I used to work in a short-lived squad formed to combat the local polygamy scourge, and we got along swimmingly. The two of us developed a healthy mutual respect for each other, and once the squad was dissolved, I was disappointed to learn that he would be returning to his former job in a part of the building that police nicknamed "the tomb." So when Wit came to me last year, and asked me to run Missing Persons, I made Myron's joining me a condition of my acceptance. Wit promptly acceded.

Earlier this year, Wit appointed a third detective, DeVoy Beckstead, to our squad. He wore eyeglasses on his cantaloupe-shaped head, was bald on top, with prematurely wilting jowls and a Clark Gable mustache that sometimes grew into a walrus one when he neglected to trim it. He had a penchant for selecting some of the goofiest bow ties I've laid eyes on. Never neckties, mind you. Only bow ties. He was frumpy, but not in a thoughtless or careless way. He was genuinely concerned about his appearance. But his tastes were decidedly passé. And believe me, nobody could ever accuse me of being a dandy or glamor boy myself.

Who was I to judge? But judge I did, as we all tend to, even if
we don't always give voice to it.

DeVoy came to us from Homicide. They couldn't stand him
anymore. My boss, Captain Wit Dunaway, begged me to take
him. There was desperation in his voice on that cool spring morning when he pleaded his case.

"Listen, Art, I hired this fuckin' clown, 'scuse the French,"
Wit said. "Him being here—that's my mistake, I admit. But now
nobody can stand to work with him. He's obnoxious as hell. He's
condescending, always grousing. He opens his mouth and out
spews the bitching, especially about his lousy apartment and how
his dentist made a mess out of his pearlies and won't fix 'em properly. And he's constantly listening to opera music. Fuckin' wop
shit. Drives the men crazy. They hate the guy."

"Why don't you fire him?"

"It's too hard," he said. "He's long past his probationary
period."

"So you're going to unload him on me?"

"C'mon. You've got a thing for strays and foreigners, Art."

"What'll I do with him?" I asked.

"Assign him to answer the telephone. Dump paperwork on
him. Hell, if worse comes to worst, send him off to see that new
Shirley Temple picture at the Rialto!" He pulled out his billfold
and handed me a dollar bill. "Here, I'll spring for it."

I gave Wit his floppy buck back. "I won't make him go to the
movies."

He put it back in his billfold, which he returned to his
pocket.

"I know he was a court stenographer at one point," said Wit.
"He's the only man I know who can do shorthand."

"You don't say."

"I'll have a stenotype sent up with him. He can transcribe interviews."

"That beats a kick in the pants," I said.

With those words, DeVoy Beckstead became the newest member of the squad.

At first, the perks of running the Missing Persons Bureau seemed readily apparent, outweighing any drawbacks. I was delighted to be working with Myron again, who brought with him a sense of humor so subtle you might not even know it existed. And DeVoy slowly grew on me. *Slowly.* And me? I no longer had to answer to Grundvig, a big improvement over my previous assignment. Wit was now my boss, and he more or less left me alone, placing full trust in my ability to run the squad.

Unlike some of my past placements in the force, the Missing Persons Bureau was strictly an 8:30 A.M. to 4:30 P.M. job. I'd work all morning, take a half-hour lunch break most days, and resume my duties until it came time to go home. About 50 percent of the job involved Myron and me pushing pencils in bureaucratic tasks, usually handled before noon.

The other half took us out onto the streets in an unmarked prowler to investigate reports and occasionally follow up on past cases. After DeVoy's transfer into Missing Persons, he helped whip us into shape administratively, and answered the squad's main telephone daily. Thankfully, most of the calls we fielded were easily resolved. They typically fell under one of three categories: 1) runaway adolescents, who were usually found in close proximity to their homes; 2) adult men or women fleeing domestic hardships or marital strife; 3) the elderly, reluctant to remain dependent on loved ones who could barely support them. The overwhelming majority of these people were quickly found, and most returned home after we encouraged them to do so.

Yet the job, I soon learned, came with a dark side, in the form of what I called "the stack"—that is, a stack of folders, anywhere from perhaps a dozen to fifteen at any given time, of unsolved cases. Cases we refused to close. These were people who vanished without a trace. No eyewitnesses to place them anywhere, no hotels or motor courts with guest books containing their names, no friends or relatives who could confirm their whereabouts, no bank account activities post-disappearance. Gone. Erased. In some instances, not even a snapshot to place in their dossier.

A typical file in "the stack" was that of Melvin Fernley Thompson, age 42, an automobile mechanic at Modern Motor Service, 635 South State Street. His stats sheet described him as five feet nine inches tall, weight 178 pounds, pale complexion, grayish-black hair, hazel eyes, and a prominent mole by his right ear. He resided with his wife, Gail, on the second floor of the Shubrick Apartments, 72 West 400 South. The two of them had lived there for at least a dozen years. Even though Thompson fixed cars, the couple did not own one. He'd board a streetcar to work. No children either, only some birds. For years, Thompson liked to take an after-dinner stroll over to Saxman's Cigar Store, a few blocks away, to buy a stogie and a copy of the evening newspaper. He'd bring his purchases home, sit on the front stoop, and puff his cigar while he caught up on the day's news. For seven years, Mondays through Fridays, he repeated this practice without fail, as well as on some Saturday and Sunday mornings.

One evening—Thursday, April 18, 1935, to be specific—Thompson and his wife finished dinner and he left the apartment, taking a couple of coins but leaving his wallet behind. That night, he never arrived at Saxman's, and he didn't come home. The next morning, Gail Thompson visited Public Safety to report her husband missing. In his typical fashion, Link Andrews left no stone unturned, going to every apartment building and business between the Shubrick and Saxman's in search of possible eyewitnesses. He interviewed Joe Saxman and his employees at the cigar store (mostly the owner's relatives), even those that weren't working that night. He talked to Thompson's fellow mechanics. He telephoned relatives of Thompson's, including the man's mother and younger sister, both residing in Spokane at the time (sadly, his father had passed away). Link found out that Thompson never touched his account at Zion's Bank after going missing. Link even visited the old garage where Thompson worked in Ogden in the early 1920s. It all added up to nothing, as Thompson was nowhere to be found. When Link finally passed the file on to me, he said with sadness in his voice, "I can't say the trail ever grew cold on this one. There was never any trail to begin with."

Every so often, I still drop by Gail Thompson's apartment, just to check in and see how she's doing. Sometimes, I'll drop off a bag of groceries—the essentials: milk and bread, eggs and lettuce, a couple sticks of butter, maybe a jar of honey or box of cookies. Gail is always grateful and thanks me profusely. She shows me her birds—a parrot, two cockatiels, and a couple of boisterous zebra finches. We'll sit out on the stoop, where Melvin once smoked cigars and read the paper, and watch cars drive by. She used to get teary-eyed and say she still expects him to come walking through the front door any day now. She no longer tells me that. She has resigned herself to the fact that Melvin is gone and isn't returning.

These days, Gail will ask me about my kids, and I'll tell her they're fine, growing faster than weeds. Sometimes I'll show her the latest wallet snapshots. I'll inquire about her secretarial job at Peoples Finance & Thrift Company, and she'll usually say it's going fine. And in the uneasy silences when we're sitting outside and a dry wind is ruffling our hair, I'm sure she's probably wondering the same thing I am: Where on earth is Melvin Thompson?

Those were the types of cases that inspired old Mr. Insomnia to pull Little Art out of Slumberland. I'd go into the kitchen and brood over a mug of warm milk. I never thought, back when I told Wit yes to the job, that working in this unit would give me nightmares, but it has. Many dreams are recurring: my children going missing without a trace; Clara vanishing from a family portrait, as if she'd been completely erased; and one terrible vision of me slowly disappearing, gradually becoming more and more transparent, until I was like that fellow in the H.G. Wells story, *The Invisible Man*. Nobody could see me. I couldn't even see myself. I'd invariably wake up from these nightmares in a cold sweat, heart pounding, pillow soaked. I found solace at the kitchen table, sipping warm milk, waiting for my demons to calm down, and taking stock of all the good things in my life, all the reasons to be happy.

All my life, I've tried to put on an optimistic face, tried to see the good in others, tried to look on the bright side. I've kept my sunny side up, so to speak, through good times and bad, telling the pessimists around me—and believe me, they're everywhere—that everything will get better, that those who persevere and work hard will be rewarded, and that even with all the economic hard times, the high unemployment, and the businesses still going under, we in America have a lot to be thankful for. I suppose I really do believe in these things, and I'm being genuine when I say them. But I also know that evil sometimes lurks in the darkness, that some people have murder in their hearts, and even in these modern times when we want everybody to be accounted for, a man or woman or child can simply vanish, never

to be seen or heard from again, as though they'd only been fig-
ments of our imaginations.

"Morning, fellas," I said, hanging my hat on the coat tree near
the door. "I hope everyone is rested and refreshed now that the
weekend is over."

"Good morning," said Myron.

"Hello," DeVoy said listlessly.

Our three-man outfit housed three huge desks, each carved
out of some kind of petrified wood and with its own chair, telephone, and typewriter. Rounding it out were several filing cabinets, a map of Salt Lake County on the wall, and a framed
corkboard outside of our door where we posted WANTED notices
for our more pressing cases. Did I forget to mention DeVoy's '34
RCA Victor Electrola combination radio/phonograph sitting on
its own table? DeVoy loved music. Not just any music. Opera and
classical music. Hence, the radio and record player combo.

On this hot, dry August morning, DeVoy and Myron watched
me as I headed to my desk, sat down in my chair, took off and
tossed my hat on my typewriter, and sat down. I retrieved a yellow pad and pen, and swiveled toward my subordinates. For
some reason, outside noises—a cacophony of streetcar bells,
horns, and traffic cop whistles coming from State Street—were
particularly loud, forming a constant din that sailed in through
the open window with the warm breeze.

"Squad roll call for the week of Monday, August 8, 1938," I
said. "My turn to take minutes. I'll get us started. As I'm sure
you both know by now, Clive Underhill has gone missing, and
it's my responsibility to find him. I'm under orders to work this
case alone, and to keep quiet about it. We don't want the press
getting wind of this, so I'd appreciate it if the two of you would

use the utmost discretion. This is big—real big. Even the FBI is involved, and I have to be careful not to step on their toes. I may end up leaning on one or the other of you—or both—for help, but make no mistake about it: this is my case." I rubbed my right eye with my knuckle, drew a deep breath, and gazed at DeVoy and Myron. "So, lay it on me fellows, where do things stand with you?"

"I spent most of last week working on the Mildred Halverson case," said DeVoy. "She's seventy-six. Went missing from the Mayfield Rest Home on, uh . . ." DeVoy searched his notes. ". . . Third South and Fourth East. Mrs. Halverson was last seen leaving the dining room on Thursday, July twenty-first, after lunch, which runs from noon to one at the facility. She hasn't been seen or heard from since. She requires routine doses of heart medication, so it is imperative that we find her at once. I've flagged her a high-priority case. So far, I've come up empty-handed, but I'm interviewing shop owners and residents near the Mayfield, as well as Halverson's relatives. This one's a real head-scratcher, I admit. I'm hoping to start back in on it after we're done here."

"Very good," I said, nodding my approval. "I'm pleased with the work you've been doing, DeVoy. Keep at it. Myron?"

Myron spun in his swivel chair and picked files up off of his desk. "I've got three runaways. All teenagers. All friends. Gayle Ostler, age seventeen; Melva Peck, sixteen; and Irene Bernstrom, also sixteen. They've been missing nine days. I've made a few calls, but I'm planning to take an unmarked out and follow up on a promising lead. An employee at the bus station encountered three young women a week ago matching the subjects' descriptions. They didn't have enough money to buy three Overland Stage bus tickets to San Francisco, and they left the depot before the ticket agent could call the police. There's another lead. One of Bernstrom's friends thinks she's staying with her boyfriend in Logan. And get this. He's supposedly twice her age. So we might be dealing with stat rape charges."

"Well done, Myron," I said. "This is a tough one. I'm sure it's especially hard on the parents of the girls."

The telephone on my desk rang.

I rolled my chair closer and lifted the phone off the hook after the third ring. "Missing Persons. Detective Oveson."

"Hello Detective Oveson," said Amelia Van Cott. "I have a feeling something really important happened in the Hotel Utah yesterday, but you ducked out before you could tell me what it was. Is that so?"

"Nope. Nothing happened. I went there to check on Clive Underhill after his accident. Everything seemed hunky-dory. I left."

"That's it?"

"That's all," I said.

"That's funny, because I get the distinct impression something is amiss in the Beehive State."

"Art!"

Cradling the telephone between my head and shoulders, I turned to see Buddy Hawkins standing in the doorway. He opened his mouth and nodded when he saw me on the telephone. I mouthed, "I'll be with you in a minute." He stepped back into the corridor, but kept watching from outside. Amelia Van Cott was waiting for some sort of response from me, but I could not remember—for the life of me—what she had just said.

"Come again?" I asked.

"I've got a funny feeling there's something you're not telling me," she said.

"Oh? What gave you that impression?" I asked, wondering how to get her off the phone without making it look like that's what I was trying to do.

"It could have something to do with that county coroner's wagon I saw leaving the parking lot, not long after you went upstairs."

"That's news to me."

"Is that all you have to say?"

"I don't know what you're talking about."

"Does that mean you have no comment?"

"Yep. 'Fraid so."

"Well, if you hear of anything, you know where to reach me."

"I do. HYland three thousand, extension . . ."

She said, "Twelve."

"Twelve. That's my lucky number."

"Is it really?" she asked, with a spark of excitement in her voice.

I hung up. Buddy took that as his cue to enter. Scanning the room with a spark of contempt in his eyes, he kept his hands in his pants pockets, and as he drew closer, I noticed he reeked of too much aftershave. Crossing to my desk, he offered something in the way of a nod to Myron and DeVoy. Rage gleamed in his eyes when he looked at me.

"I'd like to see you in my office, Art," he said. "This very instant."

"What's it about?"

"Now. Please."

"Aren't you going to give me a little hint?"

His teeth were grinding. Bad sign. As quickly as he had appeared, he left.

Ten

"All right, Art, I'll ask you again. Where is he?"

"I told you I don't know. How come you brought me all the way over here anyway? Isn't he under the covers, sleeping?"

"You know he isn't."

Buddy yanked the wool blanket down, revealing a pair of haggard pillows that'd seen better days. We were standing in the hot, dimly lit cell in the city jail where Roscoe had been incarcerated. Now, it looked as though he'd escaped. I wasn't lying to Buddy when I said I didn't know where he went. I truly had no inkling of where he might be, or when—or even how—he lit out. I should've known he might escape. If anybody could break free of this dungeon, it was Roscoe. He had worked in this building once upon a time, and he knew where the chinks in the armor were. I can't say I blame him, especially if his claim was true, that he had nothing to do with murdering Nigel Underhill. Still, I knew Buddy would order a small army, if need be, to hunt down

Roscoe. Buddy could be relentless, especially when fixated on something like apprehending a particular individual.

"According to Stroud, you visited Roscoe yesterday," said Buddy. "What did you do to help him?"

"I didn't help him," I said, facing Buddy. "I don't even know where he is."

Buddy suddenly came across as intimidating, flanked as he was on one side by Pace Newbold and, on the other, by Wit Dunaway. Maybe it was that stiff suit he was wearing, black as night, or his lantern jaw moving side to side as he ground his teeth. He reminded me of a gangster from a Warner Bros. picture, and the way he looked now, he could throw a scare into Jimmy Cagney.

"I want to know what you two talked about," he said. "And I mean everything."

"I wanted to see how he was holding up," I said. "I also happen to know he has three cats, and I asked him if there was anybody looking after them. That's all."

"Quit covering up for him," Buddy said. "Come clean. Now."

"What do you think," I said, "that I'd risk my entire career and livelihood, my . . . my family, my well-being, to cover for Roscoe?"

Pace chimed in: "That's precisely what we think."

"You keep quiet," Buddy told him. He eyed me. "Well?"

"I'm telling the truth," I said. "I'm as shocked as you are."

"I find that a little hard to swallow," said Pace.

"Shut up," said Buddy.

"Yes, sir."

Buddy reserved his coldest stare for me. "Stay away from this case. That's an order."

"Buddy."

Buddy turned to Wit. "Yeah? What is it?"

"A word," said Wit. "In private."

"Don't go anywhere," said Buddy, scowling.

"Where would I go?" I asked.

Wit placed his hand on Buddy's shoulder and steered him out into the hallway. Pace and I stayed put in the cell. He smirked at me. I avoided eye contact. We were quiet for a couple of tense minutes. But the weight of his stare got to me.

"What?"

"Where is he, Oveson?"

"Beats me."

"C'mon, don't be an asshole. I know you're hiding him. You know what they say. Once a partner, always a partner."

"Who says that?" I asked. "Ignoramuses like you?"

"Maybe you'd like to step outside."

"You two mugs will work together," said Wit, coming back in and maneuvering between us. "Newbold, you'll coordinate the homicide investigation. Oveson, you're on the missing persons detail to look for the racer. And don't go pissing into each other's gardens."

I reared my head in surprise. "I thought Buddy didn't want me to . . ."

"I reminded him you're one of the best detectives in the bureau. If anybody's going to find Underhill, it'll be you." He switched to Pace. "And you're my *numero uno* man in Homicide. Lemme know what you need to crack this one and it's yours."

"Yes sir," said Pace, trying to conceal his scowl.

"You two ladies bury the hatchet," said Wit. "C'mon. We haven't got all day."

I held out my hand. Pace grabbed, squeezed, and tossed it back like a piece of garbage. The entire time, he wore a nasty sneer on his face.

"We've got a meeting with Underhill's manager and fiancée in Cowley's office," said Wit. "I want you both behaving like a couple of choirboys. Understand?"

"Yes."

"Yes sir."

"Good. Let's shake a leg."

Chief William Cowley occupied the type of large and bright office one might expect of a powerful politician or company president. Framed pictures lined the walls, spectacular windows looked out at the mountains on the valley's east side, plush carpeting muted footsteps, and you'd get a sore neck from always gazing up at the elaborate ceiling frescoes.

Everybody in these halls knew Chief Cowley was a figurehead. Real power rested in the hands of Deputy Police Chief Hawkins. He possessed the all-consuming work ethic of my father, who also ran this police department as a deputy chief before his life was cut short by an unknown gunman. Chief Cowley may have rubbed elbows with the prominent and powerful, and constantly reassured the public—through his connections in the press—that he presided over the most honest police force in the nation. But his was an empty title, and he nearly always deferred to his deputy chief.

Still, Cowley enjoyed the nicest digs in the building. This morning, he was parked behind an art deco desk that faced a row of antique leather guest chairs. It was in these chairs that Cowley either welcomed prestigious visitors or read the riot act to inept subordinates. I'd just passed through the anteroom where Cowley's small army of secretaries typed away, walking at the head of the line, followed by Buddy, Wit, and Pace. Cowley's door was ajar. I pressed it open.

My brother, Frank, was the first person to enter my line of vision. He occupied a corner chair, adjacent to and behind Cowley, watching the proceedings like a ghost in a three-piece suit. He smiled and winked at me when we made eye contact, and I offered a single nod without saying hello.

I recognized Albert Shaw, Underhill's manager, and he rose to shake my hand. Seated beside him was a strikingly beautiful woman wearing a wide-brimmed hat over her shoulder-length chocolate-brown hair. She came attired in a striking satiny violet dress that almost appeared painted on certain parts of her voluptuous body. The hat shaded what had to be one of the most attractive faces I've ever seen. When she got up from her seat, I noticed her dress showed off a great deal of cleavage, and her stockings turned her legs a dark tan.

"Art, I take it you've met Mr. Shaw," said Cowley. I nodded, and Cowley continued: "This is Clive Underhill's fiancée, Dorothy Bliss."

"Please, call me Dot," she said, in a throaty British accent that made me swallow hard. She extended a tiny hand. I shook it gently. "You must be Detective Oveson. I have you to thank for saving Clive's life."

"It was nothing," I said.

"I've a difficult time believing that."

We released hands and I whiffed her perfume—sweet, but with an edge to it. I gestured to Pace. "This is . . ."

"I'm capable of introducing myself, Oveson."

I shrugged and made a long face, as if to say, "Be my guest."

"Pace Newbold, Homicide Bureau. Pleased to make your acquaintance, ma'am."

She aimed that dainty hand at Pace, and he gripped it for a few seconds.

"Mr. Newbold, the pleasure is all mine."

"Of course, the two of you have already met," said Cowley, eyeing Pace and Albert Shaw. They exchanged quiet greetings. Buddy walked past me and shook hands briefly with Shaw and Bliss. "And you all know FBI Special Agent Franklin Oveson."

"Don't mind me," said Frank from the corner. "I'm observing."

"Please be seated," said Cowley, gesturing to the extra chairs that his secretary had brought in from another room.

I made myself comfortable next to Shaw. Pace sat on the other side of me. Buddy picked a chair strategically located by Cowley's desk, which lent him an air of authority. I wondered if he was going to mention Roscoe's escape from jail. Something told me our British guests would not be impressed with the news. And Buddy, always fearful that the Salt Lake City Police Department might appear anything less than the world's greatest police force, would tie himself up in knots over even a hint of negative publicity.

"I'd like to thank each of you for coming here this morning on such short notice," said Cowley. "I will keep the preliminaries brief. I know you're all aware of the key details. Nigel Underhill has been murdered and he's lying in the morgue as we speak. Clive Underhill is missing, and his whereabouts are unknown. And there is one other matter." He looked at Buddy. "Do you want to tell them? Or shall I?"

"Tell us what?" asked Dot Bliss.

Buddy drew a deep breath, eyeing the pair of Brits sheepishly. "The man we arrested as a key suspect in the murder of Nigel Underhill has somehow escaped from our city jail. He is at large."

"How could something like this possibly happen?" asked Shaw.

"We're as shocked as you are," said Cowley. "I'm placing the full manpower of two entire squads behind a joint investigation of Nigel Underhill's homicide and Clive's disappearance. Special Agent Oveson of the FBI and myself will personally oversee the all aspects of this undertaking. I know I speak for all of us when I say that we will not sleep at night until Clive is found and Nigel's murderer is captured."

"I plan to be there the day that pathetic bastard Lund goes in front of the firing squad," said Pace. "He'll get his, just as sure as I'm sitting here."

Pace's comment bothered me. Cowley picked the perfect time to change the subject: "Detective Oveson, part of the purpose of today's meeting is to brief you on the case. I understand Detective Newbold, under the supervision of Hawkins and Dunaway, has already questioned Mr. Shaw, Miss Bliss, and all of the members of Underhill's entourage."

"Yes sir," said Pace. "They were all in their rooms at the time, sleeping. We've collected fingerprint samples from each one, and we'll be conducting follow-up questioning. For now, none of them are suspects, or even persons of interest."

"Have you any questions, Art?"

"Yeah, I do," I said. I looked at Shaw and Bliss. "Who was the last person to see Clive before he disappeared?"

"Nigel," said Shaw. "He and Clive . . ." Shaw hesitated. "They quarreled in the hotel lobby, after you left."

"What about?"

"We don't know," said Shaw. "A couple of hotel employees heard portions of the argument, but they weren't really sure what it was about."

"Then what?" I asked.

Buddy chimed in: "An elevator operator says he gave Clive a

ride up to his room, followed by Nigel about ten minutes later. The doorman saw him outside having a cigarette, evidently pacing, probably trying to calm down."

"That was the last time anybody saw Clive," said Pace.

"That we know of," added Dot Bliss.

Pace smiled at her. "That we know of," he echoed.

"Did the elevator operator see Clive go to his room?" I asked.

"No," said Pace.

"Did anybody see him leave the building after that?" I asked.

"No," repeated Pace. "There is an unattended stairwell, but it would've been next to impossible for a man on crutches to go down all of those flights of stairs."

"Yeah, that is highly unlikely," I said. "Unless he had help of some sort."

"I've witnessed Clive achieve feats I thought impossible," said Shaw. "I learned long ago never to rule out anything in his case."

"Well, we can theorize about that one until we're blue in the face," said Buddy. "Let's stick to matters that we know for sure, the main one being the following morning, a hotel employee found Nigel's body. We're still awaiting word from the coroner, but the m.o. appears to have been manual strangulation."

"Manual?" asked Dot.

"Done with the hands," I said.

Shaw said, "Nigel had a standing order with room service to deliver a poached egg, a sectioned grapefruit, and dry wheat toast to his room each morning at half past seven. When he didn't answer the door Sunday morning, the room service man let himself in. He found Nigel on the floor and promptly alerted the manager, who telephoned the police and then called up to my room. I, in turn, rang Clive's hotel room, but got no answer. I asked the manager to let me in with a passkey. The place was spotless. The bed was made, even though room service hadn't visited since the previous day. There was no sign of Clive. Thankfully, we found no evidence of foul play, either. I do hope he's somewhere safe right now."

Staring at me, Buddy said, "I understand you were alone with him for a good hour or more at the Coconut Grove, and you gave him a lift back to the hotel afterward. Is that so?"

"Yes," I said.

"Well?"

"Well what?"

"Did he say anything?" pressed Buddy.

"He wouldn't stop talking," I said.

Buddy glowered, as if I should've known what he meant. "Anything that'd lead you to believe that he was in danger or had any intention of going away?"

Just yesterday, I'd told Buddy about Clive's expressions of unhappiness, his desire to flee his current life and the people in it, his pleading with me to take him down to the Canyons of the Escalante, where he could lose himself, the way Everett Ruess had gotten lost four years ago. I didn't think it was wise to repeat all of those things in the presence of Shaw and Bliss. My gut instinct was to spare the feelings of those closest to him. Perhaps I hadn't made it clear to Buddy that Clive had revealed all of that information to me in confidence, and in a drunken state, probably not expecting me to share it with others. And what if he should return today or tomorrow or sometime soon, unscathed, only to be confronted by people that I'd turned against him? These matters weighed heavily on my mind, made all the more pressing by all of those people in Cowley's office staring at me, waiting for my reply.

All of these notions raced through my mind in the span of a split second.

"No," I said. "Not that I recall. He talked a lot about his upcoming attempt to break the speed record out at the Salt Flats. He was careful not to divulge too many secrets about the car he'll be driving."

"What other topics of conversation came up?" asked Buddy.

"It was all small talk," I said. "Differences between England and America, the killer heat out in the desert, and how big and open the spaces are out here in the West. Early on, Clive put the kibosh on political talk. That's about it, really."

Dot turned her glassy eyes on me. "Was he distressed or melancholy?"

"No. I found him surprisingly chipper, given what a dangerous scrape he'd been in earlier in the day." I looked directly at Dot's ethereal face, which appeared porcelain in this light. "Has Underhill ever gone missing like this before?"

"No," said Dot.

"Well, there was one time in Daytona Beach, three years ago," said Shaw. "Very similar to this. There was no sign of him in his hotel room. We reported him missing to the local police and they opened an investigation. Five days later, an eyewitness saw Clive walking along a country road out in the woods, near a little town called Kerr City, by the Ocala Forest. I promptly drove up there and found him almost euphoric, oblivious to the outside world and the consequences of his actions. The doctor gave him a clean bill of health. I told him he mustn't go away like that. He scared us out of our wits."

"What was he doing all of those days?" I asked.

"He said he went out to admire the scenery," said Dot. "We don't have that type of landscape back in England. It's all very exotic to us."

Buddy nodded. "Might he have gone on one of his nature forays again?"

Shaw shrugged his shoulders. "It's possible."

"Does he have use of a car, other than the ones he's racing?" I asked.

"No," said Shaw. "When we arrived, we rented a fleet of Buick sedans, all late-model four-doors, which we've been using for our outings. They're all present and accounted for, in the hotel parking lot. For security purposes, only myself and Clive's mechanic, Mr. Pangborn, know the exact whereabouts of the land speed vehicle."

I asked, "At any point, has Clive left the Hotel Utah unaccompanied?"

When I posed the question, I had in mind Roscoe's comments about Clive sneaking out of the hotel one night and provoking Shaw's ire for doing so.

But Shaw simply said, "No."

"What about this wreck on Saturday?" I asked. "I find it remarkable that it'd occur the day he went missing. Has anybody figured out what happened? Why the car wiped out like that?"

"His mechanic, Julian, is looking into it now," said Shaw.

"I hear Clive is supposed to unveil his new racing machine on Saturday," I said.

"That's correct," said Shaw. "If all goes according to plan, he'll break four hundred. Well, that's what he was supposed to do, before all of this happened."

"It's the same day Rudy Heinrich will attempt to set a new record," said Dot Bliss. "Rudy's car is supposed to be even faster than Clive's, according to rumors. I suppose we'll see."

"Where's Underhill's vehicle?" I asked.

"It's being kept in a warehouse locally," said Shaw.

"May I look at it?"

"I don't see what it has to do with this investigation, Detective Oveson."

"It might have everything to do with it."

Shaw nodded. "I'll consider your request."

I shifted the line of questioning: "Has Clive been threatened recently?"

As I posed the question, I thought of Roscoe's comment when I talked to him in jail yesterday, about being hired by Shaw to provide protection due to threats Underhill was getting.

"Not that I know of," said Shaw.

Either Roscoe was lying or Shaw was. I doubted it was Roscoe.

"What about Nigel?" I asked.

Pace leaned in close to me. "Don't look now, but you're wandering into my vegetable patch."

I furrowed my eyebrows at him, but Shaw answered my question.

"Nigel had enemies, no doubt, and I can say that he wasn't especially well liked. But I don't know of anyone who wanted to see him dead."

"Other than Lund," Pace mumbled.

I glowered at Pace. He imitated me.

"The other night at the Grove, someone mentioned that Nigel was working on his family history at the Genealogical Society," I said. "Enlighten me, please. Why the strong urge to sort out his family tree?"

"I don't know," said Shaw. "Nigel has always been enigmatic at best."

"I don't want to have to tell you again to drop it," Pace said to me. "Don't forget which Underhill brother you're looking for."

I pretended to ignore Pace's comment, even as it prompted me to change the subject: "We'll need access to Clive's hotel room. We have to question members of his entourage."

"I'll arrange for them to come here," said Shaw. "Give me a time suitable for you, and I'll have them driven over."

"I don't mind questioning them at the hotel," I said. "If that'd be easier."

"I prefer to remain discreet. We'd like this investigation to be handled as quietly as possible," said Shaw. "Clive is a member of a prominent British family. He's known around the world. In fact, the Warner Brothers studio in California has already purchased the rights to his memoir and they're adapting it into a movie with Errol Flynn playing Clive."

"Impressive," I said. "I imagine you want to keep the press out of this."

Shaw made a searching face. "They can only complicate things."

"The coroner's office is observing an embargo on outgoing information to newspapers and radio outlets regarding Nigel Underhill," said Buddy. "We haven't notified his parents, either. His father, Lloyd, is a newspaper magnate, getting along in years, and I understand his mother is quite frail. To hit them at once with news of Nigel's death and Clive's disappearance might be more than they can take. Am I correct, Mr. Shaw?"

"Yes," said Shaw. "Quite."

"What's going to happen to the body?" I asked.

I knew my questions about Nigel irked Pace, but at this point, I cared not at all.

"We're stalling," said Buddy. "With the hopes that we'll find Clive soon."

"The longer he's missing, the harder it'll be to keep this thing covered up," I said. "It's a small town. Word gets around. Especially with someone of his stature."

"Do your best," said Dot. "That's all we ask."

Eleven

Nearing the Missing Person's Bureau, the opera music grew louder. It rang through the halls where the second-floor Detective Bureau offices were located. *Could I not have a moment's peace,* I wondered, reaching the top of the stairs. I knew DeVoy had been playing his music full blast again, and I'm sure I was going to get an earful from my fellow detectives down the corridor. I walked into the office and went straight to the phonograph, lifting the tone arm to its resting place. DeVoy turned in his chair and seemed perturbed that I would touch his precious record-playing machine. Myron continued typing out forms in triplicate using carbon paper, pretending as though nothing had happened.

"What are you doing?"

"This isn't an opera hall," I said, tossing my hat on my typewriter.

He swiveled around, now facing me in his chair. "Do you even know what piece that is?"

"No," I said. "And I don't care."

"Take a wild guess," said DeVoy.

"Mozart," I said.

"You're about as far off as you can get," DeVoy said. "It's Jozef Sterkens performing 'Pourquoi me réveiller,' from Jules Massenet's *Werther*."

"Never heard of it," Myron taunted from his desk.

"Of course you haven't," said DeVoy. "That's because you're no different than the rest of these uncivilized brutes on the force."

"It's not Benny Goodman so I wouldn't pay a plug nickel for it," said Myron.

"Why are you two in such foul moods?" asked DeVoy, rising from his chair to slip his record back in its sleeve and into its maroon protective cover. "Did you wake up on the wrong side of the bed or something?"

"I just got out of a meeting with the chief of police," I said. I took a load off my feet, sitting down and then easing back in the chair. "Do you mind?"

I gestured to the door, and Myron got up to close it. He sat back down, and I furnished the two detectives with a recap of what happened at the meeting.

After I finished, DeVoy rubbed his hands together with excitement. "So how are we going to divide this investigation up?"

"That's just it, we're not," I said. "It's important for everything to appear to be business as usual around here. That's why I need you sticking around the office, manning the telephones."

DeVoy winced. "Aw, shoot. How come? I wanted in on the action!"

"I'm pretty sure the police beat reporters suspect something is going on," I said. "It's a small cohort. They talk to each other. If they get wind of this, there will be pandemonium the likes of which this city hasn't seen in a long, long time."

"Bigger than that murdered polygamist prophet four years ago?" asked Myron.

"Yup," I said.

"Bigger than that high-society dame that got hit by her own car?" asked DeVoy. "That caused a whole lotta ballyhoo way back when?"

"Bigger than both of them combined," I said.

"Isn't that one still unsolved?" asked DeVoy, staring almost wistfully into space. "What do you make of that? Killer still at large."

"That's ancient history," I said. "We need to sort out what's right in front of us."

"What about me?" asked Myron. "What should I do?"

"Let's go to the Hotel Utah together," I said. "We'll get a sense of the lay of the land. From there, we'll figure out how to divvy up this case."

"How come he gets to go and I have to sit here on my rump and answer the telephone all day?" asked DeVoy. "It's not fair. Let Myron answer the telephones. I want to go out on the streets and work a case for once, instead of all this bureaucratic office work. I was meant to be a man of action."

"Tell you what, I'll go and you answer the telephones," said Myron.

"Ha! Big funny of 1938," he said, sneering. "Give that man his own variety program on the radio."

"Maybe next time you can come along," I said, rising from my chair.

"I'm going to hold you to that," said DeVoy, rolling his chair back to his desk.

We left before DeVoy could squeeze in another objection.

• • •

The Hotel Utah, in all of its skyscraping white grandeur, towered above the buildings around it. We could have walked there from Public Safety. Nothing in downtown Salt Lake City is far from anything else. But at quarter past ten on a Monday morning, the temperature felt too hot to walk even a few blocks. Nearing the stately hotel, I spied Amelia Van Cott waiting out front, spiral notepad in hand, as Ephraim Nielsen stood behind her, in the shade of the awning, adjusting his bulky camera. To dodge the nosy duo, I surreptitiously circled the block and turned into the parking lot behind the hotel.

Myron and I managed to avoid being seen by her. We slipped quietly into the elevator, asked the operator to take us to the seventh floor. We exited the elevator and met a dapper, two-chinned fellow in a matching derby and chalk-stripe suit. A gold chain dangled from his vest, and he checked his pocket watch as we approached. The pouch of skin under his fat lower lip told me he was a tobacco chewer, and he probably needed the relief of a spittoon right about then.

"Oveson?" he asked.

"That's me."

We shook hands. "Hello there. I'm Dooley Metzger, house detective here at the Hotel Utah."

"Good to know you, Metzger," I said, releasing his hand. "This is my partner, Detective Myron Adler."

They refrained from shaking hands. He moved aside to let me open the door. He stared at Myron in a knowing and penetrating way, and my partner offered the closest thing to a scowl I've ever seen him make. I detected mutual hostility, and the two men seemed to want nothing to do with each other. While still out in the corridor, Myron and I slipped on thin cotton police gloves, to avoid leaving fingerprints.

"You any relation to Will Oveson?" Metzger asked me.

"He was my father."

"He used to be my boss," said Metzger. "I admired him. Say, they never did figure out who murdered . . ."

"No," I said, finishing his sentence before he could.

He arched his eyebrows and then—thankfully—changed the topic. "I keep getting calls from the press, especially that Van Cott dame. She's a pain in the neck."

"What does she want to know?" I asked.

"She keeps asking about the crash out at the flats on Saturday and Underhill's recovery," said Metzger. "I'm under strict orders by hotel management not to say a word about Underhill. As far as the press knows, he's sitting comfortably in his room, soaking his injured ankle in hot water."

"Did you see him leave the hotel early Sunday morning?" I asked.

"Of course not," said Metzger. "My shift ended at eleven P.M. Saturday night."

"Any chance he took the service elevator?" I asked.

Metzger shook his head. "No. It has a night operator."

"What's his name?" I asked.

"Haywood Arliss," said Metzger. "You needn't bother. I've already questioned him. He didn't see any sign of Underhill that night."

"What about the two regular elevator operators?" I asked.

"Raymond McCoy and Emil Dinsdale," said Metzger. "Dinsdale gave Clive Underhill a ride up to this floor after he got back from the Grove. Neither saw Underhill again that night."

"Did Dinsdale see him go to his room?"

"No."

"Underhill could've taken the stairs when he left the hotel," I said.

"Yes, that is so," agreed Metzger. "The stairs would've let him out in the lobby. The lobby is big, as you've no doubt noticed. A careful fella—late at night—could sneak out of there without being seen by the front desk man or the bellhop."

"I take it they've been questioned, too?" I half asked, half stated.

"Yes," said Metzger with a single nod.

"We'll still need to question them," I said. "It's just a formality."

"Of course," said Metzger.

"Wouldn't the doorman have noticed him leaving?" I asked.

Metzger shrugged. "There are other ways of getting out, without being seen."

"Such as?" I asked.

"Rear service entrance," he said.

"Isn't there somebody guarding that?" I asked.

"It's locked on the outside at that time of night, so you can't use it to enter the building unless you've got a key," said Metzger. "But if you're inside, you can freely use it to go outside. At that hour, it's easy to leave through that door without being noticed by anybody."

"I see. On a separate but possibly related note, I've heard that there were three eyewitnesses who saw Roscoe Lund come up here in the middle of the night to confront Nigel Underhill about money owed to him. Do you know if that's accurate?"

"Yes, it is," said Metzger, nodding. "A pair of guests—a couple from Canada—and a Negro hotel employee. It's my understanding that detectives from Homicide have already questioned each one, so that ground has already been covered."

"May I get their names?"

"I'm sure your fellow detectives will know," he said.

"I'd prefer to get it from you."

"The McKennas—Estelle and Claude—from Saskatchewan, were the two guests staying in the room across the hall from Nigel Underhill," he said. "They're here for the big radio sellers' convention. And Winston Booker is the colored bellhop. Beyond that, I don't care to say anything. You see, I know a thing or two about the law enforcement business, and, well, I don't care to pour gasoline on brush fires, if you get my meaning."

"Yeah. I get it," I said. "Thank you for your help."

Metzger tipped his derby. "I'll be in my office, ground level, if you need me."

I looked at Myron. "Ready?"

"Lead the way."

I opened the door and went inside, followed by Myron, who closed the door behind him. I switched on the lights. Between the two of us, it took less than a half hour to search the premises. It contained only the bare essentials: a freshly made bed, a closet packed with the finest clothes, bureau drawers full of socks and undergarments, a leather toiletry case on the bathroom counter, and two books on the nightstand: *The Woman in White*, by Wilkie Collins, and a dusty copy of Hubert Howe Bancroft's *History of Utah* from 1889.

Myron, meantime, opened the desk drawer. No surprises there. He found copies of the Gideon Bible, the Book of Mormon, and a telephone directory. I opened up Underhill's steam trunk, hoping to find a secret compartment or an object that would furnish a clue about his disappearance. Instead, I went through undergarments, handkerchiefs, and other such notions. A suitcase on the floor of the closet was empty. The shelves above his hanging clothes were barren. If there was anything that could be of help in our investigation, it wasn't to be found here. I went over to Myron, already peeling off his gloves.

"You were mighty quiet out there," I said, gesturing to the door. "You gonna tell me how you know him?"

I couldn't see Myron's eyes through the lenses of his glasses, but I felt them looking at me.

"There's nothing to tell. He was before my time."

"So you don't know him?"

"Should I?"

"Suit yourself, don't tell me," I said. "But I got a whiff of something earlier, and it smelled none too good."

We left room 702. I briefly considered knocking on the door across the hall to find out what the guests staying in there had seen or heard early Sunday morning. I opted against it, deciding now was not the time. Back at the elevator, a bell dinged and ornate brass doors slid open. Out walked a young mail carrier in a blue uniform and matching cap. With a canvas U.S. Mail bag slung over his shoulder, he carried a thick beige envelope in his hands that looked as if it contained a telephone directory.

"Say, you fellas know where room seven-zero-two is?" he asked.

I looked at Myron, already eyeing me, then returned my attention to the lad. "That's Clive Underhill's room," I said. "I'm afraid there aren't any visitors allowed."

The boy frowned. "Dang. I need him to sign for this. It's registered mail."

"What is it?" asked Myron.

The boy glanced at a label affixed to the package. "It's from Knopf, New York City. Says here it's a manuscript."

"I'll sign for it," I said, showing my badge. "I'm a police detective."

"Yes sir," said the boy. "I hope there's nothing wrong with Mr. Underhill."

"Not that we know of," I said. "We're on guard duty."

"Sure, of course." The boy handed me a pencil and a pad to sign. I scribbled my signature and exchanged it for the package. "Here you go, sir."

"Thank you," I said. "No C.O.D. charges?"

"It's all covered." I gave the boy two bits and he tipped his cap. "Gee thanks! Have a swell day, gents!"

He returned to the elevator and I waited for the doors to close. I ripped the package open and read a cover letter at the top of a thick stack of paper.

"It's a draft of his memoir with suggested edits," I told Myron.

Myron said, "Once the editors have picked it apart, I'm sure it'll be as bland as those vanilla cones you love."

"It's not quite there yet," I said. "Not if there are still edits left. Maybe this is the unexpurgated version."

"The honest thing would be to give it to Underhill's manager," said Myron.

"You're right," I said, looking over the package. "I'll do just that. Later."

"When?" asked Myron.

I grinned at him. "After I've read it."

Myron and I questioned several of the hotel employees on duty late Saturday night and early Sunday morning, including the bell-boy, desk clerk, night concierge, one of the elevator operators, and the doorman. The management let us use a spacious staff room in the basement, which housed a long table and several chairs around it. Unfortunately, the Negro eyewitness that Pace questioned—Winston Booker—was not working his shift while we were there, but we were still able to piece together a timeline of the night's events.

We kept the interrogations short. We encountered little variation in the accounts. Nobody saw Clive Underhill leave the hotel that night, but several witnessed him returning when I dropped him off. Even though I never asked about Nigel, to avoid overlap with Pace Newbold's case, some of the eyewitnesses mentioned seeing him smoking outside after he quarreled with his brother, and then he went up to his room in the elevator. At one point in the afternoon, Myron and I went to the building's rear and rode the service elevator up to the seventh floor, then we got back in and went down to the basement, then up once more to the main floor, to look for exits where Clive could have slipped out of the building unnoticed. A loading dock behind the building was one possible point of departure.

The Hotel Utah's rear exit doors, which opened up to the parking lot, were also left unattended in the wee hours of the morning. The doors were locked from the outside after 11:00 P.M., but hotel patrons could freely exit through them anytime. Only partially visible from the front desk, the rear doors were not always monitored by the hotel staff.

By mid-afternoon, we'd completed our initial investigation of the Hotel Utah. We drove away in the unmarked police car, now hotter than a kiln, thanks to the windows being left up in the hot sun. I'd hidden Clive Underhill's manuscript on the floor of the car's backseat, and Myron and I agreed that I'd be the one to take a look at it. We arrived at Public Safety around three o'clock. Up on the second floor, a surprise awaited our return.

Twelve

Albert Shaw made good on his promise to bring Peter Insley and Julian Pangborn in to the police station for questioning. I thanked them for coming, offered assurances they weren't under arrest, and introduced both men to Myron and DeVoy. I asked DeVoy if he'd transcribe the interview on his stenotype. He muttered under his breath about being overworked, but grudgingly accepted. Myron and I decided to question them one at a time in the office, while the other waited out in the corridor.

First up was Pangborn. Unfortunately, we could hardly understand a word he said. He mumbled unintelligibly under a thick accent. I noticed DeVoy was struggling to transcribe the interview. "Could you repeat that?" he kept asking. Meantime, I studied Pangborn's features. His hair looked even redder than it did on Saturday, and his pink lips formed a delicate oval mouth. His head bounced, he squirmed a lot in his seat, and his Adam's apple often bounced. He sat hunched with his elbows on the table. I sensed him growing frustrated with DeVoy constantly asking him to restate what he'd just said.

"It's odd that his car would wipe out the day he disappeared," I said.

Pangborn shrugged, his sentences coming out garbled and broken.

"I'm sorry," I said. "Could you speak up a little?"

"Wes a fook'n accident!" said Pangborn. "Scrattor drivin is wot it wes."

"You're saying poor driving led to his accident?" asked Myron.

More incoherent verbalizing, though I could make out the words "man a fookin' cigar." Then he added: "Steers it aal wrang. Owor corrected. Thin spun yeut." He sighed. "Ess a accident."

"So it wasn't any kind of mechanical failure?" I asked.

"Nar na."

"Did you inspect the wreckage afterward?" asked Myron.

"Wey aye."

"And you didn't find anything that seemed amiss?" asked Myron.

He tugged his ear. "Sa agyen."

"Amiss!" said Myron loudly.

I translated: "He wants to make sure that you did not find anything wrong with the car that would have caused the accident."

"Wrang? Nah. Neewt wrang wi' the screeve."

I was not certain of what he said. But I pretended to understand.

"Did Clive seem unhappy or morose in any way?" I asked.

Pangborn shook his head no.

"Did he ever say anything to you that would lead you to believe that he intended to go away?" asked Myron.

"Nah."

"How long have you worked for him?" I asked.

He cast his eyes to the ceiling. "Three, ganin on fowa yeors."

"Four years?" I asked.

"Wey aye. Abyeut that."

"Is he a good guy to work for?" asked Myron.

"Aye, decent blurk," said Pangborn. "Lightweet though. Cannit 'old ees liquor. Ah cud drink him undor the tyeble."

He began drumming loudly on the table with his hands, like playing a giant bongo. I glanced at Myron, who responded with closed eyes and a pained expression. I returned my attention to Pangborn.

"Let me see if I've got this straight, and please correct me if I say anything wrong," I said.

He nodded again and stopped that obnoxious drumming so he could hear me.

"You're from Newcastle," I said. "You've been his mechanic since roughly '34. You travel with him wherever he goes, in England and overseas. You don't have any idea where he is now. The crash out at the Salt Flats on Saturday was an accident, a fluke, probably due to faulty driving on his part. And Clive isn't a very impressive drinker, in your estimation."

"Yas startin tuh unnerstan'. Ah wes worreed abyeut yee. Worreed mebbies yor brain in't graftin properly."

"Some days I'm a little slow," I said, feigning an apologetic tone.

"Where's the Spectre now?" Myron asked.

"Undor lock an' key, wheor neebody gan get tuh it," he said, resuming his drumming. "Stop saboteurs."

Those last few words came out crystal clear. I exchanged glances with Myron. My slight nod put the ball in his court.

"Who'd want to sabotage it?" asked Myron.

"Who ya think?"

"Please tell us," I said.

"Nazis."

That came out clearly, too. DeVoy looked up from his steno-type.

"Why would they want to harm the Spectre?" asked Myron.

"Tuh win. Nar na mattor wot it teks."

"They want it that badly?"

He stopped drumming and nodded slowly. "Aye."

"Do you know where it is?" I asked.

"Aye."

"May we take a look at it?" Myron asked.

"Ax Shaw. He'll tells yee if yee gan or gannit. Ah suspects he'll say aye."

"This has been an informative conversation," I said. "Thank you for your time. Would you mind waiting in the hall while we talk to Mr. Insley?"

"Gan aheed," he said, rising from his chair. He left the room.

"Did you get even half of that?" asked DeVoy, leaning back in his chair to take a small break from his stenographer duties.

"He's got a Geordie accent," said Myron. "From northeastern England. His is particularly thick. He must've been born and raised there."

"Lucky for us the next fella talks like a BBC announcer," I said.

A tapping sounded at the door. Insley poked his head in. "May I?"

"Please," I said.

Insley walked in, closing the door behind him, and took off his Panama hat. He hung it on the coat tree and straightened his lapels. Attired in a beige linen jacket and a sky-blue shirt, he radiated confidence as he took his seat. His blond hair did not appear to be slicked back as tightly as it'd been on Saturday night. If anything, Insley seemed more relaxed now than the last time I saw him. He propped his right ankle on his left knee and his gaze bounced back and forth between Myron and me. I kept quiet at first, letting Myron ask the questions. DeVoy resumed his transcription duties behind Insley's back.

"What can I do for you gentlemen?"

"We take it you're aware that Clive Underhill is missing?" asked Myron.

"Yes. I am."

"When was the last time you saw him?"

"Saturday night," he said. He looked at me. "You were there, too, at the Coconut Grove. I haven't seen or heard from him since."

I nodded.

"Do you know where he is?" Myron asked.

"If I knew, I'd tell you."

"How long have you known him?" Myron asked.

"We met at Oxford, in the fall of '22. We were both eighteen. We boarded together."

"How well would you say you know him?" I asked.

"He's my best friend."

"Does he feel the same way about you?"

"You'll have to ask him."

"Would you consider him a confidant?" asked Myron.

"Oh certainly. Yes."

"At dinner on Saturday night Clive mentioned you're a writer," I said.

"Yes. I'm not sure what that has to do with Clive going

missing," said Insley. "But I am an avid writer. I used to be a journalist. I've dabbled in poetry here and there."

"He said you're working on a novel."

"That is true."

"Is it anywhere near being finished?" I asked.

"I've completed a first draft. I'm revising it right now."

I said, "Uh huh. What's it about? If you don't mind me asking."

"Not at all. It's about a rather sizable family in Edwardian England, and how their lives are uprooted by the coming of the war. It's rife with the usual themes. Family secrets. Love triangles. Class tensions. The protagonist goes AWOL from the Cavalry Corps to join the Bolshevik Revolution. That sort of thing."

"It sounds captivating," I said. "Do you have a title picked out for it yet?"

"My working title is *Soul in the Window*."

"I'd love to see it," I said. "I'm quite the avid reader myself."

"I'll consider it," he said. "Will there be anything else?"

"Yeah," said Myron. "What are you to him?"

Insley looked confused. "I beg your pardon?"

Myron said: "I get that Shaw is the manager, Pangborn is the mechanic, Nigel is family and probably a business partner of some sort. But how do you fit into this entourage? What practical purpose do you serve?"

"I'm his moral support."

"Meaning?" asked Myron.

"I provide encouragement and act as a sounding board. He throws ideas at me. I'm brutally honest with him. Yet I also happen to believe in what he's doing, and I push him hard to win."

"Push him? How?" Myron asked.

"I tell Clive things like it's his destiny to be victorious.

Second place is not good enough. I urge him at all times to push himself beyond the limits of his endurance. I have promised him, on more than one occasion, that I'll chronicle his achievements somehow, so that his name will live on through the ages. I am a voice of optimism when he is filled with despair. To fall back on Chinese philosophy, I suppose one could say I am the yin to his yang." He chuckled and waved his hand. "Or is it the other way around?"

"I'll assume you have it right," I said. "It sounds like the two of you are quite close. Have you two ever quarreled or fought?"

"Rarely. Occasionally we used to bicker over politics."

"What did the two of you disagree over?"

"World events. News of the day. I'm a radical. Clive isn't."

"Are you a communist?" I asked.

"If you're asking me if I'm a card-carrying member of the Communist Party of Great Britain . . ."

"Yes, I am."

"No, I'm not. I do, however, subscribe to a cooperative philosophy of living that entails a more equitable distribution of wealth, the general leveling of social classes, and the abolition of private property."

"Sounds screwy to me," said Myron. He held up his fountain pen. "If you abolish private property, what's to stop you from swiping my pen?"

"In a land of plenty, everybody will have a pen," said Insley. "There'll be no need to *swipe* them, as you put it. Besides, plenty of pens get stolen in capitalist societies. That's why banks are starting to chain them down to the counter."

"We're getting sidetracked," I said. "Let's get back to discussing the political differences between Clive and you."

"Yes, of course. Clive was once a member of Oswald Mosley's

British Union of Fascists," said Peter. "It's a vile group. Mostly unemployed street thugs who enjoy dressing up in black and going around menacing old ladies, that sort of nonsense. They look to the Nazis as inspiration. For a time, Mosley turned Clive into the human face of the organization, in an effort to try to attract new members. The two of them had a falling-out last year, and Clive left the organization shortly thereafter. Regrettably, Nigel stayed loyal to Mosley. He never came around, I'm sorry to say."

"I noticed he had a temper," I said. "Nigel, I mean."

"Yes."

"He was easily set off," I said.

"He had a penchant for throwing tantrums, yes."

"Then why bring him along?" I asked. "Why didn't Clive tell Nigel to—"

Insley interrupted: "Bugger off?"

"Does that mean go home?" I asked.

"More or less."

"OK, why didn't Clive tell Nigel to bugger off?"

Insley laughed, for some reason. "They're brothers. Clive was always protective of his younger brother. It's one of those family matters that I don't pretend for an instant to understand. Nor did I support Clive's decision to stand by Nigel. But that was his choice. And there it is."

"I understand Clive was getting threats back in England."

"Yes.

"What kinds of threats, and who was responsible?" I asked.

"They were anonymous death threats, sent through the mails, postmarked from various locations in the United Kingdom and a few spots on the continent. You know, Paris, Munich, Vienna. These threats were undoubtedly triggered by Clive's decision to openly renounce fascism last year, after publicly flirting with it for quite some time. We believe they came from fanatical true believers, probably most of them from England."

"Are there a lot of fascists in England?" I asked.

"No, I wouldn't say *a lot,* but they wield a frightening amount of influence, I'm afraid."

Myron chimed in: "There's a visiting contingent of Germans in our fair state, intent on breaking the old land speed record. As far as I can see, the only person standing in their way is Clive Underhill, so—"

"Did they have anything to do with his disappearance?" asked Insley, as if finishing Myron's sentence.

Myron shrugged. "It's not an unreasonable question. Clive is a fascist . . ."

"*Was* a fascist."

"Was a fascist. So was Nigel. They must have felt at least some affinity for Hitler and his henchmen. Or am I overreaching?"

"You may be on to something," said Insley. "Clive has spent a great deal of time in Germany. He did so under the pretext of studying their racing techniques and automotive engineering. I suspect there were ideological issues at play as well. But if you're asking me if I know whether the Germans were connected to his disappearance, the answer is I don't, but I suspect they had nothing to do with it."

"Why do you say that?" I asked.

"You have to understand the German mind-set," said Peter. "They've got a superiority complex. They always have, even before the Nazis came along. They believe they're superior at everything, and by extension, everyone else is inferior. So why eliminate the competition if you're already the best?"

"The other night," I said, changing topics, "at the Coconut

Grove, I noticed that Clive and Rudy Heinrich appeared to be friendly with one another."

"They're on good terms," said Insley. "Heinrich attended Oxford for a time on an exchange program. That's when he and Clive first met. I got to know him there, too. The three of us took a few economics and literature courses together, and we'd sometimes sit alongside each other in the dining hall."

"Is Heinrich a Nazi?" I asked.

"Heinrich is a racer," said Insley. "Everything else comes second, including ideology. If he lives in the Third Reich, he's a Nazi. If he lives in Soviet Russia, he'd be a Communist. If he lived here, in America, he'd be a Democrat or a Republican. Likely the former, as they seem to be more popular at the moment."

"Are you saying he's an opportunist?"

"Yes."

I looked at Myron. "I don't have any more questions. Do you?"

Myron shook his head no.

"May I leave, then?"

"Yes," I said. "Thank you for coming out here today."

DeVoy escorted Peter and Julian down the stairs and to the exit, where a car waited for them curbside. The clock on the wall said almost four. By this time in the afternoon, most policemen—plainclothes detectives and uniformed officers alike—were starting to wind down their shifts, calling it a day. Productivity dipped sharply after four. End-of-the-day phone calls were made, loose ends wrapped up, and black-and-white sedans returned to the lot.

As my shift drew to a close, I thought of Roscoe. Why did he pull such a foolish stunt as escaping? Where did he go? Was he in danger? I pondered these matters, and the next time I looked up at the clock, it was half past four.

I left early. Nothing more to do here today, and I knew it. On my way home, I stopped by Roscoe's place to feed his cats. The three of them appeared healthy and happy. I refreshed their food and water. They thanked me with leg brushes and head butts, and then I went out to the enclosed back porch to change the litter boxes.

My curiosity got the best of me. I tromped upstairs to Roscoe's room. On the nightstand, I examined a framed photograph of Roscoe posing with his pretty brunette daughter, Rose, in happier days, all smiles. An amusement park north of Salt Lake City served as the backdrop. I returned to the photograph to where I found it, next to a leather-bound scrapbook. I picked it up and thumbed through it.

It contained everything in Roscoe's possession having to do with his daughter, from her birth certificate to high school report cards and many items in between. Because she had dropped out of high school in her senior year, there was no diploma bearing her name. I knew this bothered Roscoe. I came to one photograph of her looking particularly angelic, in a white dress with lace and pearls sewn into it. Tiny gold lettering in the corner read A.J. MITCHELL PHOTOGRAPHY, MURRAY, UTAH, MAY 1936. I closed the scrapbook and set it down.

I left the house the way I found it. I climbed into my car, started it up, and headed for home.

Thirteen

Monday night at *casa de Oveson* passed uneventfully. Clara went to bed early due to headaches. I made dinner—my specialty, fried egg sandwiches on toasted bread, with hash browns and cottage cheese—and I found my two youngest children especially animated at the dinner table. Afterward, Sarah Jane did the dishes while her younger siblings and I gathered around the radio and listened to *Amos 'N Andy*. Then *Fibber McGee and Molly* came on. By the time the nine o'clock music variety shows started, Emily had fallen asleep and Hi was subdued. I tucked them both into bed around ten o'clock, and Sarah Jane went to her room.

I heard the faint clacking of the typewriter and noticed the thin strip of light below her door. She came by her insomnia honestly, I'll say that much. With the house quiet, I lumbered into the living room, switched on a lamp beside my favorite armchair, sat down, and pulled Clive Underhill's manuscript out of its envelope pouch. I began reading his memoirs at half past ten. I went straight through, nonstop, taking only a few breaks to use the bathroom or refill my glass of water. The prose flowed beautifully, no two ways about it. The man knew how to put a noun up against a verb. I began to wonder if Insley had a hand in ghostwriting this manuscript.

Clive told of growing up in a mansion on a sprawling estate in Weybridge, Surrey. Born in 1904, son of a well-to-do businessman, Lloyd Underhill, who'd served in Parliament for years, owned several prominent daily newspapers, and instilled in his children a competitive spirit, despite embracing Fabian Socialism and being close friends with George Bernard Shaw. The responsibility of raising Clive and his five siblings—four sisters and one brother—fell upon the shoulders of an au pair from India named Girijabai.

"I lived a youth that others only dream of," wrote Clive. "I grew up in a home filled with the finest literature and art, surrounded outside by verdant gardens. I attended symphony concerts in London and Paris. I traveled to all parts of the globe and took in sights I shall never forget. I walked through the streets of Berlin and Moscow, Cairo and Istanbul, Calcutta and Singapore, Rio de Janeiro and New York. I have shaken hands with world leaders. I have dined with the leading literary lights of our age. Famous figures from the worlds of cinema and music have invited me to their soirées. Yet these experiences have not corrupted my soul, nor blinded me to the realities of the world in which I live. I am a man of my own making. I have charted my own course in life. I have chosen a destiny that is uniquely mine. While I undeniably was born into affluence, I got to where I am by a combination of hard work, creativity, and ingenuity. In short, I may be rich, but I am self-made, which is a source of pride for me."

Clive went on to describe the years he spent attending

boarding school, where he'd go months without seeing his parents. At a young age, he developed a fascination with automobile racing. He routinely visited Brooklands, a motor raceway near his home, and dreamt of one day being behind the wheel of the fast cars he so loved. It was at Brooklands that he befriended a racer named Count Louis Zborowski, who allowed the teenage car enthusiast to drive around in one of his many Chitty Bang Bang 1 racing cars.

Zborowski took Clive under his wing and spent years teaching the boy everything he knew. Clive would spend entire summers at Brooklands, and when the fall arrived, he'd return to school to resume his studies. He and Zborowski regularly wrote letters back and forth, and Clive regarded the man as a father figure. While he was at Oxford, Clive learned that Zborowski had gotten killed after losing control of his auto and crashing into a tree at the Italian Grand Prix in Monza on October 19, 1924. The news devastated the young man.

Clive's stern father made his contempt for racing readily known to anybody that would listen. This seemed to drive his son deeper and deeper into the sport. By the end of the 1920s, Clive became increasingly interested in breaking land speed records. He admitted in his memoirs that something about taking a fast car beyond the limits of endurance, to high speeds previously unknown to man, excited him greatly. In pursuing this goal, he crashed cars on many occasions, and by his own estimation, at one time or another, he'd broken every bone in his body except his neck. By the early 1930s, he was a force to be reckoned with, already competing with the best racing motorists in the United Kingdom.

"Certain men were born to be competitive motorists, I being one of them," he wrote. "I must be clear, however, that it is not the desire to win that drives me. You have not known the fullest exhilaration that life has to offer until you have been behind the wheel of a machine capable of moving at speeds measured in hundreds of miles per hour. The flat earth coming toward you, streaking past underneath at high velocity, and unfurling behind you, provides a thrill that words cannot capture. Whether or not I am the world's fastest driver is of little importance. What I relish is the journey, that spirited race across the land, not victory itself."

The hour was late, or early, depending on how you looked at it, and I began to skim. I slowed, however, when I reached the chapter on Clive's travels through Nazi Germany. I noticed in the letter from his editor that Clive had followed the publisher's advice by downplaying his admiration for the German dictator Adolf Hitler and the Nazi Party. He agreed to cut out entire paragraphs praising the Nazis for restoring order and pride in Germany, and celebrating their willingness to serve as a bulwark against Bolshevism.

In fact, this newly revised version of the memoir did not mention the words "Nazi" or "National Socialism" or name any high-level Nazi figures by name. He simply referred to "German officials" and "German motorists" and "German engineers." No question about it: I was getting the watered-down version of Clive Underhill, stripped of all controversy, to make him more palatable to the book-buying public.

I did detect genuine warmth in the passages where he mentioned Rudy Heinrich and his wife, Gerda Strauss. Despite being a competitor with Heinrich, Clive seemed fond of the German racer, and the two grew to be close friends. The two of them had met at Oxford in 1924, where Heinrich went for a semester as an exchange student. The following year, Clive took part in an exchange program to a German university, where he met Gerda Strauss. They formed a close friendship, and he eventually introduced her to Rudy Heinrich, with whom she fell in love and later married.

I also paid especially close attention to the parts of the book where Clive discussed the members of his entourage. First up was Peter Insley, whom Clive met during his freshman year at Oxford. "Fierce, idealistic, intellectual, and intensely engaged, Peter embraced the very egalitarian principles that his wealthy industrialist father had rejected. Peter and I would argue all night and into the dawn, debating everything from alms for the poor to the nature of the 1917 Russian revolution. We did not agree on a single thing in those days, but we each of us harbored the strongest possible mutual respect for the other. Good thing we did not require ideological litmus tests for our friendship, for we formed an enduring friendship that has thrived up until and including the present."

Next came a brief history of his ties with manager Albert Shaw. The two met at a party following Clive's first-place finish at the 1931 Belgian Grand Prix. Clive asked Shaw to become his manager, and Shaw agreed. Up until then, Shaw had been a big-shot movie producer for the London-based Ideal Film Company. "We hit it off right away," Clive wrote. "There was something about his demeanor that immediately struck me as trustworthy. Our friendship and our professional relationship took hold immediately, and I have never once looked back."

Eleven pages later, Clive turned his attention to Julian Pangborn. "His bony physique, sunken eyes, nigh nonexistent chin, and crooked teeth made him not much to behold, but I could tell this intense street urchin brought with him a breathtaking knowledge of cars and how to make them drive faster. He was a master mechanic. When I first encountered him, he had been dabbling in fascist ideas and running around with some of Oswald Mosley's British Union street thugs, but his commitment to that ideology proved fickle at best. Much stronger was his commitment to automobiles, and I knew after five minutes of talking to this young man that I had to have him on my team. I am proud to say that I pulled him out of the fascist Blackshirts and persuaded him to don the mechanic's blue coveralls."

The manuscript contained numerous references to Clive's brother Nigel. The memoir depicted the brothers as quite close, and I detected no signs of hostility or resentment on Clive's part toward his sibling. Only genuine fondness came through. "Nigel and I were close, as close as any brothers I've ever known, and I made sure to include him in all of my motoring activities," Clive wrote. "He was a devoted brother, with a keen mind and a heart full of fraternal love for me. I always appreciated his presence at the many raceways where I've driven over the years. If I am a success as a motorist, it is largely because of him. Thus, I shall say it now: Thank you Nigel, now and forever, for all you have done for me."

That syrupy prose did not match up with the arrogant and overzealous young man I met on Saturday at the Salt Flats and then later at the Coconut Grove. Clive seemed to be describing another man entirely.

I noticed that the final chapter of the book, spotlighting his attempts to shatter previous land speed records by reaching four hundred miles per hour on the Bonneville Salt Flats, was only partially written. A note from the editor asked him to complete the rest of the chapter for inclusion in the book no later than October 1, 1938. I was interested, however, in his impressions of Utah from his first trip out here in 1935.

"What immediately strikes the visitor from England about this sparkling, treeless, arid desert wasteland known as the Bonneville Salt Flats is its desolation," he wrote. "It is uninhabitable. No human being could possibly survive alone out here for more than a few days. Covered with salt, this desert has been damned to be barren forever. I have heard tales of the pioneers of yore crossing this land, but they did so in pursuit of greener and more prosperous climes to the west. Fascinating, is it not, that something as heart-stoppingly dramatic as land speed racing should occur in a spot so dismal as this? I find it an ironic trick of the racing gods that out of stark landscapes these incredible feats grow."

My wristwatch told me it was closing in on 5:00 A.M. Having read or skimmed the entire manuscript, I felt completely exhausted. I placed the red rubber bands that held the pages together, then slipped the thick stack in the envelope and set it on the table next to me. A few minutes later, I'd fallen asleep.

Fourteen

"Art."

I sat upright, heart about to burst out of my chest, and caught my breath.

Roscoe stood before me. "Sorry. I didn't mean to startle you."

What time was it? I rubbed cinders and murky film out of my eyes. Watch check: A few minutes past 6:00 A.M. I got a better look at Roscoe. He appeared disheveled and in need of a shave. He wore the same clothes he had on when I saw him in jail. He sat on the edge of the davenport, elbows on knees, and stared at me for a long moment.

And the one thing I absolutely could not miss was the revolver in his hand, aimed at me.

"What are you doing here?"

"How are my cats?"

"They're peachy. About the gun . . ."

He looked down at it, and gave it a little shake, as if to remind himself he was holding it. "Oh yeah, that."

"You're not planning on shooting me, are you?"

"What the hell kind of question is that? You're my best friend."

"Good to know. It's peculiar idiosyncrasy of mine that I don't like guns aimed at me, even when they're in the hands of friends."

"The gun is purely for show, so no one thinks you helped me under your own steam."

"I see. Shouldn't you be in jail?"

"If I'd been the one that killed Nigel, then yeah."

"But you didn't do it?"

"Nope. Sure as hell didn't."

"You look terrible."

"Gee thanks." He squinted at the package on the table adjacent to my chair. "What's that?"

"A little light reading. Listen, the kids will be up soon."

"I know."

"Is there something you want?"

"Yeah, I need your help."

"If I help you, I'm aiding and abetting a known fugitive."

He held up the gun, so it was level with his head. "Not if you're being coerced into it."

"But you're not going to shoot me."

"They don't know that," he said, lowering the gun again.

"That thing loaded?"

"Uh huh."

"It doesn't look good, you escaping. It makes you seem guilty."

"It'd look a lot worse for me to rot in jail for a crime I didn't commit."

"You put me in a tough spot. If I turn you in, I'm a fink. If I don't, I'm breaking the law. I could lose my job and do time."

"No one will know I was here. And if anyone should find out, you can tell 'em I ordered you at gunpoint."

"You seem awfully sure of yourself."

"I was a cop. I know how these shitbirds think."

"Tell me why I shouldn't call the police right now."

"Our history."

He knew what to say. He had me. For my part, I was certain the man sitting across from me did not murder Nigel Underhill. No doubt he had it in him to take another man's life, and by his own admission, he had blood on his hands from his years as a strikebreaker. But that was behind us, and we were in the here and now, sitting face-to-face in my living room, in August of 1938, contemplating where to go from here. I was not about to turn him away in his moment of need.

"Besides, Art Oveson isn't a rat."

"That's good of you to say," I replied, smirking.

"I mean it."

"OK, let's talk specifics. What do you need?"

"Got any money?"

"How much?"

"Hundred. I'll pay you back every nickel of it."

"You gonna tell me what it's for?"

"Expenses. Gas. Change of clothes. A man's gotta eat."

"What about that money Nigel Underhill supposedly gave you at the Hotel Utah for your services rendered? Can't you use that?"

"It's at home," he said. "I'm not going back for it."

"Fair enough. OK. I will loan you the money."

"Thank you. I hate to sound like an ingrate, but when . . . ?"

"Now."

He arched his eyebrows. "No kidding?"

"We've got a rainy-day fund. It's in a secret place, where nobody will find it."

"You and Clara are disciplined," he said. "I would've blown it on booze and whores long ago."

"My boozing and whoring days are behind me," I said.

He laughed.

"I'll need a car, too," he said. "Could I borrow your Olds?"

"It's Clara's Olds, not mine."

"Think she'd mind?"

"I'd have to ask her."

"Is there any way we can leave her out of this?"

"She'll see it's missing. She won't be happy. What do you need it for?"

"Transportation."

"Obviously. To where?"

"Around."

"Now is not the time to hold back," I said. "I need to know."

"Somewhere where I can lay low until this blows over. How's that?"

I sighed. "I worry about you, Roscoe."

"I'm a big boy. I can take care of myself. Besides, this whole Underhill situation already stinks to high hell. Something just isn't right."

"I can't argue with you there. I'm not supposed to touch the homicide investigation, but I think Clive's disappearance and Nigel's murder are related."

"Of course they are. How could they not be?"

"The powers that be at Public Safety want to keep them separate," I said. "And they don't want the press getting anywhere near it."

Roscoe nodded thoughtfully, rubbing his hand over his bristly chin. "Because once the newspapers find out . . ."

"Pure bedlam. And make no mistake: the cops will hunt you down."

"I've got eyes on the back of my head," said Roscoe.

I checked my watch. "You'd better make yourself scarce," I said. "Before I give you a cent, or the key to Clara's Olds, I've got to know where you're going."

"I'm gonna go do some snooping around. Find out who really did this."

I studied Roscoe. No missing the desperation in his face, and that was all I was going to get out of him. I stood up and left, taking that thick stack of typewritten pages with me. In the kitchen, I found a hiding place for the manuscript, on an unused top cupboard shelf. Then I retrieved Clara's car key, dangling on a small brass hook near the sink. Next, I located the aging baking powder tin that contained our rainy-day fund. I pulled out four limp twenties and two tens, stuffed the rest of the wad back in the can and returned it to the spot where only Clara and I could find it. I went back to the front room, gave Roscoe what he wanted. He accepted it with restrained gratitude.

"There's something I didn't tell you," he said, pocketing the money.

I almost said, *I'm sure there's a lot you haven't told me.* Instead, I asked, "What?"

"The man Clive was talking to at the Old Mill Club last week was Vaughn Perry. He's a scenic tour and hiking guide."

"How did you come by that information?"

"I'd rather not say."

"I thought you said you couldn't hear them over the orchestra."

"I picked up a few fragments during the breaks. I overheard Clive asking to be taken to the Canyons of the Escalante."

"Why is it that Albert Shaw didn't mention Perry the other day?"

"Search me. Those English are screwy as hell, if you ask me." He drew a shaky breath. "Will you look in on my cats?"

"Every day."

"You may need to buy them some food and gravel for their pans on the back porch. I'll reimburse you."

"Don't worry about it."

"Thanks again, Art. I won't forget this."

I watched Roscoe leave. The revving Oldsmobile engine awoke Clara, who came walking down the hall, her slippers slapping the wood floor. She was dressed in her flannel pajamas and wore a silky maroon robe that we bought in San Francisco's Chinatown. I pulled the screen door shut, closed the front door, and faced Clara, my heart and head brimming with dread.

"Why, in God's name, would you do something like that?"

Clara and I sat on the porch steps in front of the house, resting our elbows on our knees. A warm gust fanned my brow, and I could tell it was going to be another hot day. A chorus of birds proved particularly vocal this morning. Golden rays of sunlight were spilling into the valley, and trees cast long shadows. Our children were still asleep inside.

"He needed my help."

"So you'd risk everything you have, everything you are, to help a wanted man?"

"He'd do the same for me."

"That's beside the point. He's on the lam, and you're helping him!"

"Shh! Keep it down, will you?" I whispered. "He had a gun aimed at me. Let's not forget that small detail."

"The police are going to think you're lying," she said. "They're going to ask you why you didn't report it right away. They're going to know you helped Roscoe."

"He's my friend, Clara, and I was trying to help him."

"There's a little something called the justice system, Art," she said. "You always go around telling people it works, in spite of its flaws, and all they need to do is give it a chance. But then you turn around and do a damn fool thing like this."

"I know. You're right. I'm sorry."

"Is that all you can say?"

"What do you want me to say?"

"For starters, I'd love to hear a guarantee that'll assure me that everything's going to work out fine. All of this hemming and hawing and apologizing isn't exactly inspiring confidence, Art. I mean, if you get caught, what's going to happen to me? It's my car. Does that mean I'm going to go to prison, too?"

"Nobody's going to prison, Clara. Will you stop with the dramatics?"

"I can't believe you, Art. I really can't believe you."

She patted her robe in a few spots until she found what she was looking for. She reached in her pocket and pulled out a rectangular-shaped object, the size of a deck of cards. I couldn't tell what it was at first. I craned my neck to get a better look. When I saw what it was, I almost fell over in shock. Clara held a pack of Chesterfield cigarettes and a book of matches from the Rotisserie Inn. She gave the pack a couple of shakes and caught one of the Chesterfields between her lips, then deftly slipped the pack down where it came from, lit a match, and raised flame to tip. She smoked like a veteran, not even letting out a tiny cough as she inhaled. She dropped her match on the concrete walkway, picked a piece of tobacco off of her tongue, and noticed my speechless mouth agape.

"What?"

"How long have you . . . ?"

"I took it up at age eighteen."

"How often do you do it?"

"One a day, unless it's been a tough day."

My heart raced, watching her hold her cigarette like a movie star. Smoking was forbidden among devout Mormons. The pious regarded it as taboo and sinful, and judged smokers as unworthy. Smoking itself went against the Word of Wisdom, a set of healthy living guidelines that most dedicated members of the Church of Jesus Christ of Latter-day Saints endeavored to adhere to. The Word of Wisdom advised us against consuming hot beverages such as coffee, prohibited us from smoking tobacco and taking narcotics, and counseled us to eat lots of fruits and vegetables and only consume meat sparingly. But at that particular moment, watching Clara smoke—something I had never seen her do in the decades I'd known her—I was not thinking of Church doctrines or theology. I just sat there, puzzling over how I could have not seen her do this for so long.

"How have you kept it hidden all these years?"

She took a drag and blew smoke in the air. "I do it alone, outside, away from other people. When I'm done, I brush my teeth and I gargle with Listerine."

"What other secrets have you been keeping from me?"

"After what you did this morning, Arthur J. Oveson, I'd say you don't have any business lecturing other people about keeping secrets."

She smoked her cigarette in silence for a moment, then squinted at me. "What?"

"I can't believe you smoke," I said. "That's all."

"Let's not blow it out of proportion," she said. "Forgive the pun. Besides, it's not as if I'm a chain smoker."

"But you seem so . . ." I searched for the word.

"So what?"

"I don't know. So . . . *caught up in* propriety. You know, keeping up appearances, and all that. You're the last person I'd expect to be a smoker."

She laughed as she fished out her box of Chesterfields and tilted them at me.

"You might enjoy it, once you get used to it."

"You know I don't smoke."

"I never assume anything." She put the pack away. "You had no idea I smoked."

"True."

A white cloud swirling around us made me cough. I waved my hand in a subtle fanning motion, still trying to adjust to the shock.

She asked, "Don't you have any secrets? A thing, or two, you try conceal from the rest of the world."

"Sure. We all do."

"Well? What's yours? A wife and kids in Muncie?"

"Look, Clara, I don't think this is the time or place to . . ."

"You don't want to tell me. Is that it?"

I moved to change the subject: "What do you think Bishop Shumway would say if he saw you smoking like this?"

She took one final, deep draw from her cigarette. Tobacco crackled. The tip glowed brightly. She dropped it on the ground, crushing it under the sole of her slipper. "I've followed the rules all my life." She blew one last cloud of smoke. "I obeyed my parents like a dutiful daughter. I met a boy and fell in love with him. I waited two years for him to come back home from his mission. I got married to him and bore his children. The one thing I wanted for myself, to be a teacher, to make a difference in the lives of students, I gave up. I threw it away. You know why? Others expected me to. The lobbying for me to resign was relentless, and I succumbed."

"I never asked you to quit your job."

"No, but you sat back in silence when your brothers and sisters-in-law all told me that the only way I could be a good mother was to quit my job," she said. "You could have defended me and the choices I made. But you didn't. You just sat there like a bump on a log. Why didn't you speak up?"

I had no reply to that question. The possibility that she was right—that I was a coward, and I'd failed to come to the defense of my own wife—haunted me.

"And as if all that weren't bad enough, you handed Roscoe my car keys without asking me, along with a hundred dollars of *our* money, without asking me, so he could run off and do God knows what. And please, spare me the business about the gun, because that's malarkey, and you know it. Who knows how many laws you've broken this morning? I can think of several right off the top of my head. And you have the temerity to sit there and judge me for smoking."

"I didn't judge . . ."

"Yes, you most certainly did, Art!" She lowered her voice to imitate me. "*What do you think the bishop would say if he could see you smoking?*"

"Oh c'mon, I was merely pointing out . . ."

"Does smoking a cigarette make me less of a person in your eyes, Art?"

"Certainly not! But . . ."

"But what?"

"Put yourself in my shoes. How would you feel if I'd smoked since I was nineteen . . ."

"Eighteen."

"How would you feel if I'd smoked since I was eighteen and never told you?"

"At least there'd be something interesting about you that I didn't know about before. Sometimes I wish you had a couple of skeletons in your closet, Art. It's exhausting to be married to a saint. Even Joseph Smith drank liquor and chewed tobacco and married young ladies."

Clara saw my shoulders sagging. I could not conceal the hurt I felt then. I told myself that Clara spoke out of frustration, and did not really mean what she said. But that did little to diminish the sting of her words. She reached for my dangling hand. I instinctively pulled it away. She tensed up. In that instant, a big white Cream o'Weber dairy truck rumbled past, and I could hear bottles rattling and clanking inside of it.

"It was wrong of me to do what I did," I finally said. "I'm sorry."

"I'm sorry, too, about what I said. Sometimes I feel like we don't know each other as well as we should, especially for people who've been together so long." She paused, to collect her thoughts. "When Sarah Jane came to me and told me she no longer believed in God, part of me was terribly upset. But I was also relieved."

I reared my head in surprise. "Relieved?"

"Yes. Because she isn't going to turn out like me."

"You say it like that's a bad thing. You're the finest woman I know."

"That's good of you to say. What I mean is, I'm glad she won't grow up to be the kind of woman willing to give up everything to please other people."

"Do you think that's what you've done?" I gestured to the rectangular bulge in her robe pocket. "Is that why you . . ."

The words trailed off, but she read my mind.

"It's my own little act of rebellion."

"Since eighteen, huh?"

"I took it up while you were on your mission. Remember Margo Barnes?"

"From grammar school?"

Clara nodded. "Her powers of persuasion were strong."

"I see."

Clara turned her head toward me and blinked a few times. I smiled as I beheld the splash of freckles on either side of her lean nose, so light you almost couldn't see them unless you looked close up.

"So you think he's innocent?" she asked.

"Yeah."

"You still shouldn't have done what you did."

Clara thrust herself upward with her arms, turned and faced the house, and walked up porch steps. She halted, and her hand gripped my shoulder, and I reached up and patted it softly. She released me, wood creaked under her footsteps, the screen door clopped shut, and she was gone.

I leaned down and picked her cigarette butt off the concrete.

Fifteen

I didn't bother informing Myron or DeVoy of my spontaneous decision to drive out to the Bonneville Salt Flats Tuesday morning. I figured the two of them could find plenty to do without me looking over their shoulders. They were probably happy to be rid of me. Before leaving town, I stopped at Roscoe's place to feed his cats. With that behind me, I climbed into my Dodge, started her up, and drove west, into the sun-drenched desert. On the passenger-side seat next to me sat a folded copy of today's *Salt Lake Examiner* with the front-page headline that had prompted me to embark on this trip.

HEINRICH TO REVEAL NEW RACE CAR AT
SALT FLATS TODAY

Following a dusty ninety-minute trip across an old auto trail called the Victory Highway, I reached the glittering salt-pan earth. Exiting the highway, I motored north on a primitive road and soon arrived at the sprawling tent city that stretched for a few miles. Not a tenth as many cars were out here today as Saturday, when most of the competitive driving occurred. On my way across the desert, I dropped by the tent belonging to my cousin, Hank Jensen, but it was closed up, sealed with a padlock, and his race car was nowhere to be seen.

All of the action was happening near a cluster of tents to the north. I walked across the hot ground until I came to a hundred or so onlookers that included a mix of photographers, reporters, and the merely curious. Up front was a makeshift wooden stage, and behind it, three swastika flags flapped from poles. The symbols—twisted black crosses on white circles stamped on red banners—made me queasy, knowing the aggression they symbolized, occurring at that exact moment on the other side of the ocean, thousands of miles from here.

"Cousin Artie!"

I turned to face Hank Jensen, gaunt, big-eared, and with a Thoroughbred's grin. His bright red suspenders stood out on his drab, sweat-drenched clothes. Except for the long mop of hair on top, his head was freshly shaved, and he slapped me affectionately on the shoulder with his bony hand. A few feet behind him were his trio of brothers, Murray, Gordon, and Kenneth, all wearing hats, with sleeves rolled up to the elbows. I dreaded the request coming my way in a few seconds, but I did not have the quickness of mind to feign an excuse to get out of it. So I simply smiled and gave him a playful little sock on the shoulder.

"Hank," I said. "How's every little thing?"

"I'll be better when you tell me you can make it out here on Saturday to volunteer at the tent," he said. He wasted no time. No "how's the family?" No "what brings you out here?" A master of cutting to the chase, Hank Jensen was. "It's the long-distance final. Last big outing of the summer. What do you say, Artie? Can I count on you?"

"Maybe I should check with Clara first," I said.

Behind him, my cousins laughed.

"Don't mind these fresh mugs," said Hank, jerking his thumb over his shoulder. "You go right ahead and ask her, and if you can make it, that'd be swell."

"Will do," I said.

"What are you doing here?" he asked. "Aren't the Salt Flats a little outside of your purview?"

"A little," I said. "I heard the Germans are making a big announcement."

"Yeah, it's called the P9," said Hank. "Fastest car on earth. They've got craftsmanship on their side, I'll give 'em that much."

"I'll be interested to see it," I said.

"Me too," said Hank. "Hopefully we'll see you this Saturday, huh?"

"Hopefully," I said.

I gave a last affectionate smile and parted ways with my cousins. I looked around and spotted Albert Shaw, Julian Pangborn, and Peter Insley in the crowd. No sign of the lovely Dot Bliss, to my silent disappointment. I squeezed my way toward the front of the crowd, until I came to a motion-picture camera mounted on a tripod, and a pudgy man with droplets of sweat in his bristly hair and thick beige clothing, much too hot for this weather, prepping the device for filming. A small logo on the side of the camera—white letters on a blue diamond inside of a larger red diamond—read UFA.

He scowled. "*Weg von der Kamera*," he mumbled. "*Verdammt amerikanischen.*"

"*Kripo!*" a voice called out.

I turned toward the tent, and who should step out but Rudy Heinrich. His chiseled features appeared even more pronounced under a brown leather helmet, goggles on his forehead, and a scarf around his neck. There was no missing his swastika arm-band, either. He strode past the cameraman and held out his hand, and I reached and shook it.

"What a fine surprise! I remember you from Saturday night," he said, in his thick German accent. "You were at the Grove with Clive."

"Yes, that's right," I said. "Good to see you again, Mr. Hein-rich."

"Please, let us ditch formal," he said. "Call me Rudy. What's your name again?"

"Art," I said. "Art Oveson."

"Yes, of course, Art Oveson!"

A narrow-faced man in a black suit, bald on the sides and back of his head, with a heavily pomaded strip of hair atop his skull, materialized by Heinrich's side, like a shadow. Frail in appearance, halting in his movements, he wore a lapel pin with the gold words NATIONAL-SOZIALISTISCHE D.A.P. inside of a red ring encircling a black swastika on a white circle. *No getting away from that thing,* I thought. He held out a hand and I shook it.

"Where are my manners?" asked Heinrich. "Art Oveson, this is Ernst Voss, with the Reich's Ministry of Public Enlightenment and Propaganda. Ernst, this is Art Oveson, a detective with the Salt Lake City Police Department. Did I get that right?"

"You did," I said, with a wink and smile. I switched my attention to Voss. "Good to know you."

"My pleasure," said Voss dryly, with as much sincerity as he could muster.

Someone else emerged from that Third Reich tent: a striking

woman with blue eyes, shoulder-length curly golden hair, and a shirt so white it almost blinded me. Her beige jodhpurs went with a pair of high black boots, covered with desert dust. Unlike Voss, she smiled as she came toward me, showing off a mouthful of perfect white teeth. At least she was not wearing a swastika. I was getting tired of looking at those things. Her hand was soft and cool and came with the lightest of grips, and I caught a faint whiff of perfume.

"This is Fräulein Leni Riefenstahl, one of our most renowned directors," said Voss. "She's here to make a documentary motion picture about the new land speed record that will be set by Herr Heinrich."

"I haven't broken it yet, Ernst," laughed Heinrich.

"No," said Voss, with a slight grin. "But you will."

Heinrich ignored Voss's comment. "Fräulein Riefenstahl, Art is the policeman that saved Clive Underhill's life after that terrible accident on Saturday."

"Oh, a heroic American," said Riefenstahl, beaming. "Like Charles Lindbergh."

"I wouldn't go that far," I said. "But that's kind of you to say."

She abruptly cupped my chin in her hand and forced my head to my left. It startled me, the intensity of it, and almost gave me whiplash. I glanced at her in my peripheral vision as she inspected my profile, then she placed her hand on my other cheek and pivoted my head forward again.

I wondered what this was all about?

"You have a perfect face for cinema," she said. "It's lean. It's authentic. Not excessively pretty, like Gary Cooper, but not fleshy, either. Your high cheekbones and thick hair are cinematic assets. I like a lean man. I prefer men without too much meat on their bones. Tell me, have you ever been in a motion picture?"

"No ma'am," I said. "I have not."

"You are a quintessential man of the West," she said approvingly. "I must ask you if you're partial to the novels of Karl May?"

"I haven't heard of him."

Her mouth went slack and her eyes widened. "How can that be? He is the great novelist of the American West. The Führer adores his books."

"I'll be sure and give them a look-at one of these days," I said.

Riefenstahl took out a pencil and patted herself down. She mumbled in German what sounded like an expression of frustration. When I looked at her with a puzzled expression, she said, "I forgot my card."

"Oh. I see."

She fished out a book of matches, opened it, and scribbled something on the inside for an awkward minute. When she was done, she stuffed the matchbook in my shirt pocket.

"I hope our paths cross again, Herr Oveson," she said. "Soon."

She walked over to the man standing next to the movie camera and began conversing with him in German.

Voss said, "Is there something we can do to help you, Oveson?"

"I was hoping to have a few minutes alone with Rudy here, to ask him a couple of questions," I said.

"Oh? Am I in trouble?" Heinrich asked with a nervous chuckle.

"No," I said. "It's routine police business."

"I'm in charge of Heinrich's itinerary," said Voss. "If you wish to interview him, you must submit a formal letter of request on official police stationery, as well as a list of the questions you will be asking for my approval."

"Perhaps we might loosen our rules for Art," Heinrich chimed in. "No point in making this process harder for him than it has to be."

"I'll consider an exception in this instance," said Voss. "Let's first allow Fräulein Riefenstahl to film the scenes of you unveiling the car. After she has obtained her footage, you may answer the policeman's questions. In my presence, of course."

"OK," I said. "Fair enough."

I saw Heinrich shake his head in exasperation behind Voss's back. I offered a sympathetic grin and walked away, melting into the crowd. I arrived at a decent spot from which to view the action, and I watched with my arms folded over my chest. While Heinrich made his way over to the enormous canvas tent that protected his machine from the sun and bystanders, I reached for the matchbook that Riefenstahl stuffed in my pocket. I opened it to see what she wrote. It took me a fraction of a second to decipher her scribbles, but when I finally did, my heart nearly leapt out of my chest.

BEN LOMOND HOTEL, RM 1101. MIDNIGHT. COME FUCK ME. LR

I swallowed hard and, with a shaky hand, stuffed the matchbook in my jacket pocket. I caught my breath. I wasn't sure if my heart was ever going to slow down. Nothing like that had ever happened to me before. To calm my jitters, I scanned the sea of hats around me, stopping at the mounted camera over at the front of the crowd where Riefenstahl worked alongside her cinematographer. Our eyes met, and I don't think I was imagining things when I saw her purse her lips and blow a kiss. I quickly looked away. Now I had a fierce case of the shakes.

Around me camera shutters clicked, movie cameras whirred,

and the audience "oohed" and "ahhed" as Heinrich drove the twenty-seven-foot-long silvery racing vehicle—a futuristic marvel with a low cockpit window, stubby wings, twin tailfins, and curvaceous front fenders—out of the tent garage, revving the engine loudly for show. For some reason, seeing the thing soothed my jangled nerves. While a small band played German military music with lots of horn and drum, two announcers spoke over a loudspeaker, one in German, the other in English.

"The Mercedes-Benz P9 is a miracle of modern design," said a placid-voiced female with a German accent. "This six-wheeled land racer prototype is powered by a V12 engine capable of reaching speeds of up to seven hundred and fifty kilometers per hour, or four hundred and seventy miles per hour. The building of the P9 has taken place under the brilliant supervision of Dr. Ferdinand Porsche, the famous engineer who is the driving force behind the German Auto Union."

"What are you doing out here?"

I turned to see Albert Shaw behind me, talking softly out of the corner of his mouth. The brim of his hat shaded his face to such an extent that I almost did not recognize him.

"Last I checked, I'm on the payroll of the Salt Lake City Police Department," I said, missing out on the loudspeaker chatter about Heinrich's car. "That means I don't answer to you or anyone else in Underhill's entourage."

"No need to get defensive, Oveson," said Shaw. "I asked a simple question. I was actually wondering about the progress of your investigation."

"It barely started, so I haven't gotten far. It doesn't help that you omitted a key piece of information from yesterday's conversation."

"Oh? And what would that have been?"

"You didn't mention the man that Clive met at the Old Mill," I said. "He must've meant something, if Clive was willing to risk sneaking out in the night on two separate occasions to go see him."

"I don't have the faintest idea what you're talking about," said Shaw.

"Does the name Vaughn Perry ring any bells?" I asked. "He's the tour guide that Clive was talking to that night."

"How did you know?" asked Shaw.

"It doesn't matter," I said. "What does matter is if Clive isn't back here in this very spot by Saturday to compete with Heinrich, you're going to have the press to answer to. I won't be able to cover for you or him. This mystery man I'm just now hearing about—no thanks to you—might hold the key to Clive's whereabouts. Where can I find him?"

"I honestly don't know. He's someone Clive met years ago."

"Why didn't you mention him to me yesterday, when the others were present?"

"I didn't want Dot to worry about Clive," he said. "I was trying to protect her."

"So you don't know who he is?"

"No."

"Or where I can find him?"

"No."

"Then why do you say you're trying to protect Dot? That doesn't make any sense."

"I'm not sure I like this line of questioning," said Shaw.

"Neither do I. It wouldn't be necessary if you'd come clean. I know you're holding back. I'm going to find what I'm looking for, with or without your help. You might as answer my question and spare me the wear and tear on my shoe soles."

For some reason, my comment made Shaw laugh. His reaction puzzled me.

"I don't see what's so funny."

"I find your naïveté amusing. Look around you. What do you make of all this?" When Shaw asked the question, he gestured to the P9, and Heinrich waving to the crowd. The press swarmed around the German and he began answering their questions, far enough away that we couldn't hear him.

"It looks to me like just another dog and pony show," I said.

"Is that all you see?"

"Is there more?"

"Yes, as a matter of fact, there is. This is a battle between two powers, one representing light, the other darkness."

"Oh brother," I said. "Let's not blow things out of proportion. It's just a competition to see who can drive the fastest."

"Spoken like a man who has the luxury of a big ocean separating you from Europe," said Shaw. "Hitler is obsessed with automobiles—everything about them. Engineering. Performance. Racing. Have you heard of the Autobahn?"

"Yeah, it's a big highway in Germany," I said.

"For the last five years, the Führer has personally overseen the construction of thousands of miles of Autobahn," said Shaw. "Day in, day out, tens of thousands of men toil away on it, slavishly toiling in the service of their dictator. It's one of the first huge projects that Hitler launched after he came to power. At the same time, he also offered to pay half a million reichsmarks to any German automobile manufacturer willing to develop a new generation of high-speed Grand Prix cars."

"So he wants to be the fastest kid on the block," I said. "Who cares? As long as the price of meat stays the same."

"I know you're smarter than that, Oveson," said Shaw. "Ask

yourself this: Why aren't they trying to set a new speed record on all of those miles of Autobahn track they've got in Germany? Why do it here?"

"It's Salt Flats," I said. "*The* preeminent land speed racing spot on earth."

"You're obviously incapable of thinking like a Nazi," said Shaw. "It's not good enough to be the best inside of Germany. This little spectacle happening around us is all about giving the rest of the world a good drubbing. But for a madman like Hitler, the satisfaction only lasts so long."

I grinned in disbelief. "Do you honestly think a big shot like Hitler cares about what's happening here?"

"I'll turn the question around, Oveson. Can't you get it into that head of yours that there's more to this than auto racing? We are talking about a tyrant that intends to conquer the world in every possible way, and he's made those intentions known to anybody that'll listen. It doesn't stop at fast cars, either. This man is not going to quit until the swastika flies over that state capitol of yours in Salt Lake City. He is determined. He is relentless. He is fanatical. He has vast resources at his fingertips. Millions of men and women follow him blindly and will do whatever he orders them to do." Shaw shifted his attention back to the endless, glittery raceway before us. "We live in perilous times," he finally said. "What you see here is only the beginning."

"I'll bear that in mind, Mr. Gloom and Doom."

"Don't look now, but your favorite Nazi racer is leaving."

Shaw was right. Off in the distance, Heinrich slipped into a black limousine with tiny Nazi flags attached to the front fenders. Ernst Voss, his unnerving little shadow, climbed in next and pulled the door closed. Riefenstahl boarded her own luxury car while her cinematographer disassembled the movie camera. In the meantime, a couple of oil-stained grease monkeys navigated Heinrich's P9 onto the back of a trailer attached to a truck, where it would presumably be taken to wherever the Germans were storing it.

I briefly flirted with the option of bolting to the front of the crowd to stop the limousine, so I could grill Heinrich. Then I recalled that book of matches in my shirt pocket, the one with the lewd scrawl from Riefenstahl. She gave me a room number at Ben Lomond Hotel in Ogden, a burgh north of Salt Lake City. It was a safe bet that Heinrich would be staying in the same place.

I turned to say something to Albert Shaw, but I missed him, too. Now a ways away, he and Pangborn and Insley had boarded an automobile and closed the doors, and its whitewalls sprayed salt as it sped off across the desert, toward civilization. The crowd continued to thin as car doors slammed and engines started, and all the while I watched sullen workers taking down those large red-white-and-black swastika banners.

Sixteen

When big shots visit Utah they'd typically stay in one of three hotels: the Ben Lomond in Ogden, or the Newhouse or Hotel Utah in Salt Lake City. The Ben Lomond, eleven floors of sheer elegance, opened for business in 1927 on the corner of Washington Boulevard and 25th Street in Ogden, a thriving Wasatch Front burgh on the western side of the Wasatch Mountains. Getting there from Salt Lake City was easy: a straight shot up the highway, forty-five minutes to an hour, and you would find yourself in one of the busiest railway, manufacturing, and commerce hubs in the American West.

Arriving at the Ben Lomond, I desperately sought out shade to park my car under, but found none near the hotel. So I eased between a pair of coupes, killed my Dodge's engine, and left the windows rolled down. I figured: so what if someone steals the car radio? It was one of those cheap factory Detroit numbers that came with the car anyway. I got out, slammed the door, and zig-zagged through rows of neatly parked autos. Everywhere I went, the sun's blinding reflection flashed. I entered the lobby—every bit as swanky as the Hotel Utah—and approached the long front desk, where I patted a call bell. A gentleman in a dark suit approached me and welcomed me to the Ben Lomond in a velvety, singsong voice.

"I need Rudy Heinrich's room number," I said.

He smiled ever so slightly. "Sorry sir, I'm afraid there is nobody by that name staying here."

He didn't even bother looking at a guest book.

I flashed my badge. "Detective Art Oveson, Salt Lake City Police Department," I said. "I know he's staying here. I need to have a word with him. It won't take long. What's his room number?"

"Like I said, we have no guest by that name here," he said, smile fading. "I do apologize, sir. I hope you have a pleasant day."

I drummed on the counter with my fingers for a few seconds as I contemplated my next move.

"Thank you," I said.

I headed to the exit, crossing white marble floors that reflected the chandeliers high above. I stopped at a potted palm and glanced backward, and the fellow who'd helped me at the front desk was talking to a big man who obstructed his view of me. I used that as my opportunity to make a beeline for the elevators. I remembered Leni Riefenstahl writing RM 1101 along with that lewd scrawl. If the Germans were anything like their British counterparts, they probably rented a cluster of rooms together, I reasoned. I walked inside one of the elevator cars and a green-suited elevator operator with a matching peaked cap punched a button that brought a pair of mirrored doors together.

"Which floor?"

"Eleventh."

He punched the button with 11 on it and the elevator lurched upward, stirring butterflies in my stomach. A second later, the doors opened again, and I pocketed the matchbook and muttered my thanks on my way out into the hallway. Heading past 1101, thinking of Leni Riefenstahl, made the butterflies in my stomach act up. I pressed on. The walk down the dimly lit corridor to room 1102 gave me an opportunity to contemplate my next move. Nearing the suites, I heard the door to room 1102 open, so I rushed around the next corner. I found myself in an unlit dead-end nook facing a locked door bearing the nameplate CLEANING STAFF. From this prime hiding spot, I peeked around the corner, shocked to see Peter Insley shaking hands with a burly and bespectacled bald man in a black suit and matching necktie. I pulled my head back so as not be seen, and attempted to eavesdrop on their conversation. To my frustration, I could not hear their soft-spoken words from here.

One thing that did register clearly was Peter saying: *"Auf Wiedersehen."*

That told me what I needed to know. The door closed and Peter walked off in the direction of the elevators. I waited a minute or so in that darkened corner, then crossed the hall to the tall black door with 1102 in gold numbers. I took a deep breath, balled my hand into a fist, and knocked. Seconds later, the door opened. Rudy Heinrich looked dapper in his dark blue striped suit.

"Kripo!" he said, with a toothy smile and genuine excitement in his voice. "Long time, no see!"

We shook hands and he gestured for me to enter. "Please."

I entered a large sitting room that contained a sofa and armchairs surrounding an ornate coffee table. I came face-to-face with a sinewy man in his mid-thirties with peach fuzz hair, a neck bulging with cable-like muscles, and a formfitting brown suit with a red tie. The outline of a firearm in a shoulder holster pressed through his jacket's fabric.

"Art, this is my bodyguard, Karl von Rimmelkopf."

He showed no interest in meeting me halfway for a handshake, so I quietly said, "Nice knowing you, Karl."

Two others, Ernst Voss, the petite man with the deathly pallor that I met out at the Salt Flats earlier today, and that intimidating bald mammoth that saw Insley off a short time ago, both stood and made their way over to me. Heinrich closed the door and joined us. Through a giant picture window, a distant strip of greenish-blue that was the Great Salt Lake shimmered on the western horizon. Cigarette smoke filled the room, and I spotted a big ashtray full of cigarette butts on the center of the table. The bald man puffed away on some sort of intricately carved German Black Forest pipe, and his head was as shiny as the floor of the Ben Lomond's lobby.

"Art, you remember Herr Voss," Heinrich said.

Perfunctory handshake—loose and clammy.

"And this is Hans, err, I mean, Herr Doctor Hans Meinshausen."

"This is the *polizist* I've been hearing all about," Meinshausen said, his teeth clenching the pipe. He gripped my hand tightly and shook it with an intensity that took me aback. "What a pleasure to meet you at last, Oveson. I was in the stands on Saturday when you pulled Clive Underhill out of his burning car. What a most impressive act of selfless heroism."

"Thank you," I said, subtly shaking the pain out of my hand after he let go. "That's very kind, Dr. Meinshausen."

"Let's sit down," said Heinrich. "Art, may I get you something to drink? Beer? Cocktail? A bottle of soda?"

"No, thank you," I said. "I'm wondering if I might have a word with you in private?"

I felt the weight of von Rimmelkopf's stare. Meantime, Voss approached with a frown. "As I said before, I am Herr Heinrich's manager on this trip," he told me, almost whispering. "I must be present at your interrogation, in the event counsel is needed."

"I'm not planning to interrogate him," I said. "I'd prefer talk to him alone."

"I'm afraid I can't allow . . ."

"Nonsense," interrupted Meinshausen, pulling that smoky pipe out of his mouth. He patted Voss on the shoulder as he sized me up through bifocals. "Oveson strikes me as an honest fellow. There's no need for such stringent security measures in this case. Come, Ernst, Karl. I'll buy you men a drink in the bar on the main floor."

One could plainly see that Voss was unhappy, but the jovial Meinshausen hooked his elbow and tugged him out of the room. Following them was von Rimmelkopf, who glared at us as he pulled the door closed.

I gestured to the sitting area. "Shall we?"

"Lead the way."

I ambled over and plunged into an armchair where Voss had been sitting when I first entered. Still warm. I placed my elbows on the armrests. Heinrich took a seat on the couch, kicked his right leg over his left knee, and leaned back. I noticed some minor fidgeting. He felt uneasy facing me alone in that hotel suite.

"Do you know why I'm here?"

He laughed. "No. My mindreading skills are not what they used to be."

"Maybe Peter Insley filled you in on the details."

He gave me his best confused look. "What does he have to do with this?"

"You tell me," I said. "I'm no better at mindreading than you are."

"What would you like to ask me, Detective?"

"It has to do with the Underhill brothers."

"Is something the matter with them?"

"Yes," I said. "Clive's missing. Nigel is dead."

"Oh my God. When . . ." He swallowed hard and drew a breath. "When . . ."

His response struck me as heartfelt. If he was faking it, he was a skilled actor.

"Early Sunday morning. Nigel was found dead in his hotel room. Clive has vanished and nobody seems to know where he is."

"Oh dear God. That's terrible. What do you want to know? I mean, how can I help you?"

"Was Clive ever in touch with you at all after we saw you Saturday night at the Coconut Grove?"

"No."

I decided to change my tack: "He writes fondly of you in his memoirs."

"Oh? Has it been published?"

"Not yet. I read about you in a draft manuscript. He says flattering things about you. He clearly admires you as a racer and a man."

"Does he?"

"Yes. To hear him tell it, it sounds like the two of you are good friends."

"We *were* good friends."

"Did you have a falling-out?"

"We drifted apart. I met him at Oxford years ago, in the

twenties. We got to be close when I was there. After that, he attended Heidelberg for a term, at my urging. Those were simpler days."

"Your English is marvelous," I said.

That compliment brought back his smile. "Thank you."

"Did they teach it to you at Oxford?" I asked.

"I took language courses in school in Germany so I could read the collected works of Edgar Allan Poe in the original English. I had an adolescent obsession with him."

"Heck of a writer," I said. "So is this your first trip to the United States?"

"Yes. It's everything I hoped it would be. I toured New York City for a couple of days. The press followed me around wherever I went."

"I understand you're going to set a new speed record on Saturday," I said.

"If all goes well." He held up crossed fingers.

"You must be feeling the pressure," I said.

"Yes, well, I will be glad when it's over," he said with a tentative nod. "I can finally relax. Take that ocean cruise I've been promising my wife."

"Gerda Strauss?" I asked.

He reared his head in surprise. "You know of her?"

"I read about her in Underhill's memoir," I said. "She and Clive were friends before she met you. Where are you going on your cruise?"

"We were thinking of Havana. I hear it's charming. But I have to get past Saturday first."

"It'll be easier for you now that Clive is out of the running," I said. "He's your only real rival for the world land speed record. Now that he's out of the picture, you have a clear shot at—"

"What are you getting at?" he interrupted.

"Well, here we've got the two fastest drivers in the world going up against each other at the Salt Flats, only one of them goes missing. I'd say that's pretty convenient. Wouldn't you?"

"I had nothing to do with his disappearance, and I do not know where he is," said Heinrich. "I believe our business here is concluded. I'm a busy man. I'm afraid I'm going to have to ask you to leave."

He abruptly stood and headed over to sliding twin doors, opening them to reveal a bedroom big enough to be an independent republic. He slipped in, and a minute later, came out carrying a pad of hotel stationery, a pencil, and a book. He set the stationery and the pencil on the table and he handed me the heavy hardback volume.

Mein Kampf, by Adolf Hitler.

I opened it to an inscription scrawled on the opening blank page in black ink. I could barely make out the word "Heinrich." The rest was in German of course. Even if it'd been written in English, I'm sure those scribbles would still be illegible. I assumed it was Hitler who had autographed it.

"What's this?"

Heinrich leaned in close and said softly, in almost a whisper, "*Der Führer* is the only leader in the history of the world who has stated precisely what he is going to do before actually carrying it out. It's all spelled out here, in print, for men of all nations to read. He's not always as specific as one might hope. Yet when the day of reckoning finally arrives, as I'm sure it will, nobody can possibly say, 'I didn't know.' "

I set the book on the table.

"What does this have to do with Underhill's disappearance?"

He shook his head. "You'd never make it as a *polizist* in Germany, Art."

"Oh no? Why?"

"You fail to understand subtleties," he said, still talking quietly. "Germany is not a democracy, like America. My homeland is a different animal entirely. *Der Führer* warned us that the brain grows lazy in a democracy, because of too much decadence and too many low expectations. We Germans do not have the luxury of freely stating our opinions. Everything is a puzzle one must solve. We select our words carefully. They come with hidden meanings. A sharp mind is needed in order to read between the lines, the same way a big antenna is required to pick up shortwave radio signals. If you lack such an antenna, you won't last a week in the Third Reich."

I reached for the stationery and pencil, ripped a sheet off the pad and placed it flat on the table so what I wrote would not press into the next blank sheet.

I jotted down the following:

DO THE WALLS HAVE EARS?

I handed it to him. He read it, looked at me, and nodded.

I took the paper from him, placed it on the table, and scratched out:

CAN WE FIND A MORE PRIVATE PLACE TO TALK?

I gave it to him, with the pencil. He jotted something and handed it to me.

NO PROMISES. WILL CONSIDER IT.

I folded the paper and stuffed it in my pocket.

He whispered, "Have you a business card?"

I took out my cardholder, opened it, and pulled one out.

"Please write your home telephone number on back."

I did as he asked and slid it to him. He tucked it in his bill-fold. He leaned in close, so his mouth was an inch from my ear. I caught a whiff of his cologne through the lingering veil of smoke. His words came out as softly as the flitting of a butterfly's wings.

"If I can, I'll be in touch."

He moved away, and his voice returned to its normal volume.

"Sorry I must cut this short, Herr Oveson," he said, at full volume. "Perhaps I will see you on Saturday."

Heinrich was spooked and wished to end our conversation. Perhaps the suite contained listening devices planted in key spots. For all I knew, someone might've been in the next room, monitoring our every word. I made a few minutes of small talk with him about Utah and neat places to see, so if someone were listening in, my visit would seem routine and ultimately unproductive. The last thing I wanted was to land Heinrich in trouble. But I also sensed he knew more than he was telling me, and that I'd get a more detailed explanation when—or if—he could pry himself loose from the Nazis circling him.

I caught the elevator to the lobby. On my way out, I poked my head into the smoky bar to bid farewell to the Germans I met in Heinrich's room. They weren't anywhere to be found. Outside, with the piping hot sun drilling down on me, I glimpsed Ernst Voss getting into a black Packard sedan. I got in my car and followed him out of the parking lot, in the direction of the highway.

Seventeen

I stayed four car lengths behind Voss down U.S. 91, which connected Ogden to Salt Lake City. The drive took us past roadside
diners, farms, and grassy wetlands adjacent to the Great Salt
Lake. The sun beat down on me through my windshield, so I
kept the windows rolled down. Even though hot air blew in, it
felt cool against my soaking brow. Voss exited 91 at 8th South and
headed east. I did likewise. We sped through a warehouse and
business district, then past blue-collar bungalows, and finally to
the edge of the city, where the houses thinned out into open fields
and clusters of trees. The Wasatch Mountains, in their sheer, jagged splendor, drew closer, and it soon became evident Voss was
heading up Emigration Canyon.

The road grew steep. At the mouth of the canyon, we drove
past the This is the Place Monument, a serene park overlooking
the valley and home to a stone obelisk commemorating the spot
where Brigham Young first looked out at what would become
the Mormons' new home. Across the road from the monument

was the seven-year-old Hogle Gardens Zoo, where vast enclosures and plentiful trees provided idyllic homes for animals to move about freely. I took one last glance in my rearview mirror at the city dropping behind me. The entire way, I puzzled over where the enigmatic Voss might be going.

Emigration Canyon Road wound its way between steep slopes, around pines and vertical rock walls, running parallel to a creek. I imagine the canyon probably looked much the same as it did when the Mormon pioneers passed through it in the summer of 1847, or when the ill-fated Donner Party steered their ox-drawn wagons through the passage the year previous.

Up my car climbed, past cabins and houses spaced far apart, and narrow turnoffs that led to isolated dwellings hidden back among the trees. Because this area was so susceptible to wildfires, locals generally avoided moving here. Despite that, you could still find intrepid souls prepared to give it a try, especially those drawn to the splendid natural scenery and cheap price of land.

When the black sedan ahead of me reached a sign that said PINE HILL FORK RD, it veered off the main road and accelerated up a poorly graded dirt lane. I followed, shaking violently as my car rolled over and slammed down into ruts and potholes. I'm sure my car's poor suspension took a beating as I thudded past ramshackle cottages nestled among towering Douglas firs. At the top of the hill, Voss slowed. So I slowed. He parked in the driveway of a narrow shotgun house above me. I swerved into a gravel bed surrounded by bushes and trees that would provide camouflage and much-needed shade. I killed the engine. I reached under my seat and scooped up a leather case holding a pair of binoculars. I got them out for a better look. Blurry at first, I adjusted the focus knob. Between needle-spiked branches, the green shack came into view, standing in a little coniferous nook of its own, boasting a paved driveway leading to a detached garage.

Voss got out of his car. He walked to the road and peered down the hill, toward where I was parked. I don't think he saw me, but I instinctively crouched low on the front seat, dipping my head below the dashboard. When I came back up a moment later, he was gone, but his car was still in the driveway. Presumably he went in the house. I got comfortable. I wondered how long I'd be there, squirming inside of this oven. At least I was parked in the shade, where it was a cool 87.

To kill time, I thumbed through an issue of *Street & Smith's Wild West Weekly* that I'd happened to snatch out of my mailbox on my way to work. I settled on a rip-roarin' serialized tale called "The Branded Skull," packed full of nocturnal shootouts, cowardly murderers, and miscellaneous derring-do. Every couple of paragraphs, I'd look up at the house and the sedan still parked in the driveway. Voss was taking his own sweet time. My watch told me it was coming up on three o'clock.

Just then, Voss rushed out of the hilltop house. I exchanged my magazine for binoculars. Twin scopes gave me a prime view of Voss climbing into the black car, backing out of the driveway, and racing downhill, past me, whipping up clouds of dust. Thick foliage blocked his view of me.

I got out of the car, closed the door, inhaled pine air, and crossed the dirt road. I spooked a nibbling chipmunk, sending him running for the nearest bush. I came to the green shotgun house and walked up wooden steps. A professional-looking metal sign, screwed into the door, said TRU-WEST SCENIC TOURS. Underneath that, it said in smaller print: TELEPHONE WASATCH 5292. I gave a knock on the screen door. Nothing. I trotted down the stairs and walked around the side of the house, past windows with shades drawn. I walked over to the garage and peered in a side window.

A beam of sun partially lit what I guessed to be a '35 Chevrolet four-door sedan, black or maybe dark blue or brown. I jiggled the doorknob. Locked. I returned to the house, heading directly below an open window with drapes waving inward like ghosts. I caught a snippet of a baritone newscaster from a radio inside: *"Fighting in the Far East continued yesterday as Japanese warplanes bombed a crowded public square in Canton, China. . . ."* I rounded the corner and could no longer hear the broadcast as I went up the porch steps.

I knocked on the screen door. I gave it a minute. No response. Another knock, another moment, and silence.

I opened it. A metal spring twanged. To my surprise, the door creaked open. I nudged it until the front room came into view. Couch. Armchairs. Cathedral radio. Desk along the south wall, with papers, magazines, and maps sprawled across it.

"Women across America are finding that economical, no-rubbing Aerowax makes dingy floors shine and sparkle and look like new. . . ."

"Hello!" I called out. "Anybody here?"

"And now Aerowax proudly presents Your Organ Interlude, *performed by America's favorite virtuoso organist, Eddie Dunstedter. . . ."*

I switched off the radio.

"Hello! Is anybody home?" I called out. "My name is Detective Art Oveson. I'm with the Salt Lake City Police Department."

I pushed my fedora back on my head and wiped sweat off my brow with the back of my hand. Floorboards whined with every footstep. I knew what I was doing—entering a house uninvited and without a warrant—was strictly off-limits. Still, I could not escape the nagging sense that something was amiss here.

A few framed photographs of scenic rock formations in southern Utah graced the green-and-white-striped wallpapered walls. This being a shotgun house, there was no hallway, just doors linking one room to the next. I entered the kitchen, really more of a kitchenette. An icebox stood against one wall, a stove against the other, and a pair of chairs were parked at a little round table covered with newspapers, boxes of cereal, and a porcelain sugar bowl. The sink was full of dishes, and a carton of Rinso dish soap sat near the faucet.

"Hello! I'm with the Salt Lake City Police Department! Is anybody here?"

I stepped inside of a windowless bathroom and switched on the electric globe. Tiny space, barely big enough to house a toilet, sink, medicine cabinet, and shower stall. I peeled back the shower curtain. Nothing but blue tiles, a bar of soap, and a bottle of Fitch's Dandruff Remover Shampoo.

A faint scratching noise came from the next room. I went for a look. Closed venetian blinds dimmed the room considerably. I switched on a light.

An athletic blond man, probably in his thirties, was lying on the bed, mouth agape, staring at the ceiling. He was attired in a blue dress shirt and striped tie, with dark brown corduroy trousers, and brown leather shoes that appeared to have salt caked on the bottom of them. The sleeve on his left arm was rolled up. A hypodermic needle jutted out of his arm. Above it was a rubber tube, tied around his bicep.

I pressed my fingers into the man's clammy neck. No pulse. He hadn't been dead long. He was still sweaty. Rigor mortis hadn't quite set in. Tempting as it was to close his eyelids for him, I left them open, to avoid tampering with the body.

I squatted to better inspect his arm. A caramel-colored rubber tube used to tie off the limb dangled in the spot where it had been loosened. I found no track marks. Not even a hint of past ones. That could mean a few things. Maybe he was a former addict taking up heroin use again after years of being clean. Or possibly he was trying it for the first time and injected too much or used too strong a grade. A third, more ominous, scenario had someone else administering it and making it appear to be an overdose. I unbuttoned the cuff on his other sleeve and rolled it up. No track marks on that side, either. I pulled the sleeve back down and buttoned the cuff.

I removed his billfold from his pants pocket and opened it. I held his driver's license in the light to read it.

STATE OF UTAH
BUREAU OF TAXATION AND FINANCE—MOTOR
VEHICLE DIVISION
NAME: VAUGHN HAYWARD PERRY
ADDRESS: 6010 East Pine Hill Fork Road, Salt Lake City, Utah
TEL: WAS-5292
DATE OF BIRTH: Mo. 9 Day 18 Yr. 1904
COLOR: W. **SEX:** M **WEIGHT:** 172 lbs. **HEIGHT:** 6 FT. 2 IN.
EYE COLOR: Blue **HAIR COLOR:** Blond **EXPIRY:** 09-18-40

I slipped the license back in the billfold. It was full of cash. I tucked his wallet in his pocket.

The scratching came from a phonograph needle caught on the

end grooves of a spinning record. Using my handkerchief, I lifted the needle and brought it back to its perch. When the album quit spinning, I checked the label:

WORLD'S GREATEST MUSIC

PHILHARMONIC TRANSCRIPTION

WAGNER: DIE MEISTERSINGER

Stuffing my hanky in my pocket, I looked around. On the nightstand, I came across a Ronson cigarette lighter, a second hypodermic needle, a small jade box, lid open, containing a few brown capsules, and a spoon on a strip of white linen. I'd worked in the Morals Squad long enough to know that the residue in the spoon and the capsules in the box were heroin.

I straightened and stepped to the closet door. Hanky in hand, I turned the knob and pulled it open. A row of jackets, shirts, and pants hung neatly on hangers. Pairs of shoes lined the floor. I closed the door and opened the top drawer on the bureau. Folded socks. I shut it. Next drawer: skivvies. Shut it. Bottom: undershirts. I pushed it closed.

There was a picture frame lying facedown on the floor. With a hanky I picked it up. It showed three young men, each dressed in long, flowing black robes and standing in the sunlight, with an old brick and stone building behind them. Each fellow beamed with happiness. I instantly recognized the trio. From left to right: Rudy Heinrich, Clive Underhill, and the late Vaughn Perry. There was a crack in the glass, as if it had fallen off the bureau. I returned it to exactly where I'd found it.

On the other side of the room, against the wall, sat an old steamer trunk with peeling travel decals, leather straps, and buckles. I went over to it and raised the lid with the help of my handkerchief.

The trunk contained books, newspapers, and record albums. I lifted a stack of volumes. Newton R. Perry authored each one, and the publisher was H.W. Price & Sons of New York. The titles struck me as strange: *Weeping Flame. The Serpent of the Soul. The Lost Truth. The Martyrdom of Cordell Devereaux. My Fallen Father. The Elemental's Legacy.*

The oldest was published in 1905, the newest in 1926. A dust jacket from a 1922 edition featured a photo of the author. He appeared professorial: lean, dark hair slicked back, bespectacled, black mustache, tweed jacket, and a bow tie. He bore a striking resemblance to the man lying on the bed. I assumed he was the father of the deceased, given the similar facial features and shared surname.

I returned the books to the trunk. Next I took out a stack of newspapers. Smelling of inky newsprint, they were back issues of a bizarrely named gazette called *The Platinum Patriot,* which listed itself on the banner as THE OFFICIAL ORGAN OF THE PLATINUM LEGION OF THE UNITED STATES. I pulled one out at random. The issue I perused said, VOL. 3, NO. 11, NOVEMBER 1935.

Headlines told me all I needed to know. "Franklin D. Rosenfeld Calls for Worldwide Pax Judaica." "Jewnited States Congress Orders Probe of Platinum Legion." "Fascist Revolution Coming to America" Below that, a subhead said:

**SUPREME LUMINARY NEWTON R. PERRY SAYS
UPRISING IMMINENT.**

I thumbed through a few others. They were all like that first one.

I put the newspapers back and I took out a record album. A sleeve label said:

N.R. PERRY—VOICE OF THE PATRIOT

NUMBER 179—STATION XEMR, MEXICO

TRANSCRIBED BROADCAST, OCTOBER 8, 1935

I took it over to the combo phonograph/radio console. Off went Wagner. On went Perry. I lowered the needle.

"Good evening," said a male announcer. "This is station X-E-M-R, broadcasting at 840 kilocycles from our studios in Ciudad Juárez." A bell jingled, then came melodramatic organ music reminiscent of a soap opera. "Welcome to another broadcast of *Voice of the Patriot,* a weekly report of news and views from the Platinum Legion of America. Now we proudly introduce the Supreme Luminary of the Platinum Shirts, currently numbering five thousand strong across the United States, the Exalted Chief Newton R. Perry."

The organ faded into silence and next came Perry's silvery voice.

"Good evening righteous citizens of the republic," Perry intoned. "I am Chief Newton Perry, here to share with you the one hundred and seventy-ninth broadcast of the *Voice of the Patriot.* This is a transcribed recording, made in my clandestine studio in the remote Blue Ridge Mountains of North Carolina. I am honored you've chosen to join me. Let me begin by saying that it is a unique tragedy of our times that I must carry out these broadcasts in secrecy. That's because in the United States, the so-called land of the free, our government and the press and all of the forces of coercion are firmly in the hands of the international Jew bolshevist criminal conspirators, led by that troika of barbarians Joseph Stalin, Neville Chamberlain, and our very own Franklin Delano Rosenfeld."

I wish I could say his speech took a saner turn. Perry's soft-spoken and conversational style escalated into a half-crazed rant about Jewish bankers and communist conspirators and their "Negro minions" in the National Association for the Advancement of Colored People. The whole thing made my skin crawl. I'd definitely lived a sheltered life up till then. Never before had I heard such toxic venom being spewed by anybody.

Perry singled out half of the country in his tirade: immigrants, labor union members, university professors, government relief recipients, Hollywood movie producers, Wall Street "money barons," Republicans, Democrats, politicians, lawyers, the United States Army, and the "millions cursed with the mark of the Beast." He reserved most of his animus for Jews. Jew Yorkers. Jew Dealers. Jew bankers. The "Jew-run federal government."

I lifted the needle, fearing I might hurl the record against the wall if I had to listen to another second of it. Restraint won out. I slipped it in its sleeve and put it back in the trunk. I desperately needed to go outside and inhale fresh air. Being in that room with that dead man, listening to the hate-filled invective spewed by a demagogue I assumed was his father, proved more than I could take. On my way out of that narrow shotgun house, I lifted the telephone and called the police. I reported a dead body, gave the address, and hung up without identifying myself. Then out the door I stepped, closing it tightly behind me.

Eighteen

When I entered the lobby of the Hotel Utah, I walked straight into an enormous gathering of men, most attired in fancy suits and wearing lapel name tags. A banner spanning the length of the room let me know who they were: SALT LAKE CITY WELCOMES THE FOURTEENTH ANNUAL NORTH AMERICAN RADIO SELLERS' CONVENTION. On either side of the multicolored block words, radio towers beamed signal waves, like the RKO logo at the start of the movies. I passed through blue clouds of cigar and cigarette smoke, walking by pretty ladies in glamorous dresses showing off the newest radio models. The din was so loud it began to make my head throb.

I needed to talk to the witnesses that allegedly saw Roscoe the night of Underhill's disappearance. Now that Vaughn Perry was dead, I was starting to think that Roscoe had gone off on a wild-goose chase, heading down to the Canyons of the Escalante—if that was indeed where he went. I reached my destination in a dark corner of the ground level, past the elevators. A frosted window on the door said the words HOTEL SECURITY in big, black serif letters, arched like a rainbow. A brass plate centered beneath the window said DOOLEY METZGER. I knocked. Seconds passed and the door opened, but barely, and that Roman-nosed, double-chinned fire hydrant of a man appeared in the narrow space. He wore his derby pulled low, down to his brow, and it shaded his eyes, although I could see them widen with recognition when he looked at me. He took a step back and opened the door further, and I glimpsed the inside of his office. Windowless. Sparsely furnished. Battered desk. His Smith Corona typewriter had seen better days. The only thing fancy about it was the crystal light fixture, filling the room with a strange shimmering light.

"Oveson."

"Hello Metzger. Quite the convention you've got going on here."

"It's keeping me busy, as you might imagine."

"I'll make this brief. I need to talk to those three eyewitnesses that saw Roscoe Lund confront Nigel Underhill early Sunday morning. I'd like to find out what they know."

"I thought Detective Newbold was handling that side of the investigation."

I avoided a direct response. I figured it was none of his business.

"I'd like to rule out certain things."

"Such as?"

"I've reason to believe the alleged altercation, if it indeed occurred, is closely related to Clive Underhill's disappearance."

"Oh, it occurred, all right."

"Then that's all the more important for me to speak to the witnesses."

"What else?"

"I beg your pardon?"

"Is there anything else I should be privy to?"

"Not that I know of."

"Well, I'd very much like to know why you believe the two are connected." He stepped aside and swept his hand. "Please, come in and have a seat. . . ."

"I'm in something of a hurry."

"I prefer to be kept abreast of things," he said, repressing a sneer. "In my line of work, that's essential. I'm sure you understand."

"Of course. There are some details I need to sort out. It shouldn't take long."

"I figured perhaps you'd like to share those with me."

"I'm looking for information that pertains to my investigation," I said.

"What kind of information?"

"I want to know precisely what happened between Lund and Underhill."

"Isn't it in the police reports?"

"I have specific questions I'd like to ask."

"What kinds of questions?"

"I'd like to clarify a few things and, like I said, rule out a few things."

He smiled. "I can do this as long as you wish, Oveson."

"Do what?"

"Keep asking you questions. And listen to you keep dodging them. I find you a very obstinate fellow, in your own, friendly manner."

"Sorry you feel that way."

"Sometimes sharing a little of what you know goes a long way."

"Toward?"

"You're not like your father, are you?"

"I didn't come here to talk about Will Oveson."

"So you didn't." He drew a deep breath. "Let me place a telephone call upstairs. They're guests—a couple from Canada—that saw Lund go after Underhill. I don't wish to disturb their privacy without clearing it with them first."

"Sure, that's fine. Oh, and uh, I heard there was a third eyewitness. I'd like to talk to him, or her, too."

Grinding his teeth, he looked me up and down. "I'll be right back."

The door slammed with a forcefulness that startled me. Metzger stayed in his office for a good five minutes, and his muffled voice could be heard although I could not make out his exact words. My heart raced from the rage I felt toward him at that moment. He came across as the worst combination of uncooperative and churlish, and his behavior went beyond rubbing me the wrong way. He was sanding me down raw. I heard movement on the other side of the door. A shadow moved across the frosted window. The doorknob turned and Mr. Cheerful himself stepped out, his gold chain swinging in front of his striped vest.

"I thought perhaps you could talk to Mr. Booker first," said Metzger. "He's the bellhop on duty who was on the seventh floor that night, attending to a room service matter. Right this way."

"Thank you."

I followed him through the crowd and through a set of doors into the Lafayette Ballroom. He turned a switch on the wall and a row of chandeliers lit up, infusing this giant space with sparkling light. Another one of those banners welcoming radio sellers to Salt Lake City hung from the eastern wall. Metzger walked over to a stack of fancy upholstered chairs against the curtained wall, pulled two off the top, and brought them over to where I was standing in the center of the room. He set them up, face-to-face, muttered for me to "stay here," and left me alone to marvel at the patterned wood floors. I stuck my hands in my pockets, jiggled change, and whistled a song I didn't even recognize, just to whistle something. He was gone awhile. Twenty minutes, at least. Maybe more. My legs began to ache from standing in one spot. I sat down on one of those chairs, and exhaled with relief for finally being able to take some weight off my feet.

Metzger returned shortly thereafter, followed by a nervous-looking Negro porter. As the young man approached, I saw he was brawny, with sleepy eyes, flared nostrils, and a prominent chin. He rubbed his hands together, which I attributed to a nervous tic. When Metzger gestured to the empty chair, the fancily uniformed fellow bounded over and sat down. Catching his breath, he stared at me, perhaps fearful that I might do something unpleasant, like arrest him. His nervousness came as no surprise. Most Negroes I'd encountered on my job as a patrolman harbored some sort of fear that we police were going to harm or harass them. That's why I always went out of my way to be friendly in such instances, to show I meant no harm. I smiled, which maybe broke a little ice, but not all of it. Beads of perspiration had formed on his forehead, and he was still breathing heavily. Dooley Metzger hovered off to our side, watching us carefully, like a vulture circling over the desert.

"Thank you. I can handle it from here," I told Metzger. "If you'll excuse us."

He sneered my way, then gave the bellhop a meaningful look, turned, and left. I waited until he was gone. Seated in the center of the room, we were far enough away from the entrance that I was confident Metzger wouldn't be able to eavesdrop, especially if we spoke softly.

I extended my hand and he shook it.

"Hello. I'm Detective Art Oveson," I said. "I'm with the Salt Lake City Police Department."

"I'm Winston Booker. I go by Blue."

We released hands.

"Blues?"

"Naw, just Blue. Blue Booker. I'm in a harmonica quartet, and Blue is my nickname in it. Maybe you heard of us? The King Rufus Hi-Hat Harmonica Quartet." He chuckled, more relaxed now. "We play at places 'round town. Y'all oughta come out and hear us sometime."

"I'd like that, very much," I said, with a genuine spark of enthusiasm in my voice. "Right now, I've got a few questions."

"Go right ahead, suh."

"I'm told that in the early morning hours of Sunday, August seventh, you saw or overheard an argument between two guests on the seventh floor."

"Yessuh. That is so. I seen it."

"Can you tell me exactly what you saw?"

"This fella—a big fella—he come knocking on the door."

"Which door?"

"Room seven-oh-three."

"OK. Go on."

"He come knocking, and Underhill, he answered it . . ."

"Nigel Underhill?"

"Yes. He opened the door and the two of 'em, man, they really started going at it. Hollering, getting in each other's way and whatnot."

"Can you describe the visitor?"

"Yeah. Sure. Like I said, he was big. Someone you didn't want to monkey with."

"What was he wearing?"

Blue looked up, as if thinking it over, then his eyes shot back to me. "Nice shirt. Suit jacket. Maybe black. Or dark brown. No tie. Corduroy trousers."

"What color was his hair?"

"Bald as the day he was born."

"So he wasn't wearing a hat?"

"Naw. No hat."

"Where were you in relation to him?"

He squinted. "Relation?"

"Yeah. Where were you standing when this was happening?"

"Oh. Down the hall, delivering something to one of the rooms."

"What?"

"What was I delivering?"

"Yeah."

"Extra pillows. To room seven-ten."

"Seven-one-zero?"

"Uh huh. That big guy, he was pounding on the doors, raising a ruckus. It was enough to wake up the dead."

"When you were on your way up to deliver the pillows, did you have to walk past these two men arguing?"

"Naw. It started when I was at the door to seven-ten. I give a knock and called out 'room service.'"

"And how long, roughly, would you say you were at room

seven-ten, from the time you knocked until the time the customer took the pillows and you left?"

"Coupla minutes. The guy grabbed the pillows from me, axed me to hold on, and he come back with a tip."

"So you watched the argument while he was inside fetching your gratuity?"

"Yessuh. He gimme two bits."

"I see. So from the spot where you were standing, you could plainly see room seven-oh-three, where the confrontation going on?"

"Yessuh."

"Did the man that you delivered the pillows to that night, did he see any of this?"

"I doubt it. The man just took them pillows, told me to hold tight. Closed the door. Come back a second later with the tip. That was that."

"Getting back to this argument . . . Are you sure the man that answered the door to seven-oh-three was Mister Nigel Under-hill?"

"Yeah. I know what Nigel Underhill looked like. I carried his luggage up to his room the day he arrived."

"Did he tip you?"

Blue chuckled, rocking back and forth as he did. "Naw. Now how come you'd ax that?"

"Just curious. Getting back to this argument . . ."

"Yeah."

"What exactly were they arguing about? Did you happen to overhear any of it?"

"Only part. They was far enough away. At one point, the big guy, he looks right at me, and then he starts talking softer."

"The part you heard . . ."

"Yessuh."

"What'd they say?"

"Well, see, the big guy, he wanted his money for some job he done, and he told Underhill that he'd come to collect."

"Uh huh. Did they argue about anything else?"

He shook his head. "S'all I heard."

"What time did it happen? Approximately."

"I don't know. Ain't got no watch. No clock in the hallway, neither."

"But it was late."

"Yeah. Late. Or early. Depending on how you look at it."

"Maybe two? Two thirty?"

"Possibly. Possibly three. Somewhere thereabouts."

"So while you were dropping off the pillows, you looked over and saw the big man knocking on the door?"

"Yessuh."

"And Nigel opened the door . . ."

"Uh huh."

"And the arguing began."

"Yeah."

"Did you see the whole argument?"

"They was hollering at each other right as I was dropping off them pillows, and then Underhill, I seen him go back in the room and close the door. The big guy stood there waiting, and that's when I went back to the elevator."

"Help me grasp the lay of the land right."

"Sure."

"To get back to the elevators, you had to walk past the big guy hollering at Nigel Underhill. Is that right."

"Well, that's one way of getting there."

"There another?"

"Yessuh. The long way. I didn't wanna walk past this fella. He was sore, and I was fearing he'd snap and get ugly on me if'n I got close to him, you understand. So I took a longer route to get to the elevators. Rounded a lotta corners, went down all them corridors, and by and by, I got to the elevators. Taking the long way made it so I could steer clear of that big guy."

"But the elevators are right around the corner from room seven-oh-three. Isn't that right?"

"Yes. That's so."

"OK. So you took the long way just to avoid the big man?"

"Like I said, I ain't looking for no trouble."

"Understandable. So how long did it take for you to get from room seven-one-zero all the way to the elevators, walking around the length of the hotel?"

"The long way?"

"Yes."

"Mmm. It'd take a man a couple minutes. Depending on your stride."

"It took you a couple of minutes?"

"Two minutes, three minutes. I wasn't timing it or nothing."

"When you got to the elevator, was the argument still going on?"

"Naw. I spied 'round the corner. The big guy wasn't there no more."

"It doesn't seem like he was there very long, was he?"

"Nope."

"If you had to guess, how long would you say he was there?"

"I don't know."

"And you didn't see any sign of him leaving the building?"

"Nossuh."

"Do you think if you saw this man again, in a police lineup or a courtroom, you could identify him?"

Blue shrugged his shoulders. "Like I said, I was down the hall, and it wasn't like I was staring at the man."

"Do you remember seeing Clive Underhill that night?"

"When he come in late from the Grove, yes, I surely do."

"Do you remember him going up to his room?"

He hesitated, as if cooking up an answer in his head. "No. I remember seeing him in the lobby."

"You had to think about it."

"Lots of folks ride the elevator at night. That Clive, he come and go all time, every day, and at all hours, too. So my memory needs poking."

"What did you think of him?"

"Mr. Clive?"

"Yeah."

"Oh, he's an awfully nice fella," said Blue. "Whole lot nicer than that brother of his. Mighty generous, all the time tipping. I told him I wasn't s'posed to accept it, but he says 'nonsense' in that funny way English folks say it. Always stuffing a bill in my hand, axin' how I'm doing. You won't find no one more decent than him."

I leaned back into my chair and stretched my arms. I noticed Blue loosening up, relaxing, probably relieved to be past this.

"One more question," I said.

"Yessuh."

"Remind me . . ."

"Yessuh."

"I can't for the life of me remember the name of your harmonica group."

"Oh!" He laughed. "The King Rufus Hi-Hat Harmonica Quartet. We'll be playing at the Old Mill Club tonight and again on Saturday night. Come on out and give us a listen."

We shook hands again. "Blue. It's been a pleasure."

"Pleasure's all mine, Detective."

Nineteen

"Where are you from, Mrs. McKenna?"

"Please, call me Estelle."

"Estelle." I smiled. "If you don't mind me asking."

Her floral dress, with vivid splashes of spring colors, came close to matching her red hair, which I surmised had been dyed recently. Age-wise, I'd pegged her as being in her late fifties, maybe early sixties, with the first hint of wrinkles forming in her face, and sausage-like fingers flecked with light golden age spots. She possessed a hint of the aristocratic, and spoke with a melodious accent that I couldn't quite identify. Wisconsin? Minnesota? The Canadian Prairies? In the middle of her lap she kept a shiny black handbag, and I could plainly see a familiar-looking pack of Choward's Violet Mints jutting out the top. When she came down to answer my questions in the Lafayette Ballroom, her husband was taking a nap after a long day at his convention.

"Not at all," she said. "We live in Regina, Saskatchewan."

"I've never been to Saks . . . Sawks . . . Swask . . ."

She laughed and spoke the name slowly and deliberately: "Saskatchewan."

"I've never been to Saskatchewan," I said. "What's it like?"

"Flat."

"Completely flat? Like a pancake? No mountains?"

"Not even a hill. Not for hundreds of miles."

"You're from around there?"

"I most certainly am. Born and raised."

"What brings you to our fair city, if you don't mind me asking?"

"Not at all. Claude is here for the convention."

I jabbed my thumb over my shoulder. "The Radio Sellers' Convention?"

"Yes. He owns his own business, McKenna's Radio Store. He wants to open up a chain of them. For the past month, he's been scouting around Regina, Saskatoon, and Moose Jaw, looking at storefronts. He's exploring the option of a bank loan. The time seems to be right. Radio is here to stay, and the market is expanding. Each new day, another station acquires a license to broadcast. You know what they say? Today, Saskatchewan; tomorrow, the world!"

"That pleases me to hear," I said, with a heartfelt smile. "Listen, Mrs. McK—"

"Estelle."

"Estelle. I have a couple of routine questions I'd like to ask you. Shouldn't take up much of your time, and then I'll leave you be."

"Oh, you don't have to leave me be," she said, chortling as she dipped chin to chest. "I find you a pleasant young man."

I'm sure I blushed. "That's kind of you to say. Still, business is business, and it waits for no one."

"Is it about the incident on Saturday night?"

"I understand that you and your husband witnessed a quarrel between two men."

"I saw it, through the peephole, and I described it to my husband."

"What did you see?"

"Two men arguing, yelling at one another."

"Where did this argument take place?"

"At the door to the room across the hall."

"What's your room number?"

"Seven hundred and four."

"Seven-oh-four. So you were looking out the peephole at the doorway to the room across the hall? Does that mean your husband didn't see it?"

"We took turns looking out. He saw parts of it. I saw parts. But you could hear every word they were saying through the door."

"What were they arguing about? Do you know?"

"The big man wanted money he thought was owed to him. The little man didn't want to pay him. There was quite the brouhaha."

"Oveson!"

I turned my head toward the entrance to the Lafayette Ballroom. Pace Newbold was coming toward me in a hurry, and with a furious expression on his face. Behind him, like a caboose in a three-piece suit, followed Reid Whitaker, proving he could smirk and chew gum at the same time. As Pace neared, I saw his fists clenched, as if he was preparing to duke it out with me.

"Something wrong?" Estelle asked.

"Hold on a second."

I rose to my feet and faced Pace before he could wedge

himself between Mrs. McKenna and me. As I silently predicted, he shoved me, a one-handed jab to the shoulder. I knew well enough not to let him bait me, not to shove him back, which was what he wanted and, I'm sure, expected. I stepped back, drew a deep breath, and noticed Whitaker off to the side, head cocked back, grinning as though he had a front-row seat to a big vaudeville show.

"You can't leave it alone, can you?"

"It's because they're connected, and you know it."

"I'll tell you what I know, Oveson. I know damn well what you're up to. You're not going to get away with it."

"Oh yeah? What am I up to? What sinister agenda am I pushing?"

"I'm sick of you being coy with me, playing the innocent fool."

He gazed down at Estelle McKenna, who was staring up at us, her mouth hanging open from the suspense of it all.

"Mrs. McKenna . . ."

"Estelle."

"Tell Detective Oveson what you saw through the peephole of your hotel door early Sunday morning. Remember?"

"I was about to, right before you walked in. I didn't have a chance to finish."

"Tell me what?"

She looked at me and spoke haltingly. "I . . . I saw the big fellow wrap something—a wire or a cord or some twine—around Underhill's neck and force him back into his hotel room. When they got inside, the big guy closed the door behind him."

Her words caught me off guard with the force of a horse's hoof flying into my face and cracking bone. Momentarily too shocked to speak, I had difficulty formulating a coherent response.

"What's the matter?" asked Pace. "You look like you just found out an old friend died."

I ignored Pace. I asked Mrs. McKenna: "Why didn't you call the police right away when you saw this?"

She spoke haltingly: "I was frightened and I didn't want to—"

"Butt out, Oveson," interrupted Pace. "Maybe if you spent a little less time covering up for the sorry sonofabitch Lund and a little more trying to hunt him down and bring him to justice, we might actually inch a little closer to closing this case."

"I'd like to talk to Mr. McKenna," I said. "I have a few questions. . . ."

"Drop it, I said!" shouted Pace, moving menacingly close to me.

"What about Clive Underhill?" I asked Pace. "You gonna try to tell me Roscoe had something to do with his disappearance?"

"I don't owe you any fucking explanation. Just drag your sorry carcass out of here and quit searching for an angle to get your pal off the hook."

For a fraction of a second, I considered telling Pace that I found Vaughn Perry's body in that shotgun house up Emigration Canyon. But I opted against sharing that crucial piece of information with him, mainly because at that very moment, I loathed him, and only wished to punch him in the mouth. Restraint won out, as it always seems to with me. Echoes of my dad's voice reverberated from my boyhood to the present: *Ask yourself, son: Is this really the hill you wish to die on?*

My attention returned to Estelle McKenna, staring up at me with an open mouth and expectant eyes. The last thing she needed to see, after what she witnessed on Saturday night, was a fight between two police detectives. Pace had me. I couldn't be seen fighting too hard for Roscoe. He was a fugitive now, and he'd received significant help from me, and I knew I'd face prison time if I were ever caught. I had to exercise caution and play the hand I was dealt with care. Hotheadedness would only land me in trouble.

"Sorry," I said, at last. "I guess I overstepped my bounds."

"I'd say that's putting it mildly," jeered Pace.

"Go easy on him," said Estelle. "He's a sweet fellow. He's only doing his job."

"Lady, with all due respect, you don't know this guy like I know him," said Pace.

I went over and shook hands with Estelle McKenna. "Thank you for your time, ma'am. You don't happen to know when your husband will be . . ."

Pace appeared at my side. "Get out of here, Oveson, before I personally arrest your sorry ass."

The thought of giving her one of my business cards crossed my mind. *Briefly*. With Pace standing behind me, almost literally breathing down my collar, I thought better of it. I instead offered a nod of gratitude and a tug of my hat brim. Then I crossed the ballroom, moving out into a flood of men in suits the corridor, streaming out of the ballroom next door. I walked out the rear doors of the Hotel Utah, and the late afternoon sunlight momentarily blinded me.

I tossed the dice. They stopped at the board's edge, next to one of Sarah Jane's green houses.

"Six and four makes ten!" I picked up the little metal Scottie dog and began moving him around the board. "I just passed Go, so if you please, Mr. Banker . . ."

My son Hi handed me two one-hundred-dollar bills. I put them on my stack and continued up the board. ". . . six, seven, eight, nine . . ."

"You got Vermont," said Hi.

"Spectacular!" I said. "Things have taken a distinct turn for the better."

Earlier in the evening, we'd set up the Monopoly board on the coffee table in the middle of the living room. Once again, Clara wasn't feeling well and had gone to bed early. The radio softly played a medley of big band music courtesy of *Kay Kyser's Kollege of Musical Knowledge.* I sat perched on the edge of the love seat next to Emily. Hi rocked cross-legged on the floor opposite me. Sarah Jane was reading one of her books, putting it down when it was her turn. She gazed down at the board at my triumphant landing on Vermont.

"Are you going to buy it?" she asked.

"Of course!" I said. "Given that I already own Oriental and Connecticut, I'd be a nitwit not to! What's the damage, Mr. Banker?"

"Hundred bucks," said Hi.

I passed him back one of the pretend hundreds he'd just given me. "Wait till I get some hotels up on these three babies! I'll wipe out all my competitors!"

"Don't be such a wise guy, Dad," said Hi. "Sarah Jane already owns Boardwalk and Park Place."

"And it won't be long before I put up hotels on both," she said. "Along with Marvin Gardens, Ventnor, and Atlantic. He's right, Dad. It's a little too soon to start being a hotdogger."

"Yeah, Dad!" said Emily, arms folded, with her fiercest four-year-old pouty face. "Don't be a hotdog!"

The telephone rang.

Sarah Jane noticed my posture straighten, and she shot me a look of concern.

"Let it ring," she said.

"I'd better pick it up," I said. "I'll be right back."

I hurried into the kitchen and answered the telephone. "Hello."

"Arthur?"

The voice on the other end belonged to Dot Bliss. I glanced behind me. The coast was clear. I moved close to the wall and talked softly.

"Speaking?"

"This is Dot Bliss calling."

"Hello, Miss Bliss," I said. "What can I do for you?"

"I was wondering if we could talk," she said.

"What about?"

"Some concerns I'm having."

"Can we discuss it over the telephone?" I asked.

"I'd rather talk in person," she said.

"I've got a family. And it's getting late." I checked my watch. "It's already quarter to nine."

"I don't trust these telephone lines. Is there somewhere we can meet?" she asked. "After they've gone to bed, of course."

"What time did you have in mind?" I asked.

"How does eleven o'clock sound?"

"I'll make it work. Meet me at the Airport Café. It's brand-new and open all night. You remember where the airport is, don't you?"

"Yes."

"Good. I'll see you there."

"Thank you, Detective Oveson."

She hung up.

I remained standing in that spot for a half a minute, staring at the big black wall telephone, wondering why on earth Dot Bliss wanted to talk to me at such a late hour. I lowered the phone on the hook, returned to the living room, and instantly transformed into the least popular guy in Salt Lake City when I announced bedtime, accentuating it with a triple clap. Hi and his little sister moaned, but Sarah Jane smirked with all of the self-assurance of a teenager who knew how to maneuver around bedtime rules.

I told my children to change into their pajamas, brush their teeth, gulp down their drinks of water, and climb into bed. I took Sarah Jane aside and, knowing her night owl proclivities, asked her to keep an eye on things while I went out. She eyed me skeptically when I opened my billfold and handed her a couple of floppy George Washingtons.

"What's this?" she asked.

"It's for your troubles," I said.

"Why does this feel like you're paying me not to ask questions?"

I pushed the bills back into the billfold and started to shove it back in my trouser pocket. "Suit yourself. . . ."

"No, wait!" She cracked a grin. "If you insist."

I passed her the bills and she tucked them in her shirt pocket.

"Are you going to tell me where you're going?"

"I won't be gone long."

"Does it have to do with Mom?"

I made a face. "What makes you ask a thing like that?"

"It's getting worse, isn't it?" Sarah Jane searched for the words. "Her sadness."

"You oughtn't to worry about it," I said. "Remember what I

told you? Don't carry the weight of the world on your shoulders. Everything's going to be fine."

"You say it so convincingly, Dad."

"That's because your grandma Oveson raised her sons to tell the truth," I said. "How late you gonna be up till?"

"It's a weeknight," she said. "So no later than one. Maybe half past."

I chuckled. "Chip off the old block."

"Always will be," she said. "If I don't see you later, good night Dad."

I kissed her on the forehead.

"Good night angel. I love you."

"I know. Me too, with you."

She walked into her bedroom, belly flopped on the bed, kicked her feet up, and opened her book to the place where she left off. I waited in the living room, looking at pictures in *Life* magazine, until Hi and Emily were asleep, or at least they pretended to be when I peeked in on them. Clara, too, was breathing heavily and did not respond when I whispered her name a couple of times. At about twenty minutes to eleven, I closed the front door behind me, triple checking to make sure it was locked. Then I drove off into the night.

Twenty

In a velvety booth in a dimly lit corner of the Airport Café, I peered out the window into the night, counting the lights flashing along the runway. Even at this hour—a little past eleven—airplanes still touched down at the Municipal Airport. Most of the late-night landings involved single-engine buzzers swooping out of the sky to bounce down onto terra firma. The larger commercial flights—the roaring DC-3s and Boeing 247s and Lockheed Super Electras—also arrived at the airport this time of night, but more sporadically than during the daytime. When one of the big ones came down out of the starry heavens, guided by the flashing lights on the runway and the air control tower spotlight, it was something to behold. Those powerful engines made the restaurant tables tremble, silverware clink, and windows vibrate.

Not one to loiter at an eating establishment without ordering food, I asked the waitress to bring me a banana split. A short time later, she arrived with the largest of its kind I've ever seen. I went to work on it with a long dessert spoon, digging my way down the summit. Dot Bliss arrived right at the instant I was starting to doubt she was coming. Once more, she was dressed elegantly, this time in something black that I guessed to be made of velvet, with flared elbow-length sleeves and elaborate bead designs around the bodice. A matching little black hat with bead designs around the brim topped her head. Her high-heeled shoes clacked loudly against the linoleum floor as she approached, and I stood to greet her and shake her hand.

"Detective Oveson, sorry I'm late."

"Don't think twice about it," I said. "Call me Art."

"As long as you call me Dot."

"It's a deal."

She slid into her side of the booth, I into mine.

"I hope you don't mind, I started without you," I said, gesturing to what was left of my banana split. "Want one?"

She grimaced. "No thank you. I'll have something to drink."

I flagged the waitress. A chipper brunette, young and in a blue linen dress, held a small spiral pad and a pencil poised to jot our order.

"What would you like?" I asked.

"Tom Collins, please."

The waitress did a double take. "Sorry, the bartender is gone for the night."

"Oh, I see," she said. "Have you any beer?"

The waitress rattled off a list of brands, foreign and domestic.

"Is any of that on draft?" asked Dot.

"Fisher and Becker," the waitress replied. "Both brewed locally."

"I'll gamble on the Fisher."

"Be right back."

The waitress darted off in the direction of the bar. Dot pulled an ashtray closer, lit a cigarette, and blew smoke upward. For the briefest of seconds, I thought of Clara smoking this morning, but I shook that thought out of my head.

"I hope you found your way out here without any problems," I said.

"It was no trouble at all. I took a cab."

"Good."

The waitress arrived carrying a tray balancing a mug of beer and a bowl of pretzels mixed with peanuts. She unloaded the tray, greeted by quiet thanks from Dot, and then vanished from our table as quickly as she appeared. Dot lifted the frosted mug to her lips and sipped, and the foam gave her a fleeting mustache, which vanished with a napkin's dab.

"Mmm," she said, raising her eyebrows, surprised that she'd like it.

"How is it?"

"Tasty. Crisp. Want some?"

"Oh no thanks," I said. "I'm not much of a drinker."

She smiled as she placed her beer on the coaster. "How do you pull that off?"

"It's how I've always been," I said. "I don't know any different."

"Do you eat ice cream instead?"

"I never thought of ice cream as a substitute for anything," I said. "To me, it's pure pleasure in and of itself."

She laughed in a throaty way that made her bosom quiver. I shouldn't have noticed that detail, but I did.

"What?" I asked.

"For the long journey across the pond, I brought along a book of facts about the United States," she said. "The part about Utah

boasts that it leads the country in ice cream consumption. Is that
true?"

"That wouldn't surprise me," I said. "We love our ice cream
in these parts."

"That much is obvious." She waited a beat, sizing me up with
her eyes. "Listen, thank you for meeting me out here at this late
hour. I realize Salt Lake City doesn't have much of a nightlife."

"Oh? Is your hometown hopping at the witching hour?"

"Where I'm from, the night doesn't get started until this
time," she said. "I suppose that's an unfair comparison. London
has been around for two thousand years. Salt Lake has been here
for—what?"

"Ninety-one, give or take a few months."

"Give it another millennium," she said, with a sly grin. "You
know what they say. Salt Lake City wasn't built in a day."

We both chuckled at that line. Our eyes met. She was disarm-
ingly beautiful.

"Is there something you wanted to discuss?" I asked.

"I had things I wanted to tell you. In person."

"Yeah? Such as?"

"Something isn't right."

I waited for her to continue. She stared at her beer in silence.

"Can you elaborate?" I asked.

"Yes, of course. I find the tension in Clive's entourage unbearable."

"What kind of tension?"

"The combination of Nigel's murder and Clive going missing has been too much to bear. I fear there's something sinister
at the root of Clive's disappearance. I don't believe he's gone on
an errant nature outing."

"Sinister how?"

She stared intently at me as she drew on her cigarette, and the glow of the orange tip reflected in her irises. Blowing smoke, she said, "I believe he was taken."

"As in kidnapped? By whom?"

"I don't know."

"What makes you believe he was kidnapped?"

"Intuition."

"I'm going to need more than that. If what you say is true, this thing will blow wide open. It'll be splashed all over the papers, the newsreels, the radio. Clive's face will be everywhere."

"They do love celebrities, don't they?"

I nodded. "Especially a missing one, like Amelia Earhart. It makes hot copy and sells lots of papers."

The waitress returned to our table with a smile that lit up the place.

"Is there anything else I can get for you?"

"No thank you," I said. "I'm stuffed to the gills, I'm afraid."

"Wasn't it any good? Looks like you only ate half of it."

"It was the best banana split I've ever tasted," I said. "I get full easily."

"Care for a beer?" she asked.

"No thank you."

"Coffee? Tea? Juice? A sandwich maybe?"

"I'd love a soda water, with lime and a couple of teaspoons of sugar stirred in for good measure."

"Coming right up." She looked at Dot. "Another beer?"

"No thank you," said Dot. "I'm fine for now."

"Be right back."

"Much obliged," I said.

Off to get my soda water, the waitress zigzagged around mostly empty tables—there were probably about half a dozen other people in that spacious joint. I spied Dot holding back laughter.

"What?" I asked.

"'Much obliged,'" she said, making her voice deeper and more American sounding. "You talk like they do in the cowboy pictures."

"Yeah, well, I live on a steady diet of 'em," I said, winking. "Back to your theory about Clive being kidnapped."

"Yes?"

"You haven't given me much to go on," I said. "Other than intuition, feelings of dread, and something or other about tension amongst your fellow travelers."

"Is that not sufficient?"

"You want to know what I think?"

"By all means."

The waitress delivered my soda water. I thanked her and drank half of it in one shot.

"The pressure got to Clive. He fled. Same way he ran away from Daytona Beach three years ago." I hesitated to say what I was about to tell her. "There's something I didn't mention the other day, when we were all gathered at police headquarters. On Saturday night at the Coconut Grove, Clive asked me to take him to a remote part of Utah, where there are these uncharted canyons that are difficult to explore and aren't even mapped out yet."

"Why?"

I shrugged. "He seemed to love the idea of going somewhere remote, leaving everything behind, even just for a few days. Maybe he just wanted to clear the cobwebs out of his head."

She opened her case, pulled out another cigarette, and tapped it on the silvery surface. She lit it, returned the lighter to her purse, and smoked in silence. She fingernail-picked tobacco off of her tongue.

"What part of Utah?"

"An area called the Canyons of the Escalante," I said.

"Do you believe he's alive?"

"Yes." I don't know if I really believed it, but I wanted to reassure her.

"I wish I shared your optimism," she said. "I know what these Germans are capable of."

"Germans? Who said anything about Germans?"

"They're here to stage a propaganda coup. Why do you think they handpicked Rudy Heinrich, a dashing racer who speaks fluent English? They want to demonstrate their superiority to the rest of the world, and show Americans they're really not so different from them."

"So you think they kidnapped Clive to knock him out of the running?"

"You say it as though it's far-fetched. Clive abandoned his flirtation with fascism long ago. He represents England now, whereas Heinrich is a symbol of Germany and the so-called master race. I'm sure a victory for the Germans, here on American soil, would thrill Mr. Hitler. It might even make up for the victory of your own Jesse Owens two years ago."

"I've wondered if there was a connection between Heinrich's team and Clive's disappearance. . . ."

Her eyes widened, as if she saw something, and she leaned forward and whispered, with shifty eyes: "There is a man seated over in a booth by the window, reading a newspaper."

I started to turn my head.

"Not now," she hissed. "Give it a minute."

An uneasy silence settled over our table, like a pall, giving me time to sip my drink. She slipped me her makeup compact, open with the mirror facing up. She made hand motions, advising me to use it to see the man seated over by the window, so I didn't have to turn my head directly to him. I positioned the compact on the tablecloth until a wall of newspaper appeared in the mirror. For a long while, the headlines stayed high, blocking my view of his face. When he lowered it to turn the page, I instantly recognized him as Ernst Voss, stony-faced, like Buster Keaton. I snapped the compact closed, placed it flat on the table, and slid it across to her. She slipped it inside of her purse, as if handling something top secret

She checked her wristwatch. "I should be getting back. I'll hail a yellow cab out by the curb."

"Not on your life," I said, pulling dollar bills out of my wallet and tossing them on the table to cover our bill and a little extra for a tip. "I'll give you a ride back."

"Are you sure?"

"It's on me," I said.

"I mean about the ride."

"Sure I'm sure. Let's make ourselves scarce."

She mashed her cigarette into the ashtray and the two of us eased out of the booth and headed out of the Airport Café, blending into a dense crowd of arrivals in a terminal so bright it stung my eyes.

Twenty-one

Leaving the municipal airport parking lot, I gripped the steering wheel with one hand and switched on the radio with the other. The KDYL Nite Owl Program played a horn-filled selection by Bob Crosby and His Orchestra. A smooth-voiced Kay Weber sang a sentimental love song duet with Bob called "Romance in the Dark." I thought the music might put Dot Bliss at ease, but she kept glancing backward over her shoulder, fearful we were being followed. I was not helping matters any by repeatedly checking my rearview mirror, scanning for headlights. I spotted a pair a little ways back. Who knows if that car was following us? Seeing Ernst Voss in that restaurant got to me, like it did her. Why was he shadowing me? What interest could he possibly have in where I was going? Or could he be running surveillance on Dot Bliss?

Something gnawed away at her. She was agitated. Fidgety. Preoccupied. Sighing often. I nearly asked what was eating her, but before I could, she placed her hand on her chest and began panting. In a few seconds, she was hyperventilating, and her breathing sounded labored and the hand on her chest trembled.

"Pull over," she said.

"What's wrong? Are you OK?"

"Now! Please! Right here!"

On a pitch-black stretch of road, with no streetlamps for miles, I swerved onto the gravel shoulder, and as soon as the car came to a halt, she leapt out the door and stumbled into a ditch. I killed the engine and pursued her. It wasn't quite pitch-black, but close. The sky was splashed with stars, and on the opposite side of the valley, the lights of Salt Lake City twinkled along the base of the Wasatch Mountains. I hiked down to the bottom of the ditch, where Dot Bliss was sprawled out in tall grass, still breathing heavily, but not quite as dramatically as she'd been in the car. Her hat was on the ground nearby, and I reached down and picked it up. I walked over to where she lay, sat down in the dirt, and set her hat by her side.

"Are you OK?" I asked again.

No response came from her, but her breathing slowed, and I noticed fluttering eyelids.

I lost track of how long we sat in that ditch together. It dipped sufficiently deep into the earth that I could not see the road above us, but every now and then a car could be heard zooming past. At one point, a faraway buzz of propellers hummed, and before long, an airplane roared over our heads, low enough that the glow from its open windows cast light on our grassy trench. The plane touched down on the nearby runway and its deafening engines faded, replaced by the symphony of crickets.

Dot Bliss sat up cross-legged in the grass, reached for her hat, and fiddled with the brim. Moonlight touched the corner of her face, enough to remind me of her otherworldly beauty, as if I needed a reminder. I waited for her to speak. What does one say to a young, rich, lovely British socialite sitting close by in a roadside ditch?

"I'm so sorry."

"Are you all right?"

"Yes," she said. "I wish I brought my purse. I could use a cigarette."

"I'll go get it."

I started to stand up.

"No! Stop! Please, stay here."

I plopped back down on my hind end, squirming to get comfy in the dry grass. "What happened?"

"I get these panic attacks," she said. "I have difficulty breathing. My heart starts pounding. I get dizzy, disoriented. If I'm in a car or a building when it's happening, I have to run outside to get some fresh air. Once upon a time, when I was a teenager, I used to carry around a brown paper bag, in case my breathing became labored, like I did back there. My mother told me it was unladylike to carry around a bag with me. She said no man would ever want to marry me if I kept doing it."

"Any man that'd get sore at you for carrying around a bag is not the kind of fella you'd want to spend time with. Free advice, which you can take or leave."

"You're right," she said, with a brief smile. "Thank you."

"Was it seeing that fellow back at the restaurant that brought it on?"

"Maybe. Partly. But it was more than that. I find this place unbearable."

"Well, here, let me take you back . . ."

She gripped my arm to prevent me from rising to my feet.

"Not this place here, specifically. I mean Utah, in general. Please. Sit with me here a little longer."

I sat down beside her.

"You make me feel better," she said. "You have a soothing effect on me."

"I'm glad I have that effect on somebody."

"I'm sure you've got plenty of it to go around."

"You overestimate me," I said.

"You're everything I imagined a real American to be," she said.

"I can't tell if that's a compliment. But thank you."

"Oh, it's meant as such. You're authentic. You're self-deprecating without being excessively so. You're like a cowboy. Has anybody ever told you that?"

"Until now, no," I said. "Maybe I'll go round up some little dogies."

She laughed and touched my arm. It felt nice, her doing that.

"What is a dogie anyway?" she asked. "Is it another name for a dog?"

"No, a dogie is a stray calf. Sometimes cowboys will shout . . ." I gave a loud finger whistle and hollered: " 'Git along little dogies!' "

"Impressive! That's quite a set of lungs you possess."

"Maybe I missed my calling in life. I shoulda been a dogie rounder upper."

"I'm sure you'd be exceptional at it," she said, giggling like a grade-school girl.

I smiled warmly at her. "So what is it about this place that you find so unbearable?"

"It's been so tense here since I arrived Saturday night. Even before the airplane touched down, I had this awful premonition something bad was going to happen. Now that Clive is gone, I spend every waking minute anxious. Nigel's death threw everybody into a downward spiral, and we're supposed to keep it a secret from his family back home until Clive's whereabouts are known. Albert and Peter quarrel constantly. Julian is despondent, hardly saying a word. If Clive's not found soon, I'm afraid they're going to . . ."

She stopped. Shut her mouth. Rocked gently in the moonlight.

'They?" I asked.

The only response I got came from armies of chirping crickets.

"Is there something you're not telling me?" I finally asked.

"Please don't ask me to say any more."

"The only way I'm going to find him is if you level with me," I said. "I need you to tell me everything you know."

"I am leveling with you. I'm worried about him, that's all. He's my best friend. Ours is a unique bond."

"Oh yeah? How so?"

"Clive prefers the intimacy of men over women."

Her words made my eyes widen. "You mean he's . . ."

I couldn't bring myself to say *homosexual*.

"I let him have his lovers. He lets me have mine. We cherish each other's company. We travel together, we go to the opera and museums and sightseeing. Is that too unconventional for your police detective's mind?"

"If it works for the two of you, who's to say it's wrong?"

She gave me a long and meaningful look, and I stared back, without looking away, or even blinking.

"I feel like I can tell you anything," she said.

And she did. For the next hour or so, she filled me in on all of the details of her life. She grew up in a town called Alderley Edge in the county of Cheshire. She hailed from a well-to-do family. Her father made a fortune in shrewd real estate investments, and held on to his money during the depths of hard times. She attended private schools and did her undergraduate studies at Newnham College of Cambridge University. She met Clive while they were both university students. Peter Insley, who roomed with Clive at Oxford, introduced them to each other. They instantly fell in love, but they did so, in Dot's words, "in a non-sexual way." She talked so much about herself—about her ambitions to become a journalist, her travels around the world, her earlier trips to America (she'd previously visited New York City, Chicago, and Los Angeles), and her constant worrying about Clive's love of fast driving.

She asked questions, hoping I'd reciprocate. In the past, I'd seldom confided in anybody. I wasn't used to it. Early in her mild interrogation, I furnished short answers, reluctant to divulge personal information. Before long, I found myself opening up, sharing tales about growing up in a homestead full of competitive brothers and having a lawman father that commuted by train early each morning north to Salt Lake City. I recounted highlights from my Mormon mission to Los Angeles in 1919, and explained my decision to become a policeman after years of trying to avoid the profession. I refrained from telling her about my father's murder, a defining event of my life. I decided I didn't want her feeling sorry for me. Maybe that was an excuse, a rationalization, to avoid engaging with her about something still so raw, twenty-four years later. In the middle of telling her about my life in the present, I let out a big yawn. I couldn't help it. It was involuntary. Even a longtime insomniac

like me sometimes fell vulnerable to the strong pull of drows-
iness.

"How terrible of me," she said. "Keeping you up so late. I'm
sorry. Perhaps you should take me back to the hotel now."

"Don't apologize," I said. "I'm a night owl. I'd probably be
awake at this hour anyway. By the way, you still haven't told
me . . ."

"Please don't ask me about Clive anymore. OK?"

"Suit yourself. I won't. May I ask about someone else?"

"Who?"

"Do you know a man named Vaughn Perry?"

"I know *of* him. He's an old Oxford pal of Clive's. He came
over from America. This was years ago, in the twenties. I know
he's from around here. I've never met him. Why do you ask?"

"He was seen speaking to Clive last week, at the Old Mill
Club. It's a dine-and-dance establishment down in Cottonwood
Heights."

"I thought we weren't going to discuss Clive."

"I found Perry dead this afternoon—well, yesterday afternoon—in his little shotgun shack up in Emigration Canyon."

"My God," she whispered.

"It was set up to look like a heroin overdose," I said. "I've got
my doubts."

"Are you saying he was murdered?"

"Looks that way to me."

"My God," she repeated. "Who could have done such a
thing?"

"That's what I aim to figure out."

"Could it have anything to do with . . ."

Her lips formed the word "Clive," but sound failed to come
out of her mouth.

"I suspect so. Think about it. Friends at Oxford. One goes missing. One is dead. There's something else."

"What?"

"They were both friends with Rudy Heinrich," I said. "Clive went through his fascist phase, and Vaughn Perry's father is the head of the Platinum Shirts, our own homegrown version of the Nazis, along with the German American Bund. I'm convinced that all of this adds up to more than mere happenstance."

"Are you suggesting Rudy Heinrich had a hand in any of this?"

"I don't know."

"I'd be shocked if he did," she said. "He's a gentle soul. I'm certain he'd never harm anybody, at least not intentionally."

I knuckle-rubbed my burning eyes. "It's getting late. I guess we should go."

"True. Nothing is going to be solved at this ungodly hour."

All at once, Dot shot up to her feet and extended her hand to help me up to mine. I gripped it and I rose from the ground, standing straight, face-to-face with her. The urge to kiss her hit me, and I could detect a similar impulse in her. My heart was in pain from all of the backflips it was doing. If I leaned forward four inches, our lips would've met, making her the only woman other than Clara that I'd ever kissed in my life. Those few seconds when I could've done it lasted an eternity.

The kiss didn't happen. I held back, not out of fear of being caught by Clara or rejected by Dot. My own nagging insecurities about my lovemaking skills had nothing to do with it, either. Nor were lofty religious concerns a factor. I imagined that Heavenly Father faced a host of more pressing matters than whether Art Oveson committed adultery with a beautiful Englishwoman in a remote roadside ditch west of Salt Lake City, Utah.

No, none of those variables came into play. Near enough to Dot Bliss to feel her warmth and inhale her scent, I steeled myself with the reminder that I'd have to look at my reflection in the mirror the next day, and if I made love to her, I'd have to live with what I'd done. I wasn't a cheater. Or that's what I told myself. Had I fallen for an elaborate self-deception, designed to make me feel high and mighty? I don't think so. Self-congratulation was the last thing going through my mind right then.

Perhaps it all boiled down to me being too scared to make a pass at the woman. I'd never been put in this spot before, being the seduced, or the seducer. All my adult life, I'd gone out of my way not to be in that position.

Whatever my reason for not kissing her, I stewed over my decision on the way back to the Hotel Utah, second-guessing myself the entire drive.

Crossing into the city limits, I noticed Dot had dozed off, her chest rising and falling with each breath. The glowing hands on the dashboard clock put the time around 3:00 A.M. as I neared the white tower bathed in colored spotlights. Right then, I remembered that I'd stood up Leni Riefenstahl, that aggressive Nazi documentary filmmaker. I wondered if she'd waited around for me after midnight and got sore at me for not showing up. Like Dot Bliss, the aggressive Riefenstahl did not strike me as the kind of woman that would ever have problems finding a man. That filthy note she wrote amounted to a form of female frankness the likes of which I'd never witnessed. Now it made me chuckle when I thought about it. Late at night, the strangest things could make me break into laughter.

I parked by the curb in front of the Hotel Utah. Dot woke up the instant the car stopped. Some people do that. She sat up straight, rubbed her eyes, and looked around to get reoriented.

She adjusted her hat a little, smoothed her dress, and collected her purse from the center of the seat. Now alert and ready to go, she stared at me hopefully with wide eyes.

"Would you care to come up?" she asked. "I promise I won't bite."

"Thanks, but I have to get to work in the morning."

"Certainly." She suddenly reached over and caressed my cheek. "Thank you."

"For what?"

"You're an oasis in the desert."

She lowered her diminutive hand, and I shot her a warm grin. In a rapid flash of movement, she reached for the handle, got out of the car, closed the door, and darted off in the direction of the Hotel Utah's revolving doors, all of this before I even had a chance to offer to walk her to the elevators.

That fast, Dot Bliss was gone.

Twenty-two

I tiptoed through the dark, closing the bedroom door behind me. I unbuttoned my shirt and removed it. I unbuckled my belt, opened my trousers, and let them drop to the floor. I pried off each shoe with the tip of the opposite foot and stepped out of them. I knew I wasn't going to get much sleep this morning—maybe two hours, tops. When I lowered my hind end slowly onto the edge of the bed, the springs creaked and Clara's heavy breathing ceased. She stirred and I feared the worst.

"Where were you?"

I glanced over my shoulder. "Out."

"Obviously. Where?"

"I was talking to somebody."

"Who?"

"Dorothy Bliss," I said. "She's Clive Underhill's fiancée."

"Bliss? Is that her real last name?"

"I don't know," I said. "I assume so. Why?"

"It sounds like a pseudonym cooked up by a prostitute."

I sighed at the sting of her comment. "I think it's her real name."

"What were you two discussing for so long?"

"Clive's disappearance," I said. "I think she wanted somebody that she felt comfortable talking to."

"You were that person?"

"Yes."

"I'm glad she felt comfortable with my husband."

I ignored her comment. I fell back on the bed. My head sank into the pillow's downy softness. Already I could hear the trill of the first birds at dawn performing their sweet morning song. I didn't bother getting under the covers. I would be awake soon enough. I closed my eyes, but Clara was only getting started. I felt her sitting up in bed. The bedside lamp chain clicked. A glow penetrated my eyelids. I blinked them open and looked up at Clara, hunched and staring down at me.

"What?"

"Were you seeing her?"

I pressed my fingertips firmly into my itchy eyes. "Of course I saw her," I said, opening my eyes again. "That's where I was tonight."

"No. I mean, were you *seeing* her?"

"You mean . . . Was I . . . Did I . . ."

"Yes."

"How can you ask me a thing like that?"

She furrowed her brow. "When was the last time you touched me?"

"I touch you all the time," I said. "Only you always pull away, and make it clear you don't want to be touched."

I sat up in bed, so our faces were level with each other. This conversation was significant enough to warrant sitting up.

"If you're asking, did I make love to her, I think you know the answer."

"Is it so terrible for me for to want to hear you say it?"

"No. I didn't."

She buried her face in her hands. I thought she was going to start crying. She didn't. She simply breathed heavily.

"I wouldn't blame you if you did."

I reached over and touched her shoulder. She moved it away from my hand. The rejection felt like a spear piercing me. I let my hand drop to the bedspread.

"I have a bad feeling," she said. "It's all going to come undone."

"What is?"

"Everything. All we have."

"Why do you think that?"

"I'm sure it's irrational."

"If you feel it, it doesn't matter if it's irrational or not."

She lifted her face out of her hands and turned her forlorn eyes on me.

"You're in trouble," she said. "I know it."

"Why do you say that?"

"You helped Roscoe get away," she said. "It doesn't matter that he came here armed. Nobody's going to believe he'd ever harm you."

"I did what I thought was right. . . ."

"Would you quit saying that?" Clara startled me with the force of her voice. "I don't care if you thought you were right. People think things are right all the time that turn out to be wrong. A man's judgment can be cloudy. Just because you think something's right doesn't make it so!"

"What possible reason would Roscoe have for murdering

Nigel? It makes no sense. He got the money he was owed and then he left. If he murdered Nigel, do you really think he'd go home and sleep it off?"

"You're not looking at it from all the angles, Art. You're so convinced of his innocence that you're blinded to anything that might go against your version of events."

"Like what, for instance?"

"I don't know. The police obviously had enough evidence to arrest him. There must've been eyewitnesses who saw him do something suspicious. You have to start seeing things more clearly. Quit letting your loyalty get in the way. It can drive you to extremes, like thinking that the police and the house detective at the Hotel Utah and whatever witnesses they were able to find are colluding together in some sort of conspiracy to frame Roscoe. Talk about delusional! Why would they want to frame this man for a crime he didn't commit? Because they all hate his guts? Because they're so eager to bust somebody, anybody, that it might as well be him? Oh, I know! It's because he's a rogue, unwilling to play by the rules. Or how about all of the above?"

"OK, OK. Point taken. You can stop."

She lowered her voice: "Or maybe the answer is sitting right under your nose."

I didn't respond to her comment. That was all the prodding she needed.

"How much do you actually know about his past?"

"I know all I need to know."

"That's it? That's all you're going to say?"

"I'm too tired to argue with you. I need some sleep."

My eyelids turned heavy, and exhaustion swept over me like waves of warm water. I slumped limply into bed, closed my eyes, and knitted my fingers together over my chest. Drifting off to slumber, a vision of my father appeared in my mind's eye. I yearned to ask him for his help. Countless times, I'd prayed to him, hoping he would give me a sign from above, yet I'd never felt his presence. Sometimes, I silently wondered whether he was anywhere other than lifeless and under the ground, decomposing in a pine box.

Such questions faded into sleep, at least for a sublime moment.

Then the alarm clock rang. I wanted to pick it up and throw it out the window. I reached over and shut it off.

So much for sleep.

I opened my eyes, and the sign I had prayed for appeared in my mind, as lucid as any thought I've ever had. I got out of bed and turned on my bedside lamp to help me find my clothes. Clara stirred and opened her heavy eyes.

"What time is it?" she asked.

"Go back to sleep," I said.

I didn't even bother showering or shaving that morning. I stumbled into my clothes and buttoned and snapped and buckled my way to being dressed. In the bathroom, I splashed water on my face, brushed my teeth, and managed to maneuver a shot of Mennen talcum powder to each armpit. Clara was in the doorway, blinking at me quizzically.

"What is it?" she asked.

"The answer came to me," I said, excitedly. "I needed to sleep on it."

"What answer?"

I went over to her, leaned in, and kissed her on the lips. I noticed I'd startled her as I pulled away.

"Myron," I said.

I rushed down the hall, slipped on my fedora and suit coat, and went out the door, leaving a baffled Clara behind. I decided

I'd explain it to her later. The clock was ticking, and this case wasn't going to solve itself.

Eager as I was to see Myron, I took a slight detour to stop at Roscoe's place and feed his cats. His cats seemed perfectly content, even though the skittish Captain Jack hid when he saw me. My task completed, I said my farewells, locked up the house, got in my car, and drove south. Before long, I slowed and parked in front of a tree-shrouded bungalow on a residential street in the vicinity of 900 East and 900 South and killed the engine. It was early: quarter past seven. But this could not wait. Or so I told myself as I jogged up the cement walkway and took every other step up to the porch. I knocked at the front door. Myron's wife, Hannah, opened the door. An outgoing, wiry woman with curly black hair, sparkling eyes, and a smile that could light the darkest room, she pushed the screen door outward.

"Hello, Art," she said, genuinely surprised. "Aren't you the early bird?"

"Hi, Hannah," I said. "Good to see you again. I hope I didn't wake you up."

"Oh no, not at all. We're up and at 'em at the crack of dawn. Please . . ."

She opened the screen door and gestured for me to come in.

I walked past her into an entrance hall full of wood paneling and plenty of natural light. She closed the door behind her. The house smelled of delicious aromas, as if an elaborate breakfast were being prepared in the kitchen.

"Arthur!"

"Mama Adler!"

Myron's elderly mother waddled toward me. A short woman, under five feet tall, she wore her unruly hair in a partial bun incapable of containing her explosion of salt-and-pepper frizz. Unlike Hannah, who wore something light and cottony and floral, the elderly matron preferred Old World dresses, long and dark, with sleeves down to the wrists, the kind of thing a lady might wear to Ellis Island thirty or forty years ago. She raised her hands and gripped mine and gave them a good shake, leaning in for a kiss. I bowed and gave her a light kiss on the cheek, and she pulled back with a smile that could warm even the coldest of hearts.

"Arthur, it has been a long time!"

"Yes, it has, hasn't it, Mama?"

"You will join us," she said. "Breakfast is in the dining room."

"Well, I'm sort of in a hurry," I said.

"You are in too much of a hurry to have breakfast? What is the world coming to? You can't just stop by and leave. You hardly come around anymore. Did I do something to upset you, Arthur?"

"Mama," said Hannah, shaking her head in disapproval. "Go easy on Art."

She was still hanging on to my hands, and she gave them another shake, for good measure. "Pfft! This is my number-two son!"

"Well, that's awfully kind of you to say, Mama Adler."

"It is true. Oh, and by the way, thank you for helping Myron with the family genealogy. Each day, I learn something new about my ancestors."

"I can't tell you how happy that makes me feel, Mama Adler."

"What are you doing here?" asked Myron, emerging from the dining room, eating a piece of toast. "My car got fixed. I don't need a ride anymore. Remember?"

"Yeah, I know," I said. "It's about something else."

"Tell him over breakfast," said Mama Adler, releasing my hands. "Have you ever tried *shakshuka*? Come, I will make you a plate, Arthur."

"I might have to take a rain check, Mama," I said.

She shook her head, mouth open. "What is this rain check?"

Myron said something in another language. I think it was Hebrew. Mama responded in the same language. Myron looked at me, eyes half shut and sighing.

"You have to tell her what other day you plan on coming," he said.

"And you must bring your pretty wife," said Mama Adler. "What is her name?"

"Clara."

She tugged her earlobe. "What?"

"Clara," I said louder.

"Saturday you come," she said. "You and Clara try my *shakshuka* then. OK?"

I nodded haltingly. "I'll check with the missus. I think that can be arranged."

I faced Myron and leaned in close to him. "There somewhere we can talk?"

"Front porch," he said, blowing crumbs, thanks to a mouthful of toast.

"See you Saturday morning, Arthur," said Mama Adler, with a little wave. "You and Clara and the rest of your family!"

"So long, Mama Adler," I said, reaching over and giving her shoulder a gentle squeeze. "It's great to see you again."

Myron opened the front and screen doors and headed outside. I went with him. He closed both doors, and we stood in the breezy morning at not quite half past seven, with the towering trees casting long shadows. He pulled up a wooden porch chair for me and sat down on another. Out on the street, a fancy blue Lincoln Zephyr drove past, so clean and waxed that I could see the trees and houses reflected in its door.

"What's so important that it couldn't wait another hour?"

"Remember our trip to the Hotel Utah on Monday morning?" I asked.

"How could I forget? It was less than forty-eight hours ago."

"Something was going on between you and Dooley Metzger. What was it?"

"I don't know what you're talking about."

"C'mon, Myron. Play it straight with me."

"I'm sure it's all in Metzger's personnel file."

"I'd like very much to see that file," I said.

"It's in the records room. Knock yourself out."

I nodded, silently plotting out my next move. "You used to work there."

"That's where I got my start," he said. "What of it?"

"Do you happen to know who's working down there this morning?" I asked.

"Kearney Hoagland," said Myron. "Decent enough fellow."

"Yeah, I know him."

"Why do you ask?"

"I want to see Metzger's personnel file, preferably without anyone knowing about it. If there was some other way I could get my hands on it—"

"Why all the secrecy?"

"I've got this nagging feeling that Metzger is somehow tied to Clive Underhill's disappearance," I said. "Maybe he even had something to do with the murder of Nigel Underhill. I suspect his file will be enlightening."

"You're supposed to review files in the room, unless you sign them out with the attendant on duty."

"I think this situation warrants a slight bending of the rules."

"It seems like you've been doing a lot of that lately," he said.

"I'd rather not involve the desk officer on duty."

"But you're fine with involving me?"

"I don't know where else to turn."

He waited a long moment to reply.

"All right," he said, finally standing up. "Let's get this over with."

Twenty-three

Myron fumbled for his keys in the dim light of the basement. Down here, with a cold draft whistling through the length of the hall, I briefly forgot it was summer outside. A fleeting case of the shivers even hit me. Myron unlocked and opened the door, reached inside, and pressed a light switch. I followed him in. Light fixtures sprouting out of the ceiling bathed the room with a blinding glow, illuminating rows of tall filing cabinets. A long counter, staffed during business hours, kept visitors confined to a waiting area furnished with a couple of battered chairs.

"It'll probably be in the personnel files," he said. "Which are on the west wall. Better make it snappy. You don't have much time. Sometimes he opens up early."

"I don't know my way around here. Would you mind finding it for me?"

"Me?"

"Yeah. You used to work down here. You know the lay of the land. It's all terra incognita for me, I'm afraid."

Myron's cheeks puffed out and he blew air. "I'll regret this later, I'm sure."

I gripped his shoulder and gave him an affectionate squeeze. "Attaboy! I knew I could count on you."

He rounded a corner, heading down between rows of filing cabinets. He was gone for a couple of minutes, and from where I was standing, I could hear the metallic opening and slamming of file drawers. He returned with a green hanging folder containing a cream-colored dossier and passed me the file.

"What you're looking for is in that file," he said. "I hope after this, you'll leave me out of this tangled mess."

Before he was even finished uttering his sentence, he was following me out the door and locking it up behind us.

Upstairs at my desk, I took my hat off, set it down, and opened the file—labeled PERSONNEL–M–METZGER, DESMOND V.—and began skimming. The first several pages detailed the milestones of his employment with the Salt Lake City Police Department.

I flipped pages, past minutiae about fitness exams and promotions and squad transfers and performance ratings. I came to a 1912 photograph of the Salt Lake City Police Department—six rows deep—with my father in front, and Metzger three back on the far right. I continued until I reached a form on faded onionskin paper. INTERNAL INVESTIGATION, read block lettering at the top, and it was dated Tuesday, November 1, 1921. Below that, the report read:

Detectives Wade Carlson & Robert Duncombe investigated suspect D.V. "Dooley" Metzger pertaining to allegations of his involvement in starting a local chapter of the Ku Klux Klan. Assisting them was a Klan informant who goes by the initials M.W.S. Metzger is believed to be a Klaliff (or vice president) of Salt Lake City Klavern, and editor-in-chief and contributor to the group's local newspaper, <u>The Tower Watchers</u>. Dets. Carlson & Duncombe questioned Metzger to determine if above allegations had any basis in fact. During the meeting, Metzger was forthcoming. He admitted his involvement in the secret outfit, and took pride in his role as a leader and an inspirer of his fellow man. He joined over fears of other races, namely Negroes and Mexicans, and what he called "religious undesirables"— particularly Catholics and Jews—living in our midst in ever greater numbers. When asked if he regretted his decision to join the group, Metzger responded: "Why should I?"

The initial investigation report went on for three more pages, mostly detailing the efforts of the two investigators, Carlson and Duncombe, to persuade Metzger to resign his membership from the Ku Klux Klan. Ever the true believer, Metzger refused. He sounded like an ideologue wedded to his own twisted notions of right and wrong.

I skimmed the remainder of the report—full of stilted police writing and typos—and reached a small stash of clippings from the Klan newspaper *The Tower Watcher*. The police identified columnist "Desmond Victory" as really being Dooley Metzger. Metzger admitted he wrote for the paper under a pseudonym, and with his real first name being Desmond and middle name Victor, it wasn't hard to figure out he was Desmond Victory. Most of his pieces were invective-filled diatribes directed against Jews and Negroes and bankers and "city slickers." In one column, he warned the feds were planning to confiscate everybody's firearms and planned to turn people into "slaves, like the damned forced laborers of yore." Reading it, taking it all in, I wondered if this five-and-dime demagogue was the same man I knew as the house detective at the Hotel Utah.

I moved on to a series of police reports—filed between the mid-1920s and early 1930s—that had been flagged for investigation by Carlson and Duncombe. The common thread linking the cases together is that they all involved suspects who'd died in police custody. In each case, the arresting officers were Patrolmen Grady Hedgepeth and Earl Starkey, and the supervisor who signed off on all of the reports as justifiable homicides—committed in the line of self-defense—was none other than Sergeant Dooley Metzger. I flipped and skimmed the opening lines to each report.

WED, MAY 6, 1925: Negro motorist Quentin Coleman, age 45, pulled over for broken taillight. Shot while resisting arrest.

TUE, DEC 13, 1927: Miguel Lopez, Mexican, age n.a., stopped for unknown reasons. Shot while attempting to steal Officer Hedgepeth's firearm.

SAT, APR 28, 1928: Roberto Morales, Mexican, age 38, arrested for vagrancy. Shot while fleeing arrest.

MON, FEB 18, 1929: Isaac Cohen, Jew, 32, arrested for speeding. Got out of car and attempted to strangle Officer Starkey. Shot in self-defense.

TUE, NOV 26, 1929: Arturo Diaz, Mexican, 27, arrested for possession of marijuana. Shot while reaching for a knife to stab Officer Hedgepeth.

Each report told essentially the same story: a colored person or a Mexican or a Jew, pulled over for some routine violation, ended up in the morgue, riddled with bullets, because they somehow resisted arrest. The details chilled me. Some reports included pictures of the deceased. The one that got to me the most was from the scene of an arson fire, where a man named Juan Martinez and his family of seven—a wife and six children—were burned to death in their west side home. The first men on the scene were Hedgepeth and Starkey. Once again, Sergeant Metzger signed off on the report. The fire inspector said someone had broken into the house and poured gasoline all over the main floor and started a fire with a wooden match. Martinez's crime, apparently, was that he owned a successful dry goods store on Redwood Road.

I turned pages, eventually getting past the flagged reports of suspects shot in cold blood by Hedgepeth and Starkey. I reached a document (dated Monday, October 10, 1932) that indicated, in a mercifully succinct manner, that things did not end well for the informant working with Carlson and Duncombe:

> Informant M.W.S.—who we can now reveal to be Morton W. Seegmiller—was found dead two days ago in the front seat of his automobile out by the Burmester Road, south of the Great Salt Lake, the apparent victim of multiple gunshot wounds. His body will be returned to Salt Lake City for burial in the city cemetery. Without his testimony, detectives will not pursue charges against Metzger, although it is the recommendation of these two investigators that Metzger by terminated from his employment at the Salt Lake City Police Department, posthaste.

A discovery I made near the bottom of the file gave me an unexpected jolt. The reason Metzger lost his job on the force back in '33 was because he—along with Patrolmen Hedgepeth and Starkey—assaulted a fellow police officer that used to work in the records division. The victim's name: Myron Adler. They forced him at gunpoint into a car, drove him to an isolated spot outside of the city, and proceeded to beat him so severely he spent three weeks in the hospital recovering. I cringed at the sight of eight-by-ten photos of an unconscious Myron Adler lying in a hospital bed, bruised and swollen beyond recognition, looking almost dead.

The three policemen would've gotten away with their crimes had it not been for the courage of two uniformed traffic cops, Gene Stubbs and Louis Fereday, who overheard Hedgepeth and Starkey discussing the beating at a popular police diner, the Chit-Chat Luncheonette. Stubbs and Fereday signed a statement that sealed the fate of the assailants, who were promptly fired from the SLCPD. This opened the door for legal action and jail time.

I reached for the city directory, opened it to the residential listings, and flipped pages, licking my finger along the way. My first stop was the M's. There were a few Metzgers, but no Desmond, Victor, or Dooley. I turned to the H's. No sign of Hedgepeth in the phone book. I turned to the S's and ran my finger down to the surname "Starkey." There were three of them: Bertram, Lee, and William. No Earl. I closed the directory and slid it aside.

Why hadn't I heard of this case? And why hadn't it caused a public uproar?

I soon found the reason. Myron refused to press charges. Not one of the men served a day behind bars. According to an internal report, the department paid Myron an undisclosed sum of money to not mention the incident to the press. The brass at Public Safety covered up the beatings. No big mystery as to why.

The Salt Lake City Police Department was already plagued by a scandal involving anti-vice officers found to be taking bribes and kickbacks. An avalanche of bad publicity ensued, triggering a wave of mass firings early in the decade. The higher-ups in the force desperately wanted to avoid another public outcry. Flash forward five years: Now Metzger was house detective at the Hotel Utah. Who knows what became of Hedgepeth and Starkey?

"Art."

The voice startled me out of my deep concentration. I swiveled around in my chair. The doorway framed Buddy Hawkins, hat pulled low. I could tell by his clenched jaw he was in a hard and determined way. He moved a few feet into the squad room, nodded at Myron, who stopped typing long enough to glance up at him, and repeated the gesture to DeVoy, presently hunched over his own stack of work. I was so lost in the file that I'd almost fooled myself into thinking I was the only man in Public Safety. I hadn't even noticed DeVoy arriving at work. He usually greeted me with a dour hello and some sort of grim commentary about his various maladies.

My attention shifted back to Buddy, now standing in the center of the office.

"Yes sir?"

"Cowley wants to you see you. Now."

"Yes sir," I repeated.

He left the squad room. I stood up and followed him, sticking to his heels. Myron and DeVoy stared at me as I headed out into the corridor. Buddy's request made my nervous. My mind raced: Why would Cowley possibly want to see me? Was I in some sort of trouble? I pursued Buddy down marble steps, across the lobby, down the central corridor where high-level police officials had their offices. Towering oil paintings of past police chiefs, dating back to the 1850s, adorned the walls. In the anteroom of Cowley's office, his secretary was typing what I guessed was probably another one of the chief's detailed interoffice memos. She glanced up at me as I walked by, and averted her eyes as I looked at her. Did she know something I didn't?

The interior of Cowley's office came into view, and the sight of Pace Newbold seated near a familiar art deco desk made my stomach sink. In my mind, I feared the worst, convinced I was about to be reprimanded. Sitting down, I found Cowley grim faced, elbows on the desk, the fingertips of his hands meeting, as if he'd just finished praying when I walked in. I tugged my khaki pleats upward, dropped into the chair, and kicked my right lower leg over my left knee.

"Hello again, Arthur," said Cowley. "I trust you're well."

"Hello, sir. Never better, as a matter of fact."

His face lit up with a smile, and the crow's-feet on either side of his eyes crinkled. "I'm pleased to hear."

After closing the door, Buddy crossed the room and sat down on the other side of Cowley's desk. The chief of police tilted his head in Buddy's direction, and waited for his subordinate to get comfortable. I caught Pace's gaze, but he looked away, and I scanned the room, speculating in silence as to what on earth I was doing here.

"Feel free to break the news, Charles," Cowley said.

"What news?" asked Pace.

"You're both off the Underhill case," said Buddy. "The feds are running it now."

"I got off the telephone with your brother a short time ago," said Cowley, staring at me. "He gave us direct orders to halt all investigations having to do with Clive's disappearance and Nigel's murder. That means both of you will have to stop what you're doing, and move on to other cases."

"Was there a reason given?" I asked.

"Your brother didn't say, but the Bureau is being territorial with this one," said Buddy. "And with a big shot like Clive Underhill, the feds are going to jump into this thing right away. There's a lot at stake here."

Buddy paused as if debating in his mind whether to say what he was about to say. Then he said it. "Rumors abound. There's talk of an abduction, and I've even heard that J. Edgar Hoover has taken a personal interest in the case, and that he secretly flew in last night to oversee the investigation. Apparently, he's a hands-on kind of fellow."

Cowley chimed in: "I promised your brother you'd both surrender all of your investigation notes, and that you'd fully cooperate with the Bureau men."

Cowley eyed Buddy, his way of handing it back to his subordinate. "If either of you harbor any funny notions about continuing your investigations, you'll be fired for interfering with the Federal Kidnaping Act of 1932. Understand?"

"Yes, sir."

"Yes, sir."

"Good. I'm glad you gentlemen comprehend the gravity of this matter," said Cowley. "Please don't test it. I'd hate to lose you."

"Yes, sir."

"Yes, sir."

Cowley gave a single nod. "Dismissed."

Pace and I stood up and filed silently out of the room. I pulled the door closed. We passed through the anteroom, walked out into the corridor, down to the lobby, and I gave him an opportunity to stop and get a drink from a nearby porcelain water fountain. He got his fill, straightened, and wiped droplets off his chin. His angry, furrowed-brow glance and narrowing eyes seemed to ask: *What do you want?*

"Doesn't it strike you as odd," I said, "that they plucked us right off this case, rather than—"

"You know what strikes me as odd?" Pace asked, cutting me off. "That you're such a goddamned pest, Oveson. You're unrelenting."

"What about that stiff they found up Emigration Canyon the other night?" I asked.

Pace looked at me like I'd lost my mind. "Are you talking about the stupid bastard that overdosed on smack?"

"Well, that's just it," I said. "I think it was a homicide made to look like an O.D. He's Vaughn Perry, son of Newton Perry, Führer of the Platinum Legion. There's an active chapter of it here in Utah. I'm certain the younger Perry's death is linked to all of this, but I can't be sure how."

"Christ, you've lost your marbles, Oveson," said Pace. "I saw the coroner's report. The fucking fool shot up pure-grade heroin, and now he's lying in the morgue. If you ask me, I'd say natural selection is doing its job. Now if you'll excuse me, I'd like to quit listening to you and actually go do my job."

Pace stormed up the stairs to the detective bureau. I gave him a head start before I ambled up to the morgue on the third floor, where my old friend Tom Livsey sat at his desk filling out paperwork. His thinning hair had gone prematurely silver, and his long, Lincoln-esque face exuded honesty. When I arrived at his cramped office, he was eating an apple cinnamon sweet roll and drinking a glass of milk. He brushed off his right hand before shaking mine.

"How's every little thing, Tom?"

"Can't complain, Art. You?"

"I have my good days and my bad."

"Don't we all? What can I do you for?"

"Vaughn Perry. What can you tell me?"

He inhaled deeply through his nose and considered his response. "He overdosed. Body found on Tuesday in a house up Emigration Canyon."

"Mind if I have a look?"

"No, not at all."

Tom finished off his roll, then got up and led me next door to the vast lab room where everything echoed, bleach fumes stung the eyes and nose, and sterilized tables reflected lights above. We went over to the rows of refrigerator drawers on the walls, and Tom pulled one of them—number eight—open, folding back the sheet on the occupant.

Vaughn Perry's appearance had turned waxy since I saw him last. Discoloration had set in. When I found him in his bed, he looked so alive that I thought he might open his eyes at any moment. Now he was deeply immersed in death, with sagging skin, no more facial definition, and lips beginning to curl, creating a strange smile.

"Why the interest?"

I looked at Tom. "I'd rather not say."

He smiled as he pulled the linen sheet back up over the dead man and walked the drawer closed. "Playing your cards close to your chest, huh?"

"On this one, yeah," I said. "In the words of the late, great Calvin Coolidge: 'I have noticed that nothing I never said ever did me any harm.'"

Livsey laughed as he fastened the refrigerator drawer shut. He gave me a friendly pat on the shoulder and started back toward his office. I followed him out the door of the lab and pulled it closed behind me.

"That's what I like about you, Art," he said, standing in the doorway. "Always the careful one."

Twenty-four

"Were you going to tell me?"

Myron lowered his pen and peered over his shoulder at me, blinking a couple of times, as if waiting for me to say something else. DeVoy was talking softly on the telephone, having a conversation with a police detective in Ogden about a missing woman. Crossing the room to sit down at my desk, I opted for silence, leaving the ball in his court.

"Tell you what?"

"About the beating you took?"

He shifted his focus back to his paperwork. "It's none of your business."

"Why didn't you press charges?"

"Also none of your business."

"So you let the anti-Semites win? Is that it?"

"It's not that simple."

"These men beat you within an inch of your life, and they're out there walking free."

"There are other ways of fighting back."

"Oh yeah? How?"

Now he turned his swivel chair toward me.

"By working harder. Doing a better job than everybody else,"
he said. "They're gone. I'm here. That's good enough for me."

"They ought to be in prison."

"Good luck putting them there."

"I could use your help, Myron."

"Count me out."

"Why? Don't you want to see them behind bars?"

"It didn't happen to you. Why are you so up in arms?"

"They can't get away with it," I said. "They have to face the
consequences."

"Did you ever hear of something called the Nuremberg Race
Laws?"

"No."

"They were passed in Germany, to strip Jews of their citizen-
ship and rights," he said. "The Nazis are cracking down on my
people, stealing their property, herding them into open-air prisons. Bad things are going on over there."

"What's your point?" I asked, tucking the photographs away
in the envelope.

"The men that beat me up were fired. Over there, they'd be
promoted for it. That's the difference. I have no plans to rock a
boat that doesn't need rocking. It's easy to stick your neck out
when it's never been on the chopping block."

I shook my head. "Suit yourself. These thugs will probably
just go do it again—harm some someone else, based on the color
of their skin or their religious beliefs."

"Detective Oveson?"

I turned around. The voice belonged to a young blond fellow,

mid to late twenties, standing in the doorway. He came immac-
ulately dressed in a pinstripe suit with a matching vest, and his
red-and-yellow silk tie brought out the blue in his coat.

"Yes?"

"Wallace Fitch, Federal Bureau of Investigation. I'd like to
have some of your time, if I may."

"Of course."

"Would you follow me, please?"

"Sure."

Even though my head was still back in my troubling conversation with Myron, I followed the G-man out of the office, trotting
down the stairs, to a basement interrogation room. He closed the
door behind us, and we took our seats on opposite sides of the
table. The man was thorough. He kept me in there for about two
hours, asking question after question. I walked him through everything, going all the way back to Saturday, when I saved Clive
Underhill's life from the fiery wreckage of his vehicle. During
the course of the long session, I made repeated efforts to try to
pry information out of him about what the feds planned to do.
He was not particularly forthcoming, although he did let it slip
out that a small army of agents was combing the Canyons of the
Escalante at that very moment, searching for Underhill. He was
courteous to a fault, even allowing me to go to the restroom
halfway through our powwow.

It was nearing the lunch hour when I returned to the Bureau
of Missing Persons. The office was empty. I noticed those gruesome photos of Myron in the hospital were gone. I opened a filing drawer full of dossiers containing unsolved cases. I fished
out a stack of seven or eight and went to work. An oscillating
fan on a nearby table whirred back and forth, blowing warm
fresh air coming in through the open windows. I opened the file

on top. A familiar green sheet greeted me, and my eyes dropped down to the main stats.

MISSING/UNIDENTIFIED PERSON REPORT
LAST NAME: FOSTER
FIRST NAME: GWENDOLYN
DATE OF BIRTH: 5/14/1893
ADDRESS: 1879 South 900 East, Salt Lake City
DATE OF DISAPPEARANCE: Monday, 2/10/1936
AGE AT TIME OF DISAPPEARANCE: 42

I examined her picture. The family had furnished a sepia-toned snapshot with creases and stains. I picked it up to get a better look at her sunken eyes, pug nose, slight overbite, and flowing, curly black hair. February 10, 1936. Almost two and a half years ago, I thought. Where have you gone? Why haven't we found you yet? What's the point of looking anymore?

I returned her picture to her file, closed it, and set it atop the formidable stack before me. Each cream-colored dossier represented someone who'd disappeared, probably never to be found. I went through one after the other, and their pictures blended together in my mind. Leafing through those files, I thought of Melvin Thompson, the mechanic who went missing en route to the cigar store three years ago, and a wave of despair swept over me. How could it be—in this modern industrial day and age of airplanes and telephones, automobiles and electricity—that a man or a woman could vanish into thin air, never to be seen or heard from again? God only knew. I sure didn't.

Sometime around one o'clock, Myron returned, followed minutes later by DeVoy. Before long, the latter put one of his operas on the phonograph and kept the volume turned low, so as not to incur the wrath of our neighbors in the Homicide or Morals squads down the hall. I couldn't concentrate with that racket, and with him blabbering incessantly. It soon dawned on me that he was talking to me.

"I'm particularly partial to Wagner's *Tristan and Isolde,* although I'm not too pleased with the maestro's decision to exclude *Liebestod* from Act 3. Oh well. Who am I to grouse? In my humble opinion, Stokowski makes up for that shortcoming with a sublime version of *Liebesnacht* in the second act. The 'Love Music' never sounded so absolutely magical. Riveting, absolutely riveting."

DeVoy finally quieted down long enough to look over at me. "What do you think of him?"

His words rattled me out of my sweaty trance. "Who?"

"Wagner," he said. "Weren't you listening?"

"Yeah, I was listening," I said, closing the dossier. "I just wasn't sure if you meant Wagner or the Leopold guy, that's all."

"Maestro Stokowski?" he asked, with an edge of contempt. "I'm sure he'd take exception to being called *the Leopold guy.*"

"I haven't listened to much Wagner, I'm afraid," I said.

"No shock there," said DeVoy, loosening his crooked bow tie.

I nodded. "If it's not on *Kraft Music Hall* or *Kay Kyser's Kollege of Musical Knowledge,* I probably haven't heard it."

"I'd say that makes you a philistine of the first order," said DeVoy with a snort. "*Kay Kyser's Kollege of Musical Knowledge.* Lord, what is the world coming to? We live in an age of mindless conformity."

I rolled my eyes and sighed. Once again, DeVoy had managed to depress me. This was becoming an occupational hazard thanks to him.

I put on my hat and my coat and wandered out into the heat of the afternoon, carrying a spiral notebook with information

I'd jotted after going through those files. I decided I was going to update all of these files after spending so many days away from them. I spent a few hours going from door to door, talking to the friends and loved ones and relatives of missing persons. I asked if they'd heard anything, if they had any news for me. I scribbled notes as fast as I could. My right hand developed a writing cramp. Their words, like the faces of the missing, began to blend together in my head.

Midafternoon rolled around, and I stuck my spiral notebook in the glove compartment, and drove over to the nearby Crystal Palace Market at 100 South and 300 East to buy groceries. I stocked up on the essentials: flour, eggs, milk, bread, apples, oranges, a jar of peanuts, and—just to liven things up a little—a box of candy. I feared it would melt during the drive, but I bought it anyway. I walked out of the store carrying a big brown bag full of groceries, which I loaded onto the passenger-side floor of my sweltering auto, and then I made my way over to visit an old friend.

Gail Thompson still lived at the Shubrick Apartments, 72 West 400 South, the same place she'd lived when her husband, Melvin, had disappeared back in 1935. I rang the buzzer below her metal wall mailbox in the entrance hall, and she appeared at the top of the staircase a moment later. Her face lit up with a smile when she saw me.

"Come on up, Art!"

"Thanks, Gail."

Inside of her cramped, hot place, she expressed her gratitude for the groceries—she was almost on the verge of tears when she accepted them in her open arms—and told me how much she appreciated the box of chocolates in particular, which, thankfully, had melted only a little on the ride over here.

She took me to meet her new parrot, named Ray (her previous

one had died), and reintroduced me to her cockatiels and zebra finches, and pointed to two new additions in a cage dangling above her radio, a pair of budgies, one blue-and-white, the other green-and-yellow. Moments later, we were sitting out on the front stoop. She was smoking and I was drinking a glass of ice water, which, at one point, I pressed against my sweating brow to cool off. I noticed, while I was sitting on the hard concrete step, that Gail had aged quite a bit since I'd seen her last. The wrinkles cut deeper into her narrow face, and her hair was rapidly whitening. She preferred to hang her head, bending her neck, thus making her appear even older.

"It's been three years and almost four months since Mel—" She bit her lower lip, and then took a drag off her cigarette. "It used to be that whenever I'd hear someone walking out in the hallway in the building, I'd turn down the radio and run to the front door," she said, blowing smoke. "But it'd never be him. That's the thing, it was never him."

I drank my water and listened.

After a long pause, she continued: "When April eighteenth rolled around this year, I told myself I wasn't going to keep listening for him anymore. I still have the birds. They're like my kids, really. They keep me in line. Mel and I never had any interest in having children. There are times when I regret the choices we made, but that's my bed, and I've got to sleep in it. I'm too old now to do anything about it." She reached down and stubbed out her cigarette in a clay pot full of sand sitting on one of the steps. "Speaking of which, do you have any new pictures of your little ones?"

"I sure do," I said, pulling out my wallet.

I passed it to her and she looked at the school snapshots with envious eyes.

"They grow up so fast," I said.

"They certainly do. My goodness, is this Sarah Jane?"

"Yeah. She's fifteen now, believe it or not."

"She's beautiful. Looks like her mother."

I smiled. "Thank you. She carries the weight of the world on her shoulders."

"She's like her father that way." Gail flipped to the next pictures. "Look at the three of them. They're adorable. How old is Emily now?"

"Four," I said. "And she's as feisty as they come."

Gail laughed, and then she shook her head. "Where does the time go?"

"I don't know."

She closed the wallet and handed it to me, and I stuffed it in my pocket.

"Thank you, Art," she said. "You're one in a million."

I shrugged and drank ice water. "I'm glad to see you're doing OK, Gail. You look fine, you really do, and the birds seem completely happy."

"Those are *my* babies," she said, echoing her words from a moment ago, this time with a throaty laugh. "I cherish their company."

"I'm sure you do."

For a long moment, the two of us sat on the steps, watching cars whiz by on 400 South. I checked my wristwatch. I didn't realize I'd been there so long. It was past five. Time to go home.

"I know you have to leave," she said. "Thank you for coming, and for the groceries. You shouldn't have. But I'm glad you did."

We both stood up at the same time, and I held my hand out awkwardly and she took it in hers and gave it an affectionate little shake.

"It's good to see you again, Gail," I said. "If you ever need anything, you know where to reach me."

She nodded, and her smile faded, and she stared deeply into my eyes. "He's not coming back, is he?"

"You know what I always say. It's best to be hopeful. Optimism is the key to—"

"Art?"

"Yeah?"

"He's not coming back." She swallowed hard and held back the tears. "Is he?"

Paralysis gripped me momentarily as I looked at her.

"Probably not," I finally said.

"Thank you," she whispered. She leaned in and kissed me lightly on the cheek, like the flit from a butterfly's wing, then stepped back. "Don't be a stranger. Bring Myron with you next time. I'll introduce him to Ray."

"I will. He'd like that."

"So long, Art."

"I'll see you again soon, Gail."

I crossed the street to my car, parked under the shade of a tree, and got in. I waved to Gail as I started the engine. She gave a little wave back. Then I steered away from the curb, waited for a streetcar to pass me before I accelerated, and I headed for home.

Twenty-five

My first jolt the next morning came when I spotted all of those federal agents—there must have been half a dozen of them, maybe more—camped out at Roscoe's house in the Marmalade District. Four enormous black government Ford Standard Fordor sedans were parked in the cul-de-sac, all gleaming in the sunlight. The men strutted about in stiff suits and dark fedoras, all beady eyes and lantern jaws, cold as the iceberg that sank the Titanic.

They evil-eyed me with open mouths and furrowed brows—clearly not pleased by my presence—as I walked up the porch steps to enter the house so I could feed Roscoe's cats. I was two feet inside of the house when one of them came up behind me, throwing the screen door open, gripping my right wrist, and shoving me against the frame of the door opening up to Roscoe's living room. Out the corner of my eye, I saw one of the cats dart past us and run out the front door.

"Hey, don't let her out!" I shouted, with my face pressed into the wall. "They're not supposed to go outside!"

Cold metal of handcuffs clicked tightly around my wrist. Seconds later, my fingertips began to go numb from lack of circulation.

"Roscoe Lund, you're under arrest for violating the Federal Kidnapping Act of 1932, and for the murder of Nigel Underhill at the Hotel Utah on—"

"I'm not Roscoe Lund!"

"Check his I.D.," said a nearby voice.

I felt my billfold being fished out of my trouser pocket. Whispers hissed behind my back. A moment later, the G-man loosened his grip on me. "Police dick. Got the same last name as the boss," said the agent who checked my badge and identification. "Let him go."

The handcuffs clicked and loosened. Feeling returned to the ends of my fingers as I jerked my hands loose and faced the feds. One of them tossed me my wallet. I fumbled for it and nearly dropped it.

"You let his cat out," I said, gazing into the brightness beyond the screen door. "She wasn't supposed to go outside."

A Bureau man with a deep dimple in his chin shrugged and smiled crookedly. "He can always file a complaint with Director Hoover."

A redheaded fed with big pink ears laughed stupidly, which seemed to make the spray of freckles on his cheeks and nose light up. "I say let the coyotes have at her. They gotta eat, too, ya know."

"What're you doing here, anyhow?" asked Dimple. "We got orders to bring in a sack-of-shit murderer, and that's exactly what we aim to do, and we don't particularly care to have any local yokel hayseeds getting in our way."

"I'm responsible for my friend's cats while he's gone," I said, pocketing my wallet. "I'm here to feed them. Now you've let Millicent outside. She's not an outdoor cat."

Dimple approached me menacingly, with clenched fists. "Do I look like I give a shit about his fucking cat?"

Before I could answer, the redhead with the enormous ears asked: "Where is he, Detective?"

"I don't know. And if I did, I wouldn't tell you."

"A wise guy, huh?" grunted Dimple, clearly ready for ye olde fisticuffs. "Maybe you'd like to step outside and discuss this in greater detail. Police dick."

I walked past the two men, pushing my palms against the screen door mesh. A second later, I stood out on the porch, with more of these stiff, interchangeable fellows aiming their steely gazes my way. I'd had enough of these fresh-out-of-the-academy lads and their appalling arrogance. Years of law enforcement experience taught me that the longer you could keep the FBI out of an investigation, the better off everybody would be. They had a way of fouling everything up.

I searched for Millicent. I explored weed-choked lots. I wandered into side yards. I checked up trees and utility poles. No sign of her anywhere. I'd have to come back later and seek her out again, hopefully without all of these G-men lurking. I returned to Roscoe's house to feed Barney and Captain Jack, and on my way out to my car afterward, I drew the nasty stares of the Bureau boys.

I climbed into my car and drove away. I felt so eager to escape from that dusty little nook at the base of the hill. Clearly, these FBI agents were determined to capture Roscoe and incapable of examining this case from all the angles. Somebody higher up on the totem pole—most likely my brother—had issued orders to bring my friend in dead or alive. At this point, even I was beginning to have my doubts about Roscoe. Estelle McKenna's words still echoed in my mind: "I saw the big fellow wrap something—a wire or a cord or some twine—around Underhill's neck and force him back into his hotel room." It didn't look good for Roscoe. But the man I'd known so well, and had worked with so closely for years, couldn't have done the things that McKenna attributed to him. He was my friend, and I was loyal, and I wasn't prepared to give up, despite my uncertainty.

I feared for Roscoe's safety. I still had vivid memories of the Bureau's crackdown on crime four years ago, in which my brother played a key part. The names remained vividly emblazoned in my mind from all of the newspaper and newsreel and radio coverage: Bonnie and Clyde; John Dillinger; Baby Face Nelson; Pretty Boy Floyd. What chance would an ex-cop-turned-private-detective like Roscoe Lund have of evading them? *Slim to none,* I'd guess. I had to find him before they did. But where had he gone? Where would I even begin to look?

My second jolt of the morning came when I entered the lobby of Public Safety and got swarmed by press hounds. I'd been carrying a pink box of bakery goods that I'd picked up at Beau Brummel on the way over here—treats for my men—that I nearly dropped on the ground due to shock. I tried to remain calm and collected as I made my way across the staircase. Not only did I encounter the usual suspects, namely the ever-pesky Amelia Van Cott and her gangly photographer sidekick, Ephraim Nielsen, but I noticed all manner of reporters representing national newspapers, as well as wire service fellas in fedoras with PRESS tags in their hat bands. Flashes started to burst, burning into my retinas as I closed my eyes in a futile attempt to blink out the big white dots. The pen-and paper-wielding journalists began coming at me like a school of piranhas devouring a poor wayward cow. At the head of the pack, Amelia Van Cott attempted to move in for the kill.

"What's your response to the big announcement this morning?" she asked.

"What big announcement?" I asked, spying her in my peripheral vision.

"Your brother didn't tell you about the press conference?"

I halted and faced her. She stopped and turned to me.

"What press conference?"

"This morning, about a half hour ago," she said. "Frank Oveson read a statement at the capitol rotunda. Then he left. He refused to take questions."

"What did he say?"

"Didn't he tell you?"

"No."

"Oh." She looked over her shoulders at the crowd of reporters behind her, all of them silent and listening intently to my every word. Her eyes met mine and she said, "Well, this is a little embarrassing."

"C'mon, Amelia," I said. "Out with it."

She cleared her throat meekly. Eyelashes fluttered. "He said Clive Underhill is missing. The Bureau suspects abduction, and it's focusing its search on a lone kidnapper: your former partner, Roscoe Lund. That's what your brother said."

I nodded. "I see."

"So how about it?" she asked. "Any comment?"

"No."

A reporter called out, "Can you address rumors that Nigel Underhill was found dead in his hotel room? Police are refusing to confirm or deny."

"I have nothing to say," I told the reporters, to the sound of pencils scratching against spiral pads. "If you'll excuse me."

I rushed up the stairs, deeply shaken and trying to ignore the questions being shouted out to me from below. Lucky for me, Public Safety regulations stated the press could only question police from near the building's front and rear entrances, or if there was a large enough group of journalists, they would be given access to the lobby by a supervising officer. Despite the pressroom being located on the second floor, reporters were not allowed to question detectives in any of the nearby offices without the prior written or verbal consent of the interviewee.

Doing my best to chase away thoughts of the belligerent press, I entered the Bureau of Missing Persons office to find a Negro couple—an older man and woman, likely in their fifties or sixties—being questioned by DeVoy. They were dressed formally, as if they'd just gotten out of church, and the woman's velvety hat had a net that went down over her face. DeVoy sat a few feet away from her, attempting to record her every word with a pencil and notepad.

I sneaked a better look at the couple. She was on the plump side, he was lean, but they both wore solemn expressions, and their eyes glimmered with dignity. His hair had gone salt-and-pepper, and lines were etched deeply into his face, like tiny trenches. Her coiffure was as black as the darkest night, and I could tell from her swollen eyes—which she dabbed from time to time with a hanky—that she had been weeping. As the man talked about his son in a hushed voice; they both glanced at me, then shifted their focus back to DeVoy, still scribbling furiously to keep up with them.

DeVoy raised his head and gestured to me. "This is my supervisor, Detective Arthur Oveson. Perhaps I should turn it over to him." He shot me a pleading glance. "Sir, this is Mr. and Mrs. Leon Booker."

"I'm Maybelle," the woman said under her breath. I nodded a greeting to them.

DeVoy continued: "They reside here in Salt Lake City. They say their son . . ." He checked his notes quickly. "Antoine Winston Booker"—he looked up from his scribbles—"has been missing since his shift ended at the Hotel Utah on Tuesday night."

"It isn't like him to vanish like this," said Mr. Booker. "He was supposed to play with his musical troupe last night."

"The King Rufus Hi-Hat Harmonica Quartet," I said.

"Have you heard of them?" asked Maybelle Booker, clearly surprised.

"Yeah," I said. "I met your son on Tuesday, at the Hotel Utah."

Their eyes widened with hope. "You saw him the day he went missing?" asked Leon Booker.

DeVoy rolled his wheeled chair backward, waving toward the couple, as if inviting me to join in. "You really should be the one talking to them. Not me."

I passed the pink box of pastries in my hands to Myron, then slid up a chair and sat down. "Would either of you care for a Danish?"

"No thank you."

"No, that's mighty kind of you, though."

I maneuvered my chair closer and scooped up a spiral

notepad and a pencil from my desk. I flashed the couple a reassuring smile. They returned the gesture, but only briefly.

"Where does your son reside?" I asked. "Let's start there."

"He lives with us," said Leon. "Our house is at seven fifty-two Roberta Street. Little side street, 'twixt Second and Third East, and Seventh and Eighth South."

I was jotting all this down. I nodded and looked up at them. "When was the last time you saw him?"

"Tuesday morning," said Maybelle. "Before he left for work. He ate a big breakfast, and he looked so fancy in his hotel uniform."

"Did he say if he was going anywhere after work?" I asked.

"He was supposed to play with the quartet down at the Old Mill Club, but he didn't show up," said Leon. "It isn't like him to miss a performance."

"This isn't much to go on," I said. "Is there anything else you could possibly tell me? Has he been morose lately, or has he had any troubles of any sort?"

"Nothing like that," said Leon. "But there was something else—"

Maybelle gripped his arm, "Do you think it's wise, telling the police?"

Leon turned in his chair toward his wife. "They ought to know, dear. It'll help."

"Yes, anything might help," I said. "Please tell me everything you can."

Maybelle's eyes, full of fear, met mine. "I don't know if it's right to tell you."

"My number-one priority is to find your son," I said. "Every little thing helps."

"Winston was working the early morning shift on Sunday at

the Hotel Utah," Maybelle said. "He came home that morning worried about something or other, but he wouldn't say what it was."

"He didn't give you any hints?" I asked.

"He wasn't himself, Detective Oveson," said Leon. "He started crying at one point, and he made a run for the bathroom and I could hear him throwing up. After he was through in there, I asked him what was wrong, but he wouldn't say. We could tell our son was mighty distressed about something."

"I ain't never seen him that way," said Maybelle. "Something was eating away at our boy, and I don't have the foggiest notion as to what it might've been."

"Did he mention a fella named Metzger?" I asked. "Dooley Metzger? That name ring any bells?"

They looked at each other. She nodded at him. Then he addressed me.

"We knew Metzger from the times we picked our son up at work. We were never partial to him. Something about him wasn't right. A few months ago, I went to the Hotel Utah to pick up our son. I waited out back for him, behind the hotel, by the loading platform, minding my own business. But Metzger saw me out there and he come up and told me to leave. He said, loudly, there weren't no *niggers* allowed. I says, 'Even back here?' And he says, 'Yeah, they ain't even allowed back here. Now go on, get, before I let you have it!' That's the word he used. *Niggers.* He had his service revolver poking out of his jacket in plain sight. He was fixing to use it. That's what I thought, anyhow, at the time."

"Maybe I need to pay a visit to the Hotel Utah and talk to Mr. Metzger," I said. "Find out what he knows."

"Here, Detective Oveson . . ." Maybelle reached in her purse, pulled out a five-by-seven photograph, and passed it to me. It was a close up of Winston Booker, a smile on his face and holding up his harmonica. "It was taken in October of '36, right before he joined up with the quartet."

I held the picture up closer, to get a good look. His eyes glimmered with hope, the way they did when I met him.

"Please find our son," said Leon, his lower lip quivering. He was on the verge of tears. Maybelle, convulsing with sobs, fished a handkerchief out of her purse and dabbed her eyes. Leon wrapped his arm around her shoulder and patted her lovingly, all the while keeping his eyes on me. "He's a fine young man, Detective Oveson, and we've been plenty worried about him."

"I'll do my best," I said. I turned the picture toward them. "May I?"

"Please do," said Maybelle. "We'd like it back when you're done."

"Sure."

The parents spent another ten minutes filling me on details about their son, such as when his Tuesday shift was supposed to end (6:00 P.M.), and that the desk attendants at the hotel did not see him punch out the time clock or leave the building. After they were finished, we said our good-byes, and I promised them I'd update them as soon as I found out anything. DeVoy led them downstairs, taking them to the rear exit of Public Safety. I stared at the picture of Winston "Blue" Booker for a long time. Knowing Metzger's history of violence when he was a policeman, I feared the worst for the young man. Myron and I stayed silent for a long while, and we were soon joined by DeVoy again, who returned to his desk and resumed working.

"Got any guesses as to what happened to him?" Myron finally asked.

"I don't know." I reached for my hat. "But I'm going to try to find out."

DeVoy lowered his pen and turned in his chair to observe the discussion.

"What have you got in mind?" asked Myron.

"A return trip to the Hotel Utah," I said. "Care to join me?"

DeVoy Beckstead suddenly lit up: "Hey, mind if I tag along? I'm going stir crazy in here."

I was still staring at Myron. He closed his eyes and offered a solemn nod.

"Make it snappy," I said, rising from my chair. "We haven't got all day."

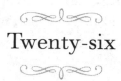

Twenty-six

By the time DeVoy Beckstead and I arrived at the Hotel Utah in the late morning, I was starting to feel like I was spending too much time there. Once again, the same colorful banner high above greeted me:

SALT LAKE CITY WELCOMES THE FOURTEENTH ANNUAL
NORTH AMERICAN RADIO SELLERS' CONVENTION.

Today, however, the crowds had thinned out to a dedicated few convention-goers milling about on the last day of the event, sitting on chairs and couches, smoking and chin-wagging about the latest models for 1939. With DeVoy behind me, I headed past potted palms and the barred windows for Western Union and various ticket agents: Union Pacific, Denver & Rio Grande Western, and United Airlines; past Jorgensen's Floral Shop and the bustling Lafayette Ballroom, where diners feasted on a ritzy breakfast buffet.

In the center of the lobby, a pair of teenage newsies hawked newspapers: "Extra! Extra! Read all about it! Famous English motorist Clive Underhill is missing!" "Don't miss the afternoon edition of the *Examiner*! Learn the details of world-famous English racer Clive Underhill disappearing!"

I leaned near DeVoy. "Let me do the talking."

"Yes, sir," he said.

"May I help you, sir?" asked a desk clerk I hadn't seen before.

"Yes, please," I said, producing my badge. "Detective Art Oveson, Salt Lake City Police. This is Detective DeVoy Beckstead."

DeVoy held up his badge as well.

"What's your name?" I asked.

"Nils Thornton," he said. "Assistant manager."

"Good to know you, Thornton. I was wondering if I could ask you about an employee of yours who's gone missing."

"Are you talking about Mr. Booker?"

"Yes, indeed."

"He's never missed a day of work in the two years he's been here. His parents dropped by here this morning looking for him. I told them I had no idea when he finished. I checked his time card. He did not punch out at the end of his shift."

"Were you working at the time his shift ended?" asked DeVoy.

"Yes," said Thornton.

"But you didn't see him actually leave the building?" asked DeVoy.

"No. At six o'clock, the Lafayette was packed, and there were a hundred or more out in the lobby."

"What about the rear entrance of the hotel?" I asked.

"What about it?"

"I'm assuming there would've been a lot of folks around there as well?" I said.

"The whole ground level was packed that time of the evening," he said.

"I see. It'd help if I could talk to Mr. Metzger," I said.

"He's no longer in our employ."

"Oh? When did he quit?"

"He failed to show up yesterday, and today, as well. I tried to reach him by telephone, but to no avail. Our night watchman, Owen Nebecker, has been promoted to head detective."

"May I speak to him?" I asked.

"Certainly. I'll ring him."

Thornton lifted a telephone. "Mr. Nebecker's office, please. Yes, I'll hold." Several seconds passed. Then: "Mr. Nebecker, this is Thornton at the front desk. Some police detectives wish to speak to you." Pause. "Thank you. I'll let them know."

Thornton hung up and smiled. "He'll be right here."

"Thank you," I said.

Behind my back, the newsies were unrelenting.

"One nickel buys you all the news you need to know! Paper, mister?"

I turned face-to-face with a kid, who couldn't have been more than thirteen, wearing a plaid newsboy cap. He held up the front page: FBI AGENTS COMB STATE FOR MISSING BRITISH RACER.

My eyes dropped to a smaller—yet still sizable—headline halfway down: EX-POLICEMAN NUMBER-ONE SUSPECT IN FED KIDNAPPING PROBE.

"Paper, mister? Only one nickel."

I reached in my pocket, scooped out a handful of coins, and dropped a dime in his hand.

"Keep the change."

"Gee, thanks, mister!"

He handed me a paper, then went back to his preferred spot to resume peddling. A photo splashed across page A-1 showed Clive Underhill's futuristic car roaring across the Flats on Saturday, before it overturned. A smaller image inserted above the car showed Underhill himself in happier days, complete with his leather helmet and his thick goggles perched atop his head.

"The phone has been ringing off the hook," Thornton said.

I looked up at him. "Come again?"

"Our switchboard has been buzzing all morning with calls about Mr. Underhill, ever since the FBI announced he's missing."

"What sort of calls?" asked DeVoy.

"The press, mostly," said Thornton. "They call constantly, hoping for updates, which of course we don't have, because we've no idea what's happening."

I nodded, holding up the newspaper. "One of the stories here suggests that Underhill may've been kidnapped."

"I'm under strict instructions not to publicly discuss either of the Underhills," he said. "I don't wish to add to the churning rumor mill. Reckless talk of abductions and murder can only undermine this establishment's fine reputation."

"Of course, I get it," I said. Right as I said that, I suddenly remembered Blue Booker telling me about delivering some pillows to room 710 in the wee hours of Sunday morning. "By the way, can you tell me if someone was staying in room seven-ten on Saturday night?"

He rotated the large guest book so he could read it, and he ran his finger down a series of lined columns, filled in with neat penmanship. His finger stopped, he made a long face, and looked up at me. "Mr. A. J. Randolph, manager of station WTAM,

Cleveland, Ohio, stayed there. Didn't leave any contact information. It lists his hometown as Cleveland Heights."

"I see," I said. "What about that couple from Canada—Claude and Grace McKenna? Are they still staying in the room seven-oh-four? I'd like to talk to them again, if I could."

He checked and shook he head as he looked up at me. "Nobody by that name staying there. The guest in seven-oh-four that night was Horace Reynolds of the Radio Corporation of America, Chicago offices. Says here he checked out the next day."

His words chilled me. "Who were Claude and Grace McKenna then?"

"I don't know. They're not in the guest book."

The new Hotel Utah detective arrived. He was younger than Metzger, likely in his late twenties or early thirties. He was a clean-cut golden boy, with a prominent chin and sinewy neck. I filled him in on Winston "Blue" Booker's disappearance, and he listened intently to my every word, nodding from time to time. At some point in the conversation, I switched gears, bringing up Metzger and my need to question him about Booker.

"Metzger's gone," said Nebecker.

"Gone?" echoed DeVoy. "You mean he skipped town?"

"I'm not sure. I tried looking for him yesterday when he failed to show up at work. I called the landlady at his apartment building. She said he's gone. Moved out. He picked this place clean. Didn't leave so much as a file folder behind. He took all of the office supplies—you know, the stapler, pen set, ruler, paper, and even the darn city directory. Good riddance, I say."

"Why?" asked DeVoy. "Was he that bad?"

"I kept my distance from him," said Nebecker. "He had a mean temper, and he was involved in some shady groups. A few years ago, he pressured me to join some hate group he's involved with. Something with legion in the name."

"The Platinum Legion?" I asked.

"That's it!" Nebecker snapped his finger. "Real scary group. They want to overthrow the government and prop up Hitler. Before that, Metzger was in the Klan, but he dropped out of it at some point. He used to brag that he started the local chapter here in Salt Lake City, but he said it dried up. I'll tell ya, he had high hopes for the Platinum Legion. Said they were gonna start a revolution. I wasn't gonna have any part of that business, I'll tell you that."

"Would you be willing to testify to any of this in a court of law?" asked DeVoy.

"No," he said, shaking his head. "Not unless Metzger's in the cold, dead ground. He's a dangerous man."

"Any chance you'd be willing to take us up to room seven-oh-four?" I asked.

"Why?"

"The other day, I questioned a woman claiming to be from Canada who said she was staying in the room," I said. "It turns out she was lying to me. Someone else was staying there. Horace Reynolds of the Radio Corporation of America. I just want to examine the place. I won't be long."

He fished a large ring out of his pocket that jangled with keys.

"Right this way."

Up the elevator we went, which opened onto to an adjoining suite and bedroom. Spotless. Elegant furniture filled the large carpeted space, and several spectacular seascape oil paintings were hanging on the walls. He switched on the lights and stepped aside. DeVoy and I found the bed meticulously made and everything in its place. We looked around the room, our footsteps muted by plush carpet. DeVoy leaned over to get a better look at the Zenith console radio in the corner of the room. I picked up a Holy Bible off the bedside table. The blue ribbon marker was holding a place in the Book of Joshua.

Finding nothing unusual about the pristine room, we thanked Nebecker for his help, and then spent an hour questioning hotel employees who had been on duty Tuesday, the day Booker went missing. Nobody had witnessed anything out of the ordinary, although the news about Claude and Estelle McKenna amounted to a major breakthrough. She was the only witness who actually claimed to see Roscoe assaulting Nigel Underhill. Now it seemed clear that the mystery woman definitely wasn't who she claimed to be.

I slowed my car on Foothill Drive when the Bonneville municipal golf course came into view. Not a moment too soon, either. DeVoy had been prattling endlessly about a series of opera records that he'd blown his last paycheck on, and he started comparing the sound quality of these two record labels that specialized in classical music. I pretended to care by nodding and saying "uh-huh" and "oh, is that so?" over and over, but the truth is, I couldn't care less about anything he was saying. So far that morning, the only encouraging development had been the movement of dark storm clouds over the valley, threatening rain. As a result, the temperatures had cooled substantially, down into the high 70s, and the air had that rainy smell.

Bonneville was a picturesque golf course up on the east bench, near Hogle Zoo and the This Is The Place Monument, at the mouth of Emigration Canyon. I found the parking lot, shut off the car, and we got out. DeVoy scanned the rows of automobiles all around us. He plucked a linen hanky out of his pocket and dabbed the beads of perspiration on his face.

"You sure he's here?"

"I've ruled out everyplace else," I said.

"After you, sir," said DeVoy.

We crossed the parking lot to the green. The freshly mowed emerald grass hummed with activity. Caddies towed bags of clubs, and golfers teed off. Most wore caps or visors to shade their eyes. I caught sight of my brother Frank at the sixth hole. He had on an airy white polo shirt with navy-colored trousers, and he wore his flat cap low to keep the sun out of his eyes. He furrowed his brow when he spotted me. It was not my imagination: He was *not* pleased to see me. His golfing partner wore a seersucker shirt, airy khakis, and saddle shoes. I did not know him, this man with my brother, but I recognized him from somewhere. His kept his dark hair tightly slicked back, and he had bulging eyes—always searching—and bulldoggish jowls. I kept wondering: Where had I seen him before?

"Hey kid," said my brother, walking toward me. "What are you doing here?"

He stopped a few feet away and eyed DeVoy.

"This is my partner, DeVoy Beckstead," I said. "DeVoy, this my brother, Special Agent Franklin Oveson."

They exchanged handshakes. "Call me Frank."

DeVoy nodded. "Will do, sir."

Frank looked at me with a raised eyebrow. "Well? How about it?"

Suddenly, the man with my brother cut in front of him, extending his right hand. "I'm J. Edgar Hoover, director of the Federal Bureau of Investigation."

My mouth fell open in shock. "Art Oveson," I managed to say. "Pleased to meet you."

"Likewise. Nice, firm handshake, son. I like that."

He released my hand and offered his to DeVoy, who proved equally at a loss for words, a rarity for this heavy talker. Hoover stepped away from DeVoy and looked me up and down.

"Your brother speaks highly of you," he said. "We recruit heavily among the Mormons, you know. They don't drink, don't smoke, don't use profanity, and don't carry on with the ladies until all hours. Yes, indeed, they represent the ideal pool of prospective employees."

"Thank you, sir," I said. "I'm sorry, I didn't know you were here, otherwise I wouldn't have—"

"Nonsense," said Hoover, raising his golf club, flashing a grin. "Quite the sport. I find it remarkably exhilarating, in its own peculiar way."

"As you can see, I'm busy at the moment," Frank told me. "Can it wait?"

"Applesauce!" protested Hoover. "He came all the way out here. Surely, there must be something we can do to help."

I hesitated, but with Hoover smiling and Frank glaring, I knew I had to say something. "It's about the Underhill investigation."

"You were ordered to stay away from it," Frank said. "It's in our good hands."

"A Negro bellhop who works at the Hotel Utah has gone missing," I said. "His name is Winston Booker. Goes by the nickname Blue. His parents dropped by Public Safety this morning to report his disappearance."

"Why are you interrupting our game to tell me this?" asked Frank.

"I suspect his disappearance has something to do with Clive Underhill vanishing," I said. "I'm convinced if we find Booker, there's a good chance Underhill won't be far away."

"We?" asked Frank testily.

I sighed. "Look, I can't be responsible for any overlap this may have with the Underhill investigation."

"Then leave it alone," Frank said.

"His folks reported him missing," I said. "I can't ignore it."

Frank hooked me by the elbow and tugged me away from the prying ears of DeVoy and J. Edgar Hoover. Near the trunk of a towering oak, he leaned in close and spoke in a near-whisper. "I see what you're up to."

"What do you mean?" I asked.

"You're trying to save Roscoe's neck. It's not going to work."

"You've got to listen to me, Frank," I said. "The house dick at the Hotel Utah, Dooley Metzger, most likely had a hand in Booker's disappearance. I know for a fact he scared Booker into giving the police a false eyewitness testimony implicating Roscoe in the murder of Nigel Underhill. Metzger also concocted a phony Canadian couple to corroborate Booker's claims. He even found a woman to play the part of the wife. I'm telling you, Frank, he's rotten to the core. Used to be in the Klan. Now he's in the Platinum Legion. I have a feeling he's in on some sinister dealings, and he scared Booker into providing false testimony in order to throw the police off his trail. Now he's gone, too. It seems like everybody's disappearing, but you can't be bothered with it."

"You know what I think, kid?"

"No. What?"

"You rubbed elbows with the rich and famous after you saved Clive Underhill's life out at the Salt Flats on Saturday," he said. "It went to your head. You don't want it to end. But there's plenty you don't know about his disappearance. For instance, Director Hoover has reason to believe Underhill's been kidnapped, and this abduction is the work of a cunning criminal who's out for the money. There are no higher principles at work here than that."

"Kidnapped? Where's the ransom note? What are the kidnappers asking for, exactly?"

"The specifics are none of your concern," said Frank. "All you need to know is Roscoe Lund is our number one suspect. He's our murderer and our kidnapper. I'm certain of it. Think about it. He's heavily in debt. His house is about to be foreclosed. He can't make ends meet with his crummy detective agency. He's got a daughter to support. I think he went there to abduct Clive, and Nigel got in the way."

I shook my head. "None of that proves anything."

"Sure it does. It all adds up to a desperate man, who'd resort to extreme measures for pecuniary gain. Believe me, kid, I know what I'm talking about. I've been around the block a fair bit more than you have, and the last thing I need is law-enforcement tips from a greenhorn like you."

"What about Winston Booker?" I asked.

"What about him?"

"I don't trust the FBI to mount a proper search for him," I said.

Now Frank was glowering at me. "Listen, I'll spell this out for you as clearly as possible, because you're no good at grasping subtleties. There are politics involved here that you cannot even begin to understand. Director Hoover expects a swift resolution to this case. Careers and promotions and funding are on the line. We're working with a great deal of information to which you're not privy. Now, if you'll excuse me, I've got twelve more holes to play with the most powerful man in America."

"I won't give up until I find Booker."

He let out a long and deep sigh, and his glower melted into a forlorn gaze. The silence allowed me to reflect. Since the time my father was murdered, when I was twelve, going on thirteen, Frank had assumed responsibility as the next-in-line patriarch, and he was not used to having his orders disobeyed. My defiance left him at a loss for words. He left me in the middle of the golf course, and as I watched him walking away, I began to wonder what—if any—consequences awaited me for my little act of rebellion.

Twenty-seven

Looking back, it probably wasn't the brightest idea to interrupt Frank's golf game with J. Edgar Hoover to announce my intention to investigate a missing persons report with close ties to the Clive Underhill case. Had I been weighing my options in a more rational manner, I would have taken an entirely different approach, like searching for Booker on the quiet. But I chose the confrontational route because I wanted my brother to know that I was not going to bow to his intimidation, as I had done so many times in the past.

When DeVoy and I returned to Public Safety, I found Buddy Hawkins sitting on my chair in the Missing Persons Bureau, with Myron pretending not to notice anything. Buddy didn't say a word as he got up and walked past me. He didn't have to. He just tipped his head slightly, indicating I should follow him, and led the way down the stairs to the ground floor.

Past the big and somber oil paintings we strode, as typewriters rattled and telephones rang in the background. Chief Cowley sat leaning back in his chair, fingers knitted, staring morosely at me. I noticed his frown, a rarity for him, which I took to be a bad sign. I sat down on one of the guest chairs, and Buddy found his seat on the other side of Cowley's sprawling art deco desk.

I feared he was going to fire me right away. He didn't. Funny thing is, I always underestimated my political clout around Public Safety. Being the son of Willard Oveson, martyred police inspector extraordinaire, came with its own unique set of perks. Foremost among them was that you could get away with murder, and a wide array of lesser felonies, and not face any consequences. But I was about to commit the worst sin of all in the world of law enforcement: taking a stand. Strong principles can quickly turn into strychnine in this line of work. And with Clara unemployed and not likely to find teaching work anytime soon, I had to make some fast decisions about how far out on the chopping block I was willing to stick my neck.

Before uttering a word, Cowley drew a shaky breath. "Your brother, Frank, telephoned here a short time ago to discuss a matter of utmost urgency. He said that you interrupted his game of golf with the director of the FBI, and that you were belligerent and told him you would not halt your investigation of Clive Underhill's disappearance, despite my dire warnings that you would be—"

"I said nothing of the sort," I protested. "I informed my brother that—"

"Let him finish," said Buddy.

Cowley nodded and shifted his weight in his chair. "Like I was saying, Special Agent Frank Oveson insists that you outright refused to stop your work on the Clive Underhill case, which is in direct contravention of the Lindbergh Law."

"Sir, you need to hear my side of the story," I said. "I never told Frank I was planning to keep working on the Underhill case. I was merely paying him a courtesy call to let him know that a bellhop named Winston Booker who worked at the Hotel Utah has gone missing, and his parents dropped by Public Safety this morning to ask me to find him. I wanted Frank—er, uh, Special Agent Oveson—to know that there might be some overlap between my case and his. That's all."

"Well, in that case, I think there may be a perfectly simple solution to this problem," said Buddy. "Delay your investigation into Mr. Booker's disappearance until the FBI has wrapped up its work on the Underhill case."

"I can't," I said.

"Why?" asked Buddy.

"Because he deserves the same treatment as any other missing person," I said. "When a person goes missing, I don't delay my investigation for any reason."

"That's a noble principle in theory," said Cowley. "But there are certain political realities that have to be taken into consideration."

"With all due respect, sir," I said, "the only reality at stake here is that a man is missing and his family is frightened."

"I think you'll find that I'm a reasonable man, Arthur, which is why I've chosen to make you an offer," said Cowley. "Hold off on looking into Mr. Booker's disappearance until such time as the FBI has completed its investigation of the Underhill case."

"Or?" I asked.

"You'll be demoted to Traffic Bureau, which means this time tomorrow you'll be ticketing jaywalkers and pulling slugs out of parking meters with pliers."

"Last time I was in here, you promised to fire me for interfering with the Underhill investigation," I said. "Do you think it's wise to make threats you have no intention of following through on?"

"Are you goading me, Arthur?" asked Cowley, with a hint of anger in his voice.

"No," I said. "Just trying to do my job."

"Is this about some sort of silly rivalry between you and your brother?" Buddy asked. "Because if so, I can tell you right now it's not worth—"

"Pardon me," I said, rising from my chair. "I need to find out what happened to Winston Booker."

"You've got a bright future here," said Cowley. "Don't throw it away."

On my way to the door, I paused to respond to my superiors.

"I like a bright future as much any man," I said. "But there's a limit to what I'm willing to pay for it."

"Before you go getting all high and mighty and start flushing your career down the toilet," said Buddy, "you ought to ask yourself if it's worth it."

I nodded. "Thank you for the advice."

"Aren't you forgetting something?" asked Cowley.

I shot him a quizzical look.

"Your badge, please."

I approached his desk, opened my wallet, and unclipped the shiny shield that had come to symbolize my professional life for the past eight years. It felt scary and disorienting to lay it down on his desk and leave. But what choice did they give me? At this stage in my life, if they weren't going to let me do my job right, then I was not going to do it at all.

The entire time I loaded my belongings into a cardboard box, my stomach churned something fierce. DeVoy blinked morosely in my direction, watching my every move, while Myron kept his back turned to me

To say I had mixed feelings about taking a stand I knew would get me fired was *the* understatement of the century. Eight years I'd given to this job. Eight years I'd shown up here faithfully every weekday morning at eight thirty, ready to put in at least eight hours—often more—of rigorous work. Eight years I'd listened to the hubbub in the corridors and the steady din from the downstairs lobby, which would occasionally erupt into out-and-out pandemonium. This had been the longest-running job I'd ever had. Despite my occasional grumblings, I loved the work I did. I felt like I was making a difference for the better, and I often found that the results of my work were tangible and, occasionally, even satisfying. While I always dreaded the prospect of finding a missing person dead, or not finding one at all, the experience of reuniting a lost loved one with his or her family, and seeing the looks of relief on the faces of kin, was gratifying, to say the least.

Was I really ready to give it all up? Was I prepared—as Buddy put it—to flush it down the toilet, simply because I refused to compromise? Somewhere in the back of my mind, I could hear Willard Oveson's voice echoing, as only a father's can: *Pick and choose, carefully, the hills you wish to die on.*

I considered such matters as I put on my hat, lifted the box off my desk, and headed to the door. I took a long last look.

"So long," said DeVoy, sadly. "Sorry it has to end this way."

I mustered a smile. "Don't worry. I'll see you around, I'm sure."

I cleared my throat. Myron stopped writing whatever it was he was writing and looked over at me.

"Good-bye, Myron."

His stone face did not change one iota. He gave a slight nod and resumed work.

I stepped into the corridor to encounter a small crowd of detectives, all in dark hats and suits and ties. I recognized most of them as friends and acquaintances from the Morals and Homicide squads, the two biggest bureaus on the second floor. I sensed the collective gloom that filled the hall—a forest of somber stares and clenched jaws, lit by the yellowish light from above.

One by one, voices sounded as I walked past, some overlapping. A hand or two reached out and patted my shoulder or squeezed my bicep.

I responded to each with a smile and a nod. Pace Newbold joined me at the stairs. He looked sharp in a dark green suit and brown fedora. His red tie was loose, and I could see the splotches of sweat on his shirt. Typical of Pace, he did not bother to ask if he could escort me down the marble steps. He assumed it would be fine. Halfway down the first flight, with the crowd of men now out of earshot if you spoke low, he leaned in and let me have it.

"The hell do you think you're doing?"

"What does it look like?" I asked. "I quit my job."

"You must be chump of the year, Oveson," he said. "Throwing away a perfectly good job over a missing Negro."

He cut ahead of me, right in my path, and turned toward me, forcing me to halt on the step above him.

"Get out of my way," I said, glaring at him, raising the box higher against my chest. "I really don't feel like getting into it with you right now, Pace."

"Why bother?" he asked. "It won't make a goddamned bit of difference, you quitting like this."

I outflanked Pace, zooming to his right—my left—to get around him to continue to the first floor. He spun around and trotted down the steps, keeping up with me as I went. We rounded a corner and descended the next flight.

"Good old-fashioned jealousy! Bet that's what it is," said Pace. "You can't stand that your brother is now running the show. Well, get used to it, Oveson. It's nothing personal. The FBI always hands the preliminary shit work over to local law enforcement. By the time we have the case damn near cracked, they step in and take all the credit."

"I said leave me alone, Pace."

"Or what? You gonna deck me?"

Reaching the bottom of the stairs, with the ornate lobby ceiling looming high above me, I glanced at Pace. In his own grating way, he was trying to talk me out of leaving. Despite deep doubts I harbored about what I was doing, at this point, I felt that it was a matter of pride that I follow through with my decision to quit. Clearly, Pace hoped that poking me would provoke an angry response—and maybe even prompt me to reconsider. But I felt too shaken and morose to challenge him. I just stood there looking at him, clinging to that box, and I flashed him a bittersweet grin.

"So long, Pace."

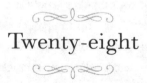

Twenty-eight

I stalled going home as long as I could. Tempting as it was to go looking for Winston Booker, losing my job left me more disoriented than I thought it would. I drove around in a daze. I kept second-guessing myself, wondering if I'd done the right thing. My heart was racing, and I broke out in a cold sweat while I was circling downtown blocks. I ended up spending an hour nursing a banana split at a corner table in Keeley's Ice Cream parlor on Main. Cold gusts of air conditioner wind against my perspiration-soaked forehead soothed me. I managed to kill another ninety minutes at the library, thumbing through various atlases and the *Readers' Guide to Periodical Literature* and old historical picture books about the Civil War. I dreaded telling Clara about my decision. Finally, I walked over to the Victory Theater to see *The Adventures of Robin Hood,* splashed across the huge screen in glorious Technicolor. The fact that its star, Errol Flynn, was also supposed to play Clive Underhill in an upcoming Warner Bros. biopic, was not lost on me as I sat in the balcony, nervously shoveling popcorn into my mouth. The picture ended around 5:00 P.M., and I knew I could not delay the inevitable any longer.

Turning onto my block, I cringed at the sight of countless autos, parked on both sides of the street and in my driveway. It was so crowded I had to park a ways away. Coming up the front walkway, I could hear a cacophony of voices flowing out of open windows, and I feared the worst. I entered my house to find it packed. Two of my three brothers and their wives had shown up, along with several of their children. So did Bishop Garth Shumway, long-faced and bespectacled, in a maroon-colored cardigan and baggy khakis. Clara's mother and father found a spot to stand in the living room, not far from her sister Joyce and brother-in-law Mac. My former partner from my days in the Morals Squad, Thayne Carlquist, even put in an appearance, shaking my hand as I walked through the front door.

"Hello, Thayne," I said, scanning the crowd. "How's every little thing?"

Before he could answer me, Clara hooked me by the elbow, pulling me past the throng of familiar people and a chorus of "hellos" and "how are yous." We ended up in the quiet kitchen, where she moved up close to me, and I could plainly see the film of sweat on her face and neck and chest.

"What's going on here?" I asked.

"Is it true?" she asked, her lower lip quivering.

"We need to talk."

"Answer my question."

"Alone. Without all of these people here."

"Is it true?"

"Look, dear, I can explain, but I'd prefer—"

"Don't *look dear* me!"

I lifted my hands, palms facing down. "Shhhh. Keep it down, will you?"

"How could you do it? And without asking me?"

"Well, to be honest, I was planning on discussing it with you tonight, but—"

"After the fact, you mean," she said. "Do you realize we barely have enough money to pay our mortgage and survive for the next two months?"

I pointed to the swinging kitchen door, now closed. "What on earth are all of those people doing out there?"

"Half of them are here to try and talk you out of your damn fool decision," she said. "I guess the rest have come to enlighten you about other ways of making ends meet. But whatever their reasons for being here, I think they all pretty much agree you're being reckless."

"Who told you I quit my job?"

"Does it matter?"

"Yes."

"Buddy Hawkins," she said. "He was kind enough to call me this afternoon, and share the news that apparently you thought I didn't need to know."

"Hear me out," I said. "I've got a good reason for quitting my job."

"Oh? Better than the well-being of your own family?"

"I can't do this. How are we supposed to have a conversation with half of the state of Utah in our house?"

"You're endangering our family with your impulsiveness," she said.

"Dad. Mom."

We both looked over at Hyrum and Emily, standing in the wide-open back door, both with fearful expressions.

"Is everything going to be OK?" asked Hyrum.

"Are they going to take us away from you?" asked Emily.

I crossed the kitchen and squatted near my children, placing a hand on the shoulder of each. "Everything's going to be all right," I said. "I'm just going to find another job, and the Ovesons of Sherman Avenue are going to be just fine."

As I finished my sentence, the crowd came funneling through the swinging door. The room filled up fast. Before I knew it, I had suggestions for employment coming at me from all directions.

"Listen, Art, I can get you on with the Provo Police," said my brother Grant. "You'd have to start as a uniformed patrolman, but you'll work your way up to the detective room in no time."

Clara's father, Bruce Snow, stepped in and pulled me in the opposite direction. "Arthur, I know the fellow who runs the management training program at Henager's Business College. Classes are starting this week, believe it or not. Now, I'd be happy to have a word with him and ask if he would—"

"If you're going to go to college, why not try the Electric College?" interrupted Bishop Shumway. "That's where my eldest, Arliss, went. The campus is downtown, in the Keith Building. Arliss got a keen job up in Ogden, wiring all the new homes for a big construction project now under way. The kid is making money hand over fist."

"I beg your pardon." Frank Oveson's booming voice came from behind us. He seemed more relaxed without a tie and vest on. He glowered at me as he moved uncomfortably close.

"Out back," he said. "Now."

I nodded. We squeezed out the back door, onto the porch, crossing the grass for some privacy. I took a few seconds to cherish the quiet, the gentle breeze, the overcast skies, and the light birdsong filling the air. Once again, Frank leaned in close to me, probably hoping his burly physique would intimidate his kid brother. If anything, his strong-arm approach merely strengthened my resolve, persuading me that I'd done the right thing.

"What do you think you're doing?"

"I quit my job," I said. "What's it to you?"

"What kind of stunt are you trying to pull here?"

"It's not a 'stunt,' as you put it," I said. "I'm tired of a lot of things—of going at this investigation with one hand tied behind my back, of the lack of cooperation between squads, of the FBI waltzing into what's for them terra incognita and laying down all of these arbitrary rules, and finally banning us from the case altogether. I'm tired of not being listened to. You didn't hear a word I said about Booker, and you don't care that Metzger was a Klansman and a Nazi, or that Estelle McKenna—the only eyewitness who claims she saw Roscoe assault Nigel—was a phony. She doesn't even exist. But the worst thing is that you called my work and ratted me out."

"I didn't rat you out," Frank said. "I advised Cowley not to discipline you. I see I was wrong."

I nodded. "I guess so."

"When did you get to be so pigheaded? Look, I just got off the phone with Cowley. He says if you ask for your job back, it's yours. No apology necessary."

"What do I have to apologize for?" I asked. "Doing my job?"

"I'll repeat what I said earlier, Art: There's a lot at stake here that you aren't aware of. Trust me, we know everything you know, and a heckuva lot more. Don't start getting cocky and thinking you're a few steps ahead of us, because you're not."

"What about Winston Booker?" I asked.

"What about him?"

"He's missing," I said. "His parents want him found. It's my job to find him."

Frank shook his head, puffed his cheeks, and blew air. "You mean all of this is going on and you're honestly worried about a nigger?"

Frank's words hit me like a punch to the stomach.

"Did you really just use that word?"

"What do you want me to say?"

"Oh, I don't know," I said, trying to hold back my rage. "Negro. Colored. Black."

"That's the difference between you and me," he said. "You're a naïve idealist. If you want to spend the rest of your life tilting at windmills, don't let me stop you. Me? I'm a realist. I have to deal with real-world practicalities. Maybe that's why I'm a contender for assistant director of the FBI, while you've spent the last eight years handing out traffic tickets and helming dead-end, go-nowhere squads. Now look at you. You're another statistic on the unemployment rolls. What do you think Dad would say?"

"I don't know," I said, giving Frank a stony stare. "He's dead."

"I bet he's looking down on us, shaking his head in disbelief that his youngest is an out-of-work bum willing to throw everything away over some lowly coon bellhop. That's what I think."

"Dad believed everybody deserved justice," I said. "And that's what Winston Booker's family is going to get. Justice."

Frank sneered, turned around, and left me there, under the tree. When he opened the back door, all of those people squeezed into the kitchen came flooding out, tramping down the porch steps en masse toward me, voices over voices, hands gesturing, eyes wide, all of them determined to give poor, misguided Art Oveson some words of wisdom about what do with his uncertain future.

• • •

Desert Lightning, a polished black arrowhead of a machine, flashes reflections of sun that burn into your retina as it streaks across the crystal landscape. Now airborne, it spins toy-like, crashing into salt encrusted earth. In seconds, it is reduced to a heap of twisted steel and jagged glass teeth. Gasoline leaks everywhere. Little fires send plumes of smoke wafting into the blue sky.

A patrol car races across the flats. Before it stops, I leap out the back door. Sprinting to the wreckage, I plunge to the ground near a broken window. I peer in to find Clive Underhill hanging upside down by safety restraints. He is as dashing as ever, despite his hair dangling down and minor cuts and bruises on his face.

"Help me."

"Take my hand."

He extends his arm out as far as it will go, but it is still too far from mine for me to reach it. I struggle to grip his hand. I grunt. I gasp. I flail. I thrust my feet into the salt below me, hoping against hope for some sort of leverage. I inch forward until our fingertips touch. He lunges and grasps my hand, squeezing tightly. But instead of me pulling him out of the burning vehicle, he pulls me into it.

In terror, I strain to break free of his grip. Flames engulf him instantly, his face vaporizes into a blinding yellow-white likeness, and then the fireball comes at me in the form of giant orange flower, consuming me until I can no longer feel or see or think anything.

My eyes opened. I jerked upright.

A figure stood in the arched doorway. Like a ghost, she glided silently into the dim yellow from a nearby nightlight.

It was Sarah Jane, clutching a clipboard as she came closer. In the darkness of the living room, I could not see her expression, yet I felt her anxiety, which must have come from finding me in the living room, in the middle of a nightmare. She sat on the other end of the couch, next to my feet, squirming to the edge until she felt comfortable. I reached for a nearby lamp and pulled the chain. A soft glow lit our part of the room.

"What are you doing in here?" she whispered. "Why aren't you with Mom?"

"She needed extra space," I said, pulling my feet away from her to give her room. "I thought I'd sleep out here on the couch tonight."

She held up a clipboard. "As long as you're awake . . ."

"What's that?"

"It's a petition." She handed me the clipboard. "Will you sign it?"

I examined it. Not a single signature. Just blank lines. I'd be the first. S.J. handed me a pencil. A WE THE UNDERSIGNED statement appeared at the top explaining it, but I shot S.J. a quizzical glance, hoping she would fill me in.

"Yesterday afternoon, I went to the Civic Club to hear Dr. Henry Wachtel."

"Who?" I asked.

"He's from New York City," she said. "He gave a speech on the need to create a colony in the Lower California peninsula of Mexico where Jews can go live in peace, and not have to worry about being terrorized, and fearing for their lives, and having their belongings and their shops and their houses taken away. All of those things are happening now in Europe, but nobody's doing anything to stop it. He recited a quote by an Englishman named Burke."

"Oh yeah?" I asked. "How did it go?"

She closed her eyes. "He said, 'The only thing necessary for the triumph of evil is for good men to do nothing.' " Her lids fluttered open. "I asked Mom to sign it, but she refused. She called it a fool's errand. Is she right?"

"There's always hope." I drew a deep breath and held up the clipboard. "So what does the petition say?"

"It calls for the creation of a homeland for Jews in Lower California," she said. "It asks the Mexican government to set the land aside for that purpose."

I lifted the pencil S.J. gave me and wrote my name on the first line, where it said PRINT NAME, and signed where it said SIGNATURE. I handed her the clipboard and the pencil. She beamed when she looked down at my John Hancock. Her joy was short-lived. She became pensive again.

"Dad?"

"Yeah?"

"Why is she so unhappy?"

"She's not. Sometimes she just comes across—"

"Dad?"

"Yeah."

"Be honest with me."

S.J. could see right through my platitudes.

"It's complicated," I finally said, itching the back of my neck.

"Try me."

"A few years ago, when Emily was still a toddler, lots of people kept pressuring your mother to quit her job."

"What people?"

"Your aunts and uncles, and various relatives and friends. Your mother put her whole heart into her teaching. She loved everything about it—the students, the work, the smell of fresh school supplies. I think she even loved grading papers. But she relented under all of that pressure. She resigned. She regretted her decision, and has ever since." I rubbed my burning right eye with my knuckle. "I feel bad."

"Why?"

"I didn't stick up for her. I should've defended her choices. I didn't."

"How come?"

"I hate conflict. Always have. I'm always so dang busy trying to make other people happy. In trying to do that, I failed her."

We shared a silence, as we both took in what I'd just said.

"Dad?"

"Yeah?"

"What are you going to do, now that you're no longer a policeman?"

"I don't know."

S.J. yawned and stretched her arms. She picked a sleepy cinder out of the corner of her eye. Then she flicked it away and raised her clipboard to her chest. "I'm going back to bed. I'm tired."

"I could use a hug," I said.

Sarah Jane rose from the couch, stepped closer, and wrapped her arms around me. I hugged her back, patting her gently, and I gave her a soft peck on the temple. She eased back and inspected me with sleepy eyes.

"G'night, Dad," she said. "I love you."

"I love you, too."

I listened to my daughter's footsteps fade down the hallway into silence. A door closed in the distance. I was alone again. Alone with my thoughts.

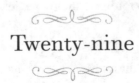

Twenty-nine

I pulled up to the Oveson homestead in American Fork at quarter past seven in the morning, after driving an hour to get there. I shut off the engine and climbed out of the car. My white-haired mother looked up from her newspaper when I closed the car door. She was sitting on her favorite rocking chair, on a day when gray clouds delivered a welcome breeze giving the first hint of fall. Mom greeted me on the front porch with an embrace, led me inside the house, and offered me a glass of ice-cold lemonade. I thanked her and said I knew she was an early riser, and that's why I dropped by at this hour. She sized me up through wire-rim glasses, smiling at the small, handpicked bouquet of colorful flowers I held in my hands, and she knew what I needed without me even having to tell her.

I followed her out the back door, down the steps, under a canopy of leafy tree branches. We headed south, beyond the barn and the tractor, the chicken pens and the canal, through an open area of grassland, until we arrived at the Oveson family cemetery. Mom unlatched the white picket fence gate and the door hinges squealed when she opened it. The grass inside was freshly cut, and I knew that one day my remains would end up here, along with Mom Oveson, Clara, and my brothers and various sisters-in-law. Mom waved her hand in the direction of the solitary headstone, in the shade of a towering tree that predated the earliest pioneers by a long shot.

"He's waiting for you."

"Thanks."

"I'll be inside, if you need me."

The gate whined again and its latch clanked shut behind me as I faced his headstone. WILLARD JOSEPH OVESON read big letters at the top, and I stooped to run the tips of my fingers over the words and numerals etched below:

OCTOBER 1, 1864—JANUARY 23, 1914
LOVING FATHER, HUSBAND AND FRIEND.
AND JUSTICE FOR ALL . . .

I got down on one knee and placed the bouquet on the grass, near the foot of the monument. Its stone surface was warm to the touch, despite the darkening skies and chill on the morning breeze. Collecting my thoughts, I inhaled deeply, filling my lungs full of clean pine scent. Returning to my childhood home comforted me, but it was not enough. I felt a deep inner need to share my troubles with my father, whether or not he was listening.

"Sorry it's been a while since my last visit," I said. "I quit my job yesterday. You probably already know that. I can't explain why. I guess I was fed up with the bureaucracy and the red tape. I was sick of worrying all the time about stepping on the toes of other detectives who'd get sore at me for trying to rob them of

their glory. And I didn't care for the indifference that my superiors were showing to this young man—a boy, really—who went
missing the other day. If I'm being truly honest, I guess what
really got to me the most was standing in Frank Oveson's shadow.
I'm a free man now. But freedom comes with a price."

I straightened the bouquet in the grass, so it touched the
headstone: "I'm not sure if I did the right thing. I'm beginning
to doubt myself. Clara's not teaching, so we have no other income.
We don't have much money saved. There's a recession on—well,
at least that's what the newspapers call it, to put people's minds
at ease. It still feels like a depression to me, if you want me to be
honest. I don't know what I'm going to do now. I considered taking out a loan and starting my own private investigation business. I'd be an operative for hire, like the fellow in the Dashiell
Hammett stories. You don't read him, I guess. He's a detective
yarn writer."

I was silent for a long moment, surveying the scenery around
me. My gaze shifted to the Wasatch Mountains on the east side
of the valley. I shifted my focus back to the headstone. I imagined
my father's long, lean face, a smile tucked away under a mustache
showing its first hint of gray. There were moments—now being
one of them—when I could not picture everything about him
with precise clarity, and it bothered me when his features were
not distinct in my mind's eye.

"I don't know what I'm doing. I wish you were here. I wish I
could talk to you. I'm scared. I'm just some puny little David who
thought he could take on Goliath. I guess I was wrong. I feel so
alone, and I don't have the faintest idea of where to go from here.
I'm not sure what you'd tell me if you were still alive. I remember you always used to say, 'Choose carefully which hill you want

to die on.' I've spent my whole life avoiding those hills. Now that I've gone and picked one, I don't know if I selected wisely."

I leaned forward, pressing my palm against his tombstone, hoping to feel something—*anything*—from the beyond, even a faint stirring. I kept my hand there a long time, but nothing came. Not even a distant vibration. What was I expecting? He was gone, and I was here—still walking this earth, tormented by doubts.

"I'll take anything," I whispered. "Is it selfish to wish for some small sign?"

No reply came to me, at least not a direct one. But the wind changed direction, and ruffled my hair like fingers, and I looked up at the western skies, where the slate-gray heavens sent bolts of lightning dancing across the dusty horizon. Maybe rain would come today, I thought, as I closed the cemetery gate behind me. The air sure smelled of it. I went inside the house and said farewell to my mother, and we embraced once again, and I got back in my car and headed north, to Salt Lake City.

Some small sign, I thought, speeding up the highway, listening to the Early Bird Serenade on KDYL.

I had nowhere to go. I did not want to return home, where I knew there was a good chance Clara might not be speaking to me. No more going back to Public Safety, my workplace of the past eight years. My mind was a swirling kaleidoscope of thoughts as I motored around downtown, contemplating my next move. Turning onto Main Street from North Temple, I glanced at an enormous brick building with steep steps climbing to a columned classic portico. Stately white words floating above the entrance caught my eye: GENEALOGICAL SOCIETY OF UTAH.

I hit the brakes. My car screeched to a halt. The air smelled of smoking rubber.

Some small sign.

Peter Insley's words from Saturday night at the Coconut Grove echoed through my mind: *"You know, Nigel here is quite the family history buff. He's already spent a fair bit of time up at the Genealogical Society on Main Street. Isn't that so, Nigel?"*

I found a parking spot and hurried up to the building. Mormons like me had been genealogy enthusiasts since the founding of the Church over a century ago, embracing the practice for a variety of complex reasons. Spiritually, tracing our family roots, we thought, brought us closer to our ancestors, drawing us together into an eternal family. We performed baptisms for the dead for men and women and children who did not have that option during their lifetimes. We believed these souls were waiting in the afterlife for this gift, and once they received it, it would enable them to spend an eternity with their loved ones.

There were other reasons, more secular, for our championing of family history. Regardless of your religious views, learning about one's forebears—their dates of birth, their histories, when they died—connects us with the past and deepens our bonds with our kin. This is one of the reasons why the LDS Church has encouraged non-Mormons to work on their genealogy. It's also why the institution has devoted so much of its resources and armies of volunteer researchers to collecting data from far-flung locales around the world—including census figures, city directories, ship passenger lists, draft cards, birth records, marriage records, death records, cemetery and almshouse and hospital records, wills and probate records, newspaper clippings, photographs, the list goes on—and compiling them all systematically in one place, the Genealogical Society of Utah, and making them available to the public, Mormon and non-Mormon alike. The collection had gotten to be so enormous over the years that nowadays the Society uses the latest technology—microfilming—to catalogue, in an orderly fashion, millions of pages of documents.

Knowing all of this, I raced up the steps of the Society's headquarters, the hub of all this humming activity. I flung open one of the heavy doors and charged inside, running across the high-ceilinged front entry hall to the information counter up front. Lowell Bendix, an aging gentleman in a dark three-piece suit and bow tie, looked up at me from his work behind the counter as I stopped to catch my breath. Lowell's thinning white hair was combed over the bald top of his head, thick spectacles rested at the end of his nose, and his expression conveyed a gentle quality. He knew me from all the times I'd been in here working on my genealogy, and he probably recalled me trying to show Myron the ropes, too.

"Arthur! How are you?"

"Lowell, as I live and breathe—"

"Which you're doing pretty hard now, I might add."

I laughed. "How's every little thing?"

"I can't complain," he said. "Well, I can, but I won't. May I help you?"

"You certainly can," I said. "I was wondering if you knew anything about an Englishman who came in here several times last week? Name of—"

"Nigel Underhill?"

"You know him?" I asked, hanky-dabbing my brow.

"Hard to forget," Lowell said. "He left quite an impression. Hasn't been in for several days, though. What about him?"

"He was in here doing research," I said. "I was wondering if you'd mind telling me what he was digging into?"

"That's confidential, Art. There are privacy issues to take into consideration."

"Sure, I understand, Lowell." I looked around, then switched my gaze back to him. "Look, what I'm about to say is strictly confidential. Nigel Underhill is dead."

"Oh my heavens."

"And the research he did here might help me figure out what happened to him."

Lowell nodded. "Of course, I see what you mean. Yes, I'll show you. Follow me."

He opened a drawer, searched about, and fished out a key. Then he walked to the end of the counter, opened a waist-high door, and stepped out to the area where I was standing. He went past me, and I tailed him across the Grand Central Terminal-like room, through a set of arched doors, and down a hall to an area where the walls were covered on either side with green lockers. He stopped at one numbered 308 and inserted his key into the lock, opened it, and pulled out a cream-colored dossier. He closed the door, pocketed the key, and passed me the file.

"I was expecting you sooner," he said.

"Oh?" I accepted the file and gave him a curious look. "What do you mean?"

"Surely you've heard the big news. It's all over the newspapers, the radio. Clive Underhill is nowhere to be found. I know you're in the Missing Persons Bureau, Art. But this is the first time I've heard about Nigel. That is terrible news."

"Yes, I know," I said. "It came as quite a shock."

He nodded. "Maybe whatever is in that folder can shed some light on it."

"May I?" I asked, gesturing to the coveted object in my hands.

"Go right ahead. Whatever is in there is quite popular."

"What do you mean?"

"Someone else came in to see it," said Lowell. "A rather large Englishman. His name escapes me."

I thought of "rather large" Englishmen. Only one came to mind.

"Was his name Albert Shaw, by any chance?"

He snapped his fingers and his face lit up with a smile. "That's the one."

"What did he say? If you don't mind me asking."

"He wanted to take the file with him," said Lowell. "He wouldn't tell me what it was about. I told him the file had to stay here, on the premises. He seemed agitated, rushed. He was only in here briefly. He said he'd come back. He hasn't—not yet, anyway."

"Nobody else has come in to look at it?" I asked. "No police? No feds?"

"Nope. You're it. Well, you and that Shaw fellow."

I nodded, opting against telling Lowell that I'd recently lost my job at the SLCPD. I hated lying, but a lie by omission was not as bad as uttering an outright falsehood. Or so I assured myself.

With Lowell standing beside me, I opened the file. It contained a stack of photostats, still smelling of fresh ink—if I had to venture a guess, I'd say probably about a hundred or so pages in total. Not a single document had anything to do with the Underhill clan. I flipped pages. The documents were all in German. Two names kept coming up over and over: Gerhardt Rudolf Heinrich and Gerda Strauss. And the two words I saw over and over again—underlined in pen, presumably by Nigel Underhill— were JUDE and JUDEN. When I got to the bottom of the stack, I found a couple of pieces of tan-colored scratch paper, provided to patrons of the Genealogical Society for note-taking, and I guessed the mostly legible cursive on them belonged to Nigel Underhill.

I looked at Lowell. "Mind if I take this with me?"

"Go ahead," he said. "Anything to help with the investigation."

"Thank you ever so much, Lowell."

I closed the file and we started off across the black-and-brown checkerboard linoleum. Lowell and I made small talk about the weather and the people that came in each day to do research and the boxes of records that were arriving here on a daily basis. On the way to the exit, I peeked in the reading room, where dozens of women of all ages—and a handful of men—pored over documents at wooden carrels. At the entrance, I thanked Lowell once more, shook hands with him, and left.

Thirty

From a distance, the engine's rumble rolled across the salt-encrusted earth, bouncing off of treeless mountains and stubby purple hills. I skirted the makeshift tent city, scanning the banners announcing the big showdown tomorrow between Great Britain and Germany. A clash of monumental proportions, the newspapers had called it. Yet news of Clive Underhill's disappearance had gone public, casting a pall over Saturday's scheduled event. This morning's newspaper had reported that Rudy Heinrich was still planning on showing up to break the old speed record. "I hope they find Clive Underhill," he told reporters. "But that won't stop me from doing what I've traveled all this way to accomplish." Albert Shaw told the press that the Brits had no intention of canceling, either, and he insisted Clive would be found before Saturday.

Still, the clock was ticking away, and Clive's disappearance threatened to eclipse Saturday's event. Already, a search of epic proportions, spearheaded by FBI Director J. Edgar Hoover, was under way. As I traversed crystals, recalling Clive describing them as "desolate," I felt the hot surface penetrating my shoe soles. Venturing out onto the raceway, I spotted a silvery dot on the horizon, where azure skies and white earth met.

This crusty landscape, devoid of life, had been named for a nineteenth-century Frenchman, Benjamin Bonneville, who crossed the Atlantic, joined the United States Army, and came out West to survey the land and trap fur. For a place not fit for man or beast, the flats teemed with signs of life on this day, as workers erected banners welcoming visitors to the raceway, and raised rows of Union Jacks, Old Glories, and twisted black swastikas on white circles in the middle of red banners. To the west, bright newsreel trucks shimmered in the sun.

I had no business being out here, in the middle of this strip of raceway. No longer a police detective, I now enjoyed the status of an ordinary civilian, with no power or authority to do anything, not even give out a traffic ticket. Still, the security guards out here in these parts knew who I was, and because I was the cousin of the legendary Hank Jensen, they left me alone. So I stood out a ways from the hubbub of the tents and the bleachers, out here where the cars drove. The shadow of my fedora brim protected me from the worst of the sun's ferocity. My left hand gripped the dossier that I had obtained earlier in the day at the Genealogical Society in downtown Salt Lake City.

As the Auto Union Streamliner—a practice car prototype—neared, its engine grew louder, until the grinding roar convinced me to move aside a ways, to the east. The sleek machine Rudy Heinrich planned to drive tomorrow had been built to break speed records on the Autobahn in more temperate stretches in

Germany. Nevertheless, it ended up out here, in the kiln-baked deserts of Utah, gleaming under the bright sun. The vehicle rocketed past me, its deafening engine noise stabbing my eardrums, and a hot wind gusted from its rear, nearly blowing my hat off my head. I watched it shrink in my line of vision and its roar fade in my ears as it whipped up clouds of dust in the final stretch.

I walked south to get closer to Heinrich's prototype. The five-minute trek took me across white diamonds that crunched under each step. To the east, where the tent city stood, a giant loudspeaker atop a high pole crackled an announcement about time trials. I tugged my hat brim low, to better shade my eyes, and I held tighter to the file folder. Up ahead, Heinrich's crew had swarmed around the car, and the German racer raised the tinted dome above his head, climbed out, and leapt onto the ground. He peeled off his goggles and helmet and handed them to a young blond-haired assistant, and his face lit up with what seemed to be genuine happiness when he saw me approaching. He squinted, offered a toothy smile, and came at me with his hand extended outward.

"Kripo!"

I headed toward him, raising my hand to grasp his, when a familiar-looking woman stepped in my path. She appeared so abruptly I nearly walked right into her. I instantly recognized her as Leni Riefenstahl. Her golden hair was made disheveled by the desert wind, and tiny flames of rage burned in her eyes with intimidating ferocity. She was wearing some sort of getup that was much too hot for the desert, involving a leather jacket, jodhpurs, and boots. Her lips were pursed. Her fists were clenched. A thin layer of sweat covered her face. Her bosoms rose and fell with each angry breath. Behind her, a cinematographer finished filming the scene and stepped away from his camera. I found Riefenstahl so intimidating that I had to back up a few steps as she advanced toward me.

"You never showed," she whispered, in her thick German accent.

"I never said I would," I whispered back.

"No *männlich* has ever turned me down."

"I'm a married *männlich*," I said, waving my wedding ring in front of her. "Pardon me, please."

As I maneuvered around her, she shot me an incredulous, open-mouthed "how dare you" look. In an uncharacteristically crass move on my part, I managed to steal a glimpse of her rear end, enough of one to know that I'd probably missed out on something memorable by not journeying to her hotel room a few nights ago. But I could bear my momentary wistful sting of regret. I can't say the same thing would have been the case had I strayed behind Clara's back. Once past formidable Fortress Riefenstahl, I went straight over to shake Rudy Heinrich's hand. His grip was firm.

"What a pleasant surprise to see you again," he said.

"You as well," I said. I gestured to the car behind him, now crawling with crew. "Practicing for the big day tomorrow?"

He glanced over his shoulder, nodding, and looked at me again. "She's not the P9, but she's the next best thing."

Just then, the phantom-like Ernst Voss chose to put in an appearance. I didn't even see where he came from. He simply cut in like a jealous husband. He looked as frail as ever, as if he'd escaped from the tuberculosis ward of the nearest sanatorium.

"What brings you out here?" he asked.

"I've come to wish Heinrich good luck tomorrow," I said.

"Thank you," said Heinrich. "We're about to pour beers over in our tent. Care to join us?"

"No thanks. But I do have a few more questions, if you have a moment."

Voss said, "All questions must be submitted in advance to my office for . . ."

"Ernst," said Heinrich, leaning toward Voss. He spoke German softly. Then he straightened and his focus—along with that big smile—returned to me. "Ask away, *kripo*. I wish to cooperate, especially if it will help in locating Clive Underhill."

"May we talk alone?" I asked, eyeing Voss's pasty face. "Shouldn't take long."

"Of course," said Heinrich. "Why don't we take a little walk?"

I noticed Voss glowering as we walked away.

We went north, away from the maintenance crew and the Nazi hangers-on. The heat was taking a toll on Heinrich. I stopped. He stopped. We faced each other. The sun bleached him and his white racing coveralls, like everything around us. I held up the file folder, and he blinked at it, then at me.

"What's that?"

"It belonged to Nigel Underhill," I said. "He loved genealogy."

"What?"

"Genealogy. It's the study of family history."

"Oh. I see." He chuckled uneasily. "Sorry, what does this have to do with Nigel?"

"Before he was murdered, he spent a lot of time at the Genealogical Society."

"What was he doing there? Researching his ancestors?"

"No. Researching yours."

Heinrich seemed even more mystified than before.

"My ancestors?"

"Yeah. He also unearthed some documents related to Gerda Strauss."

"Gerda?"

"She's your wife, no?"

"Yes." It wasn't my imagination: Heinrich was tensing up. His smile tightened. "Frau Strauss is my wife."

"So I gathered," I said. "The documents indicate that you and Strauss are Jews. I understand it's a crime to be a Jew in Germany these days."

That killed Heinrich's smile.

"You're mistaken. My mother converted to Catholicism years ago," he said. "My father was born into a long line of Catholics. That makes me a Catholic. And Gerda is a practicing Lutheran. Obviously, you don't know what you're talking about."

"Was Nigel blackmailing you with these documents? Is that it?"

He swallowed hard as he looked me up and down. "I perform a useful function to the Reich. Hitler himself called me Germany's greatest racer. He invited me to a reception at the Berghof to celebrate my Grand Prix victory at the Masaryk circuit three years ago."

"I'll ask again," I said. "Was Nigel Underhill blackmailing you?"

"The Reich authorities already know about everything in that folder," said Heinrich. "If they were going to do anything to me, they would've done it by now."

"Possibly," I said. "But there are other ways of getting to you."

"I don't follow you."

"Sir Lloyd Underhill, Nigel's father, owns newspapers in

England," I said. "Several of them. I'm sure Nigel had enough clout to persuade at least one of them to make a big stink out of this. It's one thing for the Reich bosses in Berlin to be privy to this information in private. It's a different matter entirely for the whole world to know that Rudy Heinrich is a Jew."

He turned his back on me, hands on hips, and walked out into the whiteness of salt. He stared for a long while into the distance. A faraway car thundered across the flats arrow-like, and he watched it intently. Minutes passed, and I began to wonder whether he was going to say anything. I almost broke the silence, but I thought it best to give him a chance to speak. When he looked off to the south, I saw a flash of his profile, and the smile had returned.

"Do you know what I love about this place?"

"No. What?"

"Its purity."

"What do you mean?"

"Listen. What do you hear?"

The world around us had fallen silent. Not even the wind whistled. I gazed up at the sky, so blue it almost stung my eyes to look at it. I lowered my head and set my sights on Heinrich once more.

"Nothing," I said.

"That's right. Nothing. No jackboots marching. No Luftwaffe planes in the sky. No cheering mass rallies. Sometimes we forget how beautiful it sounds, the silence."

Heinrich faced me and approached slowly. "How much do you want?"

I opened the dossier and fished out a picture. I held it up for him. "His name is Winston Booker. He's a bellhop at the Hotel Utah. His parents asked me to find him. I have a feeling he saw something over the weekend he wasn't supposed to. I don't know what it was. I thought there was a chance you might."

He glanced at the picture, then at me. "I've never seen him before. Good luck in your search."

"I'll need more than luck," I said, tucking the photo away. "I'm thinking along the lines of miracles, at this point."

"What would you say if I told you I murdered Nigel Underhill?"

"Did you?"

"What if I said I did?"

"I wouldn't believe you."

"Why?"

"Because the maître d' at the Coconut Grove confirmed my suspicions," I said. "According to him, on Saturday night—well, Sunday morning, really—you were the last guest to leave the place, along with Karl von Rimmelkopf and Dr. Meinshausen, and that would've been around three, maybe a little after. He sent you all back to the Ben Lomond in a yellow taxi because you weren't in any shape to drive. There was only one person missing from your group at the time. Ernst Voss."

"Stay away from him," Heinrich whispered grimly.

"Why?" I asked. "What's he hiding?"

"Have you ever heard of the Night of the Long Knives?"

"No. Should I have?"

He nodded. "It was blood purge four years ago. Hitler ordered mass executions of members of the *Sturmabteilung,* the Brownshirts, including its *stabschef,* Ernst Röhm. *Der Führer*'s chief executioner was another Ernst—Voss. Nobody knows how many people Voss has murdered, but I hear it numbers in the thousands."

"Where was he the night Nigel was murdered?" I asked.

"I don't know," said Heinrich. "Not with me, I can say that much."

"Not even for part of the evening?"

"No."

"One more question," I said. "Then I'll let you go."

"All right. Go ahead."

"Vaughn Perry. Name ring any bells?"

"Of course! He was my first close friend from America," he said, with a dreamy smile. "I got to know him when I was an exchange student at Oxford."

"I've got bad news for you," I said. "He's in the morgue."

Heinrich's mouth fell open. "My God. How—"

"The coroner listed the cause of death as a heroin overdose," I said. "I happen to think he was murdered."

"Who'd do such a thing?"

I dodged his question with a slight shrug, unsure of whether I could trust him if I told him I saw that it had been Voss.

"Did the two of you stay in touch over the years?"

"We wrote to each other from time to time," said Heinrich. "He stayed in Germany, and spoke the language fluently."

"How would you describe him?" I asked.

Heinrich made a long face and shrugged. "Ruggedly handsome—a bohemian type. Loved by the ladies. He practically lived outdoors. He always had a fresh tan. He loved jazz. He read literature, and had tremendous natural intellect, but not in a boastful or arrogant way. He wanted to live out in nature, like Thoreau. His father, Newton Perry, was—*is,* I suppose—a famous American fascist and radio personality. Father and son were estranged. They stopped speaking to each other years ago."

"Over what?" I asked.

"Fascism," said Heinrich. "The elder was for it, the younger against. Vaughn used to write me impassioned letters condemning Hitler and the Nazis. I'd throw them into the fire after reading them. I didn't want to get in trouble with the authorities. Of course, the censors never checked my mail because I am who I am. They've always left me alone, as long as I produced the desired results."

"When was the last time you saw or heard from Vaughn?"

"Last week," said Heinrich. "I ran into him at the Old Mill."

I arched my eyebrows in surprise. "Oh? You were there, too?"

"Yes. Clive and I frequent the same establishments."

"What about Peter Insley?"

"What about him?"

"Why was he at your hotel room the other day?"

"He's with British military intelligence," said Heinrich. "My fellow travelers were assisting him in his hunt for Clive."

"Why?" I asked.

"If it looks like we sabotaged him in any way, world opinion will turn against us. Besides, Hitler has confidence in the P9's superiority. He knows it's the world's fastest car."

I nodded, and I needed a few seconds to take it all in.

"Look, Heinrich, I'm not after you," I said. "I don't have any reason to believe you murdered Nigel. At the same time, I have this funny idea you know more than you're letting on." I checked my wristwatch—almost noon. I grew discouraged, and I could not hide it. "I'll level with you. I'm not a *kripo*, as you call it."

"No?" My words jolted him, I could tell. "Well, what . . . Who . . ."

"I quit my job the other day."

"Why are you doing this, then?"

"I thought I could do some good." I drew a deep breath. "I guess I was wrong. But thank you for your help. And good luck."

I held out my hand. He eyed it briefly then shook it. I left him, cutting across the flats to the tent city and the booming loudspeaker, the flapping banners and newsreel cameras, the bleachers and radio control booth. I returned to my car, parked among scattered vehicles, opened the door and climbed inside. I placed the dossier on the piping-hot passenger side of the front seat, pulled the door closed, and rolled down the window as I fired up the engine.

While pondered my options, I noticed a slight square bulge in my suit jacket. I reached in my pocket and pulled out a familiar matchbook. I opened it so I could reread the lewd message inside: *BEN LOMOND HOTEL, RM 1101. MIDNIGHT. COME FUCK ME. LR.* I shook my head to thoughts of that wild woman I encountered out there on the flats moments ago, and mostly I was glad I did not take her up on her offer, though a tiny butterfly of regret fluttered inside of me. I closed the matchbook and examined it. On the front flap was a cute cartoon polar bear. Right below the cuddly, smiling beast, it said:

ALPINE ICE & STORAGE COMPANY
WHOLESALE DEALERS OF ICE & BOTTLED
BEVERAGES
REFRIGERATED WAREHOUSES
REFRIGERATED INDIVIDUAL LOCKER
SERVICE
230 CANYON ROAD EAST, WENDOVER, UTAH
DIAL WENDOVER 4-4205

I checked the backside, near the coarse strip where one strikes the match.

CALL ON US FOR ALL YOUR REFRIGERATION NEEDS!

I closed my fist around the matchbook.
At last, I knew where I had to go.

Thirty-one

Wendover straddled the Utah-Nevada border. For years, it had been an obscure little railroad outpost in the middle of the desert. Everything changed when the state of Nevada legalized gambling in 1931. That was seven years ago. Since then, Wendover has expanded rapidly into a bustling town full of fancy, air-chilled hotels, shiny new restaurants, and a full-fledged supermarket with wide aisles and canned goods stacked in pyramids. Wendover was a few hours' drive on the Victory Highway west of Salt Lake City, on the other side of the Bonneville Salt Flats. Each weekend, chartered tour buses would deliver crowds of bright-faced gamblers to the burgh. They'd come with purses jingling with coins and pockets stuffed with wads of bills. They'd usually go home flat-busted broke but filled up with roast beef and liquor or, if they were Mormons, roast beef and ice cream.

Getting to Wendover involves a straight-line drive across the desert, about thirty minutes west from the Bonneville Salt Flats. High above me, cumulus clouds sailed across the sky like fluffy cotton pirate ships, casting shadows on the salted earth. Even out here, radio signals reached from afar, playing fifteen-minute-long network soap operas filled with overwrought organ music and performers reciting the kind of stilted dialogue one never hears in real life.

Too preoccupied to listen to soaps, I killed the radio on the last leg of my drive, wondering what I might find at Alpine Ice & Storage. The mere fact that Leni Riefenstahl presented me with the company's matchbook led me to believe it assumed some significance in the plans of the Germans. Before long, the facility came into view, off to my right. I pulled off the side of the road and skidded to a halt on a big strip of gravel surrounding a series of enormous, dark brown, Quonset-style arched warehouses. I shut off the engine, got out of the car, and headed straight for the front office.

"Lemme see if I've got this straight. You work for the state of Utah?"

Disbelief rang out in the kid's squeaky, almost pubescent voice. He couldn't have been older than eighteen or nineteen. On his head was a red ball cap with its visor pointing up at the ceiling. Pimples dotted his face. A pug nose, beaver front teeth, and an unruly mop of brown hair did little to boost his prospects of finding a date for Saturday night, I'm sure.

"I'm with the Board of Health," I said, spreading the lie on thick. I hated lying, but the situation called for it. "That means I answer to the governor."

As I spoke, I surveyed the room. On wood-paneled walls hung signs for nearly every major brand of soda pop and beer imaginable. In the middle of it all was a 1938 calendar advertising a Chinese food joint down the street, accentuated with multicolored dragons. A Bakelite radio played a rebroadcast of the previous day's ballgame: Cleveland Indians versus St. Louis Browns, brought to you by sparkling Dr Pepper. Bottom of the fifth. Cleveland down by two. I knew the outcome. That killed the tension.

On the counter sat a small box containing books of matches advertising the Alpine Ice & Storage Company, just like the one Leni Riefenstahl gave me that day at the Salt Flats. I smiled at the sight of the sweet little cartoon polar bear on each one.

"Ain't you got some identification?"

"Why don't you call the governor's office?" I said. "He'll vouch for me."

"Governor?"

"Look, I wish I could stand here all day and chew the cud about procedures," I said. "But I've got a doozy of a schedule to contend with. Can we make it snappy?"

"Tell me again what it is you want, mister," he said.

"I'm crisscrossing the state, inspecting refrigeration storage facilities," I said. "There's been an outbreak of poisonous bacteria along the Wasatch Front. People have been hospitalized. One lady even died. The department has traced the culprit back to bad ice. Seems somebody got careless with the temperature settings and didn't handle the product properly. It's my job to make sure companies across the state are adhering to proper refrigeration codes. That goes for this one, too."

He raised an eyebrow. "Proper *what*?"

"The temperature inside of a refrigerator belonging to a licensed business is required to be set to thirty-six degrees Fahrenheit, no warmer than forty, because bacteria sets in at forty-one," I said. "Freezers should be adjusted to a range between minus ten and plus ten degrees, to prevent spoilage in

meat and other frozen goods. Failure to adhere to these rules will
be met with a fine and or jail time, and possible confiscation of
said equipment."

He swallowed hard at the mention of jail time.

"Like I said before, mister, my manager isn't here," said the
kid. "In fact, Mr. Gulbranson doesn't even live in Wendover. He's
from Provo."

"Gulbranson, huh?" I asked, jotting his name on a clipboard
form, which I'd swiped from the vacant radio room at the Bonneville Raceway. I thought it would make me look more official.
"First name?"

"George," said the kid. "George P. Gulbranson. I think the
P is for Palmer."

"And what's your name again?"

"Does it matter?"

"Official business," I said. "Plus I find it helps—forgive the
pun—to break the ice if I learn other people's names."

"Willis Edmonds," he said. "I go by Willie. Hey, you gonna
stick it to my boss?"

"Not if he's heeding regulations, sonny," I said. "It's actually
a good thing he's not here. I find that owners get needlessly antsy
when I'm giving their place of business a good going-over. So tell
me something."

"Sure. Anything."

"It looks like Mr. Gulbranson is doing pretty well for himself," I said. "Who are his clients?"

"You'd be amazed at how many people need cold things out
in the middle of the desert," said Willie. "You know, soft drinks,
beer, spirits, dairy products, meats, frozen novelty treats, bags
of ice. We service the hotels, the big I.G.A. down the street, all
the little roadside markets, and a bunch of local customers.

Mr. Gulbranson even rents space out here, too. The man rakes in some handsome profits, enough to buy a hunting lodge up in Wyoming."

"A whole hunting lodge huh? Look at that," I said, making a *tsch* sound out the side of my mouth.

"Hey, mister?"

"Yeah?"

"Have you actually arrested anybody for peddling bad ice?" he asked.

"You'd be surprised," I said. "The state penitentiary is packed with fellows who thought the rules only applied to others."

My words spooked the lad. "Jeepers. All that for making bum ice?"

"Listen, sonny," I said, "if you just hand me the keys to these warehouses, I'll go take a gander on my own. All I have to do is take a peek at the temperature inside of each one and then I'll be out of your hair."

Off a wall hook near that Chinese restaurant calendar, he plucked a master key ring with six keys on it and handed it to me.

"They're numbered, to correspond with each building," he said. "They unlock the rear entrances. I figured that's the best way to get inside. To save yourself some time, you can just skip warehouse six."

"Why?" I asked. "What's in it?"

"The Germans rented it out," he said.

"Germans?"

"Yeah, they forked over a pretty penny for it, and demanded the whole thing to themselves." He leaned across the counter and spoke softly. "They're real private. Queer as all get-out. They come and go as they please, at all hours. I've only seen 'em two, three times. Of course, when I'm alone here in the front office, I play the music and ballgames loud, so I don't hear much of anything outside. "

"What do you suppose they're keeping in there?" I whispered.

"Beats me," he said. "They've been mighty secretive about it, whatever it is."

I nodded and wiggled the jingling keys. "So skip number six, you're saying?"

"If you wanna save time," he said.

"That I do, sonny," I said. "Thank you for the tip."

"Don't mention it."

"Back soon," I said.

"I'll 'hang a lantern aloft in the belfry arch,'" he said, quoting Longfellow.

"'One if by land, and two if by sea,'" I said, finishing the line.

"'Paul Revere's Ride,'" he said. "Did you have to read it in English, too?"

"In my day the course was called Poetics," I said. "And we had to commit it to memory. See you soon, sonny."

"I'll be here when you're done."

To the west, a thunderstorm churned. Ominous clouds hovered low in the sky and sailed toward us. Webbing bolts, so bright they burned into your vision when you closed your eyes, shot out of the heavens, dancing on the desert floor. Rarely did it ever rain in bone-dry Wendover. Right now, however, darkening skies threatened to open up with a downpour. I had to move fast. I went from warehouse to warehouse, opening back doors, peering inside, and jotting gibberish on my clipboard forms before moving on, in case the kid was looking out the window at me. I crossed a stretch of gravel, reaching the sixth warehouse, where the Germans were staying.

I slid the diamond-shaped key with a white number 6 on it into the lock, turned it, unlocked the door, and placed a stone against the frame to prevent it from latching shut while I was gone. Next, I jogged back over to the front office, housed in a flat-topped brick box with arched windows. I threw open the front door, dropped the keys on the counter, and muttered a hasty "good-bye, and thanks."

"That's all?" asked Willie.

"I'm done."

"That didn't take long."

"Like I said, I'm on a tight schedule."

"So. Is he in trouble?" asked Willie.

"Who?"

"Mr. Gulbranson." When the name did not register with me for a second, he shot me an incredulous look. "My boss."

"Oh. Him? Naw. He gets a clean bill of health."

"Shoot," he said.

"Disappointed?" I asked.

"I don't mind a good fireworks show, long as it don't poke my eye out."

I chuckled. "Later days, kid."

"So long, mister."

I returned to the dry heat of outdoors to ponder my next move. The clouds above furnished only slight relief. Earlier, when I arrived here, I'd parked my car up the road half a mile, behind a billboard for a local casino hotel. I figured it'd be safe in that spot, in case any unanticipated problems should arise. Presently, I had to find out what was in warehouse six. I moved briskly toward it, creeping inside the back door and kicking away the stone that'd been propping it open. I pressed a button on the wall and a trio of electric bulbs above my head went on, bathing the area in light. I found myself in a narrow corridor. I pulled the back door closed behind me. The temperature plunged to somewhere in the upper 30s or low 40s. I walked to the end of the corridor, where a smaller second door awaited. I turned the knob and opened it.

I slipped inside a freezing room of gigantic proportions. Poorly lit. Thirty-foot-high ceiling. I exhaled steam. A refrigeration system hummed, and air from giant fans almost blew my hat off. I opted against switching on the overhead floodlights, which I could tell would be bright. Instead, I relied on the little bit of light spilling in from the corridor behind me and the few glowing bulbs above me.

I instantly found what I was looking for. Parked in the center of the room, facing a set of double doors, the long Mercedes-Benz P9 appeared as a silver ghost, with its front tires concealed under rounded fenders, and its four rear wheels encased in long tailfins. Its wings spread outward like those of a diving bird, and it gave off a mixed scent of rubber and oil and freshly painted parts. The swastika emblem on the side was cold to the touch. I stood next to twenty-six feet of chilled, aerodynamic machinery, one of the greatest automotive engineering feats of the twentieth century, admiring it and its matching reflection gleaming in the polished concrete floor.

It made sense, storing the P9—a car more suited to a cooler, mountainous region—in a frigid place with a controlled climate. Out here, in this desert, even the most robust of cars could take a beating, and the Germans did not want to take any risks. I stepped away from the car and scanned the room. Something in the shadows on the other side of the room caught my eye. I went closer, for a better look. Eight movie cameras attached to tripods stood in a neat row. A familiar diamond-shaped UFA logo on the side of each camera reminded me of my first meeting with Leni Riefenstahl, while she was shooting her documentary. The Germans undoubtedly planned on scoring a great victory this Saturday, and they assigned a high priority to capturing it on film. In addition to the cameras, a large Moviola editing device sat atop a wooden table, and a movie projector with a reel of film threaded into it was aimed at a portable screen. I'd worked a projector before, back when I had a job in a local movie theater. I hit the ON switch, the sprockets rattled, the reel turned, and light flickered onto the screen. Black-and-white images of the P9 whizzing across the Salt Flats filled the screen, with a shrill, nasally male narrating in German, a language I could not understand. I switched off the projector, walked over to the cameras, peeked through a viewfinder. All I could see was blackness.

I backed away from the camera and shifted my focus to one of those wide and thick freezer doors on the wall, as white as the fallen snow, with a chrome handle. When I opened it, a wall of icy cold blew in my face. It was pitch-black inside. No windows in here. I reached in and switched on a set of lights. The whole room lit up. Dangling meat hooks and smaller storage freezers filled all parts of the freezer. Right then, I heard distant movement—the sound of car brakes squealing outside, followed by slamming doors. I shut off the freezer lights, slipped out the door and closed it.

Thirty-two

In the frigid darkness of the warehouse, the tinted P9 cockpit dome beckoned.

Sprinting over to it, I almost tripped over a canvas tarp spread out on the ground. I scrambled up the side, gripping a handle below the base of the dome and giving it a firm tug. The covering hissed upward like an alligator's snout opening, and when it was high enough, I dove into a black leather seat facing a maroon steering wheel. Once inside, I lifted my arms and pulled the dome down. It snapped in place, but was not all the way closed because a thin strip of light shone through the base. I was about to pull it down harder when a pair of men strode out of the shadows. I drew a deep breath, easing lower into the seat so I had just enough height to peer through the bottom of the dome at the ghostly silhouettes coming closer, their faces shrouded in darkness. They soon stepped into the dim glow of the bulbs hanging overhead. The men faced each other, and the yellowish light from above illuminated the faces of Dr. Hans Meinshausen, attired for a long Bavarian winter in a matching Homburg hat and dark suit, and Julian Pangborn, in a baggy three-piecer much too big for him and frayed around the lapels, and a battered brown fedora.

Both men raised arms in *heil Hitler* salutes, and exchanged handshakes.

"Thank you for coming all this way out here, Julian," said Meinshausen. "Tell me, are any of your fellow Englishmen aware you're here?"

"*Nein,*" said Julian, now sounding very German. "*Ich nieman-den erzählt.*"

"In English," said Meinshausen. "Please."

Julian began speaking with flawless BBC diction. "I came alone. I told no one."

"Music to my ears, Julian. Music to my ears." Meinshausen grinned widely in approval. "You know, I still remember the day you stepped off the train in Berlin, all those years ago, a starry-eyed British fascist with a mind full of high ideals, aided by a splendid letter of introduction from Oswald Mosley. Your dedication to the cause has always impressed me, not to mention your sweeping knowledge of all things automotive. There's a reason why I handpicked you to return to England to infiltrate Underhill's team. *Der Führer* wants Germany to be the world's preeminent motor racing nation. Great Britain is the main obstacle in the way of the fatherland achieving that status. You've contributed so much to ridding us of that obstacle."

"I thank you again, sir," said Julian. "I am moved by your generous words."

"Good, because regrettably, Julian, my praise is tempered with a certain degree of criticism," he said. "To date, nothing has gone according to plan. You assured me that bomb you planted under the Desert Lightning on Saturday would destroy the car and kill the driver if it detonated close to the gas tank. You said you rigged it so the explosion would appear to be an accident."

"Yes, that's true. It would have succeeded had it not been for—"

"Uh, uh, uh—please, let me finish," said Meinshausen. "I'm distressed about your failed attempt to bomb Clive's vehicle, not to mention the eyewitnesses at the hotel that saw you take Nigel's life in the wee hours of Sunday morning."

"I did you a favor," said Julian. "He was planning to blackmail you with those genealogy documents, and he was going to tell Shaw about the bomb-making supplies he found in my bag."

"Yes, I know all of that. You might've succeeded in your task, were it not for the fact that you left the door wide open for that Negro bellhop to see everything."

"I'm sorry. I said before I wasn't in my right state of mind."

Meinshausen nodded. "And what about the Canadian couple staying across the hall from Nigel who reported seeing a scuffle—"

"They weren't real," said Julian.

"Not real? What did Metzger do? Wave a magic wand and a Canadian couple suddenly appeared?"

"No, they were tramps," said Julian. "Husband and wife, living in a hobo camp out by the railway tracks. Metzger bribed them to give a false testimony to the police to back up the Negro's claims. Metzger said the police rarely ever take a colored man's word for it. He gave the bums a night in the hotel, a fresh change of clothing, a couple of free steak dinners and all the booze they could drink, in exchange for claiming to be in the room across the way from Nigel and seeing that ex-cop Lund assault him. The hoboes thought they'd died and gone to heaven, and because Metzger was the hotel detective, the police took his word for it that they were who he said they were. For all I know, they're both long gone."

"Hmm, I see," said Meinshausen. "And Vaughn Perry? What possessed you to take his life?"

"Metzger did it, not me. I just went along to help," said Julian. "Metzger wanted to steer the police away from me by strong-arming the bellhop into giving false testimony to frame that Lund chap. In exchange, I helped him get rid of Perry. Metzger set up Perry's death to look like an overdose. Metzger used to be a police detective. He said cops never look into overdoses. They always assume it is what looks like—a fool addict getting sloppy."

"A sly one, Metzger," said Meinshausen, with a tinge of disgust in his voice. "When his name came up on a Gestapo list of foreign sympathizers earlier this year, I admit I was intrigued. After all, he was head of security at the hotel where Clive Underhill would be staying. I made my first trip out here two months ago just to meet with him in private. I devised a plan that would involve him placing a tasteless, colorless, odorless poison into one of Clive's meals—a poison that could not be detected by any postmortem tests. It would cause heart failure, which is what Clive's death certificate would say. This was our backup plan in the event that your little bomb failed to do the trick. Metzger agreed to help, but demanded money. I gave him what he asked for. After Clive went missing, Metzger wanted more money to coerce the Negro into lying to the police. If I'd known Metzger's allegiance came at such a high price, I wouldn't have asked for his help in the first place."

"I never liked him," said Julian. "I don't trust him."

"Neither do I. We've a substantial dossier on him. Voss has

been monitoring his movements since we got here. It alarmed us when he quit his job at the Hotel Utah."

"He warned me he was going to," said Julian. "The police and the FBI coming around, asking a lot of questions, really spooked him."

"I'm sure you're right. Tell me. Do you know where he went?"

Julian shook his head. "Last I saw him, he said he was going to hide behind the Walls of Jericho. I don't know what he meant. He did say the Negro bellhop was planning to go to the police to confess the real story of what happened. That's why Metzger abducted him. He says he'll put the bellhop out of his miseries when you fellows pay him the money you owe him."

Hiding in that small space, I'd just heard so much that I wasn't sure where to begin. Which revelation upset me most? That Julian Pangborn—that mousy mechanic I could hardly understand—was a spy working for the Germans? That it was a bomb that nearly killed Clive out at the Salt Flats? Or that Winston "Blue" Booker was in imminent danger, and—for all I knew—might even be dead?

They all chilled me to the bone. And then add to that what I already knew or suspected: that the McKennas were a fictional creation of the sick mind of Dooley Metzger, and that Vaughn Perry's death was a murder staged to resemble an accidental overdose. But the most troubling to me was the fate of Booker, the most purely innocent figure in this whole terrible ordeal. He was a sweet kid, and he didn't deserve to die at the hands of a monster like Metzger. I desperately yearned to take Booker back home to his parents. But now I was starting to wonder if I would ever see him alive again.

"Tell me something," said Meinshausen. "Why did Metzger want Perry dead?"

I raised my head high enough to peek through the tinted glass to see Julian's surprised reaction to the question. "He didn't tell you?"

"Tell me what?"

"About the plot?"

"Plot? What are you talking about?"

"Clive, Vaughn Perry, and Rudy Heinrich. They were schoolmates at Oxford. They used to be called the Three Musketeers back in England. They were inseparable. They've stayed friends over the years. They were all in on the plan."

"Please explain this plan. I don't know what you mean."

"They were going to stage a fake kidnapping," said Julian. "They wanted to make it look like the Platinum Legion kidnapped Clive. They went to great lengths to write doctored ransom notes and find a hiding place—a cabin—way out in the wilderness, where Clive could lay low. Clive always wanted to explore some canyons that were located in some remote part of Utah. I can't remember what they were called."

The Canyons of the Escalante, I thought to myself, as I took in Julian's words. *So that's why Clive asked me on Saturday night to show him around down there.*

"Why stage a fraudulent abduction?" asked Meinshausen. "What have they to gain?"

"That all depends on who you ask," said Julian. "Vaughn hoped the kidnaping would get played up in the press and result in the FBI cracking down on his father's precious Platinum Legion. He hated the Platinum Shirts. He thought they robbed him of a father."

"And Clive?"

"It gets him out of the crowds and the spotlight, and into the wilds," said Julian. "You know they're making a movie about him now? Clive wanted to get away from all that. And besides, he saw it as a way to help Heinrich."

"Heinrich?"

Julian nodded. "Yeah. Heinrich wanted to remove Clive from the competition, thereby making him the world's fastest motorist. Heinrich planned to use his victory as leverage to escape Germany."

"That's quite a revelation," said Meinshausen. "How do you know it's true?"

"Because last week, Heinrich showed Clive a letter, written by Dr. Goebbels himself, promising him that if he set a new land speed record on the Salt Flats, the Reich would issue stamped exit visas for Heinrich's family, and his wife, Gerda Strauss, to sail to Shanghai."

"How interesting. Dr. Goebbels never informed me of such a letter."

"Heinrich has it," said Julian. "I didn't know until recently that he's a Jew. I hope something is done to knock him down a few pegs."

Meinshausen ignored that last comment. He began walking toward the P9. I held as still as I could, keeping low, yet coiled up in fear about the prospect of Winston Booker being murdered. He checked his look in the window's reflection. Had it not been tinted, he would have seen me in the cockpit. After running his hand over his head, he opened his mouth and slid his tongue over his front teeth.

"How do you know all of this?" he finally asked.

"I overheard it from a men's room toilet stall at the Old Mill," said Julian. "They thought they were alone, Clive and Rudy. They spoke candidly to each other."

"You still haven't said why Metzger murdered Perry."

Julian scowled. "I'm getting there, give me a bloody chance! On Tuesday, I rode with Metzger out to Perry's house. They quarreled."

"About what?"

"Metzger demanded to know where Clive was. Perry claimed he didn't know. Metzger called him a liar. Perry threatened to call the manager of the Hotel Utah and tell him about Metzger being in the Platinum Shirts. Metzger pulled a gun on Perry and told me to tie him up. I did. Metzger threatened to kill Perry if he didn't reveal Clive's whereabouts. Perry got scared; insisted he didn't know where Clive was. Metzger made good on his threat with a syringe full of pure-grade heroin."

"Where did he get it?"

"The Platinum Shirts sell it on the streets to raise money. They hadn't cut it yet, so it wasn't diluted. The stuff gave off quite a bang. It wasn't pretty. Perry was screaming and flailing and begging for his life, trying to get loose. But by then, it was too late. Metzger found a vein and—well, the smack killed Perry instantly. I helped carry the body into the bedroom. We set him up in bed to look like an overdose."

"What a horrid way to meet one's end. Tell me, do you think Perry was telling the truth about not knowing where Clive was?

"Yes, I do."

"Have you any idea where Clive might be?"

"I've got my theories."

"Please speak candidly," said Meinshausen.

"I think Peter Insley is hiding Clive. Insley is with Military Intelligence. I'm certain of it. I've got this theory that he called on the FBI for help—you know, to get Clive to a safe place, out of harm's way. Insley knows it would be a huge blow to England if Clive Underhill ended up dead, like his brother. You'd better bet they aim to keep him alive at any cost. That's what I think, anyhow."

"I'm sure you're right," said Meinshausen. "It's hard to say good-bye. You are rather like a son to me."

Julian shot Meinshausen a confused look. "What do you mean? I'm going with you."

"No. I'm afraid you're not."

"You promised me a position in *der Führer*'s motorcade. Remember?"

Meinshausen turned sideways and sneezed into a handkerchief. Something about it did not sound right. It seemed staged, for effect.

"I hate summer colds," he said quietly. "I wish this one would go away."

From out of the darkness strode Karl von Rimmelkopf. The dim light above his head flashed a reflection on a shiny object in his hand. He moved right up behind Julian, pressed a straight razor into the wiry mechanic's throat, and slashed it so hard I heard skin ripping and blood splashing. I watched in stunned disbelief. Unarmed, I could do nothing. At least now I knew what that canvas tarp was doing there. Julian crumpled like a scarecrow falling off of its support beam. While his body was still quivering, von Rimmelkopf began rolling him up in the tarpaulin. My heart ached from pounding. Terror filled me, down to the marrow of my bones. *Why,* I asked myself, *didn't I do anything to stop it?* It was so sudden. I didn't see it coming. I shook all over, fearful of never seeing my family again. I began to have a panic attack. I had to get out of there.

What possessed me to turn the key in the ignition, below the word ZÜNDUNG engraved on a metal plate, I will never know. The engine turned over right away. Simply idling, it sounded like a herd of buffalos.

The dashboard lit up in a burst of multicolored lights. It resembled what I imagined an airplane's cockpit might look like. Dials. Gauges. Buttons. Switches. Everything labeled in German, down to the tiniest blinking indicator.

Von Rimmelkopf rushed past Meinshausen, aiming a Luger straight at me. Meinshausen leapt at him and forced down the outstretched arm holding the firearm. The gun went off. The bullet hit the ground, spraying dust and debris and tiny pieces of concrete. *"Nein, nein, nein! Sie werden das auto schaden!"*

Meinshausen rushed to the car and began pounding on the tinted window. "Get out! Now! Hands up, where we can see them!"

Shifting in my seat, raising my arms, I almost did as he said. *Almost.* At the last possible second, however, a different notion hit me.

Thirty-three

A blue button blinked below the word FENSTERSICHERUNGEN. I don't know what it meant, but I pushed it. Hissing accompanied the movement of a series of a metal latches at the base of the canopy dome. That sealed it shut. Meinshausen struggled to open the hatch. Failing that, he smacked the window with his palm. I'm pretty sure he cussed in German.

I found a gear lever next to the seat. I bent forward, squeezed its trigger, and pulled it toward me. The P9 shot backward several feet, jerking my head forward, only to have it snap back when the rear of the car hit the wall. I pulled the lever further back, tires squealed, and the silver giant shot forward. A pair of closed warehouse doors came toward me.

I held my breath, depressed the gas pedal with my heel, and used the P9 as a battering ram. The machine smashed through doors, shattering wood, flipping a padlock and chain through space like a twirling snake. The silver bullet fired into the sunlight as I gripped the steering wheel at ten and two.

The Bonneville Salt Flats appeared as a shimmering line west of here, with faraway mountains floating above it. Getting there was torture. Rocky terrain rose and dipped and broke out into a multitude of random bumps. The P9 bounced violently, banging and thudding and rocking its way through clouds of debris and dirt. I found it unbearably jarring. I'd never driven a vehicle this huge or fast, with this many bells and whistles. The pros trained for weeks on end to race machines like this. What chance did a novice like me stand? Slim to none, I thought.

Bobbing up and down, like a buoy in a hurricane, I tried to chart my next move.

I recalled something Julian said: *"Last I saw him, he said something about the Walls of Jericho, but I don't know what he meant."* Then I remembered that before he was a cop, Dooley Metzger worked as a security guard out at the Jericho Salt Works plant, located on a lonely stretch of shoreline south of the Great Salt Lake.

A jarring thud brought me back to the present. The P9 had jumped over a mound and landed hard. The constant scraping and screeching and thwacking of desert scrub against the car's underside made me cringe. Thankfully, the ground began to level. But the Salt Flats remained a couple of miles up ahead.

I had company. To my right, at three o'clock, a sleek black Cadillac convertible raced to keep up with me. I glanced at the speedometer. I'd reached 100 kilometers per hour. I pressed harder on the gas pedal, but it wouldn't go much faster. The Cadillac caught up with me. Ernst Voss opened the back door and crept out onto the running board.

When the car got close enough to the P9's wing, he leapt onto the shiny silver surface. His hat blew off. He started crawling across the body, inching closer to the cockpit canopy. Meantime, the Cadillac sped up and swerved in front of me. Red brake lights flashed. I lead-footed the gas pedal. The front of the P9 rammed into the Cadillac's bumper. The driver, Meinshausen, hit the brakes. The P9 scooped up the Cadillac's rear. The Cadillac was now moving on two tires.

Off to my side, Voss held on for dear life. His hair blew in a hundred directions. On his stomach, he located an exterior panel near the cockpit. He pried it open with his fingers. I craned my neck to see him fish a key out of his pocket, plug it in, and turn it. The interior locks hissed. Latches slid. The loosened window rattled. He slid over to the canopy and gripped the concealed handle. A second later, the cockpit dome rose, the engine's roar sliced my eardrums, and a wall of wind hit my face. Dust filled the cockpit. A set of knuckles struck my face. Pain, sharp and intense, shot through my body. A hand from outside gripped the steering wheel.

"Halten sie das auto!" he shouted. "Pull over or I kill you!"

In front of me, the Cadillac had come free and was fishtailing. More bumper smacking ensued. Voss grabbed my collar and began pulling me. I let go of the steering wheel long enough to buckle the safety harness around my chest and lap. That was hard to do with Voss trying to uproot me. When I finally had it fastened, I grabbed ahold of the steering wheel and planted both feet deep into the brake pedal. The P9 screeched to a near-halt. Voss flew through the air, a rag doll in the blue sky. I lifted my feet off of the brake and accelerated. Voss hit the dirt and rolled. I swerved and narrowly missed him.

For a few glorious seconds, I thought I'd shaken off the Cadillac. It appeared again, though, this time to my left, at nine o'clock. For the life of me, I could not understand why the P9 would not go above 100 kilometers per hour, which was about as fast as my Dodge would go. World's fastest car? Hardly. A big, clunky Cadillac could easily keep pace with me. If I bore down on the gas pedal any harder, I feared my foot would smash through the floor.

The Cadillac's passenger door opened and Karl von Rimmelkopf balanced on the running board. He shouted, but he could not be heard above the engine's roar. He waved his hand dramatically, as if motioning to Meinshausen to steer closer to the P9. Whenever the Cadillac would close in, I'd jerk the steering wheel leftward and veer in the opposite direction. It was having the desired effect, alarming von Rimmelkopf each time.

I fixed my gaze ahead. By my own reckoning, we would reach the Salt Flats in a few minutes. Before that, it was rough earth, with bumps growing bigger, sending both vehicles leaping up and down, sparking our own mini Dust Bowl. I heard—and felt—a thump. Von Rimmelkopf had leapt onto the P9's left wing. I began swerving—left and right and left again—but his hands clung on to the edges like a vise.

He leapt over to the dome, landing against the hard glass surface. He wasted no time in digging his fingers under the handle, seizing it with his grip. He unholstered his pistol. I resumed weaving, hoping my sudden movements would throw him off. No such luck. "Pull over!" he screamed. "Or I shoot!"

Next I peered into the bad end of his Luger.

"OK!" I shouted. "I'm stopping! Don't shoot!"

I stepped on the brake and the car slowed to a halt. Von Rimmelkopf jerked his gun in little motions to coax me out. Meantime, the Cadillac had U-turned and was heading this way. I pressed the canopy upward and moved as if I were about to climb out. Out of sight, my right hand probed the floor, stopping at the oxygen tank. I unstrapped it.

"Get out! Now! *Schneller!*"

Poor guy never the saw the oxygen tank coming. The bottom cracked his jaw, making a terrific metallic "pang." Blood spurted. He closed his eyes, spat a tooth, and fired his gun into the sky. I nailed him a second time with the tank for good measure. He toppled off the side of the car. A shocked Meinshausen, now getting out of the Cadillac, slipped back behind the steering wheel. Meantime, I pulled the canopy down, locked it in place, and resumed driving. I held the steering wheel with my left hand while I strapped the oxygen tank back in its place with the other.

The speedometer climbed to 45, then 50. The Cadillac caught up to my right. Meinshausen flung open the driver's side door, steered close to the P9, then rushed out onto the running board and dove onto the right wing. The driverless Cadillac slowed and swerved off into a dust cloud. Meinshausen inchwormed to the car's rear. I craned my neck to watch him.

He lifted a hinged cover halfway between the cockpit and the car's rear. He now had access to the gigantic engine. His upper body dipped into the opening and he commenced fiddling. I swerved more—right, left, right, left—but he held on. I even slammed on the brakes, which worked on Voss, but not on Meinshausen.

The car now sped over the smooth-surfaced Salt Flats, leaving the bumpy terrain behind. All of my swerving and braking and assorted efforts to buck the stocky Nazi off the back of the car were failing. I feared he'd soon figure out a way to manually shut down the engine. I scanned the blinking, buzzing mosaic in front of me, looking for something that might help me out of this predicament.

A green button with a lightning bolt in its center looked

promising. Above it, it said: DB 603-MW 50 METHANOL/WASSER-
EINSPRITZUNG. *All I have to lose is my life,* I thought. I pressed
the button.

The whole car began to vibrate. The engine fell silent. The
speedometer needle dropped. *55 . . . 50 . . . 45 . . . 40 . . . 35 . . .*
Tiny lights blinked everywhere. A warning signal near the oxygen mask flashed on and off. Sensing something was about to
happen, I strapped it over my face, covering my nose and mouth.

In that instant, another engine began to power up, this one
far louder than its predecessor. Meinshausen hurriedly slammed
the panel shut and jumped off the back of the moving vehicle in
a mad panic. He got off in the nick of time.

The car blasted forward, a rocket on wheels, in a sudden burst
of velocity. The force thrust me deep into my seat. The speedometer needle shot above 100, then 150, then 200. Endless
stretches of crystal flats passed under me in seconds. A free-falling
sensation twisted my stomach.

Careening through space at speeds I never thought possible,
I gripped the steering wheel tightly. At those speeds, my equi-
librium unraveled. I didn't know if I was upside down, right side
up, sideways, or backward. The urge to vomit into that oxygen
mask hit me. I held back.

In the midst of all of that turmoil, a feeling of inner peace
settled over me. I no longer feared death. I gazed out at that white
surface, and the distant peaks, and marveled at the beauty around
me. My sense of balance was restored. In fact, I had never been
so calm in my entire life.

The speedometer neared 300. Closing my eyes, I inhaled fresh
oxygen. I'm not sure if what happened next was a dream or if it
was real. Opening my eyes, I found myself passing through

clouds. Coming out the other end, blue sky permeated my view. I lost track of time. Was I experiencing this for one second or one hour? I could not be sure. My father's face took shape in the glass canopy above me. His presence seemed so strong and real. I wanted to talk to him. I wanted to say all of the things I wished I could have told him in that hospital room before death took him away.

But his likeness began to fade. I barely had time to say "I love you."

All at once, the sensation of leaving the ground surged through me, filling my stomach with butterflies. The P9 was airborne. I tipped my head back, looking directly up into the dome at crystal flats that had once been below me. I realized I was upside down. Falling through space, the vehicle landed with a deafening crash, and I lost all consciousness.

Thirty-four

I was hanging upside down in a cocoon of shattered glass and twisted steel. Outside, a storm brought heavy rain. I unclipped the safety harness and plunged, falling face first against a bed of salt crystals and glass shards. Little orange flames crackled all around me, and stinking petrol fumes filled the air. In my mind, I was taken back to when I pulled Clive Underhill out of the fiery wreckage of his Desert Lightning. Only this time, there was nobody to help extract me from the P9.

I located a narrow opening. I barely fit through it, like a gopher squeezing out of a hole he had no business trying to get through. I wiggled my way outside into pouring rain. Rolling over on my back, I surveyed the damage. The P9 had jumped off of an embankment, flipped over on its back, and was now a smashed-up shadow of its former glory. Lightning flashed across the slate-gray sky as I struggled to my feet, gripping the swastika-emblazoned vehicle to maintain my balance.

The rain fell unusually hard for Utah's West Desert. I'd never experienced a monsoon, but this is what I imagined they were like. I headed away from the P9, unsure of where I was going. I walked with a limp, resulting from a sharp pain in my foot. I stumbled repeatedly. At one point, I fell to my knees and vomited. I ran my hands over my banged-up face. Blood coated my fingertips.

Through the curtain of rain, I squinted. Up ahead in the distance stood the ruins of one of the Jericho Salt Works buildings, a sprawling, forlorn hulk on the southern shore of the Great Salt Lake. I set off in that direction, practically swimming, and soaked to the marrow. Years ago, Jericho enjoyed a top spot as one of the largest salt producers in the world. In its heyday, back in the 1920s, the company owned a railway line and train, and would ship workers in from nearby Grantsville. For those small-town boys, landing a job at Jericho meant you'd made it big in the world.

Those days were gone. Now tucked away in this corner of nowhere, the main building—five stories of rust-splotched corrugated walls and shattered windows—had only its reflection in the briny lake to keep it company. Two towering salt silos dominated the factory's southern side, and below them ran a twin set of railroad tracks still boasting lines of phantom cars coupled together that hadn't been used since the start of the decade.

Pyramids of salt, a hundred feet high, surrounded the refinery. Located between the building and the lake were huge diked ponds where salt used to be evaporated. They fed conveyor belts that had been silent for ages and had eroded over time, and the white landscape was dotted with abandoned tractors with salt shovels or elevator scoops that sat decaying like mechanical dinosaurs.

I once read that, at its height, Jericho manufactured 1,200 tons of salt per week. It went out all across America and around the world. But hard times took a toll on the company, and mounting pressure from its chief competitors, namely Morton and Royal Crystal, forced it to close its doors sometime around 1930 or 1931.

I limped to a chain-link fence enclosing the building. A sign read PRIVATE PROPERTY. TRESPASSERS WILL BE PROSECUTED. There was no getting through that padlock and chain sealing the gate shut. I walked along the length of the grounds until I found what I sought: a remote stretch of fence that had been torn wide enough to accommodate a large automobile. Multiple tire tracks crisscrossed the muddy flat surrounding the plant. I passed through the opening of the fence and headed toward the imposing structure. I stepped onto train tracks and entered the building through the railroad car bay. It was a relief to finally be out of the rain. Despite being wet, wounded, and disoriented, I somehow kept my wits about me. The floor of the plant was elevated above the tracks, like a subway station. I scaled to the top on an iron ladder anchored to the wall. My feet clinked on the rungs until I reached the platform, giving me my first view of a vast room filled with steel girder columns and rows of windows on all sides. Outside, lightning webbed across the sky, and thunder's distant rumble followed.

I knew I was taking a chance, coming here unarmed, with no idea of what to expect. I'd behaved rashly back at the refrigerated warehouse in Wendover. Still, this was my only lead. I was desperate, and I hadn't thought this through clearly. My top priority was to find Booker. I gave a silent prayer that I'd find him alive, yet in my heart I feared he was dead, or missing.

I ventured deeper into the ruins. Water dripped in spots. It was hard to see, but just enough dim gray light filtered in through the giant windows, enabling me to see dormant kiln driers, pumps, long tables, industrial weighing scales, packaging machines, conveyor belts, broken glass, scattered lumber, and twisted piles of metal and rot and who knows what else. Every step I took, the floor crunched and cracked under my shoe soles. Lightning burst in the skies and I couldn't even count to ten in my mind before the thunder arrived.

I came up behind the darkened shape of a man tied down to a wooden chair, his head drooping low into his chest. I rushed over and squatted in front of him and began untying the ropes around his ankles.

"I'm going to get you out of here," I said.

A sharp pain ripped through my shoulder, accompanied by a startling gunshot. I fell over on the wet concrete ground. Blood drained out of a hole in me. A moment later, a flashlight beam left me momentarily blinded, and I squinted in the darkness to see three figures closing in on me. Unarmed, surrounded, and possibly mortally wounded, I feared for sure I was a dead man.

"Lift him up."

Two separate sets of hands—big, strong, thick—scooped me up by the armpits and lifted me, scarecrow-like, to my feet. Before I could gain my balance, a tightly clenched fist plowed deep into my stomach, knocking the wind out of me. I tried to double over, but the men on either side of me held me upright. I glanced at them. To my right was Grady Hedgepeth, lean and Roman-nosed with a cleft chin and balding on the top of his head, and to my left was Earl Starkey, crew cut, double chinned, flab everywhere. Starkey grinned, visibly pleased to be here, while Hedgepeth remained shifty-eyed and nervous. They had once been patrolmen and partners at the SLCPD. I knew not to look at either man for too long. Instead I stared blankly ahead of me, trying hard not to let the terror I felt inside show.

Once more, a flashlight beam stabbed my eyes. I blinked my way through the brightness. While still holding his revolver, Dooley Metzger reached over and poked his index finger in the bullet hole. Searing pain racked my shoulder, accompanied by the gory sound of his finger wiggling against blood and muscle and bone. It took me several seconds to realize that the blood-curdling scream I heard was actually coming from me.

"Damn," he said, pulling away his hand with the gun in it. "You ought to have that looked at."

His goons burst into laughter as I writhed in agony. Every inch of me burned with pain and dizziness, and the world around me seemed to be spinning like a top. I wanted nothing more than to fall over, curl into the fetal position, and throw up on the ground next to me. For a brief moment, I began to wonder whether I would survive this ordeal. By now, his flashlight bulb had burned its way into my retina. I closed my eyes and a bright dot vibrated in the blackness.

"How did you know about this place?" asked Metzger.

When I failed to answer, Starkey and Hedgepeth gave me a violent shake.

"The man asked you a question," said Hedgepeth.

"Tell him, ya bastard," growled Starkey.

"You used to be a security guard here," I said. "Says so in your personnel file."

"How did you know I'd be here?"

"I guessed. It's a perfect hiding spot. It's secluded, not in use anymore. Who'd think to look here?"

"You did," said Metzger. "I take it you're looking for him."

He cast the beam of light on a sight so grisly it shocked me to the depths of my soul: the mutilated remains of Winston Booker, tied down to a chair. Much of his skin and his maroon outfit had

been thoroughly shredded, and thousands—maybe millions—
of sparkling salt diamonds were embedded in the bloody red and
pink subcutaneous layers of his corpse.

"I hated to do it," said Metzger. "He sobbed like a baby when
I tied his ankles to the rear bumper of my car. He put up one
hell of a fight. You can see his claw marks on the back of the car.
Poor kid. I liked him. He was polite. Knew his place. Kept to it.
He'd repeat—word for word—everything I ordered him to say
to the police. I used him as a bargaining chip to spook the Ger-
mans. Thanks to him, I'm fifty G's richer. Yes sir, it's a real shame
I had to kill him."

"Why did you?" I asked.

He grinned for a second. I did not see his gun coming at me.
The first hit was the most painful, the most jarring, and I heard
something crack. I was dazed. Each blow struck my head hard,
and sent waves of raw agonizing hurt through my skull and out
to the rest of me. My legs collapsed. The two men on either side
of me had to hold me up to prevent me from crumpling. The
beating lasted less than a minute, yet it seemed to go on forever.
Unrelenting. Savage. Blood ran down my forehead. It collected
in my eyes. It spread across my cheeks and dripped off the tip of
my nose. I drifted in and out of consciousness. I had never been
beaten so savagely. I'm not sure I had anything left to vomit up.

"Because I enjoy doing things like that," Metzger said, laughing.

I ended up on the ground, numb all over, with a trio of men
kicking me all over my body. My legs and arms and ribs and face
took a pounding. A heel stomped my solar plexus, making air
shoot violently out of my lungs, and I tasted the warm, iron flavor of blood in my mouth. Another hard-toed shoe kicked me in
the crotch. I gazed up at steel rafters in the shadows of the high
ceiling. Metzger crouched close by and smacked me in the mouth

with the butt of his gun, cutting my lip, and blood dripped into my mouth. With his free hand, he gripped my collar and raised my head off of the ground. He flashed a grin, but there was no missing the rage in his eyes, radiating like a pair of hot lighthouse lamps. He jerked his head at his goons as he let go of my collar and let my head smack the ground.

Starkey picked me up by my biceps and Hedgepeth grabbed my ankles. They lifted my body off the ground and carried me across a loading platform to a waiting hopper car. They dropped me at the edge of the loading dock, so I was level with the top of the open, empty storage car. I peered down into the massive, rust-brown rectangular container to see a thin layer of salt at the bottom. When his thugs parted ways, Metzger walked over to me and squatted, dipping his head so his mouth was a few inches away from my ear.

"Remember when we met and I said I admired your father?"

I could not reply. I felt too weak to say yes.

"I lied. He was a fool, too blind to see there was a race war going on. But I knew it. Hell, I knew all along the niggers and mexes and kikes had it in for all God-fearing whites, waiting in line to slit our throats. That's why every chance I got, I'd bring one of those inferior pieces of shit out here and put him outta his fuckin' miseries. I had Earl and Grady here write police reports to make 'em look like they were resisting arrest. Wasn't much of a lie, looking back. If half those curs would've had the chance, they'd a knocked me off first. The way I look at it, it was self-defense, killing 'em the way I did. Pure and simple."

Earl Starkey chimed in: "Newton Perry says there's gonna be a revolution! Newton Perry says the day will come when all the race traitors will be wiped clean off the face of the earth. Newton Perry says . . ."

Metzger turned his firearm on Starkey and pulled the trigger. A little dark hole burst inward on Starkey's forehead. He toppled off the edge of the platform, and when his body hit the bottom of the hopper car, a loud, metallic "bung" rang out, echoing across the factory floor.

"He never had an original idea of his own," said Metzger.

Hedgepeth's eyes widened and he grew panicky. "Why did you do that?"

"Sorry, amigo. There isn't any room for you on this ride."

"No! Dooley! I swear to God, you'll never hear from me—"

Metzger squeezed the trigger three more times. Muzzle flashes went off like lightning. All three bullets entered Hedgepeth's body. I looked away from the carnage, but I heard him tip over the edge, and land in the hopper next to his fellow dead partner.

Metzger aimed his gun at me. The next pair of gunshots sounded distant. Metzger jerked twice, took two steps forward and fired his gun. A dirt geyser exploded inches away from my thigh. Metzger swallowed hard. He moved up to the edge of the platform, his revolver pointed downward. He plummeted over the edge, landing with the same steely thud.

Myron Adler walked out of the darkness, clutching his .38. He crouched near me, briefly glancing at the bullet wound in my shoulder, and somehow mustered a smile—which I thought he was incapable of—as he tucked his firearm into his shoulder holster.

"Thank you," I said. "How did you know?"

"Call it a hunch."

"I suspect there's more to it than that," I said. "Are you going to tell me, or do I have to guess?"

Myron scanned his surroundings. "This is where those three charmers brought me five years ago, and beat me within an inch of my life. I suspected they'd do the same to Booker, so I came back to this dismal place. I'm sorry I got here too late for him."

A groan came from inside the hopper car. Myron rose to his feet, walked to the edge of the platform and looked down.

"Goddamn Jew! I shoulda killed you when I had the chance! Fuck! I can't move! Get me to a doctor! Now!"

Myron walked over to a huge steel chute hovering above the hopper. It was connected to one of the salt silos. He reached up and pulled a dangling chain. A rumble shook the ground, followed by a massive tidal wave of salt that came pouring out of the chute. White crystals filled the air, spilling into the hopper like Niagara Falls, prompting Metzger to let out a banshee wail. He did his best to plead for his life above the din. But the steady whoosh of pouring salt continued long after Metzger stopped screaming. Myron came back over to me and knelt closer.

"You look terrible," he said.

Outside, sirens approached. Never before had their wail sounded so sweet. "Sounds like the cavalry is coming. I wonder how they knew—"

"I called for backup," he said. "I was watching this place from behind one of those salt mountains. I saw Metzger and his thugs pull up, and that's when I drove a couple miles to the nearest call box. I anticipated fireworks—maybe not quite like this, but Mama Adler didn't raise a fool. I knew Metzger wasn't going to surrender without a fight."

I smiled up at him. "Thanks. I owe you."

"Come back to Public Safety," he said. "I'm begging you. You can't just stick me with DeVoy Beckstead and then walk away."

I laughed, but then I winced in pain. "Ooo. That hurt."

"Well, then, don't laugh," said Myron. "And don't do much else, for the time being."

He took off his hat, sat down on the ground by my side, and made sure I was as comfortable as I could be on the cold floor of an abandoned factory. The once-empty railroad hopper car was now halfway full of salt as the two of us waited together in silence for the police to arrive.

Epilogue

With a clipboard and pencil in hand, I walked out to the orange cone and stood near the photoelectric device, watching the red bulb blinking on and off atop the pole that held it in place. The engine's wail rose, and Cousin Hank's newest creation, a Duesenberg Special equipped with a V12 aircraft engine, came rocketing toward me. I raised the stubby pencil in place, prepared to record the stats of his latest feat. The vehicle shot past the speed sensor, blowing my hat off, and the numbers on the device began clicking away, settling on 294 MPH, with a time of 1:06.3. I put my hat back on and wrote the numbers on the form, which was robin's egg blue this year, and carried it back in the tent. My cousin Murray was sitting on a folding chair inside, sipping a bottle of Nehi grape soda and staring glumly at the newspaper on the rickety card table. The all-caps headline, splashed across the length of the page, said it all: GERMAN TROOPS INVADE POLAND.

"How'd he do?"

"Two hundred and ninety-four, at a minute and six-point-three seconds," I said, placing the clipboard on the table near the paper. "That V-12 is making a big difference."

"Do you know what Eyston's Thunderbolt is up to? Five hundred and twenty-seven feet per second! Hank isn't even up to five hundred, by my calculations."

"He's getting better," I said. "He was a lot slower this time last year. The important thing is that he's making progress."

"Thank you, Pollyanna. By the way, the main run is in a half hour. Can you stick around for it?"

"Sure. Clara and the kids are coming out to see it. I'll catch a ride back to town with them."

I wandered out into the midmorning sunlight to savor one of the last hot days of summer. The place hummed with drivers trying to squeeze in their final runs before the end of the Labor Day weekend, the Speedway's last hurrah before closing. It entranced me, watching cars and motorcycles race across the desert, leaving dust clouds in their wake. I stood in the same spot for a long while, with the sun beating down on me, as vehicle after vehicle zoomed past. At some point, I began walking south, past rows of tents, to the bleachers and huge loudspeaker attached to the top of a steel tower. I arrived at an empty spot in a clearing where Clive Underhill's enormous Union Jack circus tent stood a year ago.

I noticed a split-second gleam in the salt. Leaning down to pick it up, I stood and dusted it off with my index finger. A British flag lapel pin.

The pin in my palm triggered a flashback of pulling Clive out of the fiery car crash last year. I had no way of knowing at the time that that incident would off a chain of events that would nearly kill me. At the end of it all, I barely made it out of Jericho

Salt Works alive. An ambulance took me straight to the LDS Hospital with life-threatening injuries. I remained in critical condition for days. In the end, it took me months to fully recover from a fractured arm, a broken leg, and a couple of busted ribs.

Only over time did I begin to fully grasp the bloody convergence of events in the summer of 1938.

Even as Nigel Underhill's life was being strangled out of him, his fellow Brit, Peter Insley—a carefully placed agent with British military intelligence secretly appointed to protect his brother, the famous motorist—was getting in touch with my brother Frank. When the Desert Lightning exploded due to the incendiary device that Julian Pangborn planted in it, that set Insley to request FBI protection for Clive Underhill. The shocking news of Nigel's death only confirmed in Peter's mind that he had done the right thing.

Special Agent Frank Oveson ordered G-men under his command to stealthily relocate Clive Underhill to an undisclosed location. Not knowing whom to trust, Frank and Peter Insley agreed to keep their decision a secret, preferring to let the police, the press, the general public, and even the members of Clive's own entourage speculate endlessly about his whereabouts.

Clive stayed in hiding until the big day. When it finally arrived, he ended up withdrawing from the competition, and the world soon found out why. With the blessing of the Underhill family, the Salt Lake City Police Department announced that Nigel had been brutally murdered. Clive experienced a massive outpouring of sympathy in the form of huge bags of telegrams, and even though I never saw it, I heard his hotel room resembled a florist's shop. With Metzger out of the way and Pangborn's body discovered out in the West Desert, Clive came out of hiding and greeted a sympathetic press, putting on a brave face. But inside, he was devastated, and in no shape to race—mentally or physically.

"There will be other competitions," he told a room full of reporters in one of the ballrooms at the Hotel Utah. "Now is the time for me to mourn what I've lost, and I ask for your understanding in this difficult time."

Rudy Heinrich also pulled out of Saturday's event. He never publicly stated why, but I knew at least one reason, possibly the *only* reason, which—due to my dismal driving—was lying in an upside-down heap of scorched steel and glass at the base of an embankment near the Great Salt Lake. I knew I had myself to blame for Heinrich missing out on the chance to break the land speed record.

For the longest time, I was haunted by my decision to steal the P9 for my getaway. It really got to me, knowing *I* was the reason why Heinrich—an innocent Jewish man condemned to living in the giant open-air prison that was Nazi Germany—could not compete. Guilt burned inside of me, turning my stomach, torturing me into wakefulness on many long nights. I often wondered what happened to Heinrich, and to the murderous Nazis surrounding him like the proverbial wolves guarding the sheep. While I was still floating in a morphine-induced high in my hospital bed, Heinrich and his small army of support personnel quietly slipped out of Salt Lake City on a flight to New York, where they boarded a Hamburg-American ship bound for Bremen. To my knowledge, Leni Riefenstahl never did complete her documentary film about Heinrich.

No records were broken out at the Bonneville Speedway on August 13, 1938, but that did not stop Warner Bros. from staging a lavish press photo shoot out at the flats to publicize its upcoming Clive Underhill biopic, *Desert Lightning,* starring Errol

Flynn, and directed by Michael Curtiz. On a huge white wedding cake–like platform, right out of a Busby Berkeley picture, with a brightly lit Warner Bros. logo suspended above it, Clive Underhill stood between Flynn and Curtiz, all smiles for the cameras. Clive did a yeoman's job of hiding the misery he was feeling over the loss of his brother and the loss of one of his closest college chums, Vaughn Perry, allegedly of a heroin overdose.

The only silver lining in the dark cloud of death that hung low over Utah that summer was that my close friend and former partner, Roscoe Lund, was cleared of involvement in Nigel Underhill's murder. He followed the story in the *Los Angeles Times,* and decided it was safe to come home. Turns out he had been hiding in a beachside motor court in Santa Monica, California, searching for his missing daughter, Rose. He returned to Utah without her, but he clung tenaciously to hope that he might one day find her. He parked Clara's automobile in our driveway with only a minor dent in the fender, which he agreed to pay to have repaired. It still hasn't been fixed.

Roscoe paid me a visit at the hospital. He'd lost a great deal of weight, and lines of anguish were carved into his face. His once bald noggin now sported a thin layer of dark brown fuzz. He cheered up when he told me that Millicent, his missing cat, had turned up on his doorstep. His felines were all present and accounted for. I assured him we would find his daughter.

Roscoe asked me to team up with him, as partners in his struggling detective agency. I initially agreed. But when Buddy Hawkins visited me in the hospital a few days later and offered me my old job at the SLCPD back, I could not refuse. Alas, a steady paycheck won out over the uncertainties of being a private investigator. Roscoe understood and accepted my regrets with his usual charm and sense of humor. I sensed his disappointment, though. And, I guess, not so deep down, I yearned for the freedom that would come from running my own business. I refused to abandon the hope of one day partnering again with Roscoe.

I once again assumed command of the Missing Persons Bureau, with Detectives DeVoy Beckstead and Myron Adler as my subordinates. The injuries I sustained in August left me incapacitated for a month, and when I did return to Public Safety, I resumed work slowly, on a part-time basis. As fate would have it, Clara had found work as a substitute teacher at a few local high schools that fall, including East High, where she used to work. Her disposition immediately brightened, sending her melancholy into retreat. What a joy to hear her laugh again, and see her smile.

Seasons changed. The long, hot days of summer gave way to shorter, crisper fall ones. Across the valley, leaves on trees turned orange and yellow and red and fell to the earth. On the second Thursday in November, Myron had my family over to his house to sample Mama Adler's *shakshuka*. Outside, the air was chilly and nighttime came early, but inside it was warm, and our families sat around the table talking and laughing and passing around a Jewish delicacy made of eggs poached in a sauce of tomatoes and onions and chili peppers.

It was all good cheer until the music playing on the living room Zenith console stopped for a news bulletin. We all gathered around the glowing gold dial as Mama Adler shushed us and turned the volume high. "Eyewitness reports are coming in tonight of mobs charging through the streets of major German and Austrian cities, attacking Jewish-owned businesses and homes, setting fire to synagogues, and murdering prominent Jewish leaders. There are unconfirmed claims that the mobs are made up entirely of Nazi storm troopers disguised as civilians. Please stand by." The radio announcer paused for a moment as a Teletype machine rattled in the background. "This just in. Dispatches from Vienna confirm that all twenty-one of the city's synagogues have been partially or completely destroyed. At least twenty-two prominent Jews in Vienna have committed suicide so far during this latest wave of violence. According to the International News Service, the eerie glow of flames across Berlin can be seen from miles away."

Mama Adler reached over and squeezed my hand. She looked up at me with sad eyes and a long face. Gone was her beautiful smile.

"This is only the beginning, Arthur," she whispered. "Worse things are yet to come. I feel it in my bones."

Mama Adler was prescient. The situation continued to deteriorate overseas with each passing month. I had to hand it to my daughter, Sarah Jane, who went tirelessly from door to door collecting signatures and contributions for a New York–based group advocating the establishment of a Jewish homeland in Lower California. I was proud of her for caring so much. It left her discouraged, however, to discover that most people did not seem to care about Jews in Germany and Austria, and did not wish to sign her petition or donate to the cause. Still, she refused to succumb to pessimism, and she found scattered handfuls of signatories, and collected a jar of rattling coins. She continued clipping articles and writing letters to the president and members of Congress, asking them to help Jewish refugees. I made it a point to tell her repeatedly I was proud of her. "It could be *our* family over there suffering," she said. "It's not enough, you know—what I'm doing."

As she spoke those words, I thought of what Clive Underhill cried out after he left the Coconut Grove. "It's not enough!" I'm still not sure why he shouted it. I wondered if maybe he was

haunted by his past flirtation with fascism, and regarded his efforts to distance himself from it and help Rudy Heinrich escape
its evil tentacles as insufficient. I realized I'd never know the answer. In the end, Clive remained an enigma to me—an intrigu-
ing man, equal parts charismatic and lonely, and I knew that
night I spent with him at the Coconut Grove and on the drive
back to the Hotel Utah afterward was the closest I was ever going
to get to him. I continued to follow his career from afar, and
hoped that—in the end—he would find the peace that seemed
to elude him in the face of stardom.

If the turbulence of that summer brought me closer to my
daughter, it had the opposite effect on my relationship with
Frank, my older brother. From the outset, Frank had tried to sabotage my friendship with Roscoe, all the while willing to sacri-
fice him as a fall guy for Nigel's murder without conducting a
proper homicide investigation. This infuriated me and alienated
me from Frank. I quit attending Sunday dinners at his house,
opting instead to deliver homemade meals with my immediate
family to my mother's homestead in American Fork. Each Thursday night, we all gathered around the long table and prayed and
then passed around food Clara had cooked in the late afternoon.
Mom accepted my estrangement from Frank with a certain
resignation. I cannot say I missed him. Frank had always been
overbearing, and it pleased me to put some distance between us.

The coming of spring the following year raised hopes along
with temperatures. A full-time teaching job in English had
opened up at South High. The principal, Mr. Carlson, asked
Clara to drop by for an interview in March, and he hired her on
the spot to start teaching in the fall. To celebrate, we splurged
and bought tickets on a cruise from New York to Havana. We
chose late May and early June to travel, before the weather turned

too hot. Clara's parents had offered to watch our children while we were gone. We took them up on it.

Aboard the ocean liner SS *Oriente,* Clara and I loved our enchanting time at sea, precisely what we needed after a long drought in our marriage. We ballroom danced until the wee hours of the morning to the swinging sounds of the Nat Harris Embassy Orchestra, held hands under the stars and watched the moon's reflection in the water, spent our afternoons taking dips in one of the outdoor tiled swimming pools, and made love with renewed passion whenever we were alone.

When the ship steamed into Havana Harbor, June 2, 1939, an ominous black rainstorm swirled low in the sky, with occasional flashes of lightning over choppy, whitecapped waters. The cruise ship director advised passengers to stay inside. The weather forecast called for heavy rains over Cuba, he said. Clara and I dined at a breakfast smorgasbord in a cavernous room full of tables draped with bleached white linen, lit brightly by chandeliers and natural light from tall windows. Halfway through a plate of scrambled eggs and fruit, I felt a strange sensation, as if something was terribly wrong. Sipping orange juice, I suddenly began to pick up on snippets of conversations at other tables.

"They say all of the passengers are Jews."

"Downright shame, in this day and age—all those refugees with no place to go."

"You see the headline in this morning's paper? 'Ship Turned Away at Havana.'"

"'Voyage of the Damned,' they're calling it. Sounds like the name of a novel."

"Canada and the United States won't let 'em in either, according to the *Herald*."

I pushed my scrambled eggs aside. I'd suddenly lost my appetite. I raised my hand and signaled the waiter, a dark-haired young man in a white tuxedo with alert eyes and a receding chin. He hurried over, and Clara shot a quizzical glance my way.

"What's this about a ship?" I asked.

"It's the *St. Louis*," he said. "It's full of Jewish refugees from Europe with nowhere to go. We're going to pass it soon, off to the port side."

"Thanks."

The waiter left, heading toward a pair of swinging doors. I tossed my napkin next to my half-empty plate. Clara watched me rise from my chair and take a sip of ice water before leaving the table.

"Where are you going?" she asked. "It's going to rain out there."

"That's OK," I said. "Don't worry about me. I'll be back."

I ducked outside through a set of fancy French doors, and tasted salt on the breeze as I cut across the freshly polished deck, glancing up at the slate-gray heavens. Cuba was visible in the darkening distance, a thin strip of mountainous land rising up from the sea. Scattered passengers still outside made their way inside or to covered areas. That gave me a choice of one of the many unused tower viewers, those big, heart-shaped telescopic devices mounted on a stalk attached to the guardrails. I put my eyes to the pair of magnifying lenses. Gripping a pair of handles on either side, I aimed the viewer to the south, and that's when I caught first sight of the leviathan of an ocean liner, cutting through the choppy waters like a gigantic axe blade.

A rain droplet tapped my arm—one at first, then another, and another, soon escalating into a steady drumming on the deck. Rushing past me, a couple, a man and woman in their thirties—like Clara and me—huddled under a single umbrella, making their way toward the dining room entrance.

"You'd best get inside, fella," said the man. "Looks like a big one."

I pulled away from the contraption. "Thanks. I'll be along soon."

I lowered my face to the tower viewer right when the *St. Louis* and the *Oriente* passed each other. Rain picked up in intensity. Bigger droplets came down faster and harder as I steadied the device. All of the decks of the *St. Louis*—upper, lower, sheltered and uncovered—were jammed with men, women, and children. Close enough that I could see open mouths and envious eyes. Passengers came in every imaginable size and age—old and young; men and women; wrinkled and smooth; robust and frail; homely and breathtaking; dark hair, light hair, no hair at all; some wore hats, quite a few held umbrellas, and a fair number pointed fingers and conversed with each other.

A downpour arrived. Rain fell in sheets. Passengers on the *St. Louis* began filing inside of the ship.

That is when I saw him, pressed against the guardrail, near a lifeboat, peering out through a set of binoculars. *Rudy Heinrich.* A pretty woman stood behind him and to his right, and I was sure she was Gerda Strauss. I stepped away from the viewer and moved adjacent to it, looking out at the *St. Louis* in the distance, so he could see my face. Then I returned to the viewer, holding the handgrips as I leaned my eyes into the lenses, just in time to see Heinrich's eyebrows arch over his binoculars. I swear I saw his mouth form the word *kripo.*

I raised my arm as high as I could and waved at him so rigorously I thought I would dislocate my shoulder. Seconds later, he responded with a similar wave, still holding the field glasses to his eyes. Rain had thoroughly soaked through my clothes, and I was as wet as I'd be if I'd just crawled out of the sea, but I did not care. *Let it rain,* I thought. *This is too important.*

I watched a long time until Heinrich's shape dissolved from view. I kept turning the viewer as far to the left—to the north—as it would go, listening to it squeak on its stalk, leaning over the rail to get a better view of the ship's rear. The *St. Louis* faded into heavy rain and mist like a giant ghost vessel, engulfed by a wall of swirling gray, as if it had never even existed. I lost track of how long I remained at that viewer, wondering if the phantom would ever come into sight again. It did not. At some point, I returned inside, thoroughly drenched, and Clara looked at me as if I'd lost my mind.

That scene has replayed itself over and over in my memories.

Out here in the middle of the Salt Flats on Labor Day weekend 1939, waiting for Cousin Hank to make a final run in his Duesenberg Special, thoughts of Heinrich on the deck of the *St. Louis* flickered through my mind once more. Shutting my eyes, I caught sight of his angular face, and that warm and gentle smile, and I recalled the day he stood by my side, savoring the peace out here on the piping hot salt pan. How clearly I still remember his words: "Sometimes we forget how beautiful it sounds, the silence."

While my eyes were still shut, Hank's car roared past me, sending a tidal wave of dust my way. The engine's heat warmed my face. I waited until its roar disappeared from earshot to open my eyes.

Alone again, I scanned the plain of sun-sparkling crystals, listening intently, but all I heard was silence.